What people a

The Alchem of Night

When research librarian Phillippa Grayson finds a peculiar old book about ancient Egyptian sex magic she has no idea that it will change her life forever—and in ways she could never have imagined. Soon after, in a box of thrift-store clothing, she discovers a linen robe and other mysterious objects that catapult her back to a previous lifetime as a priestess in ancient Egypt.

Unwittingly, she begins a journey through time, pursued by an angry entity she calls her Dark Enigma, the spirit of a malevolent pharaoh from that former life. While trying to make sense of the strange goings-on she's experiencing and her relationships with the people she knows in her present life, Phillippa learns that they're all entwined in the long-ago past and have reincarnated together in the present to resolve ancient wrongs.

As Judy Hall unravels the mystery of millennia-old lifetimes, curses, and magical workings, she presents information from noted occultists Pascal Beverly Randolph and Wallis Budge. She also combines her extensive knowledge of ancient Egypt, magic, gods and goddesses, shamanic journeying, and crystals to create a tantalizing tale full of twists and turns that can be read on many levels. *The Alchemy of Night* is not only an engaging story of intrigue and romantic suspense, it also provides a glimpse into the complex world of ancient Egyptian magic and the afterlife.
Skye Alexander, author of *Sex Magic for Beginners* and *The Modern Guide to Witchcraft*

'B*gger, b*gger, b*gger! Thought I'd have a quick look at *The Alchemy of Night* and now I'm VERY late for work… Loving it – very quirky and instantly absorbing, with the immediate knowledge of something much deeper below the surface.'
Richard Bryson, author of *Five Dark Moons*

'I found it riveting. It's a subject that's always intrigued me. I've never before read a book that brought together ancient history, reincarnation and Spiritualism without the need for sensationalism.'
Helen Baggott, copy editor

'Engaging, modern and above all different!'
Vicki Goldie, author of *Blind Justice*; area manager Bournemouth Libraries

'In this orgasmic time-slip adventure, Judy Hall takes us right under-the-skin of her young heroine, as we are simultaneously drenched in the sensuous, exotic mysteries of ancient Egypt, and dragged behind the scenes in charity shops, student flats and libraries and wild dream landscapes. What a roller-coaster ride! And I shall never see my local librarians in quite the same way again!'
Jane Skellett, community writer, prizewinning poet and storyteller with Dorset Writers and winner of The Quill Award

'A truly remarkable slide into the mysteries of ancient Egypt.'
Mario Reading, author of *The Nostradamus Trilogy*

'*The Alchemy of Night* reads extremely well. It's intriguing, pacey, very easy to picture, all the things you want – with no waffle!'
Tim John, screenwriter of *A Street Cat Named Bob*

The Alchemy of Night

A time-slip tale of sexual magic

The Alchemy of Night

A time-slip tale of sexual magic

Judy Hall

Winchester, UK
Washington, USA

First published by Roundfire Books, 2019
Roundfire Books is an imprint of John Hunt Publishing Ltd., No. 3 East St., Alresford,
Hampshire SO24 9EE, UK
office1@jhpbooks.net
www.johnhuntpublishing.com
www.roundfire-books.com

For distributor details and how to order please visit the 'Ordering' section on our website.

Text copyright: Judy Hall 2018

ISBN: 978 1 78535 830 2
978 1 78535 831 9 (ebook)
Library of Congress Control Number: 2017964343

All rights reserved. Except for brief quotations in critical articles or reviews, no part of this book may be reproduced in any manner without prior written permission from the publishers.

The rights of Judy Hall as author have been asserted in accordance with the Copyright, Designs and Patents Act 1988.

A CIP catalogue record for this book is available from the British Library.

Design: Stuart Davies

Printed and bound by CPI Group (UK) Ltd, Croydon, CR0 4YY, UK
US: Printed and bound by Edwards Brothers Malloy 15200 NBN Way #B, Blue Ridge Summit,
PA 17214, USA

We operate a distinctive and ethical publishing philosophy in all areas of our business, from our global network of authors to production and worldwide distribution.

Contents

Acknowledgements

To Vicki Goldie, Jane Skellet, Richard Bryson, Tracy Baines, Sue Joiner and all the members of Village Writers who poked, prodded, dissected, encouraged and who, above all, have given me the invaluable gift of laughter and companionship during long years of writing. My love and thanks to you all. To Dr Dan Potter for the generous use of his invaluable last-minute translation, *shukran*.

In memoriam: Mario Reading, Renaissance man, generous mentor, and all-round-bangin guy as Aidan would say. Love and respect to you. You were an inspiration!

Ancient Egyptian tomb warning
"Watch out not to take even a pebble from within it outside. If you find this stone you shall not transgress against it."
(*Trans.* Dr Dan Potter, Assistant Curator, National Museum of Scotland)

Our life is twofold: Sleep hath its own world,
A boundary between the things misnamed
Death and existence: Sleep hath its own world,
And a wide realm of wild reality,
And dreams in their development have breath,
And tears, and tortures, and the touch of Joy;
They leave a weight upon our waking thoughts,
They take a weight from off our waking toils,
They do divide our being; they become
A portion of ourselves as of our time,
And look like heralds of Eternity.
Lord Byron, 'The Dream'

Dramatis personae

Across time

The Prince Khem Yar Khepher'set, 'My Majesty' – a Pharaoh of ancient Egypt and wandering shade.

* * *

Present time

Phillippa Grayson – reference librarian and part-time charity shop volunteer.

Sebastian Warner – a customer at the library. Research PhD student specialising in pre-dynastic Egyptian threat-formula and binding spells.

Mimi van der Buerk – manager of a charity shop and head of a magical coven.

Mr McMeeney – chief librarian.

Aidan Doran – library intern.

Shelagh Slattery – a friend Phillippa met on holiday in Egypt.

Tom Ellison – budding entrepreneur and Phillippa's former fiancé.

* * *

Former time: ancient Egypt

Men'en'oferet, 'Mennie', (Phillippa's former incarnation) – a young priestess who is about to make a mystic marriage with Men'ofer.

Men'ofer (Sebastian's former incarnation) – a young priest and Phillippa's twinflame.

Agni'ti, tjaty (lord chamberlain) to the Prince – father of Men'en'oferet.

Lik'ebet – nurse to Men'en'oferet and former servant of The

Lady Yagut.

The Lady Yagut'd'eskia – high priestess and absconded Great Wife of the Pharaoh.

Mes'kia – daughter-priestess to The Lady Yagut.

* * *

Former time: Edwardian England

Sir E.A. Wallis Budge – Egyptologist, Orientalist, philologist and Keeper of Egyptian Antiquities at the British Museum. Member of the Savage and Ghost Clubs.

Sir H. Rider Haggard – author and amateur Egyptologist. Member of the Savage, Athenaeum, Savile and Authors' Clubs.

Andrew Lang – Scottish poet, novelist, psychical researcher, literary critic, anthropologist. Member of the Savage and Ghost Clubs.

Unidentified 'Egyptian princess'.

* * *

Between time: In the Otherworld

Babaanne – guardian grandmother to Phillippa.

Bertrand, 'Beloved grandpa'– husband of Babaanne and grandfather to Phillippa.

* * *

Outside time, in the pages of the book

Dr Paschal Beverly Randolph – African-American medical doctor, occultist, Spiritualist, trance medium, and writer. Founder of The Brotherhood of Eulis and author of *Magia Sexualis: Sexual Practices for Magical Power.*

Chapter 1

Lost without you

While I was alone in Luxor, a freak rainstorm had sent me diving for cover. I rushed from the Valley of the Kings, as water swirled around my feet. I felt like it was whirling me away, to goodness knows where. I give myself up to that same sensation now as the memories flood in, slipping back into that seductively scented land.

The excitement of the airport, settling in on the plane and then… What a pushover I'd been, falling for his charms like that. I'm well rid. Even if it has left a hole inside me, a grievous ache that I can't seem to shift.

It had been the first holiday we'd taken together. A romantic pre-honeymoon by the Red Sea, or so he had said. My mother had been scandalised. I soon found out that the blonde seated on the other side of Tom on the flight had wiped any idea of marriage from his mind. Marriage to me at any event. As the sun set behind us and we flew into the gathering dark, their conversation became increasingly intimate. I withdrew into myself, dreaming of this return to the homeland of my beloved grandmother. So longed for. So long forbidden.

The second time I'd caught Tom sneaking back into our room in the early dawn because he'd allegedly 'heard Samantha calling out and thought she might be in trouble,' I'd grabbed his clothes from the wardrobe and flung them over the balcony shouting, 'Get out or I'll throw you after them.'

The scattered clothes looked like confetti as they landed on the immaculate lawn. Confetti that, I told myself, would never be thrown for me.

It had been a fairytale romance. Or so it seemed. I should have known it was too good to be true. And, at twenty-four, surely I was too old for such dreams.

'You're so insipid, too inexperienced to keep a guy like me interested for long,' he'd thrown at me as he dived after his belongings.

So why had he promised so much? Made me believe he loved me. Eviscerated, that's what I've been. This cold emptiness that possesses me is what people must mean by 'gutted'. I prefer the more tortuous word. It sums it up so well. I've been emptied out, disembowelled, all my worst fears realised. Such words are my secret joy. I hug them to myself.

Swaying on her hooker heels, Samantha had watched from her balcony, smiling smugly. Her perfume drifted over and made me retch.

As I turned back into the bedroom, stifling sobs, I caught sight of a figure reflected in the mirror on the wardrobe door. Who was this wild creature? Hair whipping around her head, like snakes in a charmer's basket. Eyes blazing, red rimmed. The skimpy lace nightdress Tom had handed over as we unpacked hanging wantonly from one shoulder. This was not me! My mother had instilled the mantra 'never make a scene, never show emotion.' What would she think of me now? I was letting her down. I dragged on my old comfortable cotton pyjamas and headed to the bathroom to tame my hair. I'd just finished the mousy braid when a knock on the door startled me. Surely Tom hadn't had the gall to come back? But no...

'Why not go to Luxor, you'll enjoy the sites and we'll give you free entry on the tours,' an out-of-breath rep offered. 'I'm flying over myself later to meet a group. It's a longish trip, we'll have to change planes in Cairo, but so much nicer...' She gestured towards the window where a frantic Tom could be glimpsed scrabbling for his possessions – helped by the garden boys who secreted items under their *ghalabyas* whenever he turned his back.

'Thank you...yes...I'd like that. It's really kind. Oh, but will

I have to come back to Sharm...my ticket?' Biting my lip, I'd contemplated having to fly home with the lovebirds. 'I...' But she seemed to know what I'm thinking.

'You can fly home from there, I'll get your ticket changed. You'll get in a day earlier than the original flight would have done...'

'That's fine, it'll give me time to clear out his things.'

* * *

And clear out his things I had. There'd been plenty of time to make plans on the flight home and I got to work immediately. Tom would arrive back to find his designer suits strewn over the trees that lined the quiet street, his handmade shirts in the gutter and his prized cult classic DVD collection strung from the lampposts like bunting. My mother would not approve. Tell me I was showing myself up. But my mother wouldn't know. I'd held back from shredding his clothes. I'd been tempted, but gained more pleasure from the indelible ink messages I had secreted within them.

One of my regular customers from the reference library where I spent my working days had been passing as I heaved Tom's belongings onto the pavement.

'May I give you a hand, Phillippa?' Sebastian offered, his pale face getting pinker as he smiled down at me. His skin was so translucent I could see the blood pumping beneath a scattering of freckles that glinted like rusty pennies in the sun. He gathered up the bunting I had created. 'I shinnied up coconut trees in Africa when I was a small boy, so climbing lampposts is no problem for me.'

Gaily waving his trophies like kites catching the wind, he laughed uproariously as he clambered higher. It was a very different side of the serious young man who blushed and stammered his thanks at my desk. I'd never thought of him as having mischief in his soul. Too straight-laced for that. But, he seemed to be revelling in this.

The sight of one of Tom's immaculate white shirts lying in the dirt made the breath catch in my throat for a moment, reminding me of what I'd lost. That hole in my heart was bleeding, my belly draining, elation fading away. Best turn my attention elsewhere.

I'd absentmindedly admired the neat bum Sebastian presented as he bent to fasten more of Tom's silk ties, socks and boxers to shining discs and climbed lightly up the next lamppost with them. I was mentally checking that there was nothing left to tie me to Tom. I must remember to cancel that extra pint of milk. That or get a cat.

Thinking back to the way Sebastian had so enthusiastically helped me to erase Tom from my life I can't help wondering what's happened to him. I'd expected him to ask me out, but he'd hurried away throwing a hasty, 'Gotta go, see you, Pips, bye,' over his shoulder. He'd left behind him a wisp of creamy caramel, like the Werther's Originals of which my beloved grandpa had been so fond.

It's been over a month since I last saw him and I miss his shy smile and requests for obscure out-of-print books. I felt like a detective tracking them down. Sebastian had been so grateful, bringing in chocolates or a bunch of flowers especially for me. I'd been rather attracted to his geeky academic leanness when we first met – and his enquiring mind. Hoped he'd ask me out. I couldn't be so forward as to ask him. But his appeal had been overwhelmed by the sheer animal force of Tom's maleness. Nothing geeky about Tom. He prided himself on his gym-toned body and careful grooming.

Sebastian's attractiveness reasserted itself when he'd helped me erase Tom from my life. Now, part of me is suspended, like a half-written word hanging on a page. Waiting. Hoping…

I dream of Sebastian, though. If they are dreams? They're so real, as though he's here with me. They're getting more frequent, almost every night now. Comforting, exciting, intriguing, *physical.*

With Tom gone, the nights are long and lonely – except for those dreams. I'd always dreamt in gossamer hues, insubstantial and quickly forgotten, none of that glossy black-and-white film noir stuff other people describe. No psychological reworking of my day, and if I was exploring my subconscious, it was remarkably innocuous. But now… Romantic fantasies? Or fallacies? Maybe. Figments of my imagination? I think not. 'Chimerical'? Can I find the right word in my private store of linguistic treasures? These new dreams are different. Brilliant, luminous colour. Every detail standing out sharply, outlined in light. The sounds… The sensations... The smells… The *touch*… Each moment etched in my memory. There's no chance of forgetting these dreams, nor would I want to. I step into a parallel reality. One that if I'm truthful I'd prefer to inhabit permanently.

The days are okay. The library keeps me busy and there's the shop on Saturdays. Sundays are for a quick clean of my compact – the estate agent called it 'bijou' – flat and a long read as I soak in the bath or lay out in the garden in the sunshine. I bought the flat because the tiny courtyard was a perfect suntrap. A country girl, I need green around me and I tend my plants with care. When Tom moved in he assured me it was only for a few months until the deal he was doing came off and we could get one of the ultra-trendy flats on the river. I hadn't been convinced that a distant view of water from a balcony would be the same as sitting in my own garden, but I don't need to worry about that now. He's been 'expunged'. I love that word. It sums it up to perfection. Not quite obliterated, certainly not destroyed… merely…blotted out. Erased.

So why am I still hurting over him – and dreaming of Sebastian?

There is another man too, my Dark Enigma as I've dubbed him. The phosphorescent spectre that hangs around the edge of my dreams. All I see is the desire that flares in his hooded eyes, burning into mine before he melts back into the shadows. What's *he* all about? He doesn't appear to wish me harm. So, at the moment, I'm more curious than afraid. But I'm aware that this could change in an instant. I need to be on my guard. I remember what Lord Byron said about dreams. *'They shake us with the vision that's gone by, the dread of vanished shadows…and give a breath to forms which can outlive all flesh.'* Forms that outlive all flesh. That's a thought on which I do not wish to dwell.

Chapter 2

My heart leaps to go

Ever since the voice in a dream told me to volunteer at the charity shop I've wondered what on earth it's all about. Not that I mind being here. It had given me something to do while Tom was out with his mates watching sport, and when we broke up, I drifted into staying on. I love the treasures people donate, making up stories about their past. The people who'd drunk out of the cups and those who'd placed flowers in the vases. The souvenirs brought back from who knows what exotic lands where anything could happen.

It's the clothes that get to me, rancid with old perfume and rank with death even when they're almost new. They remind me of that freshly discovered tomb I'd been taken to in Egypt. Malodorous didn't do it justice. A fetid, honeyed-cloves and cinnamon smell mixed with sweaty trainers and something more pungent mouldering underneath had clung to the dusty interior – and to me. 'Polluted by sulphurous putrescence' was a phrase I'd found in a book a customer had returned to the library as 'too grisly for words' that summed it up so well.

For a moment, in the tomb, I'd thought I saw a bright blue flower brush along my arm, but it must have been a trick of the light because there were only a few shrivelled petals in a corner. Those and the remnants of a delicate lily frieze painted on the wall. I must have got them mixed up in the heat. It did weird things to my head. The walls wavered and wound themselves around me and the stink became so overpowering that I reeled sideways and almost fell. I was looking down on my body from above, hovering somewhere below the ceiling, scrunched up into the rock. When that gropey guide had tried to put his arm round me, I'd panicked and fled.

It took days to rid myself of the smell. Even now, when I take that dress from the back of the wardrobe, it holds the noxious memory of the tomb and makes me blench. Dry cleaning didn't work and I'd left it in the garden for several days. But it seems that neither fresh air nor pouring rain could shift that indelible scent. So I never wear the dress, which had been one of my favourites. But, somehow, I can't part with it. Touching it leaves me empty and unfulfilled, a strange unmet desire fluttering in the base of my belly. Until the stench roars in again and I stuff it back into its plastic shroud.

Shuddering, I push the memory away.

But Tom slams back into my head. Almost as though he's walking beside me. He was so suave and worldly wise. Knew exactly who he was and where he was going in his life. So many plans. An excellent dresser. So confident. Even though he was younger than me, if only by six months. He'd been my first boyfriend. My parents saw to that, guarding me closely, trying to keep me safe. Made me travel to uni each day from home. No wild student parties for me. I hadn't really minded. It gave me time to study.

When I left home to take the library job I'd always wanted, I couldn't believe it when Tom asked me out a few weeks after I arrived. Exactly what my parents had feared. They didn't think that running a reference library was the right occupation for their precious daughter. But, for me, it was perfect. Even though it might not have long-term prospects if everything gets digitised. I dread that. Spending all day amongst old books, ferreting out information no one else can access, tracking down long out-of-print works is my greatest pleasure.

Tom had bumped into me as I hurried out to grab some lunch, dropping the armful of county guides I'd taken to skim through in case of readers' questions. He'd called me Pippi Longstocking, laughing at my studiousness. Had I really want to be named after a rambunctious character in a children's book, no matter how endearing? Had Tom even read the book? Did he know her? Did he really know me? She was so far from my own character. But it had made me feel special at the time. Now I'm alone again. What am I going to do?

A waft of fragrance. The dusky perfume of a night-blooming flower. 'Best not to think of that, my dear, turn your mind elsewhere.' My guardian grandmother murmurs in my ear. Babaanne always arrives when I need comfort. And now, from the whiff of Werther's Originals and pipe smoke, it seems my beloved grandpa has joined in protecting me. Fortunately, they recede when the dreams arrive. How embarrassing it would be to have them watching. Somehow, though, I sense that Babaanne approves. So, it must be all right. Mustn't it? Surely they'd intervene if anyone meant to harm me.

Chapter 3

It is to you that I speak

'Phillippa' an imperious voice summons me. 'I'm sure I saw someone out the back. Could you check?'

As I open the door, a voice calls from beyond the rickety gate, *'Come. Find me.'* A child? But the sound is far from childlike. Creaky. Disused. *Old.* Tantalisingly close.

A glance down the alley reveals no one. Merely dustbins and black bags randomly spilling their contents. The dark underbelly of the picturesque High Street onto which the former boutique faces.

The voice comes again, rising and falling in soft cadence, *'Here I am.'*

But there's no one there.

A rustling at my feet draws my attention. A tattered cardboard box lies abandoned on the back step, a glimpse of faded red leather within. Another inappropriate donation?

My hand hesitates as I reach towards the tattered cover, disquiet running through me. The book seems to undulate, its cover rippling. But the voice pulls me on.

'I'm waiting for you... Only you.'

Wrinkling my nose at the musty smell of foxed paper, I reach towards the book. Strange, I usually revel in the aroma of old books, it's ambrosia to me. But this is different. Darker somehow. Grave-smelling. Of great import. 'Stop being silly,' I admonish myself. 'That vivid imagination of yours is working overtime again.' As I lift the book out of the carton, electric tingles run up my arm. What is it? Merely an old tome, surely? It seems to sigh. A soft exhalation of *'Found at last.'* I'm beyond wondering how pages can talk.

Taking a deep breath, I open the heavy cover. A breeze ruffles the pages but I hold them down. A faint aroma of not-quite-roses drifts up. So beautiful, such a contrast to the mustiness of its box. Bringing the book to my nose, I inhale deeply.

The air shudders and gyrates. Foul as the tomb. Bony fingers seize the book, grasping, greedy. With heart racing, and struggling to calm my racing pulse, I snatch it back with shaking hands. Wanting to run, somewhere, anywhere, but my frozen knees won't cooperate. How can spectral hands that I can't see, but most certainly *feel,* pluck at me? A delusion? Imagination? Or just another oddity in the weirdnesses that surround me?

Am I going mad? Suffering some kind of psychotic breakdown? Mental derangement? How would I know? After all that's happened, it wouldn't be surprising, but this is so real. *That smell.* There have been times lately… Those fingers are so… *solid.* As though in confirmation, blackened nails claw my arm, biting into me, compelling me. *'Give. Me. My. Book.'*

Heart scudding, I turn away and thrust the image from my mind. I long to be ordinary, untroubled – as I used to be – dull some might say, but it would appear that life has other plans for me. Since I've come back from Egypt it's as though I've been inhabiting two worlds at once.

Time to get a grip. My guardian grandmother is murmuring in my ear, *'Breathe, Phillippa, breathe.'* That's it. Breathe. Deep. Humid air cloys as it negotiates the lump of fear in my throat. *That* smell sears my tongue. But that's okay. Let it out slowly, trickling through flared nostrils… And again… Shoulders are high and tight. Drop them down… Better. Legs no longer wobbling, hands not shaking – well, not quite as much. Now, what's this is all about?

As I scan the title page, raindrops explode around me. I'll have to save a closer examination for later. I pick up the box and run into the shop, bundling the book into a plastic carrier. *A Treatise on Sexual Thaumaturgy.* How intriguing. Unravelling the arcane words will be my secret pleasure. I pay five pounds for it, putting the money in the till, along with the price of an over-large beige trench coat, all I find as protection against the sudden summer storm. I'm a small brown mouse lost in its folds.

'Anything of interest in that box, Phillippa?' the manageress calls. 'I do wish people wouldn't leave donations out there. They get damp, I keep telling them. Is there anything I should see?' Mimi van der Buerk emerges from her office, adjusting her cleavage and smoothing her too tight sweater back into place. 'Office' is a rather pretentious name for a former cupboard under the stairs, but Mrs B is full of her own importance.

I tuck the carrier into my bag, 'Only a pile of slushy romances. I'm off now. Bye.'

'Come back here, young lady.'

Has she spotted the book? Another minute and my escape route will be blocked. Should I show her? I long for a confidante, but her bossy management style, combined with a gossipy tongue, deter me. Although, even a close friend would probably laugh, tell me it was all my imagination. Some imagination!

'You never did tell me about your holiday with that nice young man of yours.' The smile is ingratiating, gratingly so.

'Oh, nothing to tell. He's not my young man any longer. Nor was he nice. Bye.'

I force my way past the nosy manageress, rushing out of the front room with its detritus of abandoned lives. The pink-and-white décor inherited from the previous occupants so at odds with the present contents. I pull the front door behind me. Don't want *her* getting her hands on the book. And anyway, what would she do with it? Mrs B is far too old for sexual wonderworking. *Let her find something else,* I add, in case anyone is listening in on my thoughts. I can't be too careful these days.

Chapter 4

Love in a beloved land

As I scurry down High Street, heading home through the driving rain, for once I ignore the somewhat dilapidated Georgian architecture and the occasional black-and-white timbered building secreted above the brash modern shop fronts. I enjoy picking out the old parts of this market town, spotting the tucked-away carvings and oddly shaped chimney pots. But I can't do that today. Head down, my vision is blurred by strands of hair escaping from a tight braid. The strands stick to my face as I try to brush them away.

Shrugging off the mac, I hang it up to dry. I'll return it to the shop next time I'm in. It's my mother reincarnated – except my mother's still very much alive. Still trying to hold me in her vice-like grip of spurious respectability. Maybe this old book will help me break free.

Taking the ancient red leather book out of its carrier bag, I finger it, curiosity bubbling through me. I open it again to the rain-splodged title page that had so excited my imagination when I'd glimpsed it. Who knows, perhaps this old tome will give me the answers I've been seeking.

The Alchemy of Night Enchiridion
A Treatise on Sexual Thaumaturgy
And the Practice thereof
The Prince Khem Yar Khepher'set,
Supreme Ruler of Khemit and the Two Lands
Being a true and accurate account of the Finding and
Transcription of an authentic papyrus from Ancient Egypt
With
A Commentary on the Practices therein

Dr Paschal B. Randolph

Ohio 1862

Foreword and Addendum notes provided by E.A.W.B.

Keeper of Egyptian Antiquities, British Museum, London

Reprinted for private circulation 1921

Thaumaturgy. Sexual magic. My body wriggles with delicious anticipation. That should liven up my humdrum life.

After putting the kettle on, I make a cup of tea and curl up on the sofa, the book on my lap quietly exuding its tantalising aroma. Breathing it in deeply, I begin to read.

> It is with great pleasure that I write this introduction to the new printing for private circulation of an ancient classic text first made available in the latter part of the nineteenth century by the Southern American Gentleman Esotericist Dr Paschal Beverly Randolph, but since lost. Herein lies a forgotten key to spiritual development through Arcane Carnal Lore that provides us with a practical method for developing the Hidden Powers of Man. Here, thaumaturgy, called by the ignorant wonderworking, reveals the secrets of creation. Love, and the nuptive moment, unlock the doors of the Spirit and disclose the secret of Eternal Life.
>
> I am sincerely grateful that this work was saved for posterity by the distinguished writer and learned Gentleman Egyptologist, Sir H. Rider Haggard of the County of Norfolk. My old friend acquired the typescript and a copy of the original papyrus on one of his expeditions to the town of Luxor in Upper Egypt. It had been left in safekeeping by the author on one of his sojourns there, but he had not returned to claim it. The hotel manager placed it into the hands of my old friend, having learned of Randolph's death.
>
> Recognising its potential value and seeking authentification of the translation of the hieroglyphs and the magical system

therein, Haggard cautiously handed the package to me one evening on the balcony of our Cairo hotel. An artefact such as this was not to be displayed before the eyes of the uninitiated amateur Egyptologist, such as is found frequenting the hotel lobby in the hope of chancing upon such a prize. And indeed, as one such rudely interrupted our exploration by climbing up from the street below, the manuscript was bundled away before I could examine it. I was not to set eyes on it for several years, the Great War having intervened in the meantime.

It was, therefore, with some trepidation and not a little excitement that, in my basement room at the British Museum, I examined the tattered, foxed and blotched pages that had suffered from being left out in the sun at some time heretofore. It looked rather as though some modern-day Egyptian fellahin had used it for his ablutions before deciding that it might be sold to a touristica…

My eyes are drooping. I'll push on and finish this page and then head for bed.

Chapter 5

Night dreams of love

I'm hurled from the depths of sleep. I've been dreaming of making slow, lazy love with Sebastian. He was giving butter-soft kisses to my ankles but he hadn't even had time to reach my knees – I discovered in an earlier dream how erotic his lips on the back of my knees could be...

But...

Sebastian is no longer here...and I'm fully awake.

My eyes flutter and I seem to see the face of my Dark Enigma smiling above me, like a cat through slitted lids. He has so much more substance now. No longer a mere aberration of light. A compelling physicality draws me inexorably towards him. Around him dances the oh-so-familiar smell of cloves and cinnamon. But sharper and less honeyed than in the tomb. Less death and decay, more a musky aphrodisiac that's an indissoluble part of this stranger who sets every fibre of my being tingling with recognition. *Why? Who is he? How can this be happening?* I was right not to trust him.

I have no time to think of that – can't think at all – as another firestorm rushes its way up my spine and out the top of my head. It takes over my whole being as a vivid flash of lightning sears my room and surges of colour burst all around. Overwhelmed by sensation, I am pure pleasure, an ecstasy so intense that it could almost be pain. Almost.

But I'm in terror too. My heart is pounding, my skin crawling, a small voice screaming and not from the intensity of the pleasure. *What is going on?* He hasn't touched me – yet. At least I don't think so. I *was* deeply asleep when this began. The thought of that mummified skin on mine creeps me out.

He's looking at me with those hypnotic eyes, they bore

into my core...and somehow he has total control over me. I'm like one of those old-fashioned puppets and he's pulling my strings. *With the power of his mind?* My mind is fighting to escape, but my traitorous body betrays me, utterly immersed in the overwhelming sensations. *How does he do this?*

As if reading my thoughts, he blinks, lazily, and the turbulence is intense, surges of pulsating fire shooting from the base of my belly. The flames move up my body in crackling waves, weaving themselves around my spine in ever increasing spirals of ecstasy. Starbursts light my now-closed eyes and cascade down to my thighs. The tight panting groans forced from my lips bear no relation to the bliss reaching my nipples, which quiver with a life of their own.

This is no dream.

And there's no time to be afraid, no space to pause and consider. This is all consuming.

My whole body ignites again, right down to my fingertips as I breathe deeper and deeper into my belly with tiny sips of air that each trigger a new tremor until I almost burst. Guttural noises burst from deep within me. Light floods my being. I dissolve into forever, melting into nothingness. All is centred round that point of ecstasy into which I'm rapidly vanishing. It's like all the life is being sucked out of me into a whirling void of urgent male lust. But it doesn't matter. Nothing matters except these incredible sensations.

Orgasm, the implacable orgasm of which Joseph Conrad spoke. This must be it.

Chapter 6

Marvelling why her roses never fade

When at last I collapse on to the bed exhausted, I breathe a long, satisfied sigh. But my mind rushes in with so many questions. It's still on red alert. My terror pushed aside for the moment, I think about sexual thaumaturgy. Is that what this is? A product of sex magic? Maybe that old book will give me the answer. And why didn't Babaanne and my beloved grandfather step in? They are supposed to protect me.

In the Otherworld, Bertrand looks to his beloved. 'Well, tell me, dear, why did we not protect the child?'

'She is no longer a child. The time has come for her to deal with His Majesty. It is time this matter was resolved. It has continued long enough.'

But...why pick me? What am I to my Dark Enigma? Does he wish me harm? He seems to be a benign mentor one moment and the epitome of malice the next.

His Majesty is all too real – and what he's done to me. I've never experienced such sensations before – sex with Tom was never great but I, inexperienced virgin that I was, hadn't known what to expect and didn't realise that his lack of skill and hasty 'let's get to the best bit' hadn't even begun to prepare me. I'd agreed with him when he muttered, 'Frigid bitch doesn't know how to respond.' Sebastian had taught me that what came before 'the best bit' could give me pleasure beyond my wildest imaginings. With him as my dream lover, I learned the delights of anticipation and delay. He crafted the pleasure slowly, savouring each moment. Almost reaching the brink and then holding back – he seemed to instinctively know when to be still

– built up layer on layer like the depth of colour that came from layering on acrylics in the painting classes I once tried. I'd loved creating moodily textured abstracts.

A musky stirring brings me sharply back to the present. That smell. It's how Tom smelled for a fleeting moment after getting to 'the best bit.' Although, Tom's post-coital aroma was a pale imitation of this potent infusion of masculine libido. It seems to reach beyond the present moment back into the shadows of time. A 'love philtre' for the soul? There's no time to find the right words. An opaque eroticism rushes through me once more, eliciting a fiercer desire than I ever thought possible. I'm exhausted, but even in my enervated state, I crave continuance. Really? My gut rolls queasily at the thought. Do I really want to give myself up to this again?

'Who are you?' I whisper warily.

'One who, once more, will teach you all, my hennu nafrit.'

The words are in my head, the voice deep, seductive... strangely familiar...the voice of the book. *Who is this man?* My capricious belly flutters with remembered pleasure like the aftershocks of an earthquake. For a moment, I give all my attention to the sensations as fierce fire plays around my spine and trickles down my thighs and outstretched arms. The dream orgasms with Sebastian were nothing like this, pleasurable though they were.

I need to get a grip on this. 'Yes, but who *are* you?'

'The Prince Khem Yar Khepher'set. Justified. Prince of Khemit and Lord of the Two Lands. May My Majesty live, prosper and throughout eternity healthy be.' He caresses my bare arm with a bright blue flower and once again waves flash through me.

'And how did you...?' I manage to gasp at last.

His face wavers and fades out of view leaving a shimmering iridescence in its wake.

'Come back! You haven't explained anything yet.' My rational head is terrified it's going to happen again. I so hate being totally out of control. I need to know what's going on.

'Read. My. Book.'

The words boom from the bottom of a deep well and I flash back to climbing down a shaft to reach that newly discovered tomb in Egypt. For a moment there, everything went still. Even the walls were holding their breath. As though I'd somehow stepped outside time. 'Don't be silly,' I admonish myself. 'How can you go beyond time?' But, I'd felt more alive than I'd ever been before, hypersensitive and somehow expanded. And – a word I love to feel bouncing along my tongue although I only ever whisper it to myself – *discombobulated* at the same time. Parts of me scattered in all directions. My senses everywhere at once. Acutely aware of every colour, each sound in the immense stillness. My clothes brushing against my skin, the breath moving across my top lip, the rank taste of that smell moving into my lungs, stealing over my skin as though alive, blood pulsing through my heart. Exactly like now. The grain of the rock had magnified, holding me spellbound. Figures moved against the walls, each surrounded by a nimbus of light. But there was a wrongness to it too, a slithering scratchiness that made my back quiver and the blood judder through my veins as my feet skittered with a desire to run, somewhere, anywhere but there. Wilfred Owen had it right, when he wrote, '*on the hot blast and fury of hells upsurge…superhuman inhumanities, long-famous glories, immemorial shames…*'

Each beat of my heart had stretched into eternity as the tiny hairs on my arms lifted themselves into goose bumps and I had glimpsed the ancient past that lingered in the rock. Until that creepy guide touched my arm and I ran. It's the same now, the air prickles with the static electricity hanging in the space where *He's* ensconsed, the Prince whatever. That strange musky fragrance, pungent and overlaid with something like roses. Yet so rank beneath. Acrid, catching the back of my throat…achingly familiar.

Why aren't I more afraid? But I am. Petrified beyond measure. My soul feels frozen, dramatic I know, and yet so true...I'm so conflicted.

A memory, tantalisingly out of reach. Is it connected, can it be...?

'Yes,' the voice in my mind sighs. *'Finally. You begin to understand. Soon everything you shall remember. My Majesty says again. Read. My. Book.'*

* * *

I'd been reading the old tome last night. But it's hard going. The language is obscure – even with my love of archaic words. The stuffy tone is so at odds with sexual wonderworking. It had taken all evening to decipher the first few pages. Not quite the pleasure I'd anticipated. But maybe the book's what triggered the dream? I'll try again in the morning. I'm free all day.

As I slip back into sleep, I'm drained, utterly weary, boneless. I've lost all substance, floating lightly above my body. Dreamily I consider again whether I'm fascinated or frightened by my nocturnal visitor. As I'm wondering what there is to remember, someone switches the light out in my mind.

* * *

Next morning, I pick up the faded red leather once more, determined to unravel what's been happening to me.

The Alchemy of Night

Preface

The Finding

In 1856 I had the greatest good fortune to travel throughout the Orient in search of arcane knowledge. During my travels in the wilderness of Upper Egypt, I was approached by a heavily veiled woman, beautiful of form, who showed me only her alluring walnut eyes. Following her beckoning finger, I was taken to a vast mudbrick hovel, the remnant perhaps of some ancient Pharaoh's palace that looked as though it would slide down the hillside at any moment. My dragoman was instructed to wait in the courtyard outside. As I entered through a low door I was astounded. The "hovel" was richly furnished and I was ushered to an opulent, gold-encrusted couch and invited to sit whilst being plied with sweet fenugreek tea in delicate gold-embossed glasses served on a tray of exquisite beaten gold. An austere gentleman in Bedouin-style robes entered and nodded pleasantly towards me. After a few moments of conversation, of which I understood barely one word, he gestured around the room and the daughter, as I presumed her to be, brought forward treasures for my delectation. Ushab'tis and funeral masks, ostraca, papyri and gemstone carvings. Larger pieces of furniture and life-size statues. All were pressed upon me. When it became apparent to my host that I had but a few words of Arabic (a situation I rectified as soon as possible thereafter) my dragoman was called in to indicate that these treasures were for sale. It was with great regret that I was forced to explain that my funds were severely limited and that I was not one of the representatives of an august foreign museum such as were to be found everywhere throughout Egypt at the time.

To my surprise, my host theretofore asked if I would do him the honour of spending the night in his establishment. He told me that he came from a venerable family of sand travellers, nomads who had settled over a millennium ago in the abandoned palace. Digging it out from the sand his family had recovered many treasures – and several tombs. He wished to explain to me the origins and purpose of some of the pieces he had for sale and to have a philosophical discussion as, so he said, he could see that I was a man of culture. Deeply flattered, I agreed. After passing a very pleasant evening in his company and learning much of the spiritual beliefs of the ancient peoples, I retired to the bedchamber indicated.

The reader may imagine my surprise when I awoke out of a deep sleep to find my host's daughter slipping into my bed. A full moon illuminated the room, its grey light sucking out all colour but bright enough for me to luxuriate in her incandescent unveiled beauty. She communicated by gestures that I should remove the undergarments in which I slept, shrugging off her own gossamer robe. What passed between us that night introduced me to the mysteries of Anseiratic communion between a man and a woman – and the powerful spiritual entities that are the gods and goddesses themselves invoked through Affectional Alchemy. Thinking back to the discussion I had had with her father, with its veiled insinuations of almost forgotten knowledge, though of necessity circumspect as it had to pass through the lips of my dragoman, I realized I had stumbled upon a primordial tradition that had clearly been transmitted down through the ages from generation to generation within a community of initiates.

When I awoke, I found myself out on the hillside. Alone. Fully clothed and clutching an ancient papyrus annotated in both demotic and Arabic script. Somehow I knew that this held the key…

Wearily, I put down the book. So wordy. But at least it's getting to 'sexual commingling.' Perhaps it will explain my experiences after all.

Chapter 7

The white magic of love

'Good morning, Miss Grayson, did you have a good weekend?' The Chief Librarian calls. With its wide glass walls and lack of a separate staff entrance, there's no chance of avoiding his watchful eye as I enter the ugly building stuck on the end of a shopping mall. Whoever designed this now decaying, brutal concrete and glass 1970s monstrosity hadn't taken officious Mr McMeeney into account. Nor have the councillors that are trying to 'close a white elephant to save money.' How can a *library* be outmoded? Surely people will always want books? At least Mr McMeeney's fighting to keep it open, suggesting innovations like writers' events. Pushing for evening and weekend opening. At his age, he'll never get another job. No wonder he's worried.

'Ah, Miss Grayson…a word if you please…'

Out of the corner of my eye, I see him fussily smoothing his comb-over and brushing off his lapels before glancing at his watch. 'Those councillors are due on another fact-finding mission. They'll be here any minute.'

Better get upstairs, make sure everything's ready, though it's doubtful he'll be showing them my outdated abode. As I head towards the sanctuary of the first floor reference section, he's a sorry figure as he fidgets with his cuffs and fingers his silly little toothbrush moustache. I'm compelled to respond, 'Fine weekend, thanks. You?'

You wouldn't believe it, I smile to myself as I round the bend in the stairs, not bothering to wait for his reply. Pushing myself up the last few stairs is hard though, my feet drag and stumble on the open treads. Strangely detached from my surroundings, I barely register the change from the glaring brightness downstairs to the dimness of the windowless reference room. Its fluorescent tubes flicker with age. That, in itself, is usually enough to make me slightly woozy. Today, my mind has untethered itself, slipped off elsewhere in search of answers. My satiated body is drained, boneless. I'm deeply weary. My legs jelly-like, as though I've had fresher's 'flu'. I haven't recovered from the drop in vitality as my Dark Enigma left. He'd visited again last night. Took all my energy with him. 'Ennui', that's what I'm suffering from. Physical and emotional 'ennui'. I've been hoping to use that word for sometime. But not like this. There's another word I favour. 'Unctuous'. 'Oily and sycophantic'. That exactly matches the tones floating up the stairs as Mr McMeeney greets the fact-finding mission.

It's horribly stuffy in here. Yesterday's sweat lingers. The faint outline of old men who come in because they have nowhere else to go. Wrapped in their overcoats despite the heat outside. That's the problem with modern buildings, no ventilation, nowhere for the smell to dissipate. It saturates the walls with their presence. Not that I mind. Most days, it feels safe being enclosed with these old books and their antiquated readers around me. But some people complain that it's claustrophobic. Such a contrast to the acres of glass downstairs that put browsers on show to every passer-by. What will the fact-finding mission make of it? Of course they'll want to shut us down. No wonder Mr McMeeney's worried.

Couldn't they make a few alterations? A window or two would make such a difference. Standing on tiptoe at the top of the stairs, I can glimpse the willow-lined river below. The stately swans in sharp contrast to the flurrying of the ducks and synchronised wheeling of a pigeon flock. Such a lovely view. The reference library could be a wonderful space if they opened up the blank wall. But the feet of those swans are paddling madly under the surface to keep them floating in the same spot. I know exactly how they feel.

As I reshelve books, dust flies up. A sneeze tickles my

nose as I inhale the smell I love beyond reason. Ancient paper and printer's ink that comes off on your fingers. The stains of yesteryear. But I feel outdated, obsolescent. My body young, but my mind outdated, like this outmoded space. I could do with a reboot, or for Sebastian to return and challenge me to find something more obscure than ever before. Something that could never be discovered hidden in a computer file.

The council could install new computers though. Free Wi-Fi. A lift. A coffee machine perhaps? Comfy seats. Like the trendy bookshops. That would draw the punters in. I've suggested a family history section, linked to county record offices and the excellent town museum. Somewhere people could search parochial church registers and burial records. We already have a great local history section. It needs to be scanned in so that people could get a sense of what their ancestors experienced. The local historical society would assist. And the museum. They do so much for children there. Really bring history to life. We could cooperate with them. We don't even have a storytelling corner in our children's section. But, when I suggested it, Mr McMeeney scoffed. So I put the idea on the back burner. It's simmering gently. Maybe I'll suggest it if the councillors come calling.

I'm reflecting on what a slimeball the so-appropriately named McMeeney can be, obsequious with the customers yet spiteful with the staff, when I bump into Aidan, the young intern.

'Alright, Miz Grayson?' he mumbles through his bright smile, although his eyes look at the floor off to my left. 'Anything I can do?'

Speaking proper English would be a start. But he's a lovely boy, even though he does seem to come from a different planet. So I say, 'I'd love a cup of strong coffee if you wouldn't mind, Aidan, I'm a bit tired this morning. But don't let those councillors see you.'

'Course not, pint of cawffee coming right up.'

Turning on the ancient computer sleeping in the corner under its 'Staff Only' notice, I remind myself to buy a new laptop. Or should I get one of those smartphones that do everything? I'm not keen on advanced technology. It's so alien to me. My old phone served me well. I was confident with it. Loved my trusty laptop too, so solid and substantial, till it died on me. Why am I so out of step with the modern world? Such a technophobe? With a sigh, I turn back to the computer.

When the machine creaks into action, I google 'Paschal B. Randolph'. There are over three thousand entries – and quite a few YouTube videos. One, by a rather delicious chocolaty voice, catches my attention but I'll have to wait until later to listen to it. It's not exactly suitable for the reference library. I'll pick up a smartphone and a new desktop on the way home. Make my study suitable for purpose. Refining my search by adding 'sexual magic' rapidly brings down the number of entries and I'm delighted to find Randolph's description of his sexual initiation.

> 'One night – it was in far-off Jerusalem or Bethlehem, I really forget which – I made love to, and was loved by, a dusky maiden of Arabic blood. I learned of her, and the experience – not directly, but by suggestion – the fundamental principle of the White Magick of Love; subsequently I became affiliated with some dervishes and fakirs of who, by suggestion still, I found the road to other knowledges; and of these devout practisers of a sublime and holy magic, I obtained additional clues – little threads of suggestion, which, being persistently followed, led my soul into labyrinths of knowledge of which the practitioners themselves did not even suspect the existence.'

Did he share those clues? Those 'threads of suggestion'? He certainly seems to know about the kind of experience I've been having. I need to discover more about this man. A job for Aidan, perhaps?

> 'Not all invisible onlookers, however, are to be counted in along with seraphs and angels... People may laugh as much as they please at the idea of wicked, mean, obsessing, tantalizing, tempting beings. My research and experience tell a far different story. When it is asserted that there is no mysterious means whereby ends both good and ill can be wrought at any distance; that the so-called spells, charms and projects are mere notions, having no firmer foundation than superstition or empty air alone – then I flatly deny all such assertions, and affirm that the conclusions arrived at are so reached by persons wholly ignorant of the invisible world about us, and of the inner powers of the human mind.'

Phew, I need to take a breath after reading that. He's verbose. Exactly like his book. Nevertheless, did that contact with the invisible world extend to being haunted by the shade of an ancient Egyptian prince? With mounting excitement, I click here and there, avoiding the more sensational tabloid sites. I'm scanning an academic article on Randolph's role in introducing sexual magic in the nineteenth century when a coffee slops on to the desk beside me. 'Hey, your man looks just like me, though he be black. He be a real beast.'

'Beast?'

'Yeah, you know. Peng. Real cool, man, er, Miz Grayson. He's got my eyes. Why are you looking at him?'

'I found a book by him in the charity shop and wondered who he was. Yes, his eyes are shaped as yours are, although his are most likely brown. It's hard to tell from this photo.' It's a pity Aidan doesn't show his eyes more often. 'Different hair though...'

The man on the screen is carefully coiffed, wiry hair tethered behind his ears to keep the springy curls in place. Aidan's blond dreadlocks are the talk of the library. Mr McMeeney demanded he cut them off but Aidan was adamant it was his ethnic right to keep them. Quite what the ethnicity behind Aidan is no one's sure, nor does anyone have the courage to ask. His surname, Doran, offers no clue. His deep green eyes are startling against his pale white skin and blond hair, which looks, to my uncritical eye, to be his natural colour. It certainly matches the fluffy soul tuft sprouting from his chin – a tuft that might one day equal the luxuriant goatee and moustaches decorating the handsome man on the screen in front of us.

'Wore I when Pharaoh My Majesty was, but that of My Majesty bigger was.'

The boastful voice is in my head again. Fortunately Aidan cuts in, 'Why not look in the Wickedpedia?'

'Because, as I've told you before, Wikipedia is notorious for the inaccuracy of its information.'

'Yeah, but it gives you the 'fo, man…sorry, Miz Grayson.' He's clearly seen the glint in my eye.

'Off you go, Aidan, I'm sure they could use some help in the back room. It's quiet in here today. Come back if it gets busy.' Unlikely, so best to keep him out of sight of those fact-finding councillors even though, in my eyes, he's an asset, and an unpaid one at that.

The photograph that heads up the article could almost be a mirror image of the Aidan of the future, seen through a dark glass. All shadows and shade. Like one of those black-and-white negatives grandpa used to keep in a biscuit tin in the dresser and insisted on showing me on Sunday visits.

'It will help her to see the world differently,' he'd said when my mother complained that it wasn't a suitable toy for a five-year-old. There was a great deal on which my mother and my irascible grandfather did not see eye to eye. Both generations had had their children late in life. He'd scandalised his family by marrying a much younger woman he met on his travels, who'd died of pneumonia soon after giving birth.

I miss grandpa terribly. He always seemed closer to me than my progenitors. He'd been quite the rebel in his younger days and he relished opening my mind to new possibilities. It was a legacy from him that had enabled me to buy a small flat and make a life for myself away from the clinging claustrophobia of the parents.

I had indeed learned to conjure faces from bleached images. I see them everywhere now, in the clouds and the stains on the old books in the charity shop. Tom laughed at me, one of the many things about me that'd made him feel superior. But I'm not going to think about that now. Especially with my new companion of the night to consider. A flicker of pleasure strokes my spine as the lingering flame bursts into life again. Pushing the sensation away, I turn back to the screen.

The handsome, dark visaged guy in the photo is nothing like my Dark Enigma. It's typical stern nineteenth century portraiture but, according to one learned academic, he was a doctor who was responsible for 'sexual thaumaturgy entering the esoteric field'. Magic of a sexual variety. Not surprising, given the sensuality of those mesmerising dark eyes and the generous bow of an amorous mouth beneath his neatly trimmed moustache. What sexual enchantments could I have learned from him? Something in the carefully contrived neatness of the photograph suggests a much more carnal man waiting to burst out from behind the stiff façade, waiting to ravish the beholder. 'Get a grip, you're talking like one of those trashy novels you weren't allowed to read as a teenager,' I admonish myself. 'The ones Mrs B probably picked out for herself from the shop.'

Savouring the word 'ravish', I swish it silently round my tongue. The roughness of the 'r' on the back of my throat and the tingle of the 'issh' as it segues from my tongue onto my lips reminds me of the dream that wasn't a dream. Ravished, that's what I've been. Ravished by my Dark Enigma. My mouth smiles ruefully as familiar tingles set me wriggling in my seat again. On the computer screen is a man who would have understood, who could have explained it, shown me what it meant to be a sexual magician. But I'm a century and a half too late. At least he left me the book.

Shivering as echoes of the firestorm that flashed through me so fiercely run up my spine once more, I turn back to the screen. Entranced, I read on, oblivious to the regular customers who come for their morning stint with the outdated periodicals. When Aidan returns to see how I'm getting on, I'm able to tell him that 'Randolph's a strange character. He was a "free man of colour" from Virginia – a mulatto as they were called then – and a friend of Abraham Lincoln's. It appears that he qualified as a doctor. His father was American. His mother an exotic mix of Madagascan royalty, American, French, African, Spanish or German depending on the person he was talking to at the time. It would have been difficult for him in the Deep South. There was still slavery, you know, and he was a fervent abolitionist. He must have been a relatively wealthy man because he travelled extensively. Not what I'd have expected at all.'

'Awesome. Sounds like me, except I ain't got no money. What else did he do?'

'He was part of a flourishing occult movement in America, started the Hermetic Brotherhood of Eulis and was involved with the Rosicrucians. Do you know about them?'

'Nah.'

'Look it up later and write a report on it.'

Aidan's written work is good. Not at all like his mangled speech. If a subject fires his imagination, he digs up a mountain of information and produces a mind-grabbing story – although I have to rein him back in the factual reports Mr McMeeney insists upon. I hope I'll kindle in him a desire to be an investigative journalist at the very least. He'd make an excellent fiction writer. But Aidan's lip wrinkles in disgust.

'You know I don't like doing those wack reports.'

'And you know, Mr McMeeney made it a condition of your internship. If you're not in full-time school, you need to be having proper training. It's not time wasted. Research is a useful skill for many things in life. You won't regret it.'

Aidan doesn't look impressed. 'Yeah, whatever. What else did he do?'

'He was an early Spiritualist and wrote a treatise on the use of hash to induce a trance state – and one about scrying with magic mirrors.'

'That's sound. He be the man. Can I do my report on that?'

'Yes, if you wish. But only on magic mirrors. I don't think the library committee is quite ready for hash-induced visions.' I suppress a grin as I picture Mr McMeeney's face. Magic mirrors are going to stretch his mindset as it is. 'I think you'll be surprised at what went on in the nineteenth century. Not as boring as you might suppose. It wasn't all stiff and starchy church stuff, you know. Here, start by reading what I've found so far.'

Scooting my chair over to my desk, I fill out a request for the biography mentioned in one of the articles. Determined to find out as much as possible about Randolph and how he'd come by his arcane knowledge. Perhaps at last I'll find the answer to those dreams. If only there was someone to explain it. But I enjoy a research challenge, so I'll dive deep into the esoteric past.

Chapter 8

Clothed in the perfect flesh of woman

'Good morning, lovey. We're going to be quiet today what with this weather and everyone being down at the antiques fair, so it's time to sort out that upstairs stock room. Okay?'

I reluctantly move towards the steep staircase. The upper floor is where the smell of old clothes is most rancid and the heat will make it stuffier than ever. A couple of poky rooms, packed with who knows what. It's where we store the donations deemed too damaged to sell, or which linger too long on the 50p sale rail. Boxes are thrust there, out of sight when the sorting room downstairs gets too full. I'd much rather be out in the sunshine looking around the antiques fair myself.

'If you don't need me today, I could always do the stock room another time, Mrs B,' I venture.

'It has to be today, lovey, the recycling people are coming to collect the rags on Monday.' The woman smirks. 'You know they pay good money for those.'

I hate that smile, so avaricious and calculating. The more money the shop makes the better she looks in the eyes of the powers that be. She doesn't seem to have any feeling for the people the charity serves. Look at her, patting her hair and smoothing her skirt. Appearance is everything with Mrs B.

'You can go through the books too. The wastepaper guys'll be here later in the month.'

It saddens me to see the old books go for pulping. I've taken so many home that my bookshelves are overflowing. In quiet moments in the library, and in the shop, I search out the antiquated words that I relish. But the first time I'd asked, 'What is the reason for that "brouhaha"?' Mr McMeeney had frowned and said with flatulent pomposity, 'We speak plain English in this library, Miss Grayson.' I savour the phrase 'flatulent pomposity', finding the explosive pop of air through my lips as I whisper it oddly satisfying. I'd discovered the phrase when browsing through a 1920s murder mystery a few days ago and immediately thought of the stuffy librarian. It describes him so perfectly, especially when faced with a 'brouhaha'. That word sounds like a commotion itself with the laughter at the end tickling my tongue. Such a shame it's gone out of fashion. I've been careful since then to keep my linguistic treasures to myself.

The thought of all those words disappearing forever breaks my heart. 'Why don't I take them round to the old people's home, give them something to read. They'll enjoy them.'

'Elf and Safety. The matron says they harbour germs. As if. But what can you do?' Mrs B shrugs, boobs threatening to jump out of a skimpy top. 'No, you'll have to sort them. Better do that stock room first though.'

Sensing the futility of further protest, I climb to the neatly labelled 'Stock Room' and push open the door. Gagging on the foul wave that engulfs me, I rush to the window. As usual I have to hunt for the key to the window locks. Whatever does the insurance company think anyone breaking in would find? There's nothing of value here. It would need an agile cat to make it this far and anyone passing in the High Street below would soon spot a burglar.

Where to start? Tottering mounds of clothes are piled among bulging bin liners and sagging cardboard boxes. The precarious heaps reach the ceiling in places. I'll set off an avalanche if I'm not careful. My heart thuds at the thought of being buried under that stench.

I plot a course of action. Pull out what I can onto the landing and sort it there. If there is anything saleable, it can go into the tiny, never used 'Staff Room' for the time being. I'll throw the rags out into the yard from the cloakroom window and bag them up later. It'll be a bit of a squeeze to get past the old-fashioned basin and lavatory cistern to the high window. Good job I'm slim. As it's unlikely to rain again before Monday, they can be stored outside. No one in their right mind would steal those fetid remnants of forgotten lives. They'd have to be desperate and, if so, they're welcome to them.

From time to time, I hear the shop door buzzer and cock my head, listening for Mrs B's call. I need something to break the silence. It's weighing heavily on me. If I'd known what I'd be doing, I'd have brought a radio to keep me company. I enjoy the travellers' tales on *Excess Baggage,* dreaming of visiting the faraway places. Although that trip to Egypt with Tom hadn't been much of a success. It still makes me queasy to remember it, despite the fact that most of the time, I'd felt comfortable among the heat and dust.

'Why be surprised when the Land Beloved was for so long your home?' The voice booms at me as the light fades.

Leaping back, I brush against a pile of boxes. Down they crash, bags, cartons and clothes sliding from all directions. Covering my nose with my sleeve, when things settle and the dust clears, my eyes are caught by a glimpse of blue. Beautiful blue. The colour of lotus petals under an azure sky... Lotus petals? How on earth do I know the colour of lotus petals? Heart thudding, I'm still shaken from my near-internment when I hear, 'The colour of initiation. Your rank as priestess. Remember you not? To earn it you studied hard.' That voice again, deep and booming, with a hint of laughter in it this time.

I'm not sure I want to know. But there's such a familiarity about this that I have to ask. 'What do you mean I worked hard to earn it?'

'You in time shall remember. Should you perhaps on it try?'

Try it on? It's bound to stink. But, despite my misgivings, I pull the heavenly blue from the pile. A beautiful linen robe is revealed. Crease-free and redolent with that almost-rose fragrance that clings to the book. Holding it to my nose, I breathe in deeply, memories stirring and shifting like snakes in a bag. I almost grasp them, but they're gone as the voice urges, 'Put it on. Revealing as those of old it is not. Under the rule of My Majesty women were proud to display their glorious bodies. But My Majesty sees that times have changed. Although perhaps, in some cases, not.'

Picturing Mrs B in her skimpy top, I hurriedly recall the frescos on the tomb walls. The way the diaphanous robes appeared to be draped under the breasts of the women. Their nipples coloured bright red. How immodest, I'd thought. But, as I drop the robe over my head, I'm longing for the freedom of those far-off times. It fits perfectly and I stand tall. Poised and confident. Comfortable in my skin. So this is what it's like to be a woman. I half turn and my lithe hips sway to a barely heard, but insistent beat as I raise my arms.

'Stop this instant. Adept you are, not a dancing girl cavorting for the pleasure of men. Dishonour not your sacred calling.' The voice is stern, but it is too late…

…Robes cast aside, diaphanous veils tied around nubile hips, caught with a girdle of clattering cowrie shells. Headbands tight to keep plaited wigs in place. Scented cones drizzling cooling oil, the weighted braids swinging from side to side. Bodies moving, sensuously, lost in the dance. Each muscle rippling of its own volition. Bellies oscillating, crimson nipples twitching. Exquisite control yet abandoned. Wild. Lascivious. Clapping, stomping. Raised arms undulating, tambourines banging, bangles shimmering, beringed fingers vibrating in time to the twin sistrums' beat. Hands roaming, touching, exploring, sharing. A splendid harp twangs. Wrought with silver, gold, lapis lazuli, malachite, and every costly stone. Leaping for the joy of our hearts. Lyres plucking harmonies from air that crackles with heka. Insistent, deeper, ever deeper. Eyes glazed. Trancelike. Mouths rejoicing, 'Hathor, Isis, Sekhmet, Bastet, Mut. Sa sekhem sahu.' Moving in unison in a

sinuous snake, central suns ablaze, raising the sekhem power before falling, limbs entwined, on to cool flaxen sheets…

If only He knew what had gone on in the privacy of our temple. How we women came together to dance, to honour the goddess, to revel in the bodies we'd been given. But even the supreme ruler Himself was banned from that sacred rite. How do I…

…oh, never mind, better get on with it.

Deflated, I turn to the disorderly heap in front of me. Have I got the energy for this? Someone's pulled the plug again. Why does that happen when His Majesty's around? But I push myself on, lured by hopes of other treasures to be revealed.

Chapter 9

The pullulating world of magic

Slipping off my shoes, I draw my feet under me and pick up young Aidan's manuscript. He may have only recently left school but I envy his confidence – and his free and easy attitude, especially towards Mr McMeeney. He doesn't seem at all in awe of him. Calling Aidan young makes me feel ancient though. There are so few years between us. He's becoming a source I can rely on. A friend. No matter how unlikely. Maybe I could open up to him a little more.

Still in search of answers, I read his report thoughtfully. There's so much to understand about this weird world into which I'm being inducted without consent. Like I'm on a 'coddiwomple'. Another word I've been hoarding as I love its clip-clopping rhythm and the suggestion of travelling purposefully towards an as yet unknown destination. It's perfect for this moment. I have more than a little curiosity and a rather disturbing flicker of excitement is coursing through me.

Magic mirrors
Aidan Doran

The use of magic mirrors for scrying – seeing what is hidden – goes back far into history. Polished stone mirrors have been found in Stone Age graves. They were popular in ancient Egypt and with the modern magicians of the nineteenth century occult revival. The Mexican god of destiny and divination, Tezcatlipoca, used obsidian mirrors as 'speaking stones'. They are truly magical.

The Goddess of Love

In Egypt, the Love Goddess, Hathor, was the patron of music, dance and beer. This lady really liked to party. She wore the all-seeing sun disk eye of her father Ra on her head. She knew everything that went on not only on earth but in the sea and the heavens – and could get into your head as well. You had to be careful what you thought when this lady was around. There was no messing with her. She carried a shield that protected you from harm but also reflected things so you saw their true meaning...

(The whole paper will be found at the end of the book)

Hmm, back to ancient Egypt again. I've got a strong feeling that's where all these weirdnesses began. Reading on, I'm soon immersed in the occult world. Aidan has certainly done a thorough job on this. Some of the uses and rituals are bizarre in the extreme. But the Mirror of Hathor looks promising. Bathing in rose oil and wearing my robe to invoke her. I can do that. The hints on how to interpret what I might see are useful. Now, all I need is a mirror.

But, goodness, how am I going to explain this one to Mr McMeeney? Sex, drugs and magic eyes. Consecrating a mirror by ejaculating on it? What's that all about? I'd better bury it deep.

Time for hot chocolate and bed. What will I dream tonight?

Chapter 10

Bright in the forehead

This time I've come prepared. A sixth sense warned me that Mrs B had plans and there's a funny little bubble of excitement fizzing in my belly. Bounding up the stairs I switch on the radio. '...who died today. Here's an extract from an interview with her in 1986.'

'It was the strangest thing. I was on the Cardiff train and this man thrust a papyrus at me. It looked genuine. I had no idea why he was giving it to me. He could not have known that I read hieroglyphs and demotic script. I was very young at the time. On my way to a singing engagement.' The voice is reedy, that had clearly been a long time ago. I turn up the volume, plastic bags and dusty boxes forgotten. Who is this?

'What did he say?' Even the interviewer seems taken aback.

'Nothing really. Merely, "I trust you will find this useful in your work." He got off at the next station. I never even asked his name.'

'Was it useful?'

'Oh yes. When I translated it – I didn't wait to get home, I got on with it there and then – it set out eight of the ten steps of the mystic marriage. Unfortunately, the last lines were torn off so we do not have the final consummation.'

'Mystic marriage? That's what your book is based on, is it not? What exactly was it?'

'It was a bonding of two souls on all levels. It pulls people together across time, what you would call a soulmate relationship. Of course, simply because you meet time and again it doesn't mean you'll be together in harmony. That needs more careful planning in the Afterlife –'

'Yes, hmm, perhaps people had better read your book to find out more as that is all we have time for today. Thank you so much for coming

on the programme M –' The time pips cut across the interviewer's voice before he names his guest.

Blast it. I'll have to check that out. It sounds as though that book could be useful. But I soon forget the mystery guest as I turn towards the sagging pile of boxes, intending to pull out the contents. A shaft of sunlight slips through the window to turn the room to gold. A stained and mouldy carton transform into a treasure chest limned in light, awaiting my eager fingers. It reminds me of what Howard Carter is reputed to have said when he squinted through the peephole into King Tut's tomb. Wonderful things, indeed. Mrs B couldn't have looked through these before piling them up.

First out of the box is a delicate mother-of-pearl-inlaid box of oyster-shell coloured candles. They remind me of Sebastian's translucent freckle-speckled skin and I hold the box to my heart. Where is he? Will he get in touch, he'd seemed so…

Reluctantly, I put the box down and lift out a tiny creamy alabaster jar whose stopper is covered in wax. The most amazing perfume drifts from it, exactly like that from the pages of the book. The almost-roses fragrance sets my heart racing and triggers a longing for something I can't articulate. It's a most effective aphrodisiac to which my whole body responds. I'm on fire again. Feminine, raunchy, ready for…

'Sufficient that is *kheroti*. Your mind pure keep.'

My Dark Enigma is back. The fire is dowsed, my energy draining away, moving towards him in a silver stream. Instinctively, I fold my arms over my belly sucking it in tight, staring at him mutinously. I'm determined not to engage with him this time. He's not going to take over my mind again. He's not.

'Examine what else in the box is, if you please.' He gestures imperiously towards the precarious pile.

It's no good, I have to ask, 'Did you put these here for me to find?'

'My Majesty may have done. Beyond the power of My puissant Majesty it is not, you know.'

Is it my imagination or is there a hint of uncertainty in the creaky voice? Is my Dark Enigma doing this? If not him, who could it be?

Tangled leather thongs catch at my fingers. Lifting them out, I see a deep red amulet carved from shining stone. Untangling it, on impulse, I slip it over my head. A moon-shaped piece nestles on the back of my neck and the closed U-shape at the front reminds me of a vulva as I look down at it. What the…?

Blinking the thought away, I recall my research. A *menat*, that's it. The feathered phallus-shaped glittering blue stone alongside must be a *sem*. It's Sebastian's, I have no doubt. It's like there's an invisible thread connecting us, pulling us together. Winding tightly in my belly. I'm quivering with anticipation, of what I'm not quite sure. But I can't wait to find out. As I slip the *sem* into my pocket, claw-like nails scrape at my hand.

'To My Majesty give!'

'No,' I reply holding onto the *menat*. 'It belongs with this and it was never yours. I'm going to give it to Sebastian – when I see him again.' I can't allow an iota of uncertainty to show or he'll snatch it out of my hands. Concentrating on Sebastian's lapis blue eyes that exactly match the colour of the amulet, I stand firm.

'My Majesty to defy you dare?'

'Yes, I do. I'm getting fed up with you looking over my shoulder all the time. Now go away and leave me to get on with this.'

A sulky silence greets my words. His Majesty is fingering something hung around his own neck. It's shimmering between the worlds. Best leave that thought for now.

Turning back to the boxes, I unearth a fragile headdress wrapped in a grubby linen cloth. It looks like gold. But it can't be, can it? The delicate filigree tiara has exquisite gems suspended like tiny drops of blood in the middle of each leaf which stand proud above a narrow central band. 'It's beautiful,' I whisper as, with quivering hands, I lift it to my hair and dash to the cloakroom. Almost afraid to look, I glance sideways to the spotted mirror above the cracked basin.

The face that stares back is not from this world. Somehow my blue robe is in place and my heavy almond-shaped eyes are outlined in darkest black kohl and shaded with brightest green malachite. The lips that rarely know lipstick in the present time are deepest red. Ebony hair is swept up under a plaited wig topped with the golden headdress. Sultry and sexy. Faintly, I hear Mrs B call from the shop below. But, for once, I ignore her insistent demand. I stare at myself. Had I really looked like this?

'Oh yes, Precious One. A temptress delightful sent from the Eternal Ones for My delectation. You My Majesty a slave to your beauty ensnared. Too good by far for that *nti hati.*' The ancient nose wrinkles with distaste as the words are spat out. Then his face brightens. 'You were as beautiful as a lotus flower ensnaring me in your petals. My Majesty a poem wrote about you, "My love is one and only, without peer, lovely above all Egypt's girls. Dressed in the flesh perfect of woman..."'

The ancient voice caresses my ears. Was this how he bound me to him? With poetry? And flattery? Potent blandishments. But surely it took more than that? Can it be true? Or is this another silly daydream?

'Come, there is still much to do.'

I plunge my hands back into the carton, trying to still an ever-deepening longing I can't wait to satisfy. If only Sebastian were here, perhaps we could...

'ENOUGH! Think not of that dog in the presence of My Majesty. You are MY *hennu nafrit.*' The face of my Dark Enigma swoops in, engulfing my lips, his greedy hands clutching at my breasts and twisting my nipples cruelly. No longer a dream ravisher, he's become so much more *physical* and, as before, my energy rushes to him leaving me weak and trembling. 'MINE YOU ARE!'

'No! I'm not. I belong with Sebastian.' I'm not sure why, after all I hardly know him outside the library and I haven't seen him for weeks. But he'll be back and when he does…

There are more urgent things to think about now though. Struggling against the peculiar lassitude that threatens to engulf me whenever *He* is near, I draw myself up and clasp my belly with one hand, thrusting the *menat* at His Majesty's face. 'Be gone. Sebastian and I are joined. You have no right to be here.' I'll cogitate on this later. After all, we've only been intimate in my dreams, never even been on a date. For now, though, I know Sebastian and I belong together for all time. And His Awful Majesty most certainly does not fit into our present day.

As though pushing my words aside, grasping hands reach out greedily once more, lusting after the lapis amulet –

'Phillippa, lovey, would you like a nice cup of tea? You must be getting thirsty up there in that dust.' The manageress's voice floats up the stairs on silken wings.

Even though I know it means 'come and make me a cup of tea,' I shout down, 'Coming right away, Mrs B.' Drawing that gnawing longing up from my belly, I intone fiercely,

'Ena'hai sh'ra khepheret dim'an'tange Ma'at
Ban'a dosert yamin heh'sieh Khem Yar Khepher'set
Ini inuit Isis
Elia whiskia fatu y Set
Ra supra mew'nit ha'wi
Yavah. Seb-en!'

Turn back the stinking face of Set is right. The words send the grizzly presence hurtling to whatever dark hole it crawled from. Trying desperately to imprint them on my mind, and still wondering where the hell they came from, I run down the stairs holding my precious finds, 'I found these bits and pieces, Mrs B. May I have them? I'll pay for them, naturally.'

'Of course you can, lovey. Tawdry bits, no intrinsic worth. But, they look like they were made for you.'

For a moment I debate putting on the headdress, showing her how regal I look. It would be good to be admired. But... No. Not when she subtly insults me like that. Tawdry indeed. Nevertheless, delighted, I wrap my precious purchases and slip them into my bag, leaving the necklace snuggled into my neck. I don't think I'll ever take it off. *It* was definitely made for me. I'll explore my treasures further when I get home. There's that documentary about ancient Egypt to watch tonight. I'll put on my finery and settle in with that and my cocoa. The evening won't be lonely then. Crossing my fingers, I hope that *He*, my Dark Enigma, doesn't intend to join me. But I can't help wishing that Sebastian were here to share it. Not something I'm going to divulge to Mrs B though.

Chapter 11

Wither shall I go?

Modern day Luxor

Shouting. Arabic. Loud and incomprehensible. Getting closer. Every conversation in this place sounds like an argument. So, nothing to worry about, surely?

The bedroom door bursts open. Men, everywhere. Guns slung over epauleted shoulders. Guns. Big guns. Black uniforms, riot shield helmets shout, 'Police!' But what…why…?

Clutching my arm, the rough command, "You, boy. Quiet. Come." Gun-prodded towards the door.

Avid hands snatch the backpack and computer from the ramshackle desk. Grabbing the precious fragments of a mummy case. A robbery? But…they look so official.

Careful, don't…no, keep quiet, don't say anything… Hustled out of the door, rancid scarf is thrust to muffle eyes still half asleep. Covering a mouth that doesn't know the words to call for help. Stumbling down steps. Concrete scraping shins. Falling. Kicked upright again. Prodded and pushed into a car, head banging against the doorframe, stars shine bright.

Yanked out…guns unslung…a blow…consciousness fades…

… Cigarette smoke and cheap aftershave over stale sweat, sewage, the metallic tang of blood. But, most of all fear. Fear so thick it is like moving through a noxious fog, the toxicity stinging the throat, searing lungs that cannot get enough air.

Hot and humid and terrified. Walls grimy and stained. Bars wriggling and writhing. Faces leering, moving, morphing. So polluted. What's gone on here? And why me…? Why can't I be home with the woman I desire above all else?…

… Restlessly pacing. Five steps one way, six the next. Nothing to sit on, only the slimy concrete floor. The incessant hooting of car horns, an ever-present backdrop. The hours marked out by the insistent wailing of the call to prayer. Lights never go off. Except when you need them most. Biting insects, swirling everywhere. No water, tongue stuck to the roof of my silent mouth, stomach cramped in pain, face swelling… When will it end?...

... Counting breaths. One, two, three, four, six. In, out, start again. Whining mozzies, forever biting, sucking away life. Scratch the feverous itching. Gouge out the poisoned blood. Cockroaches skitter and snicker. Is there any moisture under that crisp shell? Rats' tails coil like plump pink linguini, whiskers sniff and shiver around the stinking piss hole in the corner. Heart bumping. Rushing blood blots out the soft scratching and low growling. No ground beneath disconnected feet, the concrete shudders feebly. Get a grip. Throw off the shakes. Desperate thirst. Mouth dried and cracked, tongue too big, sticking to the roof. Water, please God, cool water to ease this parched throat.

Counting breaths. One, two, three, four, six. In, out, start again. Whining mozzies, forever biting, sucking away life. Scratch the feverous itching. Gouge out the poisoned blood. Cockroaches skitter and snicker…soft growling…how much longer…? Time slides away…

Chapter 12

In pursuit of *heka*

Ancient Thebes

Eyes glitter yellow, carrying the light of the sun through the gates of night. Feline claws stalk slithering scales. Cat against serpent. The ancient battle. To win the dawn, the coils of chaos must be overcome.

A green ink Apophis graffiti'd along the ancient chapel wall undulates and almost spirals forth, but is ensnared within the stone. A wax cat melts in a brazier, the coals the only light. Low chanting forms a background. The priests are at their devotions in the main temple. It does not disturb the prickling stillness.

She pounces...

A bony hand swoops down and scoops up the cat. Bastet contorts, slashing claws and spitting fury availing her nought. Her dignity has never been so assailed, her sacred task disrupted. Ruffled fur bristles as the hand strokes and soothes. Abruptly switching tactics she purrs, pushing her head against her captor, rubbing the ancient flesh with seductive ease. Confident of her charm. But the goddess shall not prevail this night. Impaled on an obsidian knife, she is thrown into a reed-woven basket and tossed aside.

'Come, my beauties, to My Majesty come.'

Out of the gloom two serpents glide, entwine themselves around the outstretched arm and hiss in the venerable ears before settling around the crown, a dual uraeus dancing and gliding in the night.

'Agni'ti come forth. My Majesty sees you in the shadows. Come. I command you. Show me how to win eternal life.'

The aged tjaty moves forward reluctantly, bowing low, arms outstretched and palms raised in the formal pose of veneration. 'Your Majesty knows that my magic is long gone, my *heka* exhausted in the battle with Yagut'd'eskia before she was vanquished. My *sekhem* power followed Her Majesty. Now I administrate.' He shrugs and spreads his hands wide. 'I am sexty, what you seek I cannot give.'

'Nonsense. *Heka* you may not bear, but where arcane knowledge lies you know – and the power of invocation. Bring forth the sacred scrolls so that My Majesty may study them for Myself.'

'But...' The tjaty falls back on reciting what had been lamented long ago. 'O Prince, my lord, I draw nigh to life's end. To me the frailties of life have come. And second childhood. Ah! The old lie down. Each day is suffering. My vision fails, ears become deaf and strength declines apace. My mind is ill at ease. My old man's tongue has naught to say because my thoughts have fled –'

'Enough. Fool My Majesty you do not. You are as sharp as ever Agn'ti. I say again. Where are My Majesty's scrolls?'

'The scrolls are gone, Majesty. Our magical library fled into the ether after Yagut'd'eskia disappeared again.'

The Prince rears up. The snakes at his brow spit and weave. 'More like she the books with her took. Why did no one My Majesty inform? I would have scoured the land for her and not rested until that *nedjem ndjmemit* was returned to my care. My Majesty would soon from her the hiding place have forced...'

'Sire, we were afraid. I sought to recover them, but my agents searched the length of Khem. Gone they are, as she has been these past years. It is too late.'

'Bring to me the Oracle. To the Gods I would speak. Go!'

'But your Majesty, preparations have not been made. The Oracle cannot speak without due process. Rituals must be obser –'

As serpents glide down the royal arms, the tjaty backs away knowing that his protests are to no avail.

'Go! On pain of death, bring him to My Majesty.' The Prince

turns his back and strides to a chair. Seating himself he waits, the plaited snakes playing as he does so.

Does Yagut'd'eskia have his great work, his precious gem culled from the long years of study. That tattered papyrus he had found in the ruined mastaba and so laboriously reconstructed. Where is that? Thank the gods he tore out the vital portions and kept them hidden. But he cannot yet complete his self-imposed task. Cannot create the sacred vessel. Not without further guidance. Yagut is aware of how he had bound their souls together in the mysteries of the night, surely? If so, why did she flee before the final act that would have made them all powerful, entwined like the snakes at his feet, alive throughout eternity? How could that *temun't* relinquish all that he offered? Abort the son that would have sealed all? He had forgiven her, but it had been a mistake. She forsook him again.

Shall he regain what has been lost? Find another vessel? Lips clenched tight, a white slash across the ancient face, he thumps a clenched fist into his palm, keeping time with his angry pacing. Why does the Oracle not hurry to his Master's command?

A tall man enters, ancient of nights but bearing his years with dignity. Robed only in a loin cloth his lean body gleams with oil. There is not a hair visible on his body. The sparse flesh clinging to his bones could be almost mummified yet glows with vibrant life. His deeply lined face sniffs the air like a hound. In one hand he carries a *uas* staff, its sekhem power oscillating bright. In the other shimmers a crystal mirror draped in cloth of gold. He walks directly to where his ruler is seated in the gloom, although his eyes are veiled by cataracts thick and milky. 'My presence as you demanded, Sire. The price demanded by the Gods shall be heavy, do you pay it?'

'Yes, yes, anything.' Impatiently the Prince waves Agni'ti forward. 'Stop lurking in the shadows, tjaty. Your presence is required also. As scribe you shall act.'

Prostrating himself before his sovereign, Agni'ti picks up the writing box left by the wall. Seating himself cross-legged on the ground, he discards the inky brush and silently commands the graffiti'd serpent to merge back into its stucco. The spell needed more power than this Prince could ever command. But who let slip the formula to reverse the natural order and draw life from the cold stone? It is not safe in this despot's hands.

Taking out a stylus and wax tablet, he murmurs, 'I await your command, Majesty.'

'Well, Oracle, what require you?'

'Only that, no matter what, you shall not protest but shall heed the Gods. Do you agree?' The veiled eyes look sharply at the Prince, their gaze hypnotic. This man, despite his blindness, sees deep into the monarch's black soul. 'But first, what seek you?'

'The key to My Eternal Life. Sufficient *heka* to keep My Majesty from the next world. To be instructed how to step into My Body of Light without passing through the portals of death. To snatch the time needed to create the vehicle that ensures My Majesty's survival for eternity on this earth. But, beyond doubt, this you already know.' The words are silky, deceptively mild.

'Naturally, I know. But the Gods from your own mouth wish to hear this blasphemy.'

'Blasphemy? How can it be blasphemy to keep My royal personage strong throughout eternity?' Angry now, the Prince rises from his seat.

'Your Majesty should be at his capital governing his subjects not skulking here in this palace in the wilderness. The entrance to the land of the dead lies not beyond this miserable cleft in the hills. It may swallow Ra at night but you cannot hold back death by lurking here. Abydos is where the power of eternity lies, as well you know. Go there to face your destiny. Or return north to your capital and tend your flock.' The old man's face is defiant. He has no fear of this man. A mere mortal now. The gods have left this royal personage, fleeing from the arrogance that presumes to defy death and seeks not the immortality beyond the stars.

'Enough of that. Speak. Tell me what My Majesty must do to ensure my eternal life on this earthly plane or my serpents around your neck shall coil. The blood of a holy man is a sweet chalice for their poison.'

The Oracle lifts his hand for silence. With a wave, he puts the serpents to sleep. 'Your threats avail you nought, Majesty. Do you wish to speak with the Gods or not? If so, sit. And be silent.'

A fist is raised, but the arm pauses in midair before reaching for the chair as the Prince seats himself once more. The Oracle throws a handful of herbs on the brazier and kneels with infinite care, holding on to his staff as though his bones might break from the mere action of folding himself. He lays out the cloth of gold between them and, stamping his staff on the floor, sways and mutters invocations as pungent smoke swirls around. The crystal mirror is reverently placed in the centre, its darkness a shimmering silent pool. Half-glimpsed colours erupt and mingle, flashing lights piercing the gloom as the crystal pool awakens. Images prowl deep in its depths. The old man places both hands on the mirror and shakes as the *heka* passes through him. With a guttural cry, the Oracle throws back his head and a woman's harsh voice is heard.

'Eternal damnation shall be the prize you claim if on this course you continue. Death you cannot avoid. Eternal life for your *khu* you could win if, after your demise, you evade the weighing of your heart but you would merely haunt this world throughout eternity. Your body would be corrupted and could not sustain life on this plane. You cannot escape the double death. Only once a magical child is conceived in which your *sakhu* can take on new life shall you find rest. You cannot from your *khu* create a Body of Light. Your heart is too black. If you must proceed on your course, and it is the greatest perversion, you must find a *wowaei* to bear this child, one to whom you are willingly bound throughout eternity in affectional alchemy. And then, through death to new life, you may proceed. But, be warned. This you cannot force. No shortcut is possible. Even though supreme ruler you be and the Great Wife with whom you passed the tests has fled, you must find someone with whom by the bond of spiritual love and service to each other you transcend that former union and make the magical child. Or else cursed and out of favour of the Gods you forever shall be. Condemned to the second death from which there is no return. Hear our words and beware.' The ancient one slumps to the floor, exhausted.

The Prince leans forward, grabbing both staff and mirror. 'This is not sufficient. You are duplicitous as always. Tell me clearly how I may gain Eternal Life, where I shall find such a one to give my *khu* that life now,' he demands peering into the mirror. It remains shrouded. Throwing it down, he thrusts the *uas* into the old man's side, 'Tell me.' The ancient frame jerks once and is still. 'Awake, damn you. Do as My Majesty orders. Give to me the *heka* My Majesty desires.'

Agni'ti dares to speak. 'You…mi…misunderstood the Oracle, sire. Death is inevitable, and I fear it is too late for *heka* Majesty, the Oracle himself has entered into the Duat.'

'Take out this *nti hati deshretyw* and to the dogs throw him. His power shall avail him nought. He My Majesty has insulted and must pay the price.'

Reverently Agni'ti lifts the body. A feather's weight now the soul has left. Already, as Agni'ti knows, the Oracle's *ba* has passed the test. His *khu* has gained the Otherworld. His heart is the lightest of the light against the judgement of Ma'at. There shall be no second death for him. It matters not where his body is left. Nevertheless, the tjaty shall see that he has a good burial. The dogs shall not have him. 'But,' the old man begs quietly, 'do not stray too far from me, brother. I have need of your assistance in the struggle to come if I am to overcome this *seba*.' As he turns to leave, he plucks up the discarded mirror tucking it deep within his robes. Who knows when it shall be needed next? Meanwhile its power must be dimmed, hidden from this avaricious ruler and his impious desire to escape the next world.

Chapter 13

O happiness is passing

'Excuse me, miss. Do you happen to have *The Idiot's Guide to Apologising*?'

As I look up, the voice goes on. 'I was a right twat. I know that now. Do you think...could you give me another chance, sweet pea?' A pleading smile – wheedling I might have called it were it not bringing back memories of what we'd once had. I'd loved this man with all my heart. Or thought I did. Once. In what now seems like another life.

'Is that really you? You look –' The formerly suave salesman appears ten years older, and way less self-assured. Unshaven beyond fashionable, hair greasy and unkempt. His clothes belong in the reject pile in the charity shop. 'Whatever's happened to you?'

'Oh, you know...' Some of his usual cockiness reasserts itself as he straightens up. 'Temporary reversal of fortune, sweet pea. Seems like that celebratory holiday in Egypt was a trifle premature. Lost a few projects. Should have stayed home to keep on top of things. It took longer than –'

'Keep on top of things? You did that out there, going off with that skank in her hooker heals.'

'No, no, that was merely a momentary aberration on my part. I realised that when I got home and met her mother.' His grimace shows yellowing teeth.

I can't bear to look. He'd been so fastidious before.

'Well, let's say I realised what I was in danger of losing...'

In danger of? More like had lost. But I can't get a word in as he rushes on.

'I had a few business deals going down. Still do. I knew I'd be able to claim you back, *Pippi*.'

'Claim me back! I wasn't lost property. And don't call me Pippi. It was never my name. Anyway, there's –' I'm about to say Sebastian, but is there really? Does he care for me? It's been weeks since he'd shinnied up that lamppost and disappeared. I'm beginning to wonder if I'm unwise holding on to the delights that filled my nights before His Awful Majesty appeared. My cheeks bloom rosily as I remember *those* dreams. Perhaps I am a thoroughly uptight frustrated old spinster – as the man standing before me had so often called me in the past. Too much time on my hands – or rather my nights. What I need is a life. With a hot, flesh and blood –

'From the look on your face you've found someone else to fill those lonely nights, *Pippi,*' he quickly retorts.

'Not at all.' I'm almost shouting, wanting to wipe the smirk off his face and that name off his tongue. So infuriating. So not me. I'm not daring, brave, uninhibited, amusing, rebellious – or defiant of authority. I succumb all too easily. Look at how I crumble under Mr McMeeney's truculent tones. As for my crepuscular night visitor, *He* seems to think he has total power over me. There's nothing remarkable about me. I don't have the fortitude of that fictional little girl.

He's smiling now, switching on the charm, softening me up. Trying to make me feel like I'm the only woman in the world. Pretending to want me. I know that look only too well. It always made my knees go a little weak. Turned my head if I'm honest. I'd so wanted to believe it. What we'd had had been the stuff of my adolescent fantasies. There'd been times he'd been so loving, so focused on me, needing me so intensely. Should I really have tossed that away so easily?

'Of course there hasn't been anyone else, except…' I falter, almost choking up for a moment. Loathe to reveal how I yearn for Sebastian. How much I'd counted on him being back by now to save me from my Dark Enigma. I don't want to tell my ex that though. I hardly think he'll be the one to save me. We used to talk for hours, but not about stuff like this. And it was a case of my listening, not sharing. Spurious intimacy, I realise with hindsight. But fingering the *sem* in my pocket, it becomes hot under my roving fingers. It's powering up. It couldn't be meant for Tom, could it? I'd been so certain it was Sebastian's.

Tom's stroking me now, whispering it will all come good. Calling me sweet pea again. How did he get so close? He says he needs somewhere to stay for a few nights, a few notes in his pocket, for all his deals to come right. Then, we'll be able to live in the country like I've always wanted. I'm leaning into him, softening, overcoming my revulsion at his unwashed state. Remembering the charismatic lover for whom I'd fallen. Sucked in by that old magic. I've been so lonely lately…

But something nags at me and I pull away. The idea of having sex with Tom again doesn't have the same impact as recollecting making love with Sebastian. Even though we've never really… How strange. I realise with a jolt that I've never actually had physical contact with Sebastian. Only dreamt it.

My knees buckle and I almost faint as, without warning, the air thrums and falls away from me. For a moment everything goes dark. I'm whirling down into that bottomless pit again. Sucked back into the past.

'Ah, yes,' a creaky voice sighs in my other ear. 'When surrender to My Majesty you do, everything else disappears.'

He's back. My Dark Enigma. That disused shade of a memory. But deeply seductive for all that. Desperately, I mutter the banishing spell and claw my way back to the present moment, pinching my arm so that the pain brings me back even faster. The light rearranges itself and I see clearly once more.

Tom puts his hand to his nose, retching. 'Whew, what is that smell? Time the drains in this place were cleared out, they're disgusting.' He wipes his mouth with the back of his grimy hand, peering around, trying to locate where the smell is coming from. He's clearly oblivious to his own body odour.

I'm not going to let on that it's not the drains. It's His Awful Majesty's own pungent presence. His phosphorescent shadow is once again detaching itself from the nearest bookcase, thin green waves radiating before him. His angry vibes spill out to fill the – thankfully, otherwise empty – reference library.

Before I can say more, hurried footsteps, the banging of the double doors and a huge intake of breath announce the arrival of Mr McMeeney.

'What is the meaning of this, Miss Grayson? One does not entertain down and outs in the Reference Room of the City Library. You know my policy. It will not do.' He draws himself up to his full but still rather insignificant height. 'Sir, I must ask you to leave immediately.' Bristling is the only word for it. Even his sparse hair is standing angrily on end where he's thrust his hand through it.

'But…but,' stammers a bewildered and somewhat chastened Tom as he struggles towards me. 'I'm her fiancé. Isn't that right, sweet pea?'

'Not anymore,' I respond with satisfaction as Mr McMeeney takes his arm to escort him down the stairs. 'Not anymore.' But the wobble in my voice denies that it is over. Tom has bounced back into my life with such confidence, despite his outward appearance. The old charm is still there. He could so easily make it right again. Do I really want to relinquish him? Sebastian seems to have vanished. Is my only chance at happiness slipping away? The relationship was all-consuming when we first met. Could we rekindle it? I need someone special in my life. I'm so confused. As Tom looks back at me, I call softly, 'Give me some time to think it over, please.' I'm not sure whether he's heard or not, Mr McMeeney is delivering a stern lecture. Should I run after him? No. Best leave it for now.

If only Sebastian would come back. Everything would slot into place, I just know it. My guardian grandmother speaks softly inside my head, *'Put yourself first. Stop relying on the men in your life, or the lack of them, for your happiness. Trust what's coming.'* Now that is something I can do.

Smiling at Aidan as he bounds up the stairs, I nod a thank-you to his proffered offering of 'caffee, good 'n' hot. Just the way you like it.' Gratefully, I bury my nose in the cup, drawing in the fragrance.

Chapter 14

If I be summoned

Fortunately His Awful Majesty has followed Tom down the stairs. The air has begun to clear until there's little more than a lingering hint of his presence. That slight aberration of light. Dust motes dancing and sparkling green in darkness where no sunlight reaches. But there's still that indefinable, constant sense of *watchfulness.* I glance over my shoulder warily. But no, *He's* clearly more interested in Tom than me. For now.

From the Great Beyond, the guardian grandparents watch as Mr McMeeney escorts Tom off the premises. The fussy librarian smirks to himself as he smoothes down spikes of hair blown upright by a sudden gust of wind. Isn't it time he let nature take its course? Surrendered to the ravages of time? They see him take out his phone, knowing he'd better report back to the boss. He's kept his end of the bargain. Run off the young whippersnapper. Now all that's left to do is find the lost golden boy. Sniffing loudly, he comments that it really is time those drains were fixed. He's oblivious to the malevolent smile that watches him turn back towards the library.

His Majesty has no need of any device. He hears the conversation clearly across the town. 'Yes, yes, I know I said we needed them to do it, Ron. But we really can't wait any longer. We'll have a go ourselves. Get the others together. We're not that old. We know the routine. It'll be fine. We'll do it at Wednesday's meeting. I'll set it up. See you then. Gotta go.'

The librarian is left listening to bottomless space. His face glum as he returns the phone to his pocket. Not too old? Of course he is.

His Majesty is content. For now. Although it is high time the young pretender returned home. His Majesty shall swat him aside. He's done it before. This time it shall be permanent. Nothing is going to stand in

His Glorious Majesty's way. Nothing at all. But he can wait. He's been waiting through eternity.

The guardian grandparents cluck anxiously, alert to the danger. Watching with care.

* * *

'Ah, Miss Grayson,' Mr McMeeney calls as he steps back into the reference room, puffing from his rush up the stairs. 'I wonder, we have some important cataloguing work to complete in the rear office. Would you mind? Maybe young Aidan here could lend a hand?'

Aidan nods enthusiastically. As we walk down the stairs, he whispers, 'I've more research on my man to share. This is the perfect opportunity.'

Chapter 15

On the horizon of my seeing

The next morning Tom's there again, blocking my way into the charity shop. Trying to pull me into his arms. People rushing to the market in the square mutter wearily as yet another down-and-out pesters a young woman on the High Street. But no one intervenes. All they care about is having to walk those extra few steps around us. I have a harder job on my hands.

'Phillippa, please. Another chance. That's all I'm asking. I'll soon be back on my feet and –'

'I'm sorry, Tom. I need time to think. Harassing me like this isn't going to help your case. Please leave me alone for now.' Once again, I attempt to step around him.

'But, Pippi, sweet pea, you know you're the only one for me.'

What a cliché. How could I have fallen for it? I push past him, almost falling into the shop as Mimi hauls open the door. Her face is furious. 'Phillippa, I've been waiting for you. What kept you?' Pulling me inside, she slams the door in Tom's face and locks it. 'One last push and I think you'll have cracked it, lovey.' The switch to a cajoling smile is abrupt. This time I'm ready for her.

'Of course, Mrs B, I brought my radio.' I'm going to put all my worries aside today. No more agonising over the men in my life, or rather the lack of them. I need space to clear my head. That stock room is as good a place as any. As I run lightly up the stairs, I'm already daydreaming of an ancient temple in a sun-dipped land. I can reach out and touch it. 'You stay away, you old fart,' I whisper as the air glimmers before me and my nose wrinkles. 'This is time for me.' Why won't these men leave me alone? Where *is* Sebastian? If only he'd come back. I hear Tom rattling the door again, but Mimi doesn't open up until he's given up and left. Maybe there'll be peace today.

Upstairs His Majesty remains out of sight, although I am aware of his watchful presence in a darkly distorted corner of the room. He's sucking out the light and trying to take me with it. Pulling my cardigan tight, I finger the *menat* before plunging into the mess before me. Hoping it's all the protection I'll need.

From the Great Beyond, the guardian grandmother watches. Standing still as night. Is this it, will she find it? Will she remember? She was well-taught. The lucent stone is deeply imbued with heka. *Will it awaken her sight?*

Once the last of the dusty black sacks have been removed, the cardboard gathered up and the contents thrown into the yard below, there's only one box to go. I've already moved it nearer to the door on the single chair I'd placed there. I'd wanted to clear the rest of the room before I explored its enticing depths. Putting the dustpan and brush aside, I get off my knees and bend to open the box. As I touch it, the back of my neck tingles and my heart races. There's a buzzing in the air. I almost see it fizzing before my eyes. This is the final tool. A magical prize. My senses tell me so.

A tangled cloth lies in the bottom. It could almost be spun from pure gold. It's so delicate, gossamer thin. At its centre is a cold, hard lump that is emanating… What? Not exactly animosity but something close. Giving out 'keep off' signals, as though determined to remain in hiding. There's a force field crackling around it that burns my fingers as I reach for it.

'Yours it is not *hennu nafrit.* This My Majesty claims.' The bony hand is back, scrabbling towards the box.

As I pull it out of his reach, I stamp my foot, saying fiercely, 'Be gone.' Pulling aside the cloth, I hear myself gasp. A pool of old-fashioned black ink has been poured into the centre and solidified. One of those magic mirrors Aidan waxed lyrical about? Wonderingly, I pick up the polished stone, which is warm, encouraging me. Dizziness rises up around me and I almost fall at the shock that shoots up my arm. I'm being pulled into its centre, down a long dark tunnel towards a pinprick of light that won't release me. As I stumble to the chair, I'm fully in that ancient land.

...A cool serpent slithers up my half-naked body, the rough skin exciting my senses. The head weaving before my eyes, tongue flickering lulling me into a fugue state. Around me, the six ibis-headed watchers with the great beaked helmets backed with feathers of gold keep guard. Or guard the secrets. I am no longer sure which it shall be. There is danger here. Am I compelled or impelled? I am certain that I see true, but know that I cannot speak it. There are times when to speak would be more dangerous than to keep silent.

Holding the mirror between my hands, gazing deep within, everything is so intense. The colours are luminescent. Shapes reveal themselves, hard-angled or softly rounded with a nimbus of light. My nose tickles as I breathe in fleeting but powerful aromas, all my senses prickling, the air buzzing and crackling against my skin as I rest the mirror on my knees. It's like the contrast has been turned to maximum on a television screen and I've stepped inside.

Television? In ancient Egypt. 'Get a grip, Pips,' I admonish myself. But that's exactly what it is. An ancient Egyptian viewing device: a portal to the past – and most probably the future too. If I dared to look. Now it's mine – again. Shuddering with excitement, I peer deeper into the stone, merging into that quondam life.

... As the mist clears a woman stands out strong and proud. Head thrown back she raises her arms and calls to the Gods. Draws on her

instruments of power and sends lightning shards ripping through the ethers into His Majesty's heart. 'Think you to bind me,' she shrieks as thunder rolls and she twists and turns. 'Nevermore shall you make me a vessel for your power. I claim mine own. No longer shall my soul be joined to yours. I call on the Gods to break the bond and set me free. You have violated our sacred trust.' Slashing all around herself with an obsidian knife, she roars, 'Take this joining from me!'

Turning, she gathers up the bundles of papyrus leaves and rolled scrolls before her and, beckoning to a servant, demands, 'Hurry, wrap these and add them to the others. Then fetch my daughter and the sisterhood. We must leave immediately.' Like a deep dark pool that's had Hekat leap into it, the image ripples and then clears again. A flotilla of boats is slipping noiselessly down the great river in the evening dusk. The image shatters as a door is thrust open and the watchers melt into the silence. 'Tell me, what you see,' an imperious voice demands. 'Where did that ha'her'sha't go?'

'Down the river, Majesty.' That is all I say. 'The image dissolved before I could see further.' Not that I'd tell you if I had. I cloak the thought as the flinty eyes look deep into mine. But, I promise myself, I shall seek out that hiding place. It is where Men'ofer has been taken, and it is there the answer lies.

Why is this so visceral? So much more than mere pictures glimpsed in a crystal mirror? I'm here. In the past. I know how to *see*, I've been trained. Why is that woman so familiar? And who on earth is Men'ofer?

Wrapping the mirror carefully, I creep down the stairs and secrete the gold-encrusted parcel in my bag. I'll pop some money in the till, but, until I've got a handle on this, I'm not going to tell anyone what I've found –and especially not what it does to my inner sight.

Chapter 16

Gloom on glooms

Racking sobs assault my ear and I thrust the phone away. 'I'm sorry, I have to take this. Please, excuse me,' I say, turning my back on Mr McMeeney who approaches me as soon as I walk through the door.

'Miss Grayson,' he blusters, 'there are things that we absolutely must discuss before the committee arrives. Your reference library is in peril...'

Impatiently, I shake off the insistent hand that seeks to pull me towards the stairs. But he reaches for me again. 'Come this way. Now!'

'No,' I almost shout. 'Not now. In a moment. Please.'

As patrons' heads turn, he tut-tuts and says, 'Miss Grayson, I really must insist.' But I hurry out of the library, bringing the phone back to my ear.

My nemesis is following me out of the door when Aidan calls him back with a hurried, 'Mr McMeeney, sir, do you think...?'

Silently thanking Aidan for spotting my predicament, I turn my attention to the phone. I'll placate Mr McMeeney later, although there may not be a reference library much longer. Not in its present form. The council has now proposed a 'community hub' instead, which pleases me, but he's right to be concerned for his future, the old curmudgeon.

'Who is this?' I ask in the gaps between sobs. 'Please talk to me whoever you are. You are clearly very distressed.'

After much gulping and sniffing, a voice says, 'Shelagh. Shelagh Slattery, from Sharm. Do you remember me?'

I barely recognise the voice, but hurry on and say, 'Yes, of course, I do. You were extremely kind to me after... What can I do for you? You sound terribly upset.'

'Yes, well, I, er…you see…I…it's difficult…' The soft barely there northern accent that I remember has thickened and clouds the words.

'Take a deep breath and tell me slowly,' I encourage, seating myself on the library steps. This could take some time.

'Well, you know that waiter, Ibra'him? The dark good-looking one…' Gulping sobs rasp down the phone again.

'Yes…he was most attentive as I recall.' He'd left me alone while I was with Tom, but any woman without a man around had seemed fair game. I recall Tom saying with a sneer that he was the kind of guy who was always on the lookout for a tip – or a bit of the other. I'd tried to give Ibra'him the benefit of the doubt but couldn't help noticing how he'd targeted the older women. I hadn't noticed him paying particular attention to Shelagh though. But I'd been puzzled when an invitation to accompany me to Luxor was turned down. She'd said how much she'd wanted to see the real ancient Egypt, not this holiday resort. But she didn't take up the offer. Was this why? It wasn't that Shelagh didn't enjoy my company, after all.

'Oh, he were, even more so after you left. Everyone else went home and there were only me until the next lot arrived. If me friend hadn't cried off at the last minute I'd … He were so kind… at first.'

I try to recall Ibra'him's behaviour as Shelagh and I had shared a table for that last lunch. Was it my imagination or had he pushed his groin against me as he brought me a plate from the buffet? I'd sat with my back to the room, trying to blot out the sight of Tom and Samantha canoodling together. I'd been grateful to Ibra'him for saving me the embarrassment of going up to help myself. I hadn't wanted to go in at all but Shelagh had persuaded me.

'Keep me company,' she'd urged, revealing how lonely she must have been surrounded by all the couples and giggling girls. The older women seemed to hunt in predatory packs, drinking even more than the young ones. Not Shelagh's sort at all. Her wispy brown hair and modest blouses were a stark contrast to blonde helmets blow-dried into submission each morning, and the clinging strappy tops that showed off saggy boobs to a distinct disadvantage. Which made it all the more surprising that she hadn't transferred to Luxor with me. Was there a hidden agenda? Ibra'him had seemed to treat Shelagh with deference, calling her madam. Fussing over her, yes, but not groping her. Not that I'd seen.

'Do go on,' I urge. 'Tell me what happened.'

'Miss Grayson, I really must insist. You have customers waiting. This way, please. Do I have to make it an official order?' The voice of the Chief Librarian is hostile. 'You have already been warned.'

'I'm so sorry, Mr McMeeney. I will be there in a moment. But this call really is important. A friend is in great trouble.' I smile at him, hoping against hope there is a soupcon of humanity in the man.

'Well, er, two more minutes and that is all. The readers must come first, you know.' With that he turns and huffs his way back through the heavy glass doors, almost toppling one of the elderly patrons in the process.

'Shelagh, I'm so sorry for the interruption. You were saying? Ibra'him…'

'Well, he …' More sobs. Then, 'Would you, do you think, we could meet like, our Phillippa? I'd find it easier to talk to your face, hen. You know what it's…'

I don't want to remember one of the worst days of my life, but it would be good to see her again even though she is so unhappy. 'Yes, yes, of course. But where are you? I'm afraid I'm working today…'

'Oh, that's all right. It'll take me a few hours to get to you and I need to pack. I booked myself into a B-and-B for a couple of nights on the off chance. I had to get away and thought I might as well have a little holiday.' The gulp that accompanies these words suggests it isn't a happy thought.

I press on. 'How about tomorrow then? Say about seven? It's our late night. Why don't we meet at the café on the corner of the main square, opposite the library? It's easy to find. We'll talk then.' Hopefully, she'll be calmer. It's so hard to make sense of the garbled sounds coming down the phone. Maybe it will be better face-to-face.

'Can't thank you enough, hen. I'm ever so grateful you gave me your number. You don't know what this means to me.'

'It will be good to see you again –' But the phone has been switched off in the middle of more wrenching sobs.

Chapter 17

Dark smoke and wicked fire

Flickering shadows weave and dance in the eldritch light of the brazier, burnished bronze gleams and shimmers in blue flame. Hypnotic fragrance drugs the air as white smoke roils and rises from the silver thurigible coiling and plaiting a doorway to the Otherworld. Chanting invocations, figures move in the eternal round, inviting the participation of the ancient ones. Calling, beckoning, beseeching, beguiling. Offerings are made, the room asperged with holy water. Velvet drapes swirl ominously in the windless night. Dusky corners guard the secret names as answer is given and those that are called come forth. Gauzy nimbuses waver around the heads of the Gods as they walk between the worlds in response to sistrums shaken, drums calling. Golden headdresses glisten as the voices weave the imprecation.

Come forth.
Join the oscillation of the ancient ones.
The recreation of creation.

A deep voice booms out from beneath upturned golden horns.

I summon you in the name of all that is holy. Come Great Ones.
Come forth through dark smoke and wicked fire.
Come forth from the starry heavens.
Make your presence known once more.

A lighter voice commands,

Come forth!
Bring out the wowaei.

The deeper one echoes,

Come forth!

The Jackal Anubis, his golden face sharp snouted below ears pricked high, steps towards the Great Horned God. Haughtily he leads forward a young woman, unchastely robed in translucent white edged with scalloped blue flowers. Her red-painted nipples stand proud in the firelight and her hair shines like the sun god's metal itself.

'Shit,' she mutters as she almost trips on her four-inch heels.

The golden phallus strapped to a feather-and-corn bedecked, green-robed god bobs and wobbles.

'It's no good. It's not going to work.' Muffled irritation rises sharply as a lion-mask is thrown down and a voice says, 'Take that sodding thing off, Ron. You look ridiculous. Min stood proud, but you've got brewer's droop. For god's sake, Meski, take that bloody net curtain off and put some clothes on. You're more like a tart than an untouched maiden. Get this lot put away.' Her finger stabs at priests, gods and trappings.

Lights flare with cruel intensity. Harsh fluorescence reveals daubed cardboard and tattered robes. A candle in a crudely painted barbeque is snuffed, seedy velvet curtains pulled down as a child's rattle thuds to the bare wooden floor, and a flour sifter spills its charcoal load. The thump of a tin drum rolling under a chair is drowned out by all too human swearing as the erstwhile god fumbles to retrieve it. Joss sticks are extinguished, and bottled water pushed aside.

'I'm doing my best, Aunty Mim. I can't help it if I'm not a virgin maiden. I've had my share of love pleasures as you well know.'

A whining voice replies, 'It was you who sent me to –'

'Yes, okay. That's enough about that. Let's see what can be done.' With a deep sigh, the high priestess turns to her books yet again.

'Some proper working tools would be a start, not the stupid bits you find in the shop,' Ron retorts as he gathers up the props and locks them in the hall cupboard. 'We might have begun as the local drama group but we're a proper working coven with serious magical intention now.'

'Anything becomes magical when infused with intent. It says so in here.' The waving of a black leather-covered book with gilt lettering punctuates the words. A few yellowed pages flutter to the floor.

'He was well named the Great Beast. Kinky sort of chap if you ask me. I wouldn't go on anything he says. I reckon that other book was the real deal –'

'It's the quality of the folks that powers the whole thing, not the props. We can't do it without the chosen ones. We have to get them to join us –'

'You'll have to find that son of yours first. Seems to me he's uncovered your plans and legged it.'

'He'll be home. Leave it with me.' The high priestess smiles. 'The plan is well in hand.'

'That's exactly like a lioness licking her lips moments before she launches into the attack. Has our esteemed leader taken that mask too seriously?' The erstwhile maiden mutters to her neighbour, who is combing hair ruffled by a cardboard headdress. 'Chosen ones indeed. The silly bitch will get what she deserves.' She gathers up her belongings and makes for the exit. 'Get it on.'

As the door closes behind her, a hollow laugh rings around the scruffy church hall. 'Challenge My Majesty, you ignorant fool? Can one whose mother had sex with a dog go against the might of My Majesty? An *asit'sow* trained not in the dark arts dares to wear the insignia of priestess? Methinks not.'

Mimi van der Buerk glances over her shoulder, pulling her book closer to her chest. She isn't sure what she heard but, one thing she does know, she doesn't want to hear it again.

'Come on, Ron. Let's go and practise a bit of this 'ere magical sex shall we? It's time we got the hang of it.' Opening the door, she ushers him through, locking it behind them. 'Your place or mine?'

A scowl splits the dusty air. 'Over my dead body, *asit'sow.* Let us see how you to a night visit by My Majesty in my eternal glory respond. Certain of your power you shall not then be.'

Chapter 18

Banishing the badasses

'Hey, Miz Grayson. I was being bothered by this rank old geezer that looked like something out of one of those old horror movies. He were buggin and it vexed me. I tried giving him the air but it dain't work so I found this spell in an old book on the net. It were real wicked man, I mean, Miz Grayson. Did it and *pfftz*, the saddo woz gone. Look, I wrote it out for you. It can be another of my reports.'

Smiling, Aidan hands me an immaculately presented – and, at first glance – properly spelled essay in English as it is most often spoken, even if the title does leave something to be desired. I must remember to ask Aidan more about 'the old geezer' later, but, for now, I can't wait to see what he has to say. 'Why, thank you, Aidan. This looks really good. If you wouldn't mind fetching me a cup of coffee, I'll read it now.'

'Course not, one pint of espresso coming right up.'

Oh dear, why doesn't his speech match his writing, I wonder yet again. And why does a pint of espresso translate to such a small cup? I must have a word with him. He could go far if only he'd lose that ridiculous way of talking, although some of his words are quite creative when I think of it. It's more that I need a specialised dictionary to understand them. I must find out what his story is, and why he adopted what cannot be a natural vocabulary.

A Ritual for Banishing the Badass Guys
Aidan Doran

Aleister Crowley (12 October 1875–1 December 1947) was a phat occultist who popularised ritual magic in the West and founded a new religion, Thelema, which he got from an

Egyptian spirit, Aiwass. Crowley was the first rudeboy. The role model for the 1920s cult classic black-and-white film *The Magician*. The newspapers of the 1920s and 1930s demonized him, dubbing him 'the wickedest man in the world'. His philosophy was 'do what thou wilt' and he appealed to people who wanted to revel in excess. He died penniless and forgotten in a boardinghouse in Hastings. But, twenty years after his death, his 'magick' was part of the crazy sex, drugs and rock 'n' roll lifestyle of the 1960s. Crowley was a heroin addict and a member of several occult organizations, setting up the Ordo Templi Orientis...

Oh Aidan, what will Mr McMeeney make of this one? Sex, drugs and rock 'n' roll indeed.

...A prolific writer and poet he was also a world traveller, mountaineer, chess master, artist, yogi, social provocateur and bisexual sexual libertine who swung both ways. Before Crowley, magic was for initiates only. It had to be earned and took years of practise. But magic – which he spelled 'magick' – to obtain wealth, happiness and power can be practised today by anyone as it isn't a secret no more, thanks to Crowley.

In his writings, the self-styled Great Beast says that you must create a safe space for ritual work – and he tells you how to banish the badass guys when they come calling.

According to Crowley, his practices stemmed from ancient Egypt and the badass guys were as bothersome then as now. Some of the Undead were real psychos. Proper whack jobs. His 'Lesser Banishing Ritual of the Pentagram' gets rid of the badass guys, but Crowley says in *Magick in Theory and Practice*, 'those who regard this ritual as a mere device to banish spirits are unworthy to possess it. With it you are sealed off from the outer world of ignorance and darkness, from the false and the unseemly, and are attuned to the Light.'

Back to ancient Egypt again. Did everything stem from there? That Banishing Ritual is exactly what I need to deal with His Awful Majesty. Eagerly I read on,

> ...The ritual uses the five-pointed star pentagram to create a safe place in the astral as well as the physical world in which you may safely engage in magick. The pentagram has supremacy over lying, deceitful spirits, in other words the badass guys and the Undead...
> *(The full text is to be found at the back of this book)*

I can easily draw a pentagram and I showered before coming into work. My clothes are clean even if I'm not wearing my blue robe, and although I'm not quite sure that the library is sanctified space in magical terms, to me it is sacrosanct. I certainly need protection from a 'badass guy'. I'm not altogether confident about using magic gleaned from the wickedest man in the world. But I'm desperate enough to try anything to clear out what's bugging me. Anything that gets the Prince out of my head and safely into the past where he belongs has to be good. Doesn't it? Quietly, I whisper the words of power, my hand tracing the four pentagrams as I turn on my chair. To be on the safe side, I invoke not only the gods of ancient Egypt but the Blessed Virgin and the Archangels of my childhood as well. Best be sure.

As yet another coffee slops onto the desk beside me, I smile my approval. 'Aidan, this is incredible. Well written and useful, too. Bring that other chair over. You must tell me exactly where you found it. You know you have to put your page references in your reports, show where you got it from. But well done, I'm proud of you. Don't forget to tell me all about that old geezer.'

'Oh, he was minging all right. He stank something chronic. Like something had crawled away and died. Rank. Tatty too, bits of bandage falling off him – skin peeling. Gaping hole in his cheek. 'Zactly like Halloween. Snakes hanging round his neck.

At first I thought someone woz having a laugh. He kept calling me Paskall and telling me to read his book. I dain't know what he were yakin on about, so I found the spell. It worked a treat.' His grin is wide and his green eyes look directly into mine.

With a shock I realise how ancient they are. With that lively intelligence, Aidan is certainly not at all what he pretends to be.

Chapter 19

The undying love of a visa

'Cooee. Over here, our Phillippa. All right, hen?'

Out of breath from the last-minute rush to usher everyone out of the library into a soggy evening, and the need to evade Mr McMeeney, who seemed intent on holding me back, I look round. I recognise the voice, but where's Shelagh? A hand beckons as a skinny woman half stands and removes dark glasses. Jet black hair is skewered high over a lined forehead, thick-coated mascara tramlines down her cheeks towards blood-red lips. Her skin has the grey pallor and limpet lumpiness of mashed potato left too long on the plate. This can't be...

'Shelagh? What's happened to you...?' As I falter to a stop, I'm pulled into a hard embrace and surrounded by a cloud of perfume that, for a moment, reminds me of that tomb.

'It's so good to see you again, hen. Let me look at you.' As I'm thrust out to arm's length, I look wonderingly at her. Gone is the fluffy mousy hair, the gently rounded curves, the discreet makeup. The collar of a black leather jacket is pulled high over a strappy top. What is it they call those older women who chase after young men? 'Cougar'. Yes, that's it. She's metamorphosed into a lean black cougar. But the eyes, behind the makeup, are the same violet-blue, although bright with pain. Smiling through the sadness, she looks me up and down.

'You look like life's agreeing with you. You're in love, I can see. Did you make it up with that spoon'ead?'

'No, not at all, I...' Time for that later. 'Tell me what has made you so distressed.' I need time to acclimatise to this accent. It's almost as hard to penetrate as Aidan's pseudo-street talk, but I say no more as I sit down.

'Long story, hen, I've been such a fool. Shall we order and

I'll tell you over a nice cuppa, though if you wouldn't mind I'd rather have a stiff drink.'

* * *

Decamping to the pub and settling in gives me time to assimilate the change in her. It's extreme, a tough disguise covering the old-fashioned soul that made Shelagh so *simpatico*. She'd been a woman who quietly presented herself to the world. Till now... What's brought the change about? More Egyptian weirdness?

Tugging down the short skirt, she vainly tries to cover her knees as she picks up her glass. Taking a noisy gulp, her voice is muffled, 'Well, hen, it were like this.' But she falters to a stop again.

I nod encouragingly. 'Do tell.'

Pulling a packet of tissues from her handbag, she says. 'Bound to need these. I've cried for the last week solid, and most of the time afore that. Pretty quickly ran out of hankies.'

I recall the delicately embroidered handkerchiefs that had been pressed on me in Egypt. They'd belonged to Shelagh's grandmother and still held a faint whiff of lavender. It's a good job we've tucked ourselves into my favourite corner. At least it's fairly private here. Better than the café. No one can see her misery. Taking a long sip of Prosecco, I settle back to listen. Shelagh had said it was her favourite drink, but I'm not convinced. It's left a sugary coating of stale apple juice on my tongue. I'd have preferred a beer. It's making my head swim too, so I'll just set it aside for now.

'You remember Ibra'him, of course.' Her face twists longingly. 'Such a good-looking fella. There were something so mysterious about him, those hypnotic eyes, drew you in.'

I nod again, not wanting to speak.

'Well, he'd been real kind to me seeing as I were on me own. Took extra trouble serving me and brought drinks to me room when I didn't feel like being in the bar. Always the gentleman though. We met in town a few afternoons, he took me to the shops, helped me barter for what I wanted, presents and the like.'

She'd kept that quiet.

'Said he'd borrow a friend's car and take me up to the monastery on his day off. I really wanted to see that place you know.'

'Yes, I remember you were upset when the trip was cancelled. But was it safe?'

'No, not really. It weren't the terrorists I had to look out for, though. It were Ibra'him. We drove for hours...'

...The red dust is choking. It finds its way through the cracked and battered windows and up her nose. Mixing with her sweat and staining her skin. It'd been so long since they turned off the wide highway and on to this dirt track into the mountains. She wishes she'd brought more water with her – and food. She'd missed breakfast as she stole out of the hotel and down the road to where his friend's car was parked. It was long before the call to Morning Prayer. He'd said they would eat at the monastery but that was hours ago.

'Ibra'him, how much farther?'

'Almost there.' White teeth gleaming. 'Soon you see.'

A few minutes later the car turns off the track towards a long low stone building. Ibra'him pulls into the meagre shade at the side. 'We are here.' His smile is triumphant.

'But...but, this isn't the monastery.'

'No. Better. Old temple. All tourists want see.'

Disappointment overwhelms her. Not again, not when she so wanted to see the monastery she'd dreamed of since she was a child. How could he?

'What is this? What are we doing here?'

He opens the door and pulls her out. She staggers when a wave of heat hits her. Like a child she grasps the arm held out to her as he helps her into the dingy building lit only by barred windows high in the wall.

'There, everything all right now. I love you, angel,' he says pulling her close. 'We made for each other. Only you for me.' Kissing her passionately, he sinks towards a pile of rags on the ground at the foot of a pillar. 'Here we be together, not risk it in hotel.' He's pulling at her clothes now, stripping away the white blouse that has become dust stained and constricting, tearing at her skirt. He kisses her breasts. 'So beautiful, beautiful lady. Lady mine. I love you.' He fingers the silvery, crescent moon scar high above her left breast matching the one beneath. 'You marked, pretty lady, belong my people. Belong with me.'

Feebly trying to push him away, not willing to think about those scars, she is overwhelmed. Her body is on fire. She's exploding. She hasn't felt like this for many years. It had never been so right. When she was married, they chastely undressed in the dark. Her husband was inexperienced and believed she was too. There'd been that other business, but she didn't want to think of that. Their inept fumblings had improved as the marriage went on, but when her husband had been killed in a road accident, she hadn't wanted another man.

She's gasping even before Ibra'him enters her, the orgasm goes on and on. He seems to know instinctively what to do, where to touch her to give her the greatest pleasure, how to prolong the ecstasy. It's so familiar, so longed for. She can't say no. Doesn't want to say no. She wants to stay here forever. Here in this dusty sweatbox with a boy young enough to be her son, younger if she's honest. For a moment reason exerts itself and she pushes at him, 'No, no, we can't.'

'You mine!' He bellows as he comes in great shuddering gouts before collapsing on top of her. 'Mine, my love forever.' As he rolls away, the scent of their lovemaking wafts up from the crumpled rags. The animal smell of warm bodies and desperate desire tying them together. But part of her can't help wondering how many others he's brought here to listen to his protestations of love...

Shelagh shudders herself out of the past, her hand straying under her jacket. 'Didn't take me to the monastery though. He took me to his family's land, way up in the mountains. It were an old temple. Told me later they kept goats there foraging for food. Spent weeks with them as a young boy dreaming of what he'd do when he grew up and could make his way in the world.' She smiles at the memory. 'He said he dreamed of meeting a woman who'd take him away to a new land. An angel. Now he'd found her.' Shelagh dabs her eyes before tucking her hands into her armpits. Hugging herself tightly.

At the next table two women settle themselves. Snatches of their conversation float towards us. '...Told him I'd only take him back if he'd stop his womanising. He promised and so...'

'Wasn't that a bit of a leap? He'd only recently met you after all?'

She blushes. 'Well, after we'd made love, it felt so right to be together.' Looking down at her lap, she twists the tissue in her hands into ribbons. 'Like I'd always known him. The sex were fantastic. Like we'd been connected a long, long time ago and now we'd found each other again. I don't suppose you'll understand...'

'Actually I do know how that feels...' It's my turn to blush.

Shelagh looks at me expectantly, but when I don't continue, she goes on. 'After that we met every afternoon in a room in town. Then the locals found out. One threw a stone at me. I came home while Ibra'him found a job in Cairo. Thought we'd be more anonymous there. I could get a flat and he could stay with me until we were able to get him a visa and come back here and get married.'

Married? That was a big step given how long she'd known him. And the age difference? 'Did you? Go to Cairo – to be with him, I mean?'

'Oh, yes. Ibra'him found me a place within a couple of weeks. Very cheap. I bought it immediately over the internet. Rented out me house and flew back.' Her smile turns bitter. 'But he didn't find himself a job, expected me to keep him though he didn't tell me till I got there. He said it weren't worth it as we could apply for a visa right away. He'd told me he were looking after his widowed mother and three sisters. That weren't true. Father came round one day berating him for being with an 'ore. Said he disowned him.' Tears trickle slowly down her face as she speaks. Her eyes are far away in that other land.

'You and me, we belong together. We marry now. Go lawyer, today. Get paper. Consulate tomorrow. Visa quick. You take me to England as husband. Easy. Yes?' His smile is so appealing, so innocent. Like a naïve child.

'But Ibra'him, I cannot marry you. I'm not a Moslem – and we've only just met.'

'You carry mark of Islam. You belong me!' He jabs his finger into her scar, pushing through the filmy fabric covering it, leaving the place raw and abused.

She rubs the place gently, trying to soothe away the memory.

Marriage? How could she... She doesn't recognise her sweet boy in the angry, insistent young man looming over her.

'The consulate would need evidence that we've been married and lived together for months, years maybe. It'd be better if you applied for a tourist visa. Came over to England for a holiday like. Or applied to a school, got a student visa. We could marry when you've established residency.'

'Residency? What that?'

What a barrier language creates. How can they be of like mind if they don't even share the same words?

'It means you've lived in country long enough to support yourself. Prove you have a job. Won't be a burden on the State. Then you get 'right to stay'.' Explaining slowly, enunciating carefully, as though speaking to a wayward child.

His face reddens. 'I no burden, I live with you. I been student. I finish hotel school!' Angrily he thrusts her aside as he leaps out of bed and pulls on his jeans. 'You no love me.' The door slams on her desperate cries.

'Took me to a lawyer's office to show me how serious he were. Said he were going to marry me there and then. An Orfi it were. The lawyer said it'd stop the police hassling us. We could legally be in the flat together and could stay in hotels if we showed our papers. I had to sign several. All in Arabic. No one translated them, so I had no idea what I were signing. I were just so glad it were going to be legal, I didn't care.'

Shelagh had married him, tied herself to that boy? For a moment, I see a different Shelagh overshadowing my friend. Dark skinned. Petite. A lined face contorted with worry as she smoothes hair from a fevered brow. Did I know Shelagh before? Is she a part of that other life I've glimpsed? Can I broach the subject? Not now, not when she's so agitated. But...perhaps later?

'I stayed as long as I could but it were like living in a nightmare. He were so jealous, wouldn't let me out of the flat on me own, locked me in when he weren't there. Said it weren't in the Orfi that I could go out alone. At first it were endearing, I thought it showed how much he loved me. But it were suffocating. He wouldn't let me talk to anyone. Hassled me for money all time, took me to the bank and had me open a joint account 'cos it were in the Orfi. Made me get the internet. Then threatened to find a younger woman who'd take him away to another country. He'd say I were ugly. "You have fat stomach, breasts hanging down, ass too big, wrinkled face and veins in your legs." So cruel.'

From the next table, a wail, 'He'd been back a fortnight when he did it again.'

Shelagh's rumpled face brightens as she recalls fondly, 'Next minute he'd say he loved only me, call me darling and smother me with kisses. Said he would never let me go. I didn't know which way to turn. I loved him so much.' Another tissue goes up to the pond-rimmed eyes.

'There, there.' Trite I know, but I can think of no other response as I lean forward to pat Shelagh's hand. I can't understand the hold these men have and yet, I've been pulled into my own nightmare. My own obsession. Is it so different? Sebastian. Or, the Dark Enigma that haunts me? What is the hold this ancient land and its people have?

'Initiated you were. Initiated you stay. Ka joined to ka, ba bonded to ba. A joining made for eternity. When you meet again, it ignites. The central suns blaze towards each other. But such passion, without temple discipline, destroys.'

It's Him. The Prince Khem Yar Khepher'set is back. The air is zinging with his noxious presence. I look at Shelagh but she's dabbing her eyes again. Muttering the banishing under my breath, my fingers surreptitiously trace a pentagram. He's gone, leaving a black hole in the corner, but I'm busy thinking over what was said. Soul bonds with soul. Passion without temple discipline destroys. Is that what it's all about? Do you instinctively recognise someone with whom you've been joined? But you have to be prepared all over again with the same kind of discipline, the same steps, otherwise it all goes wrong?

Dubiously I take another sip of wine. It tastes even more insipid now it's gone flat. I'll get a proper drink in a moment. But, does the bond really go on life after life or does it become distorted? Can it be cut? You couldn't be with the same person throughout each and every lifetime, it wouldn't make sense. If you were, you'd need to get the timing exactly right, and that would be tricky. There's still this fundamental question of whether reincarnation exists. Have I really lived previously? Been through several lifetimes?

Before I can ponder it further, Shelagh bursts out, 'The sex were still fantastic – most of the time. But then it all got so much worse. He tore up the Orfi paper. Said he divorced me. Stormed out but came back and threw me into the street. Said what was mine was his and so he'd keep the flat and I had to go on paying him. When I went to the consulate, they told me that in Egyptian law he could demand that.'

She tucks a stray strand of hair behind her ear as she goes on. 'What were worse, I were still legally married to him in Egypt and he could follow me to England if he wanted. I hadn't' – her hands sketch quotation marks in the air – 'followed the right formalities. Should have had the marriage registered so it were "properly constituted." But contract were still legal so I had to give him the flat. He's free and I'm stuck with him. It's so unfair, hen.' Once more, her face is buried in a tissue.

My mind has returned to my previous cogitations. What if you'd made two mystic marriages in different lives, what then? Say you met them both again in the same lifetime. Could the joining be truly permanent? Is it really soul upon soul, or are there degrees? Not that the Prince's book speaks about other lives, I've added that. A leap too far? But, from what I've seen, the joinings must have gone wrong sometimes. Surely not everyone was meant to be together life after life in an eternal round. What a mess. The conundrum spins around my head making me dizzy. Do I really want to believe in this nonsense? It's too complicated. One life is enough to cope with.

'Now he says he's coming to England. To be with me.'

Chapter 20

Coming forth from yesterday

'Hey, Phillippa, how's it going?' The familiar voice whirls me around, elation surging through me. I have to do a double-take, though. Who is this garishly T-shirted stranger with close-clipped black hair and a neat beard? His startlingly pale face and arms are red-blotched and lumpy, the tips of his ears bright pink. But, one look at his rusty-penny freckles and lapis eyes and I'm convinced. He's here – at last. Leaping up from the desk, I rush across to greet him.

'Sebastian! Where've you been, I missed you so much' – my voice falters as I realise what I've said, but I rush on – 'it's been pretty dull without requests for those boring old books of yours.' I can't stop the grin spreading across my face.

Seeing the inquisitive looks from the regular customers, who are clearly puzzled by their normally placid librarian looking like she's stepped on an ant hill, I head towards the top of the stairs. It's brighter there and we can talk without being overheard. Sebastian follows more slowly. The light from the window invests him with a halo of orange light, like the rising sun.

'I was in Egypt. I've got quite a story to tell.' He blushes. Then rushes on, and asks, 'Could we meet when you've finished work?'

'Of course. How about the pub round the corner at six o'clock?'

If I nip out at lunchtime I can buy myself a new top. Perhaps even get my hair done. I'll have time to change and put on some makeup before we meet. Pity I'm wearing these flat shoes, they make my legs...

Realising how quiet Sebastian is, I look up. He's leaning

against the grubby wall. Eyes closed. Faded posters beneath his head. I really must take those down and look for something brighter. His face is drawn. He didn't have those lines before. A few laughter lines, yes. But these are deeply etched. So thin. He's always been lean and wiry. Now his jeans hang on him. I was so excited at hearing his voice, so caught up with possibilities – and those memories – that I hadn't really *looked* at him. He's exhausted. As I move closer, he exudes a sour smell, like the old clothes in the charity shop. 'But what happened to you? You don't look like someone back from a holiday in the sun.'

'It was no holiday. I've come straight from the airport, travelled overnight. I need to go home, soak in the bath and sleep. I'll be fine by tonight. See you later, Pips.' With a wave, he's gone.

* * *

The rest of the day passes in a blur. One or two readers look askance when I am slow to respond to their queries, but I guess the glow of happiness around me makes it impossible for anyone to be annoyed with me for long. He's back! Inside, I'm hugging myself. Now perhaps I'll find answers.

But, as I run down the steps into the market square, a dishevelled, swaying figure steps forward, blocking my way. Not another beggar, they really are getting to be a nuisance. So many in the market square these days. I usually put a pound into the outstretched hand to be rid of them. This one waves a beer can at me and shouts my name.

Risking a quick double-take at the grimy face, I say, 'Not now, Tom. I really don't have the time. I'm on my way to an appointment.' How has he sunk this low in such a short time?

Any incipient sympathy is quickly cut off as he sneers, 'With *him* I suppose. The one who ousted me.' His voice has more than a drunken slur to it. His fury is blocking up the words and they are slithering out of the corners of a tightly compressed mouth. 'He...'

'For one thing, it wasn't me who went off with a bimbo.' I rather like that old P.G. Wodehouse word. It describes Samantha and her hooker heels so well. 'It was you.'

'But...but...it was only *temporary.* You could have waited, sweet pea. You knew you were the one...' Grabbing my arm, he tries to pull me towards him.

I really don't have time for this. Sebastian is waiting. Thrusting off the grasping hand, I say, 'I simply don't fancy you anymore. Goodbye, Tom. My decision is for all time. Do not attempt to speak to me again. My heart is taken by another. Go.' My adamant finger points in the opposite direction to the pub. I'm still laughing at myself as I head into the bar.

* * *

'Here you are, Pips.' Sebastian puts the brimming glasses on the table and pulls out a chair. His creamy caramel smell is back, so comforting and *normal.* Before he sits down, he picks up his pint again. Takes a long gulp, grinning with satisfaction through the froth. 'That's what I've been dreaming of, good British beer. That and...something else.' A tide of red suffuses his neck and he tugs at his collar as the glow rises up into his face. It's like he's been coated in *karkady*, that syrupy sweet Egyptian welcome drink I enjoyed so much. 'I, err...' He drops into his seat, hiding his face in his pint.

The dreams...surely not...is Sebastian having them too? Not certain I can deal with the complications of that right now, I ask, 'So what were you doing in Egypt?' Desperate as I am to get to the bottom of those dreams, I want to know why he's in such a state. I need to be sure before I share the weirdness of my nights – out loud anyway. We've shared so much already, unless it's all my imagination. But not from the way he's blushing. The karkady tide roaring in again. His ears fiery red behind the big pint glass. The memory of our nocturnal lovemaking echoes under my skin.

Shaking myself out of the reverie, I examine him closely. Although he seems more rested, there's still desperation in his pinched face. 'Come on, Sebastian. Do tell.'

'I went out to undertake some on-site work for my PhD. My supervisor was in charge of the dig on the tomb of an unknown early Pharaoh, found last year, and he invited me along. The transition between the pre- and very early dynastic period is my thing, you know. Everyone believed all the tombs in the Valley of the Kings had been mapped and they didn't realise it'd been in use so early. When workmen broke through into this one –'

My mind flicks to the fetid tomb I'd been taken into. That had recently been discovered. Could there be a connection…should I tell him?

'– said they were trying to drain away floodwater but we reckon they knew about the tomb and were hoping to loot it before anyone realised.'

'Was it down a side alley, tucked behind a bulge of rock, bit of a scramble to get down and a rickety wooden ladder to descend?'

Putting down his pint, Sebastian leans towards me, lapis blue eyes peering intently into mine, 'Yes, but how did you know? The news hasn't been officially released yet.'

'Oh, I was taken in there when I was in Egypt at Easter. I'd just returned when you helped me dispose of Tom's things.' Briefly I consider how low the owner of those things has fallen. I still can't believe it's possible.

Sebastian's face relaxes and he laughs as we recall the expensive bunting we created. But it becomes serious once more as he says, 'Security's even more lax these days. As a matter of interest, how much did it cost you to go in?'

'Ten pounds Egyptian. I think he was hoping for a bit more than money but I felt faint and rushed out to get some air.'

Should I tell him about those strange sensations? Better wait till I hear what he has to say. 'Did you find out who was buried there?'

'Yes, we did as a matter of fact. It is a much older tomb than the one above it, little in the way of decoration or artefacts to go on. What is there was puzzling, but there was a rough inscription scratched over the door.'

'The Great Prince Khem Yar Khepher'set, Justified, blessed be His name, may the Gods keep His Majesty safe on the far side of the Otherworld. Your Majesty does not exist, nor does your body. Your Majesty does not exist, nor does your soul. Your Majesty does not exist, nor does your flesh. Your Majesty does not exist, nor do your bones. The place where you are does not exist. Your name is not among the living. What a contradiction. He was buried with blue lotus flowers. I saw one.' It's out before I can stop it. I don't dare look at Sebastian.

'How could you possibly know that, Pips? Did someone translate it for you?'

Not sure I can articulate what's rushing through my mind right now, I say, 'No... not exactly... Look, why don't you tell me your story first, then I'll explain.'

'Okay, let me get another pint, but I warn you, Pips, it's going to take some time. May I get you something else? You've hardly touched that one.'

'No thanks, this is fine.' Best to keep a clear head, it sounds like I'm going to need it. Taking a deep breath to steady myself, I realise how tense my shoulders are. If only I could relax and tell him everything.

Inky black. No sound except the living rock. Breathing. Slowly. Barely perceptible. But there. Crackling. Moving. Rock. Tons of it. Hovering above my head, plunging deep beneath my feet. Pressing. Shifting ever so slightly. Waiting. Disgruntled air moving, slyly. That – and the presence. Sighing in the darkness. Evil personified. What did he do this

Prince who was so abominated that he was bound through all time?

A breeze brushing past. A perturbation of the air. How...? Who...? Chest so tight. Blood booming across ears that don't want to hear. The smell. Getting stronger by the minute. Carrion. Rotting flesh. Is there some wild beast in here, have I stumbled into a jackal's lair? They mark their territory with urine and store the old bones. Breathe through the mouth, cautiously, slowly. Uck. Foulness beyond imagining. Must get out before I suffocate. God help me.

I'm still contemplating how to recount my experiences when Sebastian puts down his new pint, his trembling hand slopping froth on to the table.

'Seb? What is it, you've gone awfully pale?'

'Nothing, merely old ghosts stirring.' Sebastian rubs his cheek as if to push away the memory before sitting down.

'Initially, I was only going to give them two weeks. Then I was asked to stay on – I sent a couple of postcards to the library but I suppose you didn't get them. Not surprising the way the post is out there. They found another chamber at the rear of the tomb shortly after I arrived. At first it seemed to be intact. Then we realised that it must have been opened, emptied and resealed shortly after the burial took place.'

'How could you tell?'

'The seals were from the same period.'

'Oh.' I shuffle in my seat, not sure how to phrase my next question. 'What happened to the body?'

'At first we thought that the priests had probably reburied it somewhere else. They did that if a tomb was looted – or if the spirit was unsettled. That happened quite a lot. If the proper offerings and spells weren't made at the appropriate time – that's my speciality as you know, threat formula, early burial and binding rituals. Oh, and curses. I've been examining the evidence for those for my thesis. Not that there's much of it,' he shrugs.

'But there's sufficient anecdotal evidence to suggest it may have been a wider belief than we give credence to right now. King Tut's curse is well known, of course, even if not accurate. It's what got me started. The Curse of the Pharaohs. I was obsessed with the idea when I was a kid. That might have had a lot to do with my experiences later. Repressed memories. The curse of us all.' His eyes are probing.

'Yes I... But...no, carry on. I'll tell you later.' I nod to him to continue.

He takes a big glug of beer before continuing. 'Once I began to study it properly, I realised that the artefacts were ephemeral. Papyrus and potsherds don't necessarily last. But there are other tomb inscriptions. The Egyptians believed that the dead never really left. The *ka* lived on in the tomb and could trouble the living if it wasn't placated. Especially if there was something it wanted.'

Don't I know it, but I'm not quite ready to voice the thought aloud. 'What do you think was troubling this particular Pharaoh? Surely his priests would have ensured a long and happy afterlife for him?'

'That's just it, Pips. The burial seems to have been rather hasty. Of course, we don't know what the outer door looked like because it had been broken into recently. There were traces of another binding text painted below that inscription you seem to know all about.' He cocks an eyebrow but, when I keep silent, goes on.

'It's most unusual. Extremely early. That's why I was asked to take a look. The day before I was due to leave we found a stone tablet with another binding spell buried in the middle of the second chamber in a shallow trench, right where the body would have been. It was on top of bits of mummy wrappings and a few fragments of a wooden coffin. Underneath was a pile of crumbled dust. From the look of it, the case had been smashed and the mummy pulverised. Whoever did it clearly wanted to obliterate his soul.'

Taking another gulp of beer, he continues. 'That's when the trouble began.'

Chapter 21

All fragrant and dear

'To desecrate the resting place eternal of My Majesty and to bind My Majesty forever they dared. My *heka* stronger than all their pitiful mumblings were. The ignorant fools could not destroy the power of My Majesty.'

The contemptuous voice is so loud, Sebastian must hear it. But, although he glances over his shoulder, he carries on, 'My supervisor got sick, heart attack. There were rumblings in the roof. The workers said the place was cursed and refused to go in again. I have to say, it felt awful in there, Pips. The stench was appalling and it was impossible to breathe.'

Bang the flashlight. Fading batteries flicker with one last burst of light. There! Quickly. Pick up the pieces and stuff them in the backpack. Squeeze through the narrow slit in animate rock that snatches at shoulders pushing through, closing as it inhales. Head for the ladder. Quickly, while you still can. What was that? I'm here alone so why that... footstep...? Behind me? Tiny hairs prickle upright. The back of my neck knows feral fear. Is it...how could... Stand still, press into the rock, every muscle rigid, let it pass. No, no, that's wrong. Move. Now!

Thrusting upwards with all my strength. Stones rattle down on my head, the flashlight falls. Hands reach to pull me up.

'Mr Seb, sir, what is wrong?'

'Nothing, nothing. A touch of claustrophobia.' But I know it is more than that. In my heart I know the forces of darkness have been unleashed, melodramatic though it may sound. This is experiential archaeology at its worst. This is what they *feared. Those ancient ones who sought to bind this forgotten ruler into tombtime. Professor, what have we done?*

Sebastian's face still bears red blotches, which stand out against his translucent skin. 'So I took the tablet and a few of the bigger fragments of mummy case with me to my hotel to study. That afternoon the roof caved in.' His voice is bleak.

All those tons of rock waiting to come crashing down. My heart jerks and stutters. What if he had been buried alive?

'Just punishment, the *nti heti*. My Majesty has plans for this *desh'retu cymotrich*.'

The voice is in my ear and I shake my head to thrust it aside. Even though most of the dye has washed out of his coppery hair, Sebastian isn't an evil red-faced, curly headed Son of Set and he certainly isn't a senseless fool. Pushing away a fleeting bewilderment as to how I know what the insult means, my attention is caught by Sebastian's hollow voice. 'Then the police came calling.' His fingers weave themselves together like nervous, restless snakes. Icicle eyes look into the distance.

'What? How did they know?' My voice is sharp, intruding into his memories. Seeing his whole body shake and the colour draining from his face, I lean over the table and put my hand on his arm. He grasps it tightly, interlacing his fingers with mine like a drowning man reaching out to his rescuer. I want to reassure him that I'll be an anchor for him, hold him here with me, but I daren't voice the sentiment. It sounds so histrionic. Better to keep silent. For now. Instead, I take a deep breath, drawing in his creamy caramel smell although it has a sharper burnt edge to it now. More like that dark treacle toffee my mother used to make as a bonfire night treat. His trembling ceases and colour returns to his face. Eventually he raises his head, his eyes seeking mine, his face desolate.

'You tell me. The only thing I could think of was that one of the workers had seen me put the tablet in my backpack. He probably thought he could've got a good price for it himself. If only he'd known.'

The air splits over his shoulder and my Dark Enigma smiles.

Entwined snakes writhe around his head like a satanic uraeus. The malevolence in his face as he turns to Sebastian could curdle a soul. I slump back against the solid wood of the settle. Once again, it's like He's pulled the plug on my energy. It's rushing towards him and I wedge my hand over my belly, desperate to hold on to it. Why can He do this? What power does He have over me? Feeling the settee's reassuring strength cradling me, and sensing my guardian grandparents' quiet presence in the background, I take a deep breath, pull in my belly, and sit up again.

I am reaching across the table for Sebastian's hand once more when a voice in my head sneers, 'My Majesty ensured that the local *shem* priest heard about the theft and took steps. My Majesty wanted that tablet destroyed and that ignoramus cur out of action as long as possible put. My Majesty still has influence you know, and My Majesty is not finished with that son of a dog.'

'So it was all your doing. Go away, you don't belong here, you callous bastard.' Quickly, I trace a pentagram on my lap. *'Ena'hai sh'ra khepheret dim'an'tange Ma'at, Ban'a dosert yamin heh'sieh Khem Yar Khepher'set, Ini inuit Isis, Elia whiskia fatu y Set, Ra supra mew'nit ha'wi, Yavah. Seb-En!"* I shout – silently I believe, but Sebastian looks over his shoulder and asks, 'What is it, Pips. What do you see?'

How to explain? He'll think I'm deranged. 'It's nothing, look, I'm starving, how about you? Why don't we order some food and then you can tell me the rest of your story. There's so much I still want to know.'

Chapter 22

To hear your voice is pomegranate wine

After our food is ordered, Sebastian begins again. 'They took me to the central police station in Luxor. A horrible, grim concrete building behind its showy façade. Although virtually new, it smelled almost as vile as the tomb.'

My nose wrinkles in sympathy.

'I can still taste it.' Grimacing, he takes another gulp of beer swishing it round his mouth before swallowing. 'It wasn't so bad at first. They shoved me in an empty room with high barred windows like letterbox slits that looked out on to a mudbrick wall. Told me to wait for the Inspector. Hours went by. It got hotter and hotter. So airless. There was no water and I'd had nothing for breakfast. They'd burst in as I was about to go down for it.'

'Couldn't you ring someone? Your mobile must've worked out there, mine did. Cost a fortune, but I could use it.' Not that I'd had people to ring, only a few reassuring calls to the parents.

'No, they'd taken my phone and my laptop so I couldn't contact anyone. I've never felt so helpless in all my life. Thought I'd never get out. In the end, I must have passed out.' As he scratches absently at a bite on his arm, his eyes slip out of focus as he stares through the table into another world.

Calling on the gods to assist. Every name I can recall: Ra, Horus, Min, Isis, Osiris, Thoth, Ptah, Sekhmet, Khonsu…

A voice not quite in my head, not quite outside. Yet. A voice. In my head. Or is it? 'The Great God Anubis is Master here. All hail the Jackal! No gods here for you, eibata. *No one here to help you. In my power you are.'*

Trying to stand. Boneless legs wobbling. So weak. Blackness closing in. A growl arousing me. Or is it my own feeble groaning? Before I focus it's gone. Breathe out, slowly...deep slow breaths. One, two, three, six, that's the way. Snarling, tearing at my ears. How could a jackal get in here? I'm in a police station in the middle of a modern town for God's sake.

'That for the sake of the Great God should be. I say again, Anubis is master here.' That voice again. High on the ceiling this time.

The jackal's eyes shine bright, intelligence flaring in careful assessment. The body tenses, muscles flexing. It lunges snarling, its rankness growing ever nearer...

With sweat breaking out on his face, Sebastian's eyes stare blankly at me as he wraps his arms around himself and hunches down in his seat. The tendons stand out on each side of his neck and a pulse beats fast under the blotchiness of his translucent skin. For a moment I am held spellbound by the rhythm of the jerking blood. Pulling myself together, I rush to sit next to him and draw him into my arms.

'It's okay, you're safe now. You're with me and I won't let anything happen to you,' I assure him fiercely, thankful that the sour unwashed smell has been replaced. Wholesome, that's what I've always associated with him. Wholesomeness – and that shy intelligent sexiness of his. Such an attractive package.

He burrows closer, tense and agitated until, slowly, he relaxes and tension of a different kind begins to build. Each fibre in his sweater crackles with electricity under my hand. The hairs on my arm lift. For a moment, I catch again the lingering scent of that old tomb, the spiciness stirring another memory of honeyed bitterness, blue lotus flowers heavily laced with... But I can't quite grasp it... Lifting my head, I'm fascinated by a tiny, heart-shaped freckle on his cheek, below the corner of his eye, exactly like I'd seen in those dreams. My fingers itch to trace its shape but his head is moving nearer, his eyes enquiring. The strange golden glints in his irises look like falling stars smouldering in an Egyptian night sky. His mouth's straying towards mine. I'm breathing his sweet, beer-laced breath when once more the air thrums and the light fades.

'You can leave right now, you don't belong here. Go away. SEB-en!' I whisper fiercely, not wanting the other patrons of the pub to hear. But this time it doesn't work. The malevolence lingers on and I fall back, drained of energy once again.

'Pips, what is it? Can you see him?'

'Yes.' There now, I've said it.

Staring straight ahead, he mutters something in a language I can't quite grasp. So similar to my own incantation. But darker, guttural and more intense. The air snaps tight.

'What was that, Sebastian? It seems to work. What did you say?'

'The binding spell from the tablet. I'd made a copy. It was in my pocket when they took me. Although they'd grabbed the things from my desk and my backpack, they didn't search me. I suppose as I was so obviously just out of bed, only wearing jeans they didn't think it worth it. I had plenty of time to translate it later. It's come in useful a few times already. It doesn't seem to hold though.'

'Mine doesn't hold either.'

'Where did you get it?' That cocked eyebrow draws me in again. Surely I can trust him now? Isn't this what I wanted? To share everything. He's clearly had experiences of his own, even if he isn't being entirely honest with me yet. I've noticed how his eyes keep sliding away. It's hardly surprising if his experiences are anything like mine. Perhaps he wants to forget. But, I can make a start, open things up between us.

'It came out of my mouth. It worked the first time. He was taken unawares. But since then he won't leave me alone. It's like he's stealing my energy. The nights are the worst. It's been happening in the daytime too.' My face is hot as I recall those grasping fingers plucking at my breast.

'That lecherous old goat. What a piece of work. Sheesh.'

'You've seen him too?'

'It's like stepping into my own personal horror movie...'

...Slithering, slipping, scaly air restlessly oscillating. A three-headed snake breaks through the wall. It feints and lunges, seeking the throat. Another weaves lazily around the body curled on the floor. Others watch in the shadows. The Devourer of Souls lurks, patiently waiting. Is that really my body down there lying in its own stinking filth? The Jackal God Anubis hovers over me. Like a tomb painting come to life. Waiting to pull me into the void. A great beast of a crocodile glides through the bars as though they are made of silk. Bronze-plating glistening, black eyes bright with malice, mouth agape. Sixty-eight ivory adzes waiting to snack on my leg, or crunch me whole. I count each one. There are many opportunities. Water trickles from its aubergine and avocado skin. Give me a drop, please, I beg. Jaws snap.

'Welcome to the Chamber Torture of My Majesty, desh'retu cymotrich. *My Majesty is become like a crocodile. I am Sobek. My Majesty seizes prey like a ravening beast. My Majesty the Dweller in His Terrors is restored. Your life is forfeit you interfering* nti heti.*'*

The voice booming from over my shoulder. The dry husk of an imperious face leering at me, haloed in faint green phosphorescence. Rotten bandages hang from his eyes, dripping like snot from the sunken nose. His fetid breath rolls over me. The Prince Khem Yar Khepher'set in all his tattered glory. Where did he come from? Straight out of an old horror movie from the look of him. That one the babysitter was watching when I was small. 'The Mummy' or some such name. I woke up, took one look at the screen and screamed until I was sick. Slept with the light on for months.

Is that what this is? Memory playing tricks? Is my interest in banishing rituals a way of exorcising that memory? Keeping it at bay? Or did it plant the seeds of possibility? The dead living on? That was the theme of that movie. I never really believed it could be true though. He should be interred deep in his tomb and kept there. But no, I removed the binding tablet. The words scratched on the stone are somewhere in this building. He was released and now he hovers near. All too real. He's tangible, I could reach out and touch him. Taller than in life – or death. His face closes in on mine. The rank smell rolls over me and my breath hitches in my throat. His dust is on my tongue. I want to retch, to spit him out, but there is no moisture left in me. All I can do is cower away, heart gunning as my head reels and sickness threatens.

Darkness roils in. The piss hole belches. Something scrapes against the bars. Scales brush my bare foot, fur snags on my jeans. A taloned hand reaches out to snatch the heart jumping from my chest. This horror movie is all too real. Get a grip. Think. I know how to beat this. Deep breaths, slow and deep. One, two, three, four, six. Reeling back. Croaking, 'In the name of Osiris I fetter and destroy the hidden serpents, which are about my footsteps. My nest is invisible. My egg is unbroken. I am the seeding of every god. I am mighty, Lord of every strength. I have overthrown the ashmia fiends. I have come to lighten darkness. It is light. I have delivered myself from evil things. I have driven away my foes. Horus comes to me. I am at peace.'

A great golden hawk pecking at the snakes, dashing the heads against walls turned to stone. Fur shredded, blood gushing. Light flashing. The Devourer of Souls slinks away. The crocodile is driven back, but who knows when he will come again. Night after night, and daylight too. So many tortures…so many days…

'Sebastian?' My voice is gentle as I call him back. Luring him into the familiar noise of the pub again. The dark beams and yellowed ceiling, painted by centuries of nicotine low over his head. The rattle of glasses. Everyday reality. That's what he needs now.

'Oh yes, when I was in the cells he often came to visit, to taunt me. When he appeared it was as though gravity shifted. A deep dark shaft sucked all the air out of the place and he filled the space. An image straight out of my worst nightmares. Gruesome.

So gross. Does that happen to –'

Actually, when I see His Majesty, despite everything, he's rather handsome. Imperious, mesmerising eyes…but… Catching up with what he's said, I recall what I've heard about Egyptian gaols. The dreadful way the prisoners are treated. 'The *cells*? Don't tell me you were sentenced?'

'No, I was never sentenced. The Inspector insisted I'd stolen the tablet and the fragments and then brought the roof down deliberately to cover my crime. When he could get nothing from me, he had me thrown in a holding cell until he –' Sebastian sketches quotation marks with his fingers '– had time to be more *persuasive*. He left me there. If it hadn't been for that cleaner…' He shakes his shorn head, his face ashen. I miss the wayward curls that made him look so poetic. Like Lord Byron sculpted from fresh bronze.

'How long were you there?'

'I lost count. It must have been several weeks. It felt like months.' His voice is toneless. In the silence that follows I am acutely aware of every sound standing out sharply around us. The muted tinkle of glasses a crescendo, a chair scraping across the floor chalk on a blackboard.

'No one noticed when you went missing?'

'I was due to leave the next day, and with the professor evacuated to England for medical treatment, I suppose everyone assumed I'd gone too. The hotel knew, of course, but the police must have told them to forget me.'

He picks up his glass, realises it's empty and pushes himself off his chair, ducking his head to avoid a particularly low beam. Arriving with our food, a waitress smiles at him. 'Let me get you a refill, sir. You eat this while it's hot. Looks like you need it.' Putting the plates on the table, she takes his glass and goes to fetch his drink.

Reaching for the neatly wrapped cutlery, he says, 'If it hadn't been for the cleaner, I would have starved. He enjoyed practising his English with me. Joseph was a Coptic Christian, employed to do the most menial of tasks. From what he said he hadn't been paid for months. But he hung on to his job and brought me water and the local bread. He cleaned me up and took care of me. Luckily there were a few Egyptian pounds in my jeans and I gave him all I had.'

Opening his napkin, he spreads it carefully on his lap. 'He even brought me a pencil and some paper so I could work on my translation. I owe him my life. In the end he retrieved my things and got me out of there. An amazing man. I'm determined to go back and thank him one day.'

'Come on, eat up. Tell me the rest when we've finished – if you can finish. They must have thought you were famished.' Laughing, I point at his overloaded plate.

'No problem, Pips, I've got a lot of time to make up for.' After dowsing ketchup over the enormous steak pie and chips, he picks up his fork and digs in. As I watch his long expressive fingers and remember with a quiver how they'd seduced me in my dreams, I see again how thin he is. He's clearly got a long way to recover from his ordeal, physically and psychologically. Such a scarring. But talking it out could be cathartic, surely.

* * *

'Tell me more about the guy who rescued you. Joseph, you said? How did he manage that?'

Sebastian pushes away his immaculately cleaned plate, sits back, rubs his stomach, sighs contentedly, and says, 'I dreamt of that too you know…'

Uh-oh, the tricky subject of dreams again. I sit quietly, waiting for him to continue, smiling expectantly.

'In the end it was easy. Joseph had taken my jeans to be washed – given me an old *ghalabya* to wear. Apparently the Inspector had been called to Cairo and hadn't returned. As Joseph had the keys to the office, he simply opened it up and found my backpack in the cupboard where the Inspector had stuffed it after that first interview. My phone had died, of course, and they hadn't picked up the charger so I couldn't call for help.'

'So how did you get out? There must have been guards.'

'There was a fight on the streets. All the policemen rushed out to quell it. We walked out of the rear entrance straight into Joseph's brother's barber shop for a freshening up. I had matted hair and a long beard when I went in – I came out looking like this. Mikael even darkened it for me.' Sebastian strokes his close-cut hair again, grinning. Thankfully he's shaved off the clipped beard. The dye had made him look like something out of a Spanish medieval painting, ascetic and a bit sinister. I'm glad it's gone.

'Hardly recognisable, wouldn't you say? My jeans were at the shop. We thought anyone would be so blinded by a fluorescent T-shirt that they wouldn't examine my face. The Inspector hadn't found the hidden pocket in my backpack where I kept my passport and return ticket – I'd told him they were in the hotel's safety deposit box. But he hadn't had time to check before he left for Cairo. Joseph called his cousin's cab and I headed straight to the airport. No one stopped me.'

Unrecognisable, indeed. But I still have so many questions. Unsure how to put them, I ask, 'But what about your ticket, wasn't it out of date?'

'Oh yes, but I explained that I'd been holed up in a grotty hotel on the West Bank for weeks with Pharaoh's Revenge. My thinness and the emergency Egyptian hundred pound note tucked into the old ticket seemed to convince them. Thankfully, the whole country runs on *baksheesh,* though I wouldn't have wanted to try it on that Inspector.'

Twitching his shoulder as though to brush off the possibility, he goes on. 'Luckily, I also had my airline lounge pass so I went and had a long hot shower when we changed planes at Cairo.

I wanted that more than food. I'd had a strip wash at Joseph's brother's place, but it wasn't the same. I'd fantasized about that shower for weeks. Couldn't get the unwashed smell out though. A bit of that old tomb stench lingered too. Didn't do to get too close. I couldn't stand myself.' His nose wrinkles. 'But the plane was almost empty, not many tourists there now. I kept going into the loo to wash. But that put an awful chemical tang on top. The cabin crew must have thought I still had Pharaoh's Revenge because of the number of visits I made. Then I got home and saw you again.'

His face lights up and this time his lips find mine. Soft, gentle, questioning, the kiss is like old friends rediscovering each other after a long absence. He pauses for a moment, whispering, 'Why are you so familiar to me, Pips? Have we met before?'

Pulling him close, I murmur, 'I'm sure all will be revealed in time.'

Eventually…'Here,' I hand him the *sem*. 'I found this in the charity shop along with my *menat*. I'm sure it was meant for you. You'd better wear it.'

As he slips it on, I notice silvery scars around his neck. They stand out against his pale skin. 'Sebastian, your neck. What happened?'

'I don't know. I was born with them. A kind of birthmark, they said.'

Chapter 23

So tangled in you

Shelagh bounces into the tearoom looking so much more like her old self that I do a double-take. She's softer, fluffier, younger. Wearing quietly stylish clothes, her bobbed hair is a glossy honey-blonde. It highlights her beautiful violet eyes, no longer red rimmed and sorrowful. Her old voice is back, still that northern accent, muted now. Less...*broken*. I'm pleased we agreed to meet in this lovely spot by the tranquil river instead of in the pub. That's been the scene of so many dramas recently and I'm not a drinker at heart. Too many eyes – and ears – there.

When the waitress has taken our order, I turn to Shelagh. 'You're looking really good, what's happened?'

'Met a woman at a psychic fair. She told me I needed to tie-cut with Ibra'him, now and in the past, and offered me a session.' She grins. 'Once she'd explained what it were, I snapped it up.'

'Well it certainly has made a difference. You look fantastic. Your hair's great by the way.' It has a sheen to it that reminds me of that line of Egyptian love poetry I found on the net, 'like honey plunged into water.' I must read more of those verses. They give an insight into the everyday life of that ancient culture. Bring the Prince's book to life. But not, I suspect, in a way of which His Awful Majesty would approve. Best not think about him now though. 'Sounds like that tie-cutting could be useful. You must tell me all about it.'

'I will, hen, but first what about you. You're looking a little fraught around the edges if I may say so. Here, I brought you a present.' She hands over a tiny glass vial of perfume, so potent I can smell it without unstoppering. Egyptian oil. It carries so many memories, but I brush them away – for now. Later, I'll inhale it deeply and let it open the floodgates. Later.

'Thank you, it's wonderful, I...' Will she think I've lost my mind, gone into a kind of psychic shellshock? But given what she's been through herself lately, maybe she'll...it would be such a relief to talk it over with someone who understands. Or who listens with an open mind, that's all I'm asking. To be heard and not judged. Sebastian's great for that, but he's as involved as I am with His Malodorous Majesty and objective distance is what I need. In any case, Sebastian's gone off to see his PhD supervisor, and isn't sure when he'll return. There's a lot to thrash out apparently. His PhD is in peril. He has to 're-envisage' it. Come at it from a different angle. Not easy after what he's been through.

Aware of Shelagh's puzzled silence, I rush on. 'You'll probably think I'm mad,' I say, still trying to find the words. 'But I...it started in Luxor... I went into...'

When I grind to a halt, she smiles encouragingly. 'Come on, spit it out, hen. You can tell your Auntie Shelagh.' She pats the seat next to her. 'Move over here and tell me everything.'

I scoot round to sit with my back to the room. If only this old sofa could talk. It's probably seen all the dramas life could devise. It gives me confidence to go on.

'I seem to have picked up the shade of an old Pharaoh. He came from Egypt with me, or at least I think he did. Haunted the edge of my dreams and then became very...physical.' My cheeks burn, knowing how intimate that contact had become.

'Oh, you mean sex on the astral.' She laughs. 'I know all about that. It's *very* physical.' Her elbow catches me in the side and she winks.

Sagging with relief, I rush to ask, 'Do you? Do tell.' Finally I've found someone to talk to about my weird nights. With a look of such understanding that I tear up and have to wipe my eyes, Shelagh begins.

'Well, it were a long time ago. I were only a teenager when it started. John Lennon'd just been murdered and the whole of Liverpool were in mourning. We had to draw a face for homework and I choose him 'cos his picture were in me dad's paper.' She makes sketching motions. I realise for the first time that she's left handed. 'Something about him caught me attention. Mesmerising he were. Those eyes of his, like they caught hold of you and wouldn't let go. The energy…' She pauses, her thoughts clearly somewhere else. 'So sexy, he were fizzing.'

She breaks off as the neatly starched waitress approaches. 'You don't see many aprons like that,' she notes with a smile, piling sugar into her cup, 'although we do have a few up north, keeping up the traditions like.'

* * *

When we've sipped our tea and finished the delicious cake, chasing the last few crumbs around the plate with wetted fingers, I begin again. Thankfully the quaint tearoom is empty, the visitors gone for the day. No one to see. No one to judge.

'So what happened, how did you get from a sketch to… sex on the astral?' I must think about that term later. I haven't heard it before. It's so appropriate. Something else to google. For a librarian, I'm woefully ignorant, even though I did do that course on erotic literature at uni. But that was fiction, what our lecturer called 'salacious imagination'. This is real life. How many people are having sex on the astral? Something else to ponder later.

'I looked up and he were standing in the corner of the room, looking at me. Solid as you and me. Well, almost, I could see a bit of the door through him. There were a woman next to him, but she were more shadowy, wispy. I reckoned later it were Yoko.'

'Yoko? But isn't she still alive, how could she…?'

'Don't ask me, hen. I can only tell you what I saw. She were watching him watching me. Excited like. Her face alight with glee. She were urging him on. Then me mother called me for me tea and that were that.' Shelagh's grin has quite a bit of excitement in it too. She's shivering, not from cold though, not if the gleam in her eyes is anything to go by. It's more like a ripple, a current running under her skin. I almost hear the crackle. See the hairs standing up on her arms.

'The dreams started that night. Only they weren't dreams. But I were too young to understand what were going on.' Her glance towards me is sharp.

'Not if they were anything like I experienced, no. I don't think "dream" is the right word at all. I'd been "dreaming" about my new man – I'll tell you about him later – but his place was usurped. I was most definitely awake...' My cheeks burn again, 'It was very...physical. All too real. Then creepy if you know what I mean. Sucked all the energy out of me. Didn't feel right at all.'

'Exactly. Same with me. Wouldn't leave me alone. After a while it weren't only the nights. It were during the day too. I'd be in school and have to rush out, say I felt sick, needed the toilet. Couldn't stop the spasms. Couldn't keep quiet either. Panting and screeching. Happened on the bus home once. Driver thought I were off me face like. That were a right embarrassment. Threatened to call the police. Had to walk home.' Shelagh shakes the memory away, grimacing. 'I'd one or two boyfriends. Silly kids stuff. No sex...nothing could've prepared me for him, I were too young.'

Wedding bells toll. My new phone. I haven't had time to change the ringtone yet. Why they should have chosen this particular carillon to signal an unknown caller, I cannot comprehend.

'Better get that, hen. It might be your young man.' Her smile is knowing.

But when I press the screen, I rear back in horror. How on earth...who could have...

'Here, let me see.' She takes the phone from me and snorts. 'Sexting. Something you might have to get used to.'

Shaking my head in bewilderment, I ask myself why on earth I hadn't changed the number as the pushy salesman suggested. He'd licked his lips as he said I never knew what I might find now I could receive images. Didn't realise he meant *this.* But I'd thought about my elderly parents. What if they needed me in an emergency? They might not remember. It wasn't as though many people had my contact details. I never imagined… No wonder I dislike technology so much.

I'd recognise that slightly lopsided tumescent lump anywhere… How could I ever have fancied him? Quickly I reach out to switch it off. But Shelagh gets there before me. 'From the look of you, you don't want to see that again. Not exactly amazeballs is it. Here, let me block the number. Looks like you've got a lot to learn, kid.'

A few impressive finger movements later, she hands back the phone. 'Put that away for now. Tell me who that were. Not this new man from the look on your face.'

'No, an old one come back to haunt me more like.' I slide the phone into my bag. 'I don't want to think about that now. Can we get back to what we were talking about, please, Shelagh? How long did it go on?'

I've only had a few weeks of it and it's exhausting me. I'd much rather be making love to Sebastian, not fighting off the randy old bastard. He's there every moment I let my guard down. The banishing spell never seeming to hold. I'm surprised he isn't listening in on this conversation.

'Four years, give or take. Always worse in winter around the anniversary of his death. Funny thing is, he never spoke. Touched me with his eyes and wham, off I'd go.'

'Did he…er…seem to get anything out of it other than tormenting you?' I'm not quite sure how to put it. But she quickly catches on.

'Oh yes, he were gruntin' an' groanin' even though he had his clothes on. Didn't seem to need to take them off. Right weird it were. She were there too sometimes, always wispy but definitely her. I kept seeing him in different costumes, like in a movie. Old Egyptian stuff mostly.'

'I remember reading he was heavily into Egypt. Believed he and Yoko had had a former life there. Bought her a mummy in a case and kept it in the Dakota in another flat. Now that would be creepy.' My thoughts flick to that Canadian author, what was her name, oh yes, Jewelle St James. She'd written a book about being haunted by Lennon. It's tucked away in one of the boxes in my unnecessary garage. I hadn't had time to unpack them before Tom moved in. It's time to get them sorted. My former life is still encased in there. What if I have a previous life in my mind too? Is that really what this is all about?

The air shimmers for a moment over Shelagh's shoulder. It's him, His Malodorous Majesty is back. I don't need the smell to tell me that. Quickly, I trace a pentagram and mutter the banishing spell, pushing him back across the centuries. If only I could close time permanently. At least John Lennon was contemporary with Shelagh, well almost. There weren't thousands of years between them.

But my mind goes back to that 'ennui' he created. The book says, 'love-starvation', the longing for the twinsoul, is the most terrible evil that can oppress the soul. That each soul needs its complement at the highest level of being. But I don't think His Awful Majesty is what will complete me. I'm not suffering from love starvation. Not while there's the possibility of Sebastian to consider. I long for him and sense how he would fulfil me. Thinking about him makes me complete. It seems more likely that I've been undergoing what the book calls, 'magnetic and vital fluid exhaustion.' The book says there's a need for 'electrical, magnetic, and chemical reciprocation.' I certainly don't have that with His Majesty. He most definitely does not adhere to the 'naturally waxing and waning cycles of sexual power, passion and interest.' With him, the act is forced. Maybe with Sebastian the 'sexual commingling of natures' will be fully restorative. It was getting that way in the dreams before His Majesty intervened. Maybe once he's back from Oxford...

Shelagh is looking at me quizzically. 'Gone somewhere else, hen?' She laughs. 'Back to sex on the astral?'

'How did you guess?' Was I blushing again? 'But tell me, how did you get free?'

'Cancer. The chemo wiped him out. Almost wiped me out too, I can tell you. Somehow when I came out of it, he weren't there no more. I got myself on a special access to education programme, was going to college but then I met me husband. I haven't thought about Lennon in years.' Patting her renovated hair, she says lightly, 'Thought I'd grown out of it. Sex on the astral, that is. Until I met Ibra'him. He were always at it – till I did that tie-cutting.'

I need to know more about that tie-cutting. But... 'Cancer? You never told me you'd had...' I'm horrified. There's so much I still don't know about her. But then, I don't know her at all, not really. Only a few days in Egypt. Yet there's this sense of having always known her. Rather like Sebastian. More to think about later.

'I had a tumour in a lymph node. Up under me collar bone.' She fingers the scar I'd glimpsed under the skimpy top. 'The surgeon took it out. Insisted I needed chemo to be sure it hadn't spread. But it came back. Had to have more treatment.' Seeing my worried face, she says quickly, 'I've been fine since. Don't you worry, hen. I'm not going anywhere.'

She fishes in her bag. 'Here, you'd better have me new number. Tossed the old phone in the river so Ibra'him couldn't reach me anymore. Now, how about going somewhere quiet so we can do that tie-cutting?'

'Yes, I'd like that. But, do you think, could you explain a bit more about it on the way? What exactly is a tie-cutting?'

'It clears the karmic bonds between you, all the vows, pacts, promises, and unfinished business from the past, in this or any other life, that's binding you together. It uses graphic imagery… can be rather startling. But come on, best I show you.'

* * *

'Make sure you're comfortable, hen. This could take a while.'

Shelagh's wrapped us both in Egyptian pashminas 'to keep us safe.' I don't feel particularly safe though. I'd prefer my robe. I can hold onto the menat though, that feels protective. She's lit a couple of scented candles, but I'd rather she'd turned the lights up. Darkness loiters in the corners of the room. I've never been in this room before. Don't know how safe it is. Surreptitiously, I trace a pentagram and whisper the banishing just in case *He's* skulking somewhere. Surely His Majesty will have got wind of this through the ethers and attempt to intervene.

Thinking back to that scene I'd glimpsed in my mirror where an ancient Queen screamed her defiance and used magical tools that crackled with power, I can't help wondering whether an obsidian shard in a cosy B-and-B will have quite the same effect. Shelagh's bought it with her from her own tie-cutting. We've cleansed it with salt and dedicated it to the gods and goddesses of ancient Egypt. But my eyes are darting everywhere as she picks it up and stands beside me. Is it my imagination, or has she taken on a different mien? She looks…more *certain,* confident. Does she have the power? Does she really know what she's taking on?

'May the gods and goddesses of the blessed land keep us safe and assist us in our endeavours. Receive our offering and hear our petition. We come before you to request assistance at the separation of Phillippa and the Pharaoh Prince Khem Yar Khepher'set, a union that was out of time and against the natural order. A violation of her sacred calling.'

Incense perfuses the air as Shelagh lights a joss stick and passes it around the room, chanting, *'Keep us safe, keep us protected, make us holy, thanks be to the divine ones who draw near.'* Briefly, a part of my mind hopes that the smoke won't trigger the fire alarm, which would most certainly alert His Majesty. Another part urges her deep into the shadows to pentagram them and root Him out. But there's nothing stirring as she moves towards me and spirals the sweet-scented smoke from my head down to my feet. *'Cleansed and purified you are. May the ancient ones protect you and grant your petition. So be it.'*

Satisfied, she glances round the room and smiles, moving to stand behind me. 'We are in a dedicated temple. No harm can come to you. Now, first off, close your eyes and visualise a circle of light round that chair you're sitting in. Picture it really strong. Make it a cylinder of light you can quickly pull up.'

I settle back in the chair. Eyes closed, breathing tremulously. Will this...can this...finally? Shelagh seemed so less burdened after her tie-cutting, freed. It *must* work for me. She seems to know what she's doing, or is she just parroting what was said to her? Will it matter? Waves of trepidation roll around my gut and I quickly cross my hands over the void.

'Relax. Breathe deep into your belly. Take the air right down and let it out slowly. Practice pulling that cylinder of light up and letting it down again. Know that you're quite safe.' Her voice is reassuring, pitched deeper now. It's taken on a different cadence, a familiar one nonetheless. 'Now, picture another circle of light in front of you. Make it big enough to hold His Majesty. Don't let it touch yours though. You need to keep it separate. Better make it a cylinder of light too.'

I can do that. It's strong, the picture is clear. Two separate circles of light. May the goddesses protect me.

'Invite Himself into the circle. Picture Him held there. You'll need to...'

No time for anything, His Majesty is in the circle and it's racing rapidly towards me.

'Peg the circle down if it moves towards you. Pull up the

cylinders of light.'

How did Shelagh know that was going to happen? The pegs and cylinder keep Him firmly fixed in place now though. Brilliant.

'Now ask that the ties between you be shown.'

It's horrible. Like being buried under a massive fishing net. So tangled. Can't breathe, going to suffocate. Hooks cutting into me. Need to fight my way out of this, right now. Remembering that ancient Queen and calling on her to assist, I raise my arms, trying to slash it away with the obsidian shard. If only I could recall the words she'd used. The shard's getting hot, cutting into my hand. There's so many strands to this net and those hooks are deeply embedded. Got to get out!

'Breathe gently, hen. Take it easy and ask for help to cut the ties. Pile them up outside the circles. Take them off yourself first and then him.'

It's not that easy, I'm enveloped. 'Help me, please.' I'm not sure who I'm calling out to, maybe that ancient Queen. Succour must be somewhere near at hand.

A lion-headed woman roars in, spitting fury. She breathes fire on His Majesty and melts the net between us. He looks like He's coated in sticky plastic that's fused with his skanky skin. He's more concerned with getting it off than with hanging on to me. Neat distraction. She's taking more care with me, gently melting every strand and hooking it out. Then she breathes healing light on where it's been. It's taking a long time. But that's okay, His Majesty is still busy trying to free Himself and she's pulled the cylinder of light up around me. I'm cocooned. Like a butterfly waiting to emerge and fly free.

'Make sure you get all the ties, especially those around the back and in the hidden places.' Shelagh prompts. She sounds anxious. It's been awhile since either of us spoke.

Ouch, that was a bit sudden. Didn't expect my liberator to go ferreting in my vagina and pull out that tangled lump. Nasty hooks on the ends of those strands. But it's great now she's pouring light in instead. Hmm, a bit orgasmic, it would be so easy to let go. But I'd better not. Next time I'm going to be in control, follow the directions in the book.

''Have you got them all? Check there's nothing left on either of you.'

'It's okay, thanks, Shelagh. I've had a lot of help. But His Majesty's still got… oh no, cancel that. He's had them blasted off him and he's been kicked out of here, escorted by a couple of lions.'

'Good. Now gather up the ties. Light a big bonfire and burn them.'

'Er, that's been done for me. Have you ever seen a lioness roaring flames? There's not a lot left.'

'That'll be the Lady Sekhmet. Very useful she is. If there's any ash, wash it away.'

'Oh no, I don't need to do that. She's breathed on it and created a beautiful diamond that she's offered me to put in my heart.'

It's so soft, not at all what I expected. But strong too. Like my heart's been gently annealed. I've got a shield round me that will keep *Him* out. And now Sekhmet is wrapping me in a fiery cloak.

Just as I think My Lady has finished, she breathes a stream of fire into my belly. '*Sa Sekhem Sahu. Power, my child. Reclaim your gift of power.*' The void is filled. My body expands, tingling as the fire flashes through every cell, and then curls around my sacrum, the sacred bone. A firesnake poised to awaken. Power indeed.

'My deepest thanks to you, My Lady.' I bow to her as she departs and the obsidian shard shatters in my hand. Opening my eyes, I look across to Shelagh. 'He's gone. I can never thank you enough.'

'Just one more thing to do, hen. Repeat after me, '*I hereby revoke all former vows, promises, pacts and debts between myself and*

His Majesty the Prince. I relinquish all unfinished business and karma between us. I open my heart to let forgiveness flow to him, and receive his forgiveness in return.'

Doing as I'm bid, as I repeat the words a part of me can't help wondering, have I really seen the last of His Awful Majesty? I may have cut the ties with him, but I sense further theurgy will be required to return him to his own time. Now that I've got my power back, surely it will be possible to do so. I may need to learn to use it wisely first though. I won't share my doubts with Shelagh just yet. I'll wait and see if *He* materialises again first.

'Let's close things down properly.' Lighting another joss stick, Shelagh spirals it around me and then into the corners of the room.

'It'll make all the difference. Make room to let real love in, mark me words, hen. Now, let's bury those obsidian pieces and then give thanks to the divine ones. Make an offering of beer to My Lady. It were her favourite tipple.'

Chapter 24

Who guards her steps

Nestling into my comfy sofa, I take out the obsidian mirror. I've not deliberately invoked a past connection to someone before. But I'm confident it'll work. A bit like 'mirror, mirror on the wall.' Hopefully, with less fearful consequences. It could explain so much. I'm not ready to do Aidan's Hathor ritual yet though. That's a bit heavy. I'd rather see what happens when I simply gaze into the mirror again. It seemed so natural the first time. But, to be on the safe side, I murmur a quick plea to my guardian grandparents to watch over me.

Maybe some perfume will assist. Inhaling deeply, I bring Shelagh's gift up to my nose. It inundates me with memories, but they flash past so fast I can't separate them.

The almost-rose scent fills the air as, breathing softly, I mist the shadowy surface of the mirror. Then, I wait for it to clear.

A room, whitewashed and cool. Gauzy curtains grace tall windows opening on to a fountained courtyard where water gently splashes. But the tranquil atmosphere does not allay the terror in the room. A tiny woman sits at the side of a pillowed bed, anxiously soothing hair from a fevered brow. Her lined face is puckered with anxiety.

'Here my little one, drink this. It will cool and restore you. Drink.'

A few drops are trickled between lips that are cracked and bleeding…

I hardly recognise my former self. If indeed it is my old self and not some mirage. Gone is the beautiful young woman I'd glimpsed previously. In her place lies someone broken and torn. Eyes that need no kohl to blacken their rims, hair that is clumped and lank. And thin, so very, very thin. The *menat* around her neck looks lustreless, deprived of all power.

Feebly the girl pushes away the cup. 'Lik'e'bet, leave me be. Let me join my beloved in the Otherworld.'

'No, no, my darling child. It is not yet time. His Majesty is soon to depart this world and you can be free. But drink you must. We cannot have you carrying a child of His Majesty. This shall ensure there is no issue.' Tenderly, she proffers the cup again.

'He is too old for that now. Too far gone in his wickedness. His reed is diminished. He barely penetrates my body and never shall I give him my soul.' Greedily she drinks, wincing at the bitter herbs hidden within the honeyed beer. 'No child of his shall I bear…'

The old nurse wrings out a cloth and bathes her charge's face.

'Peace, Mennie. Be at peace my child. I am here for you and it shall always be so.'

So, Shelagh was my nurse. I did know her before. A promise across time, could it be true?

Chapter 25

Darkness weighs upon the dwelling place

Scooting my chair up to the antiquated computer, I enter 'ancient Egyptian ghosts'. Once I'm past 'the mummy's curse', most of the entries are online games and spooky-rubbish sites. But I find a few useful books and articles. *The Penguin Book of Myths and Legends* confirms that 'night assaults' from the unquiet dead involve touching, kissing and even sexual intercourse. A more scholarly work propounds the offerings and prayers required to control them – including binding spells. I might try those when next I see His Malodorous Majesty.

My mind goes to my next puzzle. Are there really previous lives? Do they run parallel with the present? Is it possible to cross time zones? Tangled timelines? Is that the explanation for all that's been happening to me? Putting 'reincarnation' into the search engine pops millions of entries on to the screen. Where to start? For once I turn to Wikipedia. 'Reincarnation is the religious or philosophical concept that the soul or spirit, after biological death, begins a new life in a new body.' Well yes, I've definitely established that possibility – been forced to believe it could be true. But I'm still to be totally convinced. Part of me hopes it isn't so. Do I really want to be a reincarnated priestess with a story out of Mills and Boon?

There's a whole section on 'false memory syndrome', which apparently explains people's vivid plunges into other lives. But 'recovered memories' constructed from what has been seen or heard in childhood cannot explain the intensity of my experiences surely? The textures, tastes and sheer tactileness of every tiny detail. I know olfactory memory is powerful, aromas releasing hidden memories. But memories creating smells that strip the lining from your nose? A film doesn't contain those, or a book. How about knowing what's around the corner in a place you've never been before? Being haunted by someone, in my own time, who belongs in the past? Much as I'm resisting the idea, having lived before and bringing the memories back might have credence. As does the notion that someone can walk through time in either direction.

How could I describe it? I recall what Douglas Adams said in *The Restaurant at the End of the Universe.* 'One of the major problems encountered in time travel is simply one of grammar. The event will be described differently according to whether you are talking about it from the standpoint of your own natural time, from a time in the further future, or a time in the further past.' I'd so enjoyed listening to Adams's sly satirical humour on the old tapes my beloved grandpa had treasured.

When Aidan comes over to see what I'm researching, I explain, 'From what I've already read on reincarnation' – it's not the time to go into hauntings and the sexual proclivities of ancient Pharaohs, let alone my own involvement – 'it would seem that the Egyptians believed in the concept. Pharaoh was viewed as a reincarnation of the god Horus, which gave him his power.'

Realising I'm lecturing, I glance sideways, but Aidan looks interested, so I go on. 'The *ka* was believed to travel between the worlds and there was the *akh* – a kind of transfigured spirit – which could be activated after death. It seems to have been able to get up to all kind of tricks. But sadly there doesn't seem to be much in the ancient literature that I can find.'

'That's wicked. I'll do a report on that if you like. I've been looking up the Undead but dain't know about *akhs.*'

'Well, thank you, Aidan. Yes, that would be a good topic. I'd like to see what you make of it.'

To my surprise he asks, 'Could groups, you know, reincarnate together like?'

'I haven't found much about groups of souls incarnating

together as yet, but read my Jewelle St James book if you're interested. She seems to be saying that souls travel in groups and meet time – and potentially time – and again.'

As Aidan retreats to the far corner with the book, I scan quickly through the search results. Many entries talk of karma, coming back together to pay off debts, or to make reparation. But finally I find one headed 'Unfinished business'. A rather dry account, it does seem to open the possibility of carrying a theme or entanglement across several lifetimes. A rather more lurid site goes into curses and hauntings that could well be the script for a horror movie. Maybe I'll be able to write my own once this is over. If it doesn't turn out to be a figment of my fevered imagination. Or, I could suggest it to Aidan. He seems to have been grabbed by the idea.

'Ah, Miss Grayson, could you possibly...?' One of my old dears is hovering anxiously.

I close the computer down. Now is not the time. But I'll pursue this later.

Chapter 26

Their places are gone. What has become of them?

'I kind of went off track, like, Miz Grayson,' Aidan says as he hands over the report. 'But after that old geeza that was bothering me went away, this took my fancy. I tried to be more scholarly in my approach like you said. It's rather long. I hope you'll find it interesting.'

'Indeed I will, Aidan. I'll take it home and study it tonight. It looks fascinating. Well done. I hope you remembered to put your sources and the relevant page numbers.'

Aidan squirms. 'Yeah. Most of it is from the net and I still need to verify some sources.' His fingers sketch airy quotation marks. 'But I will, Miz Grayson. You'll see.'

Ghostly goings-on in Ancient Egypt and elsewhere
Aidan Doran

(The full text of this report is at the end of this book)

Most of what we know about the dead in ancient Egypt comes from the tombs, the Book of the Dead and other texts, and from letters written from the living to the dead – or the Undead. The post-death state wasn't that different from life. People feasted and played, had sex, and life carried on almost as normal – most of the time.

Many of the magical practices of the Egyptians were concerned with preventing or counteracting disturbances from the actions of the Undead. The ancient Egyptians believed the dead lived in the Otherworld. They demanded respect to keep them content. The relatives visited the tomb regularly and made offerings. If not, the dead were vexed. They became the Undead...

Reading on, I'm engrossed in the story. That ancient civilisation clearly suffered the same kind of problems that are troubling me. But was it only the priests and important people...

> ...Hauntings happened to ordinary guys too. A husband wrote a formal letter to his dead wife moaning about the troubles she'd brought upon him. He reminds her how well he'd treated her when she was alive. How he doesn't deserve her evil because he is one of the good ones. He sets out what he's done since she died three years ago and reminds her that he hasn't had sex with any other woman since. He has to write the letter, go to her tomb and read it, and then tie the papyrus to the statue of her in the tomb so that her *ka,* who lives in the tomb, would understand. We don't know whether the letter worked.

Now, there's an idea. I could write a letter to his Malodorous Majesty. Reluctantly, I lay the report down and head for bed. But, somehow, I don't think that a letter alone would do it. That minging old bugger, as Aidan puts it, needs more. Perhaps we could tie it to the binding tablet and that bit of mummy case Sebastian brought back and leave it in his tomb. Seb said it was in his bag when he returned home, although he had no idea how it got there. He's been talking of returning it. It's a long way to go on the off chance though. Right now, I'm too tired to concentrate on anything but sleep – and hope for sweet dreams. I set the alarm clock an hour early so I'll have time to finish reading Aidan's report before going in to work.

* * *

The Undead on their travels

> The Undead could travel, especially when attached to an object or a part of their previous body. In his memoirs, Sir

> Alexander (Sandy) Hay Seton, 10th Baronet of Abercorn, tells how in 1936 he and his wife Zeyla travelled from Edinburgh to Cairo. This trip made Sir Sandy believe that his family was forever cursed…

Oh Aidan, where did you find all this? So many examples. You really would make an excellent researcher. These 'ghosts' really do travel then, they aren't tied to the land of their birth. That explains so much – oh, and what about this – looks like they aren't merely connected to artefacts either –

> It is reported that the disused platform of the former British Museum tube station in London is haunted by a mummy wearing only a headdress and a loin cloth. Apparently, while the station was still open, a national newspaper offered a cash reward to anyone brave enough to spend a night alone there. No one was.

Or, it would appear, tied by any kind of time either if Aidan's next piece is to be believed. This is much more recent. Well, comparatively speaking. This could well relate to His Awful Majesty. Maybe I'll talk to Aidan. Or should I wait until Seb gets back? It's too convoluted to go into on the phone…

> **The Priestess of Death**
>
> There are other reports of ghostly happenings within the British Museum itself caused by a haunted mummy case lid – often said to be cursed as well. At the time, Sir E.A. Wallis Budge, keeper of the collection, refused to comment on what he experienced saying he'd take it to his grave, but his staff were loud in their protests. One keeper reported seeing a horrible yellow face rising up from the case. Other staff heard 'wracking sobs and loud knockings'. Budge is even said to have suggested that the mummy caused the First World War…

That's a bit far-fetched, although that face sounds awfully familiar. What's this though?

Peter Underwood in Haunted London (1974) states, 'It does seem indisputable that from the time the mummy case passed into the possession of an Englishman in Egypt in about 1860, a strange series of fatalities followed its journey and even when it resided in the Mummy Room at the British Museum, sudden death haunted those who handled the 3,500-year-old relic from Luxor.'

'It is certain that the Egyptians had powers which we in the twentieth century may laugh at, yet can never understand.'

Sounds about right! But this mummy stuff seems to have become something of an obsession at the height of the nineteenth century.

> ...The reconstruction in Piccadilly of Seti I's tomb, in 1821, was a sensation and started a craze for 'mummy unwrapping'. Notable surgeons publicly unwound mummy bandages and chiselled away at the bitumen preservative for hours on end in front of fascinated audiences. This morphed into horror stories in film and fiction where the dead unleashed vengeance on the living. Boris Karloff played the reanimated magician Imhotep in the 1932 horror film *The Mummy*. It was but one of a long line of tales which culminated in Indiana Jones and his 'Temple of Doom'.

Hmm, reminds me of Edgar Alan Poe's *Some Words With a Mummy*. But that wasn't exactly a horror story, although it had elements. The mummy was reanimated by electricity having, if I recall correctly, been embalmed whilst still alive for exactly that purpose. Rather like ancient cryogenics. He gave an erudite explanation of life in an advanced ancient Egypt civilisation. Did that happen to His Awful Majesty? I'd better take another look at it. I haven't read Poe since uni. Come to think of it, quite a lot of nineteenth century Gothic literature was based on weird occurrences where ancient Egypt interpenetrated the present day. Conan Doyle penned *Lot No. 249,* in which a mummy was animated to carry out the will of a modern black magician. Richard Marsh published that extraordinary vision of London struck by a biblical plague spread by vengeful ancient Egyptian priests. Bram Stoker's *The Jewel of Seven Stars* used recently discovered radium to reanimate a woman pharaoh, resulting in nuclear annihilation. And, of course, H. Rider Haggard wrote *She.* The immortal African queen who crosses time to be reunited with her reincarnated lover – whom she killed in a previous life. Was *She* a Victorian fantasy cougar as one academic called her? Or was the novel based on something else entirely? After all, didn't Haggard say in *She* that the oldest man on earth was but a babe compared to Ayesha. That the fruit of her wisdom was that there was but one thing worth living for, and that was love in its highest sense. Shades of Randolph and the teachings from the Prince's book in that declaration. Wonder if Haggard read it? Did he meet Randolph in Egypt? His books are full of ancient magic and antediluvian curses. Did he step back through time, or did time come forward atavistically to meet him? Perhaps all those authors were having the same kind of time-slip experiences I am? Better see what else Aidan has to say.

> Douglas Murray was a member of the Ghost Club, a group of ardent Spiritualists. From the upper echelons of society, he knew many diplomats, colonialists, painters and writers and was a friend of Wallis Budge and William Flinders Petrie. He drew on his contacts to spread the story of his curse.

So, creative imagination? Or real-life experience? I'm inclined to go for the latter, with more than a smidgen of poetic licence and the need to sell newspapers added. Exactly like the modern day.

What the Egyptians believed and what could be done

> ...The god Osiris was in charge of the *akhs* and if they misbehaved he could be called on to keep them in order. Being bad seems to have been common. According to the *Penguin Book of Myths and Legends* night assaults by the Undead involved touching, kissing and sexing as well as illness, misfortune and nightmares. In trying to prevent this, nothing was left to chance. Spells had to be performed in the correct way and the pronunciation had to be perfect.

Is that where my banishing spell is going wrong? Would a different way of saying it make it stronger? I'll practise a few variations. See if it makes a difference.

> There were texts to repel 'every dead man, every dead woman, every male enemy, every female enemy who would do evil.' All the wack-jobs and the badasses. One spell says, 'Get thee back enemy, dead man. Do not enter into his prick so that it goes limp.' The *Papyrus Leiden* contains spells against nightmares and night terrors and 'adversaries in the sky and earth'. According to the Chester Beatty *Dream Book*, to keep bad guy nightmares away you had to invoke Isis, then rub bread marinated in beer, herbs and incense on your face. You need to know the name of the bad guy – and where possible the secret name – to make the spell work.

Yuck. I don't think I fancy that on my face. But I could burn incense and see if that'll help things along. I've got those smudge sticks that came into the shop and smelled wonderful. I'll give those a go.

> If the spells and letters didn't work, then 'execration figures' were made from clay or bowls inscribed with the deceased's name, or the name of an enemy to be overcome. The figure

> or bowl would be smashed, destroying the evil through substitution.

Aha, are we getting somewhere at last? I guess he's talking about a kind of *ushabti* figure. I could make one of those, smash it. Add it to the pile in His Majesty's former abode. Would that be enough? Something else to discuss with Sebastian. I wish he'd come home.

> An important part of Egyptian closing rituals after banishing the Undead was to make a necklace out of carnelian, lapis lazuli, serpentine, 'spotted stone' or 'very spotted stone', shiny silex, breccia and 'little jasper' beads. This was worn around the neck for seven days. Then the badass guy was well and truly banished and could not return.

That's worth thinking about. I could wear an additional necklace. I'm pretty sure the *menat* is gem quality carnelian, often used for protective amulets, described as the 'Blood of Isis' in my crystal book. It says that the stone helps to remove the 'veils of Isis' that cloud spiritual clarity and true sight. So, wearing it constantly must be having a powerful effect on my inner sight. It's supposed to help one become a truly wise woman. I can't wait!

The stone assists in remembering the lost and forgotten parts of yourself too. Could it reach previous lives? Is that why I've been getting glimpses? Apparently it accelerates an inner marriage that unites the inner masculine and feminine. One of the steps of the mystic marriage. Is that why it was chosen for my *menat* all those centuries ago?

Seb's *sem* is lapis lazuli. Another protective stone – it recognises psychic attack and returns the energy to its source. Could we turn his Awful Majesty's energy back to him? Use it to propel him into the past. Is that the secret? Lapis teaches the power of the spoken word, so it could link to the banishing spells. It reverses curses, or disease caused by not speaking out in the past. From what I've glimpsed of the far past that could be useful for Seb. He didn't have much chance to speak out and His Majesty certainly cursed him. I like that lapis bonds relationships. That must be why the *sem* is the complement to my *menat.*

There's that new shop that's opened down Traders' Alley, maybe they'll have the beads I'd need. But what on earth is 'shiny silex'? I'll look it up once I've finished Aidan's paper.

And finally, another contemporary ghost story

This tale is on a ghost story site on the internet but the writer insists it's a true account of being haunted by the ghost of an ancient Egyptian. It bears out what the previous information shows, the 'dead' are very much alive in another world and can interfere with the living in the present time no matter when they lived. The writer describes an ancient Egyptian figure that holds her down at night and 'takes advantage of her'...

I know only too well what that poor girl was going through. Sexual subjugation across the centuries. It's good to have confirmation that I'm not the only one to whom it's happened. Now, all I need to do is discover how to make it cease.

Chapter 27

A touch of lotus

Hesitantly, I open my towelling robe and reach down as far as I'm able, sliding warm fingers between moist thighs. The pleasure is immediate, hot and urgent. That silky, salty, rose-scented bath prepared me – as did contemplating raising the fires of Mut. Hips thrust to front, side and back to an insistent beat as the book had instructed delighted and aroused me. Like the belly dancing I'd witnessed in Egypt. Wondering for a fleeting moment if that's where it began, a twitch in my *kat* draws attention to my body. I'm ready. But...discomposed. This is something I've never done before. Are the curtains tightly closed? Those French windows give great access to the garden during the day, although lately I've been a little afraid at night. But the 'guest bedroom-cum-study' tucked away upstairs is too claustrophobic.

Wanting to keep such pleasure for the right moment had always stayed my hand. Oh yes, I'd had those teenage promptings. I'd been tempted. But I'd resisted. Although nothing had ever been voiced, it had been forbidden. My mother wouldn't have dreamed of speaking of it. She was much too embarrassed. The lack of information, and – I have to admit – a certain prissiness, had been enough to make me hold back. Taking that erotic literature course at uni hadn't given me any more insight, more like furious embarrassment when the tutor went into salacious detail.

I'd blushed and walked away, ducking my head, when the girls at school discussed such things. One of them had flaunted the vibrator she'd bought for herself on a trip to London – until it was confiscated by a passing teacher. 'Silly bitch probably needs it for herself, I don't suppose she's getting any,' the girl had muttered. I hadn't been convinced that a lump of rubbery plastic could possibly be fun. In any case, I never felt truly alone. Never enjoyed total privacy. There was always the comforting awareness of my guardian grandmother and the less-than-comforting presence of a watchful mother in the next room. As a small child, I believed that my mother could actually see through the wall. Her calls of 'Phillippa, what are you doing, stop that now' invariably coincided with innocent acts of mischief. My mother never really trusted me, or thought me competent to run my own life. A view to which I'd acceded. Until now. But, still hesitating, I wonder. Am I truly alone? To be on the safe side, I whisper the banishing ritual yet again.

Outside the wind howls, the banshee moan adds to my unease. A storm's been forecast. It sounds like it's on the way. Nevertheless, now I've been instructed by the book – and those dreams – I'm determined to begin *The Alchemy of Night*. So intoxicating. I've anointed my 'central suns' with the wonderful perfume from the alabaster jar. They are glowing.

It's time. I reach out to the bedside table and pick up the shining shiva lingam I'd bought that morning. I'd anointed it with oil, enjoying the slippery roundedness, running my fingers up and down it and sliding it against the palm of my hand as I cupped the basalt hardness. My palm had tingled and sent signals shooting between my thighs. I'd taken it into the bath so it was warm, almost like flesh. I'd experimented with it. Rubbing it between my legs and slipping it so smoothly into my *kat*. In seconds I was gasping. But I couldn't control the burning. The book said I had to master the fire. There was no chance with this stone. So, reluctantly, I'd put the lingam aside.

I put it down again now. I'd better learn the art of 'prestidigitation' first. What a delicious word. For a moment my mind strays, playing with the sound. But pressure in my 'God's Plenty Below' brings me back. My Hathor finger is tingling fiercely, the serpent fire connecting it to my heart tracing out the pathway of love. The ancient Egyptians were so poetic in their naming.

A crash of thunder shoots cannon fire overhead. Bright light splits the air. Water hisses and boils as the promised rain meets hot paving slabs. Shivering, I glance at each corner of the bedroom. It's not anticipation of pleasure that's uppermost in my mind now. The candlelight creates shadows that could hold anything. Stark lightning betrays every night creature waiting to pounce as the curtains at the window billow in the rising wind. Ghostly invaders swirling through dark air. My rational head knows it's an illusion. My heart is not so sure. I'm vulnerable to intruders. No walls, nor anything else, have kept His Awful Majesty at bay.

The large pieces of black tourmaline I've placed in the corners will, I'd been assured in the crystal shop, keep out anything untoward. As would the even larger pieces of rose quartz around my bed. These will call my twinflame to me. Support me and keep my enemies bound fast. Thunder drums again as the room lights up like the charity shop window. Mrs B does so like her fairy lights, leaving them in place all year round. As another lightning flash illuminates the room, I check every corner. I'm too inhibited to do this with the bedside light on so, cautiously, I switch it off. Clutching the *menat* in my free hand, I murmur the banishing ritual once more before giving myself up to the pleasure of my fingers.

It begins slowly. A prickling, tingling that is almost tickling, amongst the burning waves. An itch to be satiated. Sending shards of near-pain to my nipples. Nipples that I want coloured with the warmth of henna and carmine. The fiery juice of love. My flesh is engorged, throbbing, keeping time with the thunder rolls overhead. This must be what it's like for a man, recalling how I'd watched fascinated as Tom had sprung into vibrant life. Instantly ready for 'the best bit'. But I remember Sebastian, my gentle dream lover. How slowly he moved. I never saw his *henn* awaken. He'd always been aroused. But he held back to give me pleasure. Now I do the same for myself.

As instructed by the ancient book, my Hathor finger moves languorously over my Mound of Mut, pulling the tingling up towards my belly where tantalising sensations twitch and dance. Toes curling, I surf the pleasure waves without quite giving in to the ultimate release. Ten, twenty times. How is this possible? Pulling my gut down as I strive to hold the energy in place. Driving the fire up my spine and into my head, to curl back down into my belly, before starting the circuit again. My whole body becomes fire. Colours cascade and coalesce behind closed eyelids drenching me in blue, red and green, gilded by the afterglow of lightning flashes that surge along my skin to tickle my toes. I don't know where I end and the lightning begins. How can lightning be inside my head? I've never felt anything like this. Those dreams didn't even come close. Every cell of my body and all the spaces in between have been filled up. I've never felt so powerful before. I could do anything. I'll burst with the energy. When His Awful Majesty brought me to climax, it was the orgasm of which Joseph Conrad spoke, 'The implacable orgasm, of which we are the victims – and the tools.' This is different.

I wish Sebastian were here.

Chapter 28

A fire colder than the flames of my longing

In his narrow garret bed, Sebastian groans and twists. Overhead the thunder roils and lightning bolts shoot into every corner as the rain hisses and the wind howls. The room is the only one his college had available at short notice. He's had to return to 'defend his thesis.' His supervisor is concerned about his progress, or rather the lack of it. The room had been his when he was a lowly first year. He loves its position tucked up against the chapel roof with the glimpses of a horse chestnut tree through the high-set dormer window.

But he isn't thinking of the view. He's awoken just in time to pull back. To hold in the racing seed that threatens to spurt over the rumpled sheets like the water spouting from the gargoyles on to the roof below. He's been dreaming of Phillippa. But not a Phillippa he recognises. This one is wanton and abandoned, threshing in the throes of a pleasure he didn't know was possible. His body throbs so much it is painful.

Sebastian's no stranger to the lonely pleasures of masturbation. He's spent many a night in his otherwise celibate student bed, hoping and wishing. But this is different. A continuation of the sensation he'd had earlier when gyrating in the student bar to a thumping beat. Reliving his youth, he'd laughingly told himself when calling in to look for his supervisor – although he'd tended to skulk in the corner rather than brazenly strutting his stuff in those days. His body convulses again and he grabs the *sem* around his neck, pulling at it to hold on to the dream. He hasn't taken it off since Phillippa gave it to him. He'd feel naked without it. He must remember to look into its deeper significance next time he's in the library. The urgings of his body make it difficult to concentrate. The lightning gives an unreal black-and-white film cast to his room. Is he still dreaming?

He remembers what he'd read in the short time he'd had to examine the Prince's book. Phillippa's promised to scan it for him, but she hasn't yet sent it over. *Non-seti:* orgasm without ejaculation. That's the key. The first step to sacred sexual initiation. Just in time, he squeezes hard on his perineum. Locking the semen in place as his body bucks and quivers in time with the lightning flashing through the window. Wave upon wave cascades up his body. Dropping back down his arms and into his belly. His whole being is buzzing as a particularly fierce flash fireworks into the room. He's been electrified.

Wow, this is so good. He's never had intercourse, except for a teenage fumbling that didn't go anywhere. To his embarrassment he'd come in his pants before they'd even started. The girl had laughed and he crept away ashamed of his lack of control. After that, girls seemed to avoid him. Even at uni, he had been considered too studious. No fun. He'd once tried online dating. He was okay at the virtual chat-up. But didn't have the courage to actually meet anyone. He dreamed of it though. Longed for it. Then Phillippa came along. She seemed like the answer to his prayers. But he was too shy to ask her out. So he…

He feels Phillippa reaching out to him, minds rushing on the wings of lightning to meet across the night. The power of the *sem* and *menat* amulets around their necks entwining their souls, pulling them into oneness as the thunder claps. So this is what raising the Fire of Min means.

As he's dropping exhausted into sleep, thunder shouts him awake once more and the sensation begins again – and again. Throughout the long night Sebastian learns mastery. Raising the fire at will. Finally he allows himself release. 'That's got me up to speed' is his last thought as he drifts into sleep and the storm moves on, birds in the chestnut tree heralding the dawn.

On a roof beside the tree, a dark cloud buzzes and batters futilely at the invisible barrier thrown up by the ancient chapel.

The Prince Khem Yar Khepher'set, supreme ruler of Khemit and the Two Lands, has no power in these hallowed precincts, despite the storm he has raised. *'Wait, nti hati, wait and be mindful what My Majesty can do when you leave this temple, as leave you must. She is Mine.'* The birds rise with a great clatter, screeching a warning. But Sebastian is too deep in slumber to pay heed.

Chapter 29

Love has penetrated all

Temples Mut and Min, Thebes

Flickering shadows dance around whitewashed walls, cast by oil-lit lamps of gleaming basalt. The heavy scent of cinnamon, cloves and frankincense suffuses the air. Murmuring voices chant to the insistent beat of a drum. The light is mellow. But, in the shadows, dark gods displace the air and break through to grasp at the young man as the evening light dies. It is the perilous moment when time takes a breath. Pauses. Stands still. At any moment the Sun-God will leave the world of the living to enter that of the dead. Journeying on the Boat of the Sun through the darkest passages of night to fight his enemies. Casting off Apophis, the serpent of chaos. Striving to be born anew. The young Adept incants, 'My *ka* has prevailed over my enemies, my *ba* knows the ways that lead to the gate that conceals the Sight. I am Adept.'

The dark figures recede. Men'ofer shudders with excitement and more than a little fear. Finally she shall be his. It has taken so long to reach this point. So many years of careful study. So many stages undergone. So many days – and nights – peering at the ancient texts, preparing himself for this night. So many higher joinings made. So much restraint, withholding the pleasure of nedjemit for the greater union. They are bound together. He can't fail now. The loss would be too great. It is time.

Hands reach out, shaving his head of its plaited sidelock and his body of every tiny hair, anointing him with the sacred oils and wrapping his henn in a loincloth of finest linen. The lapis *sem* is placed around his neck. A garland of heady blue lotus shrouds his shoulders. He drinks the bitter mandrake-laced lotus wine. The air shimmers and shakes as his body shudders with power. He has become the God. It is time.

* * *

Flickering shadows dance around the walls, cast by flames from pots of finest alabaster. Cinnamon, ambergris and blue lotus flowers perfume the air. Murmuring voices chant to the insistent beat of a dream. The light is mellow and the Goddesses move closer, calling to her as they reach through the last of the evening light. 'We are with you *kheroti,* you who has never been opened in childbirth. Be brave, be bold, be powerful.'

It is that delicious moment when time takes a breath, pauses, and stands still before turning to night. Through the narrow window, the shining silver of the crescent moon gleams. Isis is waiting to be born anew. Men'en'oferet laughs and stretches out her arms, the nine concentric rings that signify an initiate of the great Goddess gleam in the lamplight. 'Welcome, My Lady, welcome.' She pulsates with sensuous delight as her attendants rub her skin with the sweet-smelling oils, paint her *kabits* and lips with carmine and tie a transparent blue robe beneath her firm young breasts. A garland of blue lotus is placed around her shoulders and a delicate golden-leafed headdress holds back her long dark hair. The gems hanging from it twinkle in the flames, stars coming out to play. The Blood of Isis *menat* is placed around her neck. She drinks the bitter mandrake-laced lotus wine. The air shimmers and shakes as her body shudders and fills with power. She has become the Goddess. At last the waiting is over.

* * *

Two processions set forth. From Temple Mut, the sistrums thrum, high female voices rise and fall in joyful harmony. The waters of the sacred lake sough as the white ibises take flight like kindly ghosts in the night. From Temple Min, the drums throb, insistent and deep. Male voices chant long and slow. The waters of the sacred lake hiss as the night birds swoop in. Shadows from the Otherworld. Fishes rise to catch the last lingering insects of dusk, ripples going out like the eternal circles of the stars surrounding the Great Red Hippopotamus of the North. The torches lighting the processions weave their snakelike paths across the darkening night towards the sanctuary of She Who Is Powerful.

'Who comes through the night to risk the Foes of My Lord?'

'The youth Men'ofer who has fulfilled the nine initiations and seeks to make the final joining with the flesh of his chosen one. I have never known *nedjemit ndjemu* and it is time. My *ka* has prevailed over my enemies, my *ba* knows the ways that lead to the gate that conceals the Sight. I am Adept. I am become the God. For this I was born.' Men'ofer proffers his shaven head, the marks of initiation clear for all to see.

'Who comes through the night to disturb the peace of My Lady?'

'The *wowaei* Men'en'oferet who has passed the nine initiations and seeks to make the final joining with the flesh of her foreordained one. I am *kheroti.* My *ka* has vanquished my enemies. My *ba* knows the ways that lead to the gate that conceals the Sight. I am Adept. I am become the Goddess. For this I was born.' Men'en'oferet proffers her beringed arm.

'My children, are you aware of the grave sanctity of this act? That with this mystic marriage comes a joining for all time? That you shall never be free from each other again, no matter where your souls may wander throughout time in this world and the next?'

'We are and we seek to claim our birthright. For this we were born.' The two voices ring out without hesitation. This night is the culmination of nine years of study, a lifetime of loving and denial. Of preparation and withholding until, at last, tonight they are free to unite their bodies – and their souls. The Gods draw near, gleaming nimbuses of night. Stars come to earth to take on corporeal form. Divinity made manifest.

'Enter the sacred portals, make your offerings and complete your initiation. May the Majesty of the Gods be with you.'

A door opens. Hand in hand the two initiates move forward. Placing their offerings of beer, bread and spices on the altar before them, they move ever deeper into the sanctuary until they stand before Their Lady. In this arcane place where so much has gone before. Solemnly they turn to face each other, taking the garlands from each other's neck and placing them reverently around the neck of the towering leonine figure. Raising their hands above their heads, they prostrate themselves full length on the ground for a long heartbeat of silence...

The goddess smiles her blessing.

Standing once more, Men'ofer takes Men'en'oferet's left hand in his, raises it to his mouth and kisses the palm tenderly. Solemnly, he touches it to the secret place where the Goddess's thighs conjoin and then to Men'en'oferet's own God's Plenty Below, 'I am joined to you in the Central Sun of Physical Being ruled over by the Lord Osiris who rose again and his Lady Isis. We are joined by right of birth. We were chosen by the Gods for this moment before time began. My *henn* is joined to your *khat*.'

The night holds its breath as he moves her hand to his own place of Plenty Below and pauses as she unties his loin cloth and lets it fall saying, 'My *khat* salutes your *henn*. In the joining, the *nedjemit ndjemu* that is to come, we shall be reborn.'

Lifting her hand away, he moves it to the gently rounded belly of the Goddess and then to Men'en'oferet's magic eye of the belly. 'I am joined to you Sekhem to Sekhem in the Central Sun of Creation ruled by the Lady Isis-Mut who breathed life into her husband once again in order that the Young God be conceived and the old transmuted into the new.'

'My Sekhem is your Sekhem. In this, by the Lady Isis-Mut, we are joined.'

Taking her hand to his own belly, Men'ofer intones, 'By the

Great God Min, fountain of all fertility, may he bless this sacred union. In this we are joined.'

Kissing her palm once more, the young initiate takes Men'en'oferet's hand first to the solar plexus of the Goddess and then to her own, 'By the Young God Horus-Khonsu, product of the union of Mut and Min, Isis and Osiris, I am joined to you in the Central Sun of the Will by the deepest emotions of my being. My *ka* is joined to your *ka*.' As he moves her hand to his own body, a breath sighs out from him in deepest contentment. 'For this I was born.'

Reverently he unties her gown of gossamer linen and lets it fall, kissing her carmined kabits. Men'en'oferet's breath catches in her throat as she responds, 'My will is your will, my *ka* is your *ka*, love eternal.'

Moving his hand up to the hearts of his ladies, Goddess and priestess, Men'ofer gazes deep into his consort's eyes. Each places the middle finger of their left hand on to the other's heart centre. 'I am joined to you in love eternal *ba* to *ba* in the Central Sun of the Heart ruled by our Lady Hathor, in the seat of our souls. Let them be united in love forever, let our veins of love be intertwined.' As he moves her hand flat against his own heart, Men'en'oferet feels its beat quicken.

'My heart is yours. *Ba* to *ba* for evermore.'

Touching her hand to the throat of the Goddess, to the priestess and to the young initiate, Men'ofer intones more quickly now, 'I am joined to you in the Great Central Sun of Communication, *khu* to *khu* by the Recording God Thoth from whom nothing is hidden and by whom all is known: past, present and future. May he bless our union, which has been written since before time began. May the Gods hear my love for you.'

'My *khu* salutes your *khu*, in this we are joined as it was written.'

They are standing close now, this priestess and the adept to whom she has been promised from birth. Silky oiled skin touches slippery softness. His smooth caramel and lotus aroma surrounds her. His lapis blue eyes gleam in the dusky light. Slowly, oh so slowly, he kisses her palm before reaching up to touch the forehead of the great black basalt figure. Transferring Men'en'oferet's hand with due deference to the Goddess's forehead and to his own, Men'ofer whispers, 'I am bound to you through the great all-seeing eye of the Central Sun where the Goddess Neith ensures that time spins out its thread in its pre-ordained pattern. It is she who holds the balance of the universe in her hands. She knows that our love endures forever and she bestows on us the ability to see past, present and future. I am joined to you *akhar* to *akhar*. Our souls –'

A dense black cloud moves briefly in front of the eyes of this priestess who has already seen so much of worlds hidden from the others' sight. Blinking her eyes, she pushes it away but cannot hold back the involuntary shudder passing through her. Men'ofer pauses and looks at her intently, but she nods encouragement quickly repeating, '*Akhar* to *akhar* are we united.'

There is only one more connection to make. Urgently, she raises her hand with his and, standing on tiptoe, takes it to the crown of The Lady.

'May the Central Sun of our father Min bless us, join *sakhu* to *sakhu* and connect us to the Eternal Ones. We are become Divine. United our souls shall be beyond the gateway of death.' As their linked hands touch her crown and his own, she exhales a long sigh of relief.

'My *sakhu* is joined to your *sakhu*. Blessed are we by the Gods Eternal.'

Reaching down to touch the feet of the Goddess, they both intone, '*Sakhu* to *sakhu*, we are inviolable souls, united we are joined on Earth by the Gods Below as it is Above. We have united with the Eternal One. Our love is sealed.' Standing, each stamps their right foot firmly on the worn granite floor.

It is done. The joining is sealed. The consummation can go

forward without hindrance now. She brushes away a foolish fear from a corner of her mind...

His arms tight around her, Men'ofer ardently kisses her lips and pulls her towards the pillowed bed laid out on the floor. 'At last, Mennie, at last. You are mine.' The heavy scent of lotus blossom enfolds them as their kisses, no longer illicit, deepen. Her lips press back eagerly, her knees buckling with the pleasure to come. She has waited nine long years for this moment. To complete on the physical plane what has been carefully charted on the metaphysical as each Central Sun was awakened in herself and in her beloved, as their souls moved inexorably towards the unity of the Sakhu and the sacred marriage. To enact in the flesh what had been stirred in the imagination by illicit embraces stolen behind temple pillars in the fleeting moments they were alone. Young they may have been, but desire had snared them from the start. The guilty kisses had been all the more delicious because they were prohibited. Now, the ever-deepening longing wants to burst forth but the discipline holds. The ritual will be completed without haste. The moment will be savoured in all its sacredness.

Amidst the silken covers, he turns and begins to kiss her feet, butterfly caresses moving with infinite slowness towards the God's Plenty Above.

Chapter 30

Come boldly into her den

'Out of the way *nti hati,* wretched child of Set. She is Mine. My Majesty claims her! With her you shall not walk in the blessed *auma,* nor enjoy the shade of the sycamores and the scent of the lotus as you linger by the sacred pool. Here, with My Majesty, she shall remain.'

A flail swats Men'ofer out of the way as though slapping at an irritating insect stinging in the night. The *sem* is torn from his neck overcome by the irresistible power of the *sema* around the Prince's neck. As the young man crumples to the floor, a predatory face swoops towards Men'en'oferet. Hot and burning, the urgent lust of an intruder's kiss claims her lips. Her soul is chained to eternity.

The images slip and shatter as a door swings open with a rush of hot air. I whimper in frustration as I try to grasp the pieces sliding through the fingers of my mind. I need to make sense of all those intertwined gods and the sudden desecration. It was indubitably me, not a dream of someone else or something inspired by the book. It was so clear, so *me*. Not a 'hallucination', or a 'fantasy in fancy dress'. Possibly a 'reverie'. Or a 'remembering'. Mayhap a 'recalling'. But how can I reconcile what I used to believe is possible with what's happening to me now? I'm part of the story. Reliving my own life. A life that took place in another time. But my life nonetheless. Mine – and Sebastian's – and the Prince's…

Had I been scared, frightened by the overwhelming power of this predatory invader? Or was I exhilarated, excited at the prospect of what was to come? A fiery tingling at the base of my belly suggests the latter, although my heart rebels queasily at the knowledge. It reminds me of those dreams secreted in the night.

But this is mid-morning. It's never happened in daylight before, not this way…they clearly weren't dreams at all but memories. All too real. I've stepped into the past.

Is it because I've been looking in the magic mirror? Opening other worlds? What hidden promise – or threat – did that meeting hold? What could the desiccated Prince want with a young priestess with all her life before her? What link does it have with that incomplete ritual at the end of the book? What was all that about joining central suns with a young initiate whose face is so tantalisingly familiar? He was so like Sebastian. Darker skinned, burned by the desert sun. But those lapis eyes. I'd know them anywhere.

His hair. Deep burnished copper rather than ginger, kissed by fire, definitely red. Not polished jet like all the others. How do I know? His head had been shaved… For a moment I see him again, younger now, laughing uproariously as we play tag around stone pillars. His springy coppery curls so similar to Seb's. Almost African in their ringleted tightness. No wonder the Prince called him a red-haired son of Set. Is this why I feel I've known him forever? Were we bonded in a former life? Playmates – and so much more. If only I could bring the images back – or put a camera in my head. Now, that would be useful. One thing is certain though, that predatory face is that of my Dark Enigma, the Prince Khem Yar Khepher'set himself. Unquestionably, this explains –

'Miss Grayson? Are you quite well? You do not look at all yourself. Might I be of assistance?' The whiny voice of Mr McMeeney sweeps away the last shards of my memories. 'I came to inform you that the library committee has decided to make another inspection. This time they are coming into your domain. So this daydreaming simply will not do.'

Opening my eyes, for a moment I don't recognise him. His pinstripe grey suit and flowery tie confuse me, although the hand fussily smoothing the comb-over is all too familiar. But where are the cool comfortable desert clothes, the loin cloths and gauzy kilts that let in the caressing air? The naked bodies displayed without shame. Squeezing my eyes shut as present reality re-establishes itself and the full horror of Mr McMeeney decked in a loin cloth, his toothbrush moustache and little else briefly manifests itself, I push away the image.

'No, thank you. I'm merely a little tired that's all. It was rather warm last night. I couldn't sleep. If you don't mind, I'll go out and get some fresh air. Pick up an iced coffee round the corner. That will clear my head. I'll be back before the committee arrives. Everything is ready for them.'

I have no intention of discussing my reverie, my other life with this old fusspot. He'd never believe me in a million years. I'll talk to Sebastian later. Surely he'll believe me. I hope so. I need reassurance that I'm not going crazy. He'll be back in a day or so. Cheered, as I run down the stairs and out into the glorious autumn sunshine, pulling out my new phone, I text, 'Seb, I've had the strangest thing happen. It was exactly like my book. It explains everything. Call me.'

* * *

Sitting quietly at home in the dusk, the book beside me, gazing into the mirror, I watch the clouds clear to reveal a now familiar scene.

...As he slides between my tender young thighs, the Prince Khem Yar Khepher'set plucks one of the bright blue lotus flowers that has been so carelessly let fall and languidly brushes it along my arm. 'I claim you, hennu nafrit, light of my heart. Mine for all time you shall be.'

Shuddering, a fire starts deep in my belly as the fragrance of the lotus roils heavily around me mingling with the Prince's pungent aroma of honeyed cinnamon and musky cloves. This union is unwritten, out of time, unblessed by priests or gods, but I can no more prevent it than stop the Great God Ra in his track. A fleeting glance is cast at the fledgling adept, so callously swatted aside before the avaricious Prince's lips plunge on to mine and I surrender to pleasures that will tie my eager soul to him for an eternity.

'Oh Seb, what happened to you?' I whisper as I wait for his call.

…Night after night, the joyful torment continues as the Prince visits me. The day is for drugged sleep, the nights claimed by a sexual rapacity that knows no boundaries. 'Mine you are forever' is intoned so fiercely and so frequently that I come to believe it with all my heart. My soul is consumed by a delirium of longing that wipes out the memory of my beloved, wherever he may be.

How could I? How could I forget all that you meant to me? Abandon you like that. Who was the young woman who took you away? What place did she play in this? I batter futilely at the barriers in my mind. The mirror is silenced, the past cancelled out – for now. But it's stirring in its shroud. If only I could *see*. Break through my credulity. Expand my mind. See what was. I must!

Chapter 31

The desperation of love

Ancient Khem

Slipping from a spyhole in the temple rooftop, the veiled watcher murmurs with satisfaction, 'It is done. Men'ofer is mine alone. Closer to him than a sister I shall be when I console him in the pleasures of the night.' Mes'kia hurries down the worn stone stairs, evading the temple guards. 'Worry not, my dearest love, I come to rescue you.'

As she tugs the young adept to safety and hustles him into a boat, she covers his mouth as he cries out in protest. 'No, stop, I must save…'

'Hush, do you want His guards to discover us? We must leave now. Quickly, *im bar*.' Picking up the paddle, she drops her veil over him as he lies naked and forlorn, curled in the bow neither knowing nor caring where he is going. He has lost his twinsoul, the one he should be with forever. What is there left for him now? Silently he calls to his beloved, reassuring her, 'One day I will make it right again. I will set you free. Wait for me!'

Drifting noiselessly through the dawn, the boat slips downriver past guards drowsing over their watch fires. As the Sun-God lights up the sky, fishermen casting nets on khaki water slap their paddles to drive unwary fish, but pay no heed to the fugitives passing by. Great Nile crocodiles beached like fallen palm trees on muddy sandbars begin to stir, mouths stretched wide to test the morning air. They too slip into the river, mother of this land of Khem.

Mes'kia steers the boat towards a reed-shrouded bend of the river, pushing through the clinging stems with her paddle until she reaches the island sheltered from the gaze of casual passers-by – and those who seek to penetrate its secrets. She ties up the boat and shakes her unwilling passenger.

'Men'ofer, wake up. We have arrived.'

The young man is reluctant to stir. He's dreaming of his beloved, safe in his arms at Their Lady's feet. Somewhere in his mind he knows that if he awakens he will have to face a future that is impossible without her, but he pushes the thought away. He cannot go on if she is not there. His heart will be ripped from his body, his guts spilled for crocodiles to devour. Better dead than this. If he holds the dream, he can stay with her. But his tormentor is insistent.

'Wake up!'

Pierced by unbearable pain, his body is raw and grieving, Gaping holes and bleeding sores leave him half a man. Turning, he mumbles, 'Leave me be, let me sleep.' He fights to get back into his dream, clinging to it with a desperation born of the sure and certain knowledge that he cannot survive without the keeper of his heart. He must reach her.

'No, you cannot sleep here, you must come with me. We have to get to sanctuary. Come.'

Reluctantly, clutching his belly, holding himself together, he stumbles to his feet and glances around. He sees nothing but head-high papyrus stalks, a forest in miniature, crumbling stone steps rising high above him.

'Where are we?'

'At the temple of my mother. We are safe here. This way, quickly.'

As they mount the steps Mes'kia utters strange shrill warbling sounds that break off abruptly and begin again like a startled bird. Soon they are answered by echoing calls and hands reach out to grasp them as they emerge into the sunlight. Men'ofer looks around in dazed amazement. The reeds give way to a courtyard, vast and stone-walled with a squat pillared building at the far end and small mudbrick huts along the sides. Statues of His Lady are all around. Older, wilder, more ferocious than the ones he has known. This grimalkin is no beneficent healer. This is the destroyer of men sent out by her father-god to wreak havoc on his subjects. This is She Who Must Be Obeyed in all her awful glory. Instinctively he falls to his knees before her, imploring, 'Help her, My Lady. Save Men'en'oferet. She is yours.'

'It is too late for that, to His Majesty she belongs. He shall bend her to his purpose. Beyond the help of anyone in this world she is. Or the Gods themselves.'

The harsh voice startles him. Looking up, he sees a woman, tall and opulent with hair the colour of dried papyrus, robed in deepest saffron with a vast golden headdress bearing the face of the Lady set atop all. Her green-rimmed amber eyes glare at him, malice in their depths.

'No, no, that cannot be true. We have to save her.'

'I say no.' The look she gives him says that she is not used to being defied. But Men'ofer tries once more.

'Then let me go, let me return to be with her no matter what may occur.'

'Take him. A night with Our Lady will his mind soon change.' Snapping her fingers at a cowering *eibata* she points to the squat stone building. 'Enclose him in the sanctuary of The Giver of Ecstasies.'

A draught of bitter herbs is forced between his lips, heavily perfumed oil rubbed on his heart as he is stripped and laid on a bed of softest linen.

'Worry not,' whispers the *eibata*, 'the Lady is not as fearsome as some would have you believe. She has compassion in her heart for those who suffer the desperation of love.'

An oil lamp is extinguished, leaving blackness beyond measure. Heavy doors slam. In the darkness something shifts, a rank feline smell assails his nostrils. Desert lion? Surely the Gods have not shut him in with a lion? What kind of ecstasy would that be?

Light flares. The pungent scent recedes.

'I am here, my dear one. Sleep safely. I shall watch over you.' She settles herself beside him. Waiting.

* * *

Sebastian groans. The dream still vivid as he wakes. There's no chance he'll forget this. Fumbling for his phone, his fingers shake as he texts, 'Call me in the morning'. No sense in waking Pips at this hour. He slips back into sleep and the dream that is not a dream.

* * *

Men'ofer writhes as the drug takes hold, muttering then shouting as he relives the loss of his beloved, his heart torn out by the roots, his soul shattered. There are craters at the centre of his being. He is a husk of a man, a failed initiate.

The rank lion smell is back. His heart pounds in fear. The grimalkin is fierce. Her power cannot be stayed. Her presence fills his heart. He bucks and twists to escape. To no avail.

'Be still. Be at peace. All is well.' Gentle fingers stroke his brow. A scented cloth wipes the sweat from his body. Smooth skin touches his. Arms enfold him. Soft murmuring soothes him. Feline scent is replaced with one he knows so well. Deep, hypnotic, firing up the senses. Assuring there is nothing to fear. Slowly he relaxes burrowing into the arms that hold him.

'Mennie. Is that really you, my love?'

'Shush now, peace. I am here.'

Fingers play up his spine, caressing, comforting. Arousing. Pulling the fires of Min from their resting place. Featherlight kisses on his chest stir his heart. His henn rises. He is thrust on to his back, guided into her and ridden towards *seti*, crying out aloud with the joy of it. She is here. She is his. They are joined.

Opening his eyes at the last moment to savour his beloved,

his tender look turns to horror.

'Mes'kia. What are you doing? What sorcery is this? Nooo...'

Desperately he tries to roll out from under her, to hold back the flood. But his protest is too late. The consummation is complete. The enchantment complete. They are joined.

'You are mine,' she exults. 'Mine alone.'

'Mennie... no...' His despairing cry falls into darkness and he knows no more.

* * *

Quiet hands rouse him. 'Sir, sir. Please to sit up.' Water is dribbled between his lips and he is helped on to cushions that enfold him in smothering softness. Memory overwhelms him.

'No, get off me –' He lashes out catching the *eibata* on the face. Brown eyes gaze imploringly into his.

'Master, please, be still. Let me tend you. The night is over.' A sheet covers his nakedness. Weak beer and soft flatbread is offered but let fall.

'But you do not understand. I believed it was her, Mennie, my beloved, but...'

'You must understand. Yagut'd'eskia is mistress here. Mes'kia is her daughter and what she wants, she shall have. It is done.'

What on earth is he going to tell Phillippa when she calls? He wishes now he'd not sent that text. But it's too late.

Chapter 32

Lest thy name appear putrid

Ancient Khem

Breath rasps through the acrid air, the labouring chest barely rising and falling. Propped on linen pillows, His Majesty is diminished. Incapable of rising. The goose feathers rustle as he moves restlessly from side to side, coughing and hawking. The bitter herbs the priests burn are failing in their task. The Prince is nearing his end. But his will is indomitable still. He shall have his way. Physical death he may not cheat, but his *ka* shall be infused to carry out his plan. His Majesty shall survive. A bony hand reaches out to grasp Agni'ti. 'Fetch her, fetch her now. It is time.' The Prince's body may be failing but he has gained otherworldly strength. *Shezmu* possesses him already. A push sends the old man tumbling towards the entrance. The tjaty hurries away, rubbing at the livid marks on his wrist.

Men'en'oferet is pushed into the room and towards the bed, her hair tangled and dirty, blue robe torn, body unwashed, nothing like the nubile young priestess who had gone so willingly to her initiation. This is a woman drained of power, a husk of her former self.

'Look upon My Majesty and weep *hennu nafrit*,' the creaking voice compels. Stubbornly she keeps her eyes to the ground. She will not look on the man who stole all she held dear and who has abused her these long months.

'Is the *wowaei* with child?' the Prince demands of Agni'ti.

'I fear not my Lord, the nurse saw blood on her rags again this month and the barley has not sprouted.' Agni'ti is careful to stay out of range of that bony hand. He does not dare utter his belief that His Majesty has lost his potency, or his suspicion that the nurse has been secretly feeding Men'en'oferet abortant herbs. But he knows that there were no stains on the bed linen after the young woman was dragged into the Prince's bed night after night. No magical child, no young Horus shall be born into which the ruler's *ka* can transfer. Not in this life.

'Bring her close,' the ancient voice demands. 'Let me look on her.'

As Agni'ti ushers her forward, like a snake, the Prince strikes. A gleaming quartz knife cracks open Men'en'oferet's chest and a bony hand is thrust inside to pull out her heart. Slicing through the filaments that anchor it, he passes it to Agni'ti. 'See that this heart is interred within My Majesty's body not mine own. Place it within my mummy before my journey to Abydos to my House of Eternity. My Majesty must pass the test. Feed My Majesty's heart to the swine to satisfy Ammit and let mine have the judgement of Men'en'oferet's innocence, and' – pointing to the young girl's body still spilling its blood on the floor – 'take that away and burn it and be sure that the ashes are placed within My bandages. Mine throughout Eternity she shall be. Ensure that you the first of many sacrifices are. I demand you serve me throughout that Eternity. That you remain with me within the tomb. You and your *heka,* which must indubitably return after your death. Heed me or suffer the consequences.'

The Prince falls back on his pillows with a creaking sigh. Dead but not gone. The tjaty sees all too clearly the desiccated *ka* hanging in the air over the innocent young girl's heart that is still warm within his hand. There shall be no peace unless he carries out his Lord's orders, this he knows. Those ancient eyes still see all. But a way must be found. It will be easier with the Prince lying at this minor palace in the Theban Hills. There are few of his court to question the actions of his tjaty. The local embalmers will not know the rituals as intimately as those who would normally tend the royal personage, and the high priests who would accompany him beyond his death into the judgement of the Afterlife are far away from this god-forsaken place.

Reverently Agni'ti wraps the girl's heart in fine linen and places it inside his robe before picking up the young woman's husk. Calling for the night priests, he goes out to spread the word that His Majesty is no more.

Later that night, he joins the jackal-headed embalmers in the fragrant darkness of the *ibu* tent. The palm wine washed body has been readied for these last rites. Slit open, its entrails are packed into canopic jars filled with aromatic herbs. Only the heart is left in place. Once the body has been released from its holding tank and packed with natron, the priests file out, leaving Agni'ti to dim the lamps. As he does so, the fragrance of the herbs dissolves leaving…what? A musky sweetness clinging to the roof of his palate with something deeply foul beneath. Sulphur sears the roof of his mouth and scours his nose. As he suspected, the Prince has not begun his journey to the Afterlife. He is here in all his majestic awfulness.

'Do it, do it now fool or suffer the consequences throughout Eternity.' The voice is already failing, but a wilder energy compels it.

As guards are placed outside, Agni'ti turns back and, reaching down through the salty mass, quickly severs the Prince's heart replacing it with Men'en'oferet's brighter one. He covers it with a scarab carved from the finest turquoise. 'Lest your name appear stinking and putrid before the Lord of the Otherworld,' he murmurs as he replaces the natron.

'There, Master, it is done.'

A quickly muttered holding spell repels the gruesome presence, for the time being. Agni'ti knows that it won't last. He must prepare the requisite ceremonies before the burial takes place. Only if the Prince is forever entombed will there be an opportunity to save his daughter's soul. Only if he finds a way to inter the body far from the Prince's House of Eternity can that dangerous force be fettered.

'Worry not, Mennie, a way to release you I shall find. You

cannot be bound to His Majesty forever.'

When the forty drying days have passed and the body is bandaged, only he will know what's occurred. But he'll have to ensure the Prince is interred with more than the usual precautions in a place no one will suspect. 'We do not want that old *seba* coming back,' he mutters, shielding himself in case His Majesty is listening. He hurries away to prepare his great deception.

* * *

'Rest in peace, my daughter,' Agni'ti whispers as he takes Men'en'oferet's body to a secret cave known only to him. With one last kiss, he lays her in the welcoming grave. A single tear trickles down his cheek and, infinitely slowly, he wipes it away and places the finger to his lips, tasting salt. He burns hot with anger but, as he calls on all his occult skill to master himself and his grief, it shrinks and freezes, an obsidian needle piercing his heart.

His child's body has been soaked in costly perfumed oils and packed in natron before being tenderly wrapped in the finest linen bandages. He has replaced her heart with one carved from the finest cornelian to give her *ka* vitality, her story engraved upon it. Her simple acacia wood coffin is beautifully decorated with the prayers and maps of the Otherworld. It shall guide her, as it would him had he occupied it as planned. The insignia of her caste are in place. Amulets nestle at each of her central suns. It is the closest he can give her to the embalming and elaborate burial that would most certainly have protected her. But he is certain the gods will heed his plea for her safe passage through the Duat. His innocent child shall unquestionably pass the test.

'Your ashes with His Majesty shall not mingle, even though your heart he has claimed,' he assures her. 'But I shall do all I can to return it to you and, when the time comes, Men'ofer shall join you here. You shall be united in death as you could not be in life. This I promise.' Weeping silently, he turns and closes the rock-cut door, sealing it with the insignia that no man shall dare to violate.

Chapter 33

Softened by love-longing

'I'll make us some coffee, shall I? I'm unaccustomed to all that wine.' Laughing, I open the door to the flat. I am a little lightheaded as I fill the kettle and put it on to boil. But I'm glowing with happiness, fizzing with joy as I look back over the evening. An excellent meal, lovely surroundings. Waiters attentive, though discreet. Waiting to fulfil our every 'gustatory pleasure'. But I hadn't shared that thought with Sebastian. He doesn't seem to embrace my pleasure in obscure words, although he espouses the tortuousness of academic language when it suits him.

The intimate ambience encouraged us to hold hands, gazing into each other's eyes, savouring one another as much as the food. Voices muted as we discussed the events that brought us here and then sliding away into the myriad and one everyday details that await discovery. Favourite music, places – although I hadn't been to anywhere near as many as he, I'd had my dreams. Shyly nuzzling up to each other as only those newly in love know how. It's so good to have someone who really listens – and who doesn't think me crazy for what I've been through.

There's an urgent pulse between my thighs that stabs at possibilities. My inhibitions are loosened by the wine, floating away like soft feathers. My need for him is painful, darts of pleasure running through me as my clothes caress me as I move. I'd taken out that favourite dress from the wardrobe. Somehow it didn't smell noxious anymore, holding a faint aroma of almost-roses. Clinging to me alluringly, it's sensuous, womanly, like putting on my blue robe. My new silk bra and knickers are everything the woman in the expensive boutique promised. But I'm conflicted, unsure, vague doubts that I try to push away invade my belly. Would it be right? Is this really it?

Snuggled up on my enormous sofa, bought more for comfort than style, I feel him tensing. He's pulling back, looking at me with those lapis eyes. I could melt into them, and try to pull him close again. But he holds back.

'No, Pips. You promised to tell me what was going on with that homeless guy? It's time to spill all.' Sebastian lifts his questioning eyebrow. My finger yearns to smooth it.

It's a pity that Tom had pushed his way in, spoiling our last few moments as one of the waiters helped me on with my coat while Sebastian visited the loo. The aggressive stance and smelly clothes had instantly attracted attention – as did the beer can being waved in my face. Other diners drew back in horror. This wasn't what they expected in one of the town's best restaurants. I'd looked round helplessly, torn between desperately needing Sebastian's help and not wanting to involve him. I hadn't had time to explain Tom's return yet. Or, rather, had hoped it would go away. He'd given up lying in wait for me at the library so I'd relaxed my guard. Too soon it seemed. Why hadn't I done a tie-cutting with him when I did the one with His Majesty? Not that that had fully worked. I've felt those watchful eyes on me a few times since then. I'm so confused. Why me? What do I have that makes these men want me so?

A couple of waiters had escorted Tom out. I hoped that would be the end. But, of course, he'd been waiting as we'd exited. Ignoring Sebastian, he'd tugged and pulled at me demanding that I take him back. Saying I belonged with him. He was even more of a pest than His Awful Majesty. Looking round, Sebastian had signalled to a passing taxi and we jumped in as it pulled into the kerb. Seeing how I was trembling, Seb had put his arm around me, pulling me close and nuzzling my neck. 'What was that all about, Pips? Or rather, who was that? He seemed to know you? I didn't want to confront him in case he became violent.'

'I'll tell you later. It's complicated. Let's go home for now,' I'd said. Reaching up, I'd kissed him and he quickly responded.

So immersed in each other were we that we barely heard the muttered 'get a room' from the front of the cab. By the time the short journey was over, I'd pushed Tom to the back of my mind again, revelling in being with Sebastian. Finally!

But no, he's gone back to that tricky subject yet again.

'Please, Seb, leave it for now. I will tell you, I promise. For this one night, couldn't we pretend everything's normal. That we've recently met and are out on our first date? Getting to know one another? Enjoy being together.'

Hesitantly, he nods and I offer, 'I'll get that coffee then, shall I?'

But, as I reach for the cups, he groans, pulling me towards him, crushing me close. Then holds me away as he delicately undoes the buttons that keep him from the skin he clearly itches to touch. 'I don't think I can wait for coffee, Pips. I want you too much. This doesn't feel like a first date. It's like I've known you forever.'

Slowly, he draws the dress off my shoulders, butterfly kissing the exposed skin and fingering the *menat* that lies so softly around my neck. Doubts gone, I help him as he fumbles with my new bra, dragging the straps down and pushing it away until he cups my breasts in his hands. He slides the soft fabric of my dress over my thighs and I step out of it, flinging it aside with my foot even as my hands are tugging at his shirt.

Behind us, the kettle reaches a head of steam and then quietly subsides. Switching itself off, it won't be needed now. Superfluous I would have said, if I could think. For once my head is not full of words. My whole body is bursting. I'm drowning in exquisite sensations.

Running my hands over the downy copper hair on his chest, I plunge them to his belt and release him from his jeans in one eager motion. Struggling to stand on one foot while he extricates himself from the tangle around his ankles, he almost falls but I hold him upright. Kissing him as he fumbles with his socks.

Finally!

Skin to skin, he clings to me. Breathing in my scent. His downy hair tickles my chest sending shivers down my spine. He inches me towards the sofa, trying to lower me gently, but I grab at his hand, pulling him over on top of me, laughing out loud with the joy of it. Only the translucent silk of my new knickers is between us. 'At last. Oh, at last.' As I wrap my legs around him, for a moment everything is quiet, stillness holds us in its thrall.

We lie together with arms and legs entwined, like lovers who know each other's bodies intimately. Each curve, every surface, all the softness – the hardness beneath – are so familiar. This far surpasses the dreams. We have all the time in the world. Idly, I trace the line of his jaw with my tongue and the curve of his cheek with my fingertips. His creamy caramel smell has darkened again to the burnt toffee of desire. His lapis eyes gleam, darkening as he draws me in. Leaning back, he finds my face with his hands, fingers tenderly exploring its contours. He strokes my eyelids as his tongue flicks inside my ear. I quake with remembered pleasure. My breath comes in short gasps as electric shocks pass down my body, swirl around my belly and flow out through my toes, only to curl up and stream through the crown of my head once again. I grope for the words to describe it. A 'frisson of desire'? No, no, something much more. That doesn't do justice to what's happening. This is a tsunami, paroxysm, ferment, maelstrom...a 'cauldron of concupiscence'. Yes, that's it. My belly is a cauldron, but the erotic force is more than mere lust. It's creation itself. A cliché? I don't care.

Sebastian pauses at my lips, gazing deep into my eyes to catch my thoughts. Lifting a finger to his mouth, he transfers a kiss to mine. Mmmm, I sigh as my lips close around his finger, sucking gently. He picks up my hand and kisses each finger in turn until his tongue flicks at my palm like a sand lizard's, slowly, lingeringly, feather-light. The tip of his index finger brushes my wrist, the familiar firestorm rushing up my spine.

Hungrily, I reach for him but his whispered, 'Wait. Let me,' makes me pause. Softly, so softly, he massages my neck, hands caressing my shoulders before moving down to the swell of my breasts. He lingers there until his lips replace his fingers, sucking at nipples standing erect, while his fingers move over my belly raising whirlpools of fire as I moan deep in my throat, before his hands slide around to match the curve of my buttocks and pull me closer. Those beautiful new knickers are still between us. He eases them down so that I can impatiently flick them away. All-consuming hunger flashes through me but, as he lifts me towards him, I stiffen and pull back, biting my lip as I recall my conversation with Shelagh and the ancient Prince's interruption. Is this really the way to do it?

'What's the matter, Pips? What is it?' His hand moves to caress my cheek, tilting it towards him. 'Are you worried about being a tiny bit drunk? You know I wouldn't take advantage of you. Don't you want to?'

'Yes, of course, but… I know this is silly. But would you mind, Sebastian?' My hand stills him. 'Do you think…could we…could we follow the stages in the book? I'd like to do it right this time. This is our last chance.' I move to arm's length, calm now that the rapacious hunger has given way to something more mellow, an inner certainty that what I'm doing is right. 'I'm not saying no, but…could we wait, please.'

'Well,' he says, the confusion on his face giving way to a grin. 'I reckon I've raised the Fire of Min and held myself back. Have you been consumed by the blaze of Mut and managed to hold out?'

I nod, the blood rising in my cheeks, 'I had to, couldn't stop myself, couldn't wait any longer. It happened while you were in Oxford.'

His eyes crinkle. 'Oh yes, I remember that night. I didn't get any sleep till dawn. What with the storm and…' His face is an even brighter red. 'That was quite an awakening. I've mastered the art of *non-seti* that's for sure. What's next on the agenda?'

'We've got a bit ahead of ourselves. Have you opened the secret chambers of the central suns?'

'No, don't forget you haven't copied the Prince's book for me yet. What are the central suns anyway?' He raises his eyebrow in the way I love.

'As far as I can make out, they equate to the chakras or energy centres used in yoga, with an extra anchoring one at the feet. I have to say, getting them activated made quite a difference to my raising the Fire of Mut – and to controlling it.' I look down at my naked body, *remembering*.

'How does one do that?' Sebastian is looking at my body too and lightly brushes his knuckle from my shoulder to my hip.

My body is desperate for him. Can I hold to my decision? Perhaps we should simply get on with making love the way I yearn to? But no, something tells me it would be better to follow the instructions in the book – as long as *He* doesn't interfere. My Dark Enigma. The tie-cutting and the latest banishing ritual seems to be holding, for now. 'Why don't I show you? Wait a minute.'

Getting up, I step into my bedroom, collecting the precious alabaster pot. Although the thought of modesty flashes through my mind for a moment, I rather like the way Sebastian's eyes follow me as I move towards him, unscrewing the top of the jar. 'Stay there so I can reach you.' There are advantages to having your inhibitions loosened by good wine. I've got power over him, I inwardly exult. Sniffing the oily contents, a deliciously sensuousness passes through me as the perfume takes hold. My body is voluptuous, feminine. Sexy. Potent. An entirely new experience for me. It was never like this with Tom, although I had glimpses in those dreams. This is what it means to be a woman. This is what they knew in the Temple.

Kneeling beside him, slowly, tantalisingly, I massage a morsel of the cream between my breasts, the intense glow burning through to the core of my being. The *vena amoris,* the pathway of love, is aflame. No wonder the Egyptians believed there was a direct connection between the Hathor finger and the heart.

'What's that fragrance?' He's enthralled. 'I've never smelt anything like it, and yet I know it. It's not rose is it?'

'No, it's heavier than rose and it has an erotic edge to it that's beyond sensual. It brings your whole body alive. Egyptian blue lotus. Here, I'll show you.'

Dipping my Hathor finger in the pot again, I move to his feet and intone, *'This is the Anchor governed by Geb the god of Earth. The Anchor unites Above with Below, forming a great chain of being, so that the Gods may be made manifest on the earth and the work of the adept be brought into manifestation on the physical plane.'*

Where's this coming from? It's in the book, but why do I remember it so clearly. It's so familiar and yet sounds so strange? My voice has a cadence and rhythm I've never heard before. So much richer. So much more depth. Is it the effect of the perfume, my head is certainly swirling with it? Or is that the remnants of the wine? I'm so confident of my power.

As I rub the cream on to the soles of his feet, he squirms at the first touch of my finger as though ticklish. But he relaxes into it as the cream takes hold.

Moving up, I slide my hand between his legs, cupping his silky balls in my hand and intoning, *'This is the God's Plenty Below governed by the great green god Osiris, the Lord of Silence and Sky, and his wife the Mistress Isis, Guardian of Dreams and Healers. The power of this Sun must not be squandered by the unrest which men miscall delight nor be turned towards satisfaction of mere lust.'*

I'm beginning to moralise, sounding like one of those old-fashioned Bible thumpers. Should I stop? Could I stop? It's like something is pushing me on faster and faster. My belly is fluttering with anticipation or – is that fear? This isn't really me, and yet I know it is. Curtains swish open in my mind. Tall pillars, a silken bed, two figures entwined in that delicious smell. I've done this before.

'The God's Plenty Below is the source of all creativity, the primal mound of creation and the waters out of which all arose.'

Sebastian's *henn* had been rising before I'd even begun the massage. Now he quivers. Then lies still as the words penetrate his mind and my becreamed finger strokes his perineum. Even though naked, I sense I have taken on a different mein, as if robed and bedecked with ritual sanctity. My voice is charged with authority. I make one short stroke across the head of his *henn* and move to his belly button as his whole body ripples.

'This is the Magic Eye of the Belly governed by the great Mother Goddess Mut from whom the cosmos was formed, bearer of the Womb of Life, and the great god Min. This is the seat of Sekhem, soul power, the generative force.' My finger gently circles below his navel.

Eyes glazed and turned inward, he's immersed in this ritual anointing that is older than time itself. Feeling a robe swish around my legs as I move, I reach his solar plexus. *'This is the Eye of the Will governed by the great god Khonsu, He Who Travels with the Moon, Watcher through the Night. Here lies the source of the common will which must be mastered so that the spiritual will is called forth from the higher realms to manifest below.'*

I place my hand below his heart. *'This is the Seed of the Heart governed by the great goddess Ma'at, begetter of cosmic harmony. Here, the ability to determine your destiny becomes a reality.'*

Destiny. Yes. This is so right, it has been written throughout time. I *knew* I belonged with him.

He is completely still now, turned deep into himself, although his skin twitches under my hands as I move seamlessly to his heart, tracing the symbol of infinity above and below. *'This is the Seat of the Soul governed by the Lady Hathor, Mistress of the West, Queen of the Dance and of Joy, the source of unconditional love.'* My hand lingers over his heart, but a fluttering of the air makes me hasten on. His Malodorous Majesty is near. I taste his presence. The sooner Seb stands in his power the better. I need him to help me fight off the avaricious one.

Quickly I anoint his throat. *'This is the Voice of Divine Intelligence governed by the great god Djehuti, One, Self-begotten, Self-produced, who established the heavens, the stars, earth and everything in them, who directs the motions of the heavenly bodies, without whom the Gods could not exist, knower of all, measurer of time.'*

Sebastian swallows convulsively as I massage his Adam's apple before moving on to his forehead, the air brooding over my left shoulder as I do so. *'The All Seeing Eye governed by the great lady of wisdom Neith, Mysterious and Great who came to be in the beginning and caused everything to come to be. When this Sun opens all is revealed. The adept sees through the veil of creation into the true being of matter, spirit and gods.'*

My voice is even darker now, authoritative and stern as I move up to the crown of his head intoning, *'This is the Great Cause of Light governed by he who before All was director of the motions of the heavenly bodies…*

'Stop! My Majesty this outrage forbids.'

Gods of ancient Egypt, pentagrams and Archangels notwithstanding, he's back. The serpents around his head hissing venomously, tongues flickering towards us. His eyes skewering us to the floor.

A taloned hand reaches out to snatch away the pot. But I'm quicker. Turning, I raise my hands. I spit out, *'Arescht, linari, achungti, delightio, abrash yaru. Ixak ib, yesh! Seb-EN.'* My voice rises and then deepens emphatically on the last syllable, shouting out the banishing.

As the air snaps closed again, his voice booms from the bottom of the well of time, 'My Majesty you defeat cannot.'

Oh yes, I can. Now I've got my twinflame, I can do anything. I've finally got the intonation right on that last word. I'd been emphasising the first syllable before, should have realised that earlier. They clearly used a different tonality to the modern day. I… The air shifts uneasily. Better think about the mechanics of sound later.

Quickly I intone, *'I am the things that are, that shall be, and that have been. When this gateway is open Nuit the Goddess of the Starry Heaven reveals herself and her milk nourishes the earth below.'* As I massage the cream into the crown of his head, Sebastian fountains Nuit's milk from his *henn* crying, *'Deshiti seti Min,'* as spasm after spasm squeezes him dry, his body heaving and bucking with the force of the orgasm. His face a rictus. But it's not pain, not if his guttural cries of pleasure are anything to go by.

A shaft of white hot flame rushes up my spine and out of the top of my head before I can control it. My hand strays to my *kat* wanting to join in the outpouring of his libation to the gods. Wishing I could be one with him in this sacred moment. It would only take one touch. Something stays my hand, holds me back. This is his moment. His initiation.

When he finally collapses back on the rug, Sebastian's eyes are rueful. 'Sorry Pips, I'm not sure that was meant to be part of the ritual.'

'Oh, I don't know. It looked pretty authentic to me.' I hand him the alabaster jar. 'Now it's my turn.'

Chapter 34

Carrying a red fish

Ancient Khem

Silently, Men'ofer slips through the reeds. Evading his guards has not been easy. It has taken many weeks to gain their trust. Many hours of playing *mehen, aseb* and *senet.* Games of strategy at which he excels. Now his pocket is packed with his pickings, wrapped in cloth to prevent jingling. As soon as he reaches a village, he will purchase a passage to where Mennie is waiting. No fellahin will be able to resist a few copper niblets. The rings would make him rich beyond measure. The bangle from the Chief Guard should be sufficient to gain entrance to the palace. No one could spurn such a beautiful piece of workmanship.

If only he could save it as a gift for his beloved. He knows she would be delighted by the craftsmanship needed to fashion the delicate fluted silver edging to the chunky silver, set with carnelian and turquoise. A gift to bring good fortune from the far-off land where it was created. What a journey it must have made with its trader-master. But he knows that to penetrate the palace of Prince Khem Yar Khepher'set will require inducement on a grand scale, as well as guile. He will sacrifice her pleasure at receiving such a gift for the possibility of gaining access to her.

Glancing at the sun, he reckons he must have been walking for a good two hours. He must reach a village soon. His legs are flayed and torn from the papyrus leaves that line his path. The mud through which he walks is deep, squishy, pungent with decay and laced with buried reed shards that shred his soles. His sandals had offered little protection to his feet. He'd cast them aside some time back. The bleeding wounds are attracting flies and small red fish that leap and nibble. The humming whine of night-biting insects is rising, replacing the cicada symphony that accompanies the slow descent of the sun. Mosquitoes bite and chew, absently he slaps at them, his own blood squishing through his fingers as he flattens them. But nothing matters if it takes him to his beloved.

Wearily he plods on, desperate to reach a village before nightfall overtakes him. He's heard crocodiles grunting in the distance, and the swish of water as they slide in to the fast-flowing river beyond the reeds. He'd hate to step on My Lord Sobek in the night. Judging by the height of Ra, darkness will not be long coming. The birds are falling silent now. Twilight is all too short in this land of abrupt contrasts. Ra versus Apopep. Day or night? He knows which he prefers, but hopes to find a boat to spirit him away into the gloom.

Another hour and he is still wading. He deliberately chose the dark of the moon but now he is desperate for even a flicker of light. Only his feet are keeping him poised between the land and the river. There is no bank to speak of. The papyrus stalks thrusting out of the water guide him, their roots catching at his toes. Step too far from them and he will be lost to the swirling waters of the Mother of Egypt. Carried who knows where. He doesn't even know whether he should be travelling upstream or down. With the current or with the wind? He'd hoped those living in the village could tell him in which direction his destination lay. He has no memory of his journey to Yagut'd'eskia's domain. His attempts to question the guards led nowhere. Since his refusal to make *nedjenit* with Mes'kia again, she has shunned his presence and his *eibata,* though willingly cooperating in his escape plan, knew not where they were.

'I was blindfolded when brought here. We all were,' the servant had said. 'The Lady considered that if we knew not where we were there would be no point in us trying to leave. In all my time here, no one has escaped.'

But Men'ofer is determined. He has to go. There is no point

to life without Mennie, without the holder of his heart. He will do anything to find her.

A flicker of light breaks through the darkness ahead. He picks up his pace, no longer feeling the heavy mud slick at his feet or the swordlike leaves flensing his flesh. Help is at hand.

'Welcome home, you poor blundering fool.' The voice flays him and he staggers and drops to the ground. The formidable figure before him is utterly naked but for a huge green-stoned ring. Totally hairless except for a pale yellow mane tumbling down her back. Clearly female, a lionskin mask hides her face but those amber eyes are unmistakable. It is Yagut'd'eskia as he has never seen her – or any woman – before. Shaman priestess. Keeper of the mysteries. Power crackling from her bare skin sends shocks through his unresisting flesh.

He had no idea such a thing was possible. She points at him with her snake-encrusted wand and raises him to his feet. The gold glitters and slithers despite the darkness. 'Did you not know you were on an island? Whichever direction you had taken, you would have returned to my welcoming arms. My homing ritual merely returned you to my presence a little earlier than otherwise. Come,' she commands as she places her wand and a carved ivory adze into an elaborate chest of ebony and electrum. The crouching lion atop it looks like it will spring at any moment. He pulls back, but she beckons him on. 'There is much to tell you.' She leads him into her lair. Unwilling, drawn by an invisible thread, he stumbles behind her.

Chapter 35

Nipple berries ripe in the hand

Turning over in the dawn light I smile, seeing Sebastian's face on the pillow beside me. I slept so well wrapped in his arms. Didn't think I would, being sure I'd find his nearness unbearable. Yes, I was the one who'd decided to hold back...urged him to do the next ritual from the book instead. But I'd been nonplussed when, afterwards, he'd said, 'Let me hold you. Let me stay. After that experience, I'm so deeply connected to you, yet widely expanded at the same time. Literally blissful. I've been plugged into something so much bigger than the pair of us. We're such an integral part of it. I want to be with you. Don't let the magic go.'

As we'd slipped into bed, I almost gave in. Then, as he stroked the back of my neck, I fell asleep instantly. From the quiet, contented look of him, he'd quickly followed suit.

As his startling blue eyes flicker open, a huge grin lights up his face. 'Pips. I thought it was another dream but you're really here. Did we...we didn't, did we?' The blush that suffuses his cheeks is the wildest yet.

The heat almost scorches me as I kiss him softly. 'No, you agreed to wait. To do it by the book. We seem to be getting the stages a bit out of order, although I think that's okay.'

His nod is thoughtful. 'So what's next? Better get out that sacred tome of yours. I'd rather like to get on with it.'

Picking up the familiar faded red leather, the place is already marked. 'Well, the next stage is supposed to be done after fasting all day and in the light of the full moon. It's up there somewhere. It was full last night.' I recall how the room glowed with pale light as we'd moved to the bed, creating a nimbus around us. 'Guess that's close enough. We may not have fasted but we never did drink that coffee.'

'It's hours since we had that meal. But I'm much too excited to think of breakfast. Are you finally ready to…?

'We need to activate those central suns again.' But' – I wag an admonishing finger that's at odds with my wide grin – 'remember, no *seti-ing* this time.' I reach for the anointing pot.

'Ah, Pips…' This time it's his turn to hesitate. 'That homeless guy? There's something you're not telling me. Who was he?'

'That was Tom. You know. The guy you helped me expunge.'

'You were with a vagrant? Not quite what I expected from his stuff.'

'Yes. No. You see…he wasn't homeless when he was with me. He had all these deals going down. He had a really good job and everything. But apparently it all went belly up and his new relationship didn't work out…his flat got repossessed so he had nowhere to go.' Aware I'm gabbling, I really don't want to talk about this.

'Slow down, there. Tell me. Why did he say you belong with him? Come on, tell me.' Sitting on the bed, he pats the place beside him. But I move to a chair, where my head will be clearer.

'You see, when we were first together, everything happened really fast. I'd only known him a week or two when he moved in. I'd been so lonely. I was blown away by him. Young and foolish describes me, more in love with the idea of being in love than in actual love. You know how silly people are when they think they're in love.' A pleading glance at Sebastian's thunderous face shows me that no, he doesn't know. I hurry on.

'To be truthful, I was already having doubts when we got on that plane to Egypt. He was so arrogant, never asked what I wanted. What happened over there proved what a dickhead he was. He tried to keep both of us on a string.'

'Well, you'd better snip it, Pips, once and for all. We can't go on until you have. Are you ready to do that?'

With no hesitation at all, I say, 'Yes, I am. You're the one I want to be with, now and forever.'

A pair of golden scissors appears in my mind and *snip* the cord tying Tom to me is gone. It's so much better.

As one, we turn towards the rustling wind that surges through the window, shouting the banishing at the top of our lungs. As the sound recedes, Seb stands up and pulls me to him once again.

'I claim you, Pips. His Awful Majesty can't have you. You'll be safe with me.'

Giving me a hug, he turns to light the candle I keep on the bedside table. As the flames begin to flicker and a potent aroma suffuses the air, I read the invocation. '*We are become Divine, the Great God and the Great Goddess incarnate.*'

To my astonishment, he joins in. His voice deepening as he intones the ancient words. Without being told, he lies on his right side, holding out his arms. 'Join with me, Pips.'

As I lean against him, my heart beats in time with his. His hands go to my centre, touching my soul. Reverently, I cover his hands with mine.

For a long, long heartbeat, all is still. Not a muscle moves. Not a sound is heard. Time pauses.

We breathe in unison. Deep and rhythmical. One single being. The Fires of Mut and Min rise up our spines, intertwining as they go. Male and female. Energies synthesising. Coming into harmony. Our central suns ablaze and connections are forged. We raise the flames higher and higher. Breathing, holding, pulling up, souls reaching out to each other. Our heart centres fuse. Burning, burning in the ecstasy of divine love exactly as the book promised. A cosmic orgasm of the heart.

'Yours forever, Pips,' Sebastian says softly.

'With all my soul,' I reply,

'My heart is burning with love.
All I see is this flame.
My heart is pulsing with passion like waves in the ocean.

I'm at home, wherever I am.
And in the room of lovers,
I see with closed eyes the beauty that dances
Behind the veils intoxicated with love,
I too dance the rhythm of this moving world.'

'That's beautiful, Pips. Where does it come from?'

'It's Rumi. I studied him at uni. I'd forgotten it until now. He's talking about the mystical flame that encompasses him when he's one with God. An all-encompassing, cosmic orgasm. It seems to apply equally to a union of hearts and souls. Sacred orgasm. I know the Sufis were in Egypt. I wonder if they inherited some of the ideas in the book.'

'Sounds likely, these things always cross fertilise. We can think about it later though. Let's enjoy the aftereffects of that cosmic orgasm for now.' He tucks his chin into my shoulder and breathes gently beside my ear, absent-mindedly caressing my nipple with his free hand.

Quietly we float, utterly at one.

Futilely His Awful Majesty attempts to batter his way in. But this time his will cannot prevail. Our soul bond has been sealed. All that remains now is to send him home. And then…

In the Great Beyond, the guardian grandparents smile at each other. 'It won't be long now, beloved, our time is coming. Then we can rest together forever. It's about time.' A contented sigh is all the confirmation he needs.

Chapter 36

The place where truth has the weight of a feather

The Hall of the Two Ma'ats

Standing at the gate to the Otherworld, the Prince shudders before taking a deep breath. Placing his hand where Men'en'oferet's heart resides safe within his wrappings, he intones the formula confidently,

'I, the Prince Khem Yar Khepher'set, life, health and honour be Mine, whose word is truth, say My heart is with Me, and it shall never come to pass that it be carried away. I am the Lord of Hearts. I live in truth, I have My being therein. I am Horus, the Dweller in Hearts. I am the Dweller in the Body. I have life by My word, My heart has being. My heart shall not be snatched away from Me. It shall not be wounded. It shall not be put in restraint if wounds are inflicted upon Me. I have not done that which is held in abomination by the gods. I shall not suffer defeat for My word is truth.'

The gate swings open. In a flash, he is through. He has passed the first test. Silently he is taken by the hand and led deeper by the jackal-headed god Anubis. As he pauses before the Lady Ma'at on her throne, the Prince says solemnly,

'Homage to you, oh great goddess, Lady of Truth. I have come before my gracious Lady that I may be judged before you. I know you. I know your secret name. I know the names of the Two-and-Forty gods who live with you in this Hall of Ma'at, who keep watch over those who have done evil, who feed upon their blood on the day when the lives of men are reckoned up in the presence of Osiris. In truth I have come to thee. I have brought Truth to thee. I have destroyed wickedness for thee.'

As the Prince hands over Men'en'oferet's heart to be placed on the Scales, Ammit restlessly pads below the pans. The dreaded Devourer of the Dead, whose forepart is that of a crocodile with crunching jaws, her middle that of a lion, the hind quarters those of a hippopotamus, senses that something is out of place. Wrongness pervades the air. She sniffs with eager anticipation and pushes at the Prince's legs. Certain that this soul that is so full of sin shall be hers to devour within a moment. He shall never walk the earth again.

Seeing this abomination before him, as the heart is set upon the left-hand pan, silently the Prince recites to himself the ancient plea to Men'en'oferet's heart to substitute for his own and not reveal the deception,

'O my heart of my very being, of My Most Beloved, do not rise up against me as witness, do not oppose me in the tribunal. Do not reveal the truth. Do not rebel against me before the Guardian of the Scales. You are the ka *within my body, the pure one who prospers my limbs. Let us go to the good place prepared for us. Do not make my name stink before them lest your heart be destroyed as well as mine soul. Before the great god, the Lord of the West, your uprightness shall be my vindication!'*

Breathlessly, he waits as the feather is placed lightly upon the right-hand pan. Can Men'en'oferet's heart pass the test when tainted with his own blackness? Will its sojourn within his mummy condemn them both? Swiftly, he shouts out the negative confession, knowing it for the pack of lies it offers but certain that the innocence of the heart before him shall protect his soul.

'I have not sinned against men. I have not wronged my kinsfolk or my people. I have not committed evil in the place of truth.'

In the secret burial place, Agni'ti listens with an ear to the Great Below, grunting and working quickly to fulfil his task as his eyes rake the darkness.

'...I have not domineered over others...'

Oh, how cunningly this Prince lies. No mention of the young priest and priestess deprived of the birthright their long initiation had won for them.

'...not done the things which the gods abominate.'

Nothing could be more abominable than the acts of this Prince who wishes to snatch eternal life by deceiving the gods.

'I have made no man weep.'

With his far sight, Agni'ti sees how Men'ofer weeps constantly for his lost beloved, how his heart is torn by the grievous loss.

'I have not repulsed the gods in his manifestations. I am pure. I am pure. I am...'

Agni'ti smiles. It is time.

Chapter 37

Ensuring no ghost looms

Then

Agni'ti reaches through the mist to snatch the heart of his daughter from the Otherworld. The impassioned voice fades away, the Prince's lies dying on his tongue as he is pulled back to the world from which he came. Pushing the heart deep within his robes, Agni'ti recites, '*Oh snake, take yourself off, for Geb protects me; get up, for you have eaten a mouse, which Ra detests, and you have chewed the bones of a putrid cat. Be gone Your Majesty and trouble her not. May the gods and the Lord of Fire protect this, the heart of my daughter, from the forces and fiends that seek to displace it.*' His hands trace symbols in the air to the gods of the four winds and above and below.

That is all the protection he has time for now. Later, he will make the amuletic plaque and inter her heart with her body.

Now

Idly, I finger the air-dry modelling clay I found in a box of children's toys in the shop. Moist and malleable, it's so tactile. I love its sensuous feel. Dreamily my hands shape a crude human figure. The feet wrapped together like a mummy, the head and arms bandaged into sausages. An execration figure from Aidan's report. A bit rough, but it will do. To my horror, I've also formed an over-large, erect phallus. I know from my research that male mummies were carefully bandaged to remain upright. All part of the symbolism of fertility and rebirth apparently. But the Prince doesn't need another weapon with which to carry out his evil intent. Moulding the clay back into the body, I turn the figure over. Maybe this will reduce his sexual prowess. With my fingernail, I incise the Prince's name and titles. Placing it on the window ledge to dry in the sun, I'll smash it with due ceremony later. Maybe paint it before I do. Would that make it more powerful? More *Egyptian?* Perhaps my books will guide me.

Then

Turning to the bandage-wrapped figure on the bare ground before him, Agni'ti quickly spits on it, stomps it with his left foot and smites it with a lance through the cavity where the heart should be, pinning it to the earth. He fetters the soul with spells and incantations. He shall ensure that this soul does not pass the test. The Prince shall not be free to move into the Otherworld, nor to return to this one. Stamping on the dried-out body until it is more dust than substance, he places a binding tablet where the mummy had been. The Prince's *ka* roars and roils, battering at the old priest's action with ineffectual hands. His Majesty's power is lost – for now.

Agni'ti stamps until the wooden mummy case itself is reduced to splinters. The debris is thrust under the binding tablet and he scoops in more dust and rocky chips from the floor to fill in the shallow crater he's created. He cannot be too careful. Quickly he intones, *'Your Majesty shall not exist, nor shall your body. Your Majesty shall not exist, nor shall your soul. Your Majesty shall not exist, nor shall your flesh. Your Majesty shall not exist, nor shall your bones. The place where you are shall not exist. Your name shall not be among the living.'*

Turning, Agni'ti pushes the rock door into place and seals it with plaster and further binding spells. He repeats them at the entrance and quickly scrambles up the ladder, throwing it down into the hole and scuffing out all traces of his passing. Now he must fabricate His Awful Majesty's funeral.

Chapter 38

How beautiful are the words that fly from his lips

'Good day, Miz Grayson. How are you this fine morning?'

'Aidan? Is that really you?' I can hardly believe my eyes as I stare at the figure in front of me. Blond hair neatly brushed, dreadlocks replaced by a cascade of rippling curls. Laser sharp intelligence flaring from eyes formerly veiled. The same faded T-shirt, hoodie and slouchy jeans but the accent…so cultured… almost public school posh. With a hint of something lilting underneath. Cultivated. It's the only word that will do. Can this really be Aidan? Putting down my coffee, I pat the step beside me. 'Come, sit here a moment and tell me what brought about this change.'

'I suppose it's quite a common story these days, so it is. My Da was a property developer, a highly successful one with projects in Dublin, part of the tiger economy. He was ballin. The Irish crash hit him hard, although he'd foreseen it and shifted his major base of operations over to London just in time.'

So that's where the lilt in his voice comes from. Southern Irish. Soft and misty. As though it's been passed through a feather cushion.

'Are you Irish? You don't sound it, although there's something…?'

Nodding. 'Yes, but I was sent away to school in England as soon as my Da made his money. The snooty little skanks at the prep school laughed at me. I quickly learned to speak like them. I was teased something awful when I went home in the holidays,' he says, smiling ruefully.

'How difficult for you.' I'm at a loss what to say. My heart goes out to him.

Another nod. 'It was much worse the second time. The bank foreclosed on Da's projects. Office blocks and industrial units weren't good investments in the current climate. He'd diversified but not into the right areas apparently. He lost everything, the mansion, Mum, it all went. We moved to a sink estate and I had to go to the local comp. You can imagine what I went through there?' The pain on his face is raw as he winces with remembrance. Now he's begun talking, it all tumbles out. He can't seem to stop himself.

'I had the dreads done, quite liked them, you know. Something different. Soon learned the street talk. Exaggerated it like. Had to use it all the time in case anyone was listening. But it was constantly updating, and I never quite fitted in. After a few fights they learned to leave me alone – being karate champion of your previous school has its advantages. I was lucky not to get knifed in a dark alley. It actually happened outside the school gates – the guy said he was vexed at me carrying a book. Fortunately a teacher intervened in time.'

Knifed? What kind of a life was that? Especially for a sensitive boy. How can he be so cool about it? I desperately want him to slow down. Give me time to take it all in. I need to say something though. Those eyes of his are starting to hood over again, as though he's afraid I'll reject him now the truth is coming out. Better find some safe ground.

'You were fortunate to escape. But how did you come to be down here?'

'My Da got a temporary driving job. He had a project he'd had to leave in abeyance. They hadn't thought the land was worth anything so he'd managed to keep hold of it. He was determined to clear the site in his spare time. He knew Ron, Mr McMeeney, from way back and Ron got me this internship so I wouldn't have to go to the local comp – I needed time out.'

Mr McMeeney? He was behind Aidan's presence in the library? They certainly kept that quiet. All those disapproving jibes? Was that camouflage? What did he, Mr Mc – I can't believe Aidan calls him Ron. What had he made of those 'reports'? If indeed he'd read them. I'd buried them deep in a file in the hope they would get overlooked.

'But why didn't you say something? At least give me a hint? You could have dropped the street talk with me.'

'Couldn't risk anyone overhearing, you know. Your man made me promise to keep our knowing each other a secret. Tried to get me to tidy myself up a bit and drop the talk. I rather enjoyed winding him up though. Bit of a pompous windbag as I'm sure you've noticed.' Aidan beams his wicked smile towards me, but goes on. 'A good heart though. The only housing Da could afford was in one of the rougher areas so I kept the dreads as well as the talk, man, sorry…I mean, Miz Grayson. Old habits die hard.' He grins ruefully, the startling green eyes looking straight into mine.

'Don't you think it's time you called me Phillippa, or Pippa if you'd prefer.' I'll think about Mr McMeeney later. There's obviously more to him than the surface snippiness would suggest. Surely it can't hide a kind heart, as Aidan suggests. Can it?

'I'd like that, sure I would.' His broad smile is reward enough. Perhaps that constant looking down was not shyness but an act of self-preservation. Hiding himself away. I know all about that.

Standing out here in the square leaves us open to scrutiny from behind the huge glass windows. Any moment now 'Ron' – somehow that name suits him so well – will be out to chivvy us for being late. Standing up, I gesture to Aidan to walk into the library with me. I want to hear the rest of the story without interruption, so I steer him quickly up the stairs. Once safely in the reference room, I ask, 'But look at you now, what's happened?'

'Da's project came good. He sold the land to a supermarket – they're the only people who're buying these days – bought us a house in a much nicer part of town. Now we've moved, I've returned to my real self. I don't have to put on that street face anymore, though I've kept the clothes for now. They help me blend in – and they're comfortable.'

I'm not so sure, but I'm not going to say anything – yet.

'Da says I can go to sixth form college. But I'll miss the library.'

Seeing his dejected face, I assure him. 'There's always Saturdays and holidays. We'd be sad to lose you altogether.'

'Thank you, yes. But, as soon as I've finished college, I'll be off to the States to uni. I'm going to be a writer like you hoped. That fellow, Paschal Beverly Randolph, I want to follow up on him and that'll be the best place to do it. I think he has a lot to teach me, even though it is from the other side of the grave.'

Looking at me sideways, he says hesitantly, 'Would you think me fanciful if I told you I have an affinity with the man. I've begun to think I was him in another life. His reincarnation. He is so familiar to me.'

'Oh Aidan, I wouldn't think that fanciful at all. If only you knew. Look, we'll be having a get-together once Sebastian returns. Why don't you join us?'

'I'd be honoured. In the meantime, why don't you read my report on who I woz.' Laughing, he hands over another set of neatly presented pages. I skim it quickly.

Paschal Beverly Randolph
Sexual Magician, Occultist and a Bangin Guy
Aidan Doran

(The full text of Aidan's report can be found at the end of this book)

Paschal Beverly Randolph has been described as the greatest unknown metaphysician of the nineteenth century. An alchemist, sex magician, magic mirror salesman, mason, Supreme Grand Master of the Rosicrucians, abolitionist, doctor and psycho-phrenologist, archaeologist, politician,

Civil War activist, world traveller, poet and writer, he was the founder of the Ansairetic Mystery System of sex magic. He had a huge but forgotten influence on Aleister Crowley and Western Occultism. He was a guy who made enemies very easily…

In 1873 he published *The New Mola* which revealed a great deal about his supernatural work. He describes a Toledo circle in which seven people sat in twilight. The mediums were a lady and a gentleman (Randolph). 'A phantom hand moved through the air, across the table, pulled at a gentleman's beard and faded away in dim phosphoric vapour.' He also describes, 'the most magnificent spiritual pyrotechnics and *thousands* of electric scintillas dancing mazy waltzes about the room…broadening out into sheets of living vapour, irradiating the room with pearly light.'

…Randolph died in Toledo, Ohio at age forty-nine under suspicious circumstances. An eyewitness, Mrs Worden, told the local paper that he was acting strangely that morning. He apparently said that, in less than two hours, he would be dead. When she moved away she heard a shot and turned to see Randolph falling. It was ruled suicide from a self-inflicted wound to the head. However, it is also said that he was in a magical duel with Madame Blavatsky and she turned a pistol on him from a distance. Allegedly R. Swinburne Clymer, a Supreme Master of the Rosicrucian Fraternity, made a deathbed confession stating that, in a fit of jealousy and temporary insanity, he had killed Randolph…

This one is really going to freak Mr McMeeney out. Even if he is Aidan's Da's best friend. Perhaps I'd better file it for now. The pile in my drawer is mounting. But that 'dim phosphoric vapour' sounds exactly like His Majesty appearing – and what about those 'dancing electric scintillations'. I know that sensation all too well. It's interesting that Randolph was aware that souls could be bound together by what must be sexual activity of the kind I've experienced – and that it's an ancient concept. Syria is close to Egypt, so the secret could have travelled. Something like that could have happened to me when the Prince broke into the ritual and took Men'ofer's place. Maybe I was bound to His Awful Majesty as well as to Sebastian. It looks as though Aidan picked up that biography I ordered; I'd better ask him for it. See if there are more clues in there.

Chapter 39

Wailing saves no man from the pit

Ancient Khem

'Quickly now, careful be with His Majesty. We must reach Abydos by noon if he is to be interred before Ra departs for the night and the Lady shows her face.' The funeral cortege must be swift, silent and convincing as it leaves the riverside temple where it had paused for the night. Agni'ti directs the coffin bearers on to the royal barge, praying that the carefully weighted sandbags will fool the bearers once again. He needs to get the ersatz mummy below ground as fast as possible. He has already sent his trusted stewards ahead to prepare the grave. His promise that they would not be sacrificed is sufficient to ensure their silence throughout eternity.

How fortunate it was that His Majesty should die so far from his court. The Great Plan could not have worked had the officious civil servants been present and the High Priests would instantly recognise the deception. Nor had the Lady Yagut returned from her self-imposed exile. Word had been sent to her secret refuge but she had not yet replied. A box of sand would not have fooled her vigilant eye. She had once loved His Majesty beyond reason, and he her. Once the coffin is interred, there will be no fear of discovery. His Majesty will remain safely confined in his Theban cave. Not that Yagut would condemn him for his actions. She, of all people, has reason to wish His Majesty rendered powerless. The dangerous force contained for all time.

The cortege is met with all the ritual panoply the funereal heart of Egypt can muster. Ululating mourners uttering the sounds of jubilation line the route. *Muu* dancers gyrate robotic movements to a beat only they hear. Drums and shawms sound as the shaven-headed *kher heb* and *shem* priests, in their spotless white robes, surround the simple wooden coffin and lift it from the barge. Agni'ti prays that the disguising spell holds. It will be a disaster if their eyes penetrate its inner darkness. Solemnly, the coffin is placed on its flower-decked sled for its final journey into the landscape of the dead. As the ropes are lifted and the ranks of young priests begin the seemingly endless trudge, mourners tear their clothes and throw dust over themselves, ululating their grief. Perfumed oils are asperged before the sled, lubricating the way. It will take several hours to reach their destination. The beaten road to the hastily erected mudbrick enclosure travels into the desert, veering towards the land of Wepwawet. Not quite reaching that sacred portal to the Duat over which the Opener of the Way stands guard.

Many fall by the wayside, overcome by heat, thirst and intensity of emotion. Ra is relentless in his desire to shine down on his subjects, crushing them into the hot desert sand. Those that fall are quickly replaced by hands eager to have the honour of hauling His Majesty to his final resting place. Barren magenta sand dunes at last give way to sheer white limestone cliffs that smudge the horizon as far as the eye can see. Before a narrow slit in the folded hills stands the Prince's House of Eternity. At the enclosure's centre, a deep shaft awaits. At its boundary, high wooden gates in thick walls protect the dead and hold the living at bay. Better that it should protect the living and hold the dead at bay. He will do all in his power to ensure it is so.

As the sun falls towards the horizon, the *kher heb* priests step forward bearing gleaming agate sickles. Agni'ti holds up his hands.

'Forgive me, fellow servants to the Gods. It was His Majesty's last wish that only those of his household be present at his final rites. We shall open His Majesty's mouth. Then we shall inter His Majesty and make sacrifices of us all. We follow our Lord into the Otherworld and take refuge in his House of Eternity forever. Pray, leave the offerings here and return to your temple to beseech the Gods in perpetuity for the welfare of the soul of His Majesty.'

Agni'ti knows that the now silent priests have no inkling of how necessary are those prayers for the old *seba.* But he says nothing, instead nodding graciously as the heavily laden baskets are placed before him. The simple grave goods shall suffice for his purpose after the priests have retreated.

'Please.' He smiles. 'Once these offerings have been removed into the enclosure, seal the doors behind us. Leave us to our preparations for serving our master in the Great Beyond.'

As the huge gates slam, the reverberation bellows throughout the netherworld. Ammit paces and roars her frustration at being deprived of her prey. No evil one has escaped her obliteration of the heart…until now.

Under smoking torches, with reverent ceremony, His Majesty's casket is lifted. The trusted retainers bring in the offerings. Perfumed oil is poured. As the doors are sealed, the lector priests outside intone,

The het-bird comes, the falcon comes;
They are Isis and Nephthys,
They come embracing their brother, Osiris…

The voices fade as, drums beating softy, the lector priests turn east, holding aloft the torches to guide them through the welcome cooling of the desert night, heeding the warning to return to their temple to begin the imprecations that shall guide their departed lord through the perils of his own night journey. In the distance, a jackal howls a last farewell. The youngest *wabet,* running up and down the long line with his water jar, shivers and glances anxiously over his shoulder, but the great gates remain firmly closed.

As the jackal's howl fades, Agni'ti turns to his companions.

"Quickly now. Lower His Majesty into the pit. I myself opened his mouth in the mortuary chamber. And do not forget to lower in the basket of *Ushabtis* after it. His Majesty must have servants to do his bidding in the afterlife.'

They must not hear how ragged his breathing has become, how his heartbeat threatens to explode. The words can hardly rise against the tension in his chest. Trusted retainers though these may be, he is not going to reveal even to them that His Majesty is not in the coffin that is now being lowered out of sight to the accompaniment of murmured prayers. All it contains is sand, the Pharaoh's mummified heart and a tablet with its brief binding inscription, *Ena'hai sh'ra khepheret dim'an'tange Ma'at, Ban'a dosert yamin heh'sieh Khem Yar Khepher'set, Ini inuit Isis, Elia whiskia fatu y Set, Ra supra mew'nit ha'wi, Yavah. Seb-En!'*

Eyes darting anxiously, ears pricked for the slightest sound from outside the walls, he prays that this most ancient spell will suffice. So lost in the mists of time is it that no one now living fully understands the words brought into the present day by his oracle brother. But Agni'ti recognises its potency. That this, the most audacious of risks, shall prove to be worth the taking, and that the binding shall hold, is all that his mind can think of at this moment. Catastrophe must be averted.

While Agni'ti stands motionless, heart and mind fully engaged in his vigilant watch, incense is lit by his companions to convey the Pharaoh's soul between the worlds. Sweet-smelling flower wreathes are flung in to ensure a good rebirth into the world that is to come. No need to tell his companions that this is in vain. The Pharaoh's soul is elsewhere. 'Place those three offering baskets there beside him and then fill in the pit. Build the mastaba over it. Hurry, there is still much to do.'

Chapter 40

Overtoned with gold

As we enter the cluttered front room with its gold-braid trimmed suite and mismatched floral carpet, Sebastian says, 'Mum, Meski, I'd like you to meet my friend Phillippa. Pips – meet my family!'

Mum? Meski? What is he on about? I stare in horror, unable to grasp what he's saying. How can this woman with tarty blonde hair be his mother? And why's she never said anything about having a son?

'But...but...Mrs B... She's your...*mother*?'

'Hello, lovey, bit of a surprise, hey?'

'It certainly is. And as for that one' – my finger points at Meski – 'that bitch stole my fiancé and you helped me throw out his stuff! How could you?' Torn between fury and embarrassment, I turn towards the door, angry tears spurting from my eyes as I fumble for the handle, my nails biting into my palm as I try to get a grip on myself.

'Pips, please...'

'Don't be silly, lovey, wait.' Mrs B puts out a hand, pulling me back into the room. 'Sebastian didn't tell you? It was me that brought you together, you know.' She smirks that familiar cat-that-got-the-cream, lip-licking smile on her gloating face. I want to claw it off.

'Didn't tell me what?' I raise my eyebrows at Sebastian.

He shrugs. 'No, I wasn't going to tell her about your silly trick to make her dream of me. All that spell stuff wasn't needed once we'd really met. I...'

'Dream about me? Do you mean those dreams...' Searing heat rises in my face. 'Those dreams were because of Mrs B?'

How could he be a party to it? The dreams were so...graphic. Hiccupping, I try to stem the sobs rising in my throat. Mrs B knew about those dreams? I'll never be able to look her in the face again.

'I didn't intend to upset you. Sebastian didn't know. It all got out of hand... didn't know my own magical strength.' She puts her hand on my arm, but I shake it off and back away.

Mrs B knows? All those intimate details sent by her? 'How dare you!'

'Sebastian didn't know what? What do you mean, Mum?' His eyes are dark with bewilderment, cutting across the tirade I'm gathering breath to throw at my erstwhile boss. I won't be going back to the shop after this fiasco.

'It was all part of the great plan. When you started talking about the quiet girl from the library you fancied so much, but didn't have the nerve to ask out, I sent her a dream to come and work at the shop at the weekend.'

'What great plan?'

'I found it in one of the old books that came into the shop. How to make a magical child. That's why I formed my group. I've had experience, you know. I'd dabbled in magic before. Thought I'd take it more seriously this time. Following my old practical magic book – like you've been doing with yours.'

Distinctly uneasy at that thought, the word *dabble* has connotations I don't want to think about. My book warned against meddling unless you'd been properly trained. Mrs B is clearly anything but...although that vision of the Lady Yagut d'eskia flashes into my mind. There were similarities. Surely she can't be...but before I can protest, she goes on.

'I needed two people who'd been united before, who'd made a mystic marriage in the past. Two innocents who'd awaken together, like in the old days.'

'Oh my god, what are you like? Mystic marriage? You said you were going to cast a "drawing us together spell," not pull Pips into your silly games. I should never have trusted you.' Turning away, Sebastian tucks me close into his side, whispering reassurances in my ear.

'Well, yes, initially. But this way, I could keep an eye on her and make sure she had all the magical tools she'd need. Then she let slip a guy had moved in and they were going on holiday together. Never saw that one coming. So I sent Meski after him. By that time, I'd put two and two together and –'

'And came up with ten as usual.' Sebastian sighs wearily. 'You were supposed to give her romantic dreams. Help her see me as a prospective boyfriend. I wanted a date, not to make magical children. I'm so sorry, Pips.'

His arm around my shoulder is comforting, but I'm not prepared to relax my guard yet.

'Well, yes, I did, sort of…maybe the spell was a bit too strong.' Mrs B is looking chastened. Not a look I'm accustomed to seeing on her snooty face. She's worrying at a fingernail too. Is she really as sure of herself as she appears?

I recall those early dreams, the butterfly kisses Sebastian bestowed. How it was before *He* intervened. My Dark Enigma. Where did he fit into all this? Had his book been amongst those Mrs B read? Was it left deliberately for me to find?

As though reading my mind, she gives that infuriatingly ingratiating smile and says, 'As soon as that batch of magical books came in, I knew it was meant. I went to see a woman down at the Psychic Fair. She told me you two had been together in a life in Egypt. You'd been tied together for all time. But you hadn't had a chance to complete the mystic marriage, let alone the magical child. Something had intervened. But now it was time to do it again. It was your destiny.'

She holds her hands out, pleading, 'You have to see, I was doing it for you, lovey. That's why I left you the book – and those other things. They were in the same boxes as the books arrived in, so I figured they must be part of the plan.'

I finger the *menat*. I haven't taken it off since it slipped so easily around my neck. Even wear it when I shower. The crescent at the back is a bit inconvenient for sleeping but I can't be parted from it for a moment. Looking up, I see Sebastian touching his *sem*.

'Looks like you were right, Pips. These were part of that ceremony you remembered.' His tentative smile is soft.

'Where did they come from?' Overcome by a burning desire to know more, I almost shout the question. I've been manipulated for so long, it's time I took control.

'All I know, lovey, is they were brought in from a house clearance. An old lady died. She was a bit of a recluse, had no family, so the social services people brought her stuff to us. They'd not bothered looking through the boxes. They were that dusty, no one had touched them in years.'

'May I see the rest, Mrs B? I must know what the other books said.' Glancing round the room, my anger is overtaken by eager curiosity. 'Where are they?'

'Safely tucked away upstairs. I wouldn't leave them down here for anyone to see.' She glares at Samantha. 'This silly cow believed she could be the one to birth the magical child. Fell in love with that jumped-up ex of yours, though that didn't last long when he realised Meski lived in one of the few council houses left in this town. Nobby twat.'

I laugh, glad to release the tension. 'You're much better off without him, Samantha, believe me. But why do they call you Meski?'

'She called herself that from when she was a little girl.' Mrs B doesn't give her time to reply. 'Always said her parents had got it wrong. That it was her real name. When she came to live with us, we got so used to it, it's difficult to think of her as Samantha now.'

What's the story about Samantha coming to live with them? But…it can wait. I have to see what else was in those boxes. 'Mrs B, I wonder, could you possibly bring those books down?' The knowledge will be power. It's way past time I recovered mine.

Meanwhile, there are still things I need to know. To get this complicated family straight in my head. 'Your surnames are different. Warner's a long way from Van der Buerk. Where did that come from?' While Mrs B heads off to get the precious box, I turn to Sebastian once again.

'It's complicated.' He fidgets uneasily. 'Um, Mum married again but I kept –'

'You don't even sound alike…worlds apart.' I bite my tongue but it's out before I can stop it. I can't seem to get my head around any of it. I'm discombobulated for sure.

'No, that's because when Mum married again she lived in Africa with my stepfather – and his daughter, Meski.'

I'm not certain I believe him, something is off. Surely I can trust him though, can't I? But the funny squirming in my belly suggests it's deeply wrong. And, Sebastian's mother or not, I'm going to need more time before I risk opening up to my erstwhile tormentor. I don't trust her one iota, even if I do desperately need those books. She's clearly using me for her own agenda. Best to withhold judgement for now and simply listen.

'He was a mining engineer – I told you I'd lived there. I used to visit in the long hols but I spent most of my time in boarding school. I soon learned to speak like everyone else.'

Seeing his rueful grin, I can guess what he's been through, ginger haired and *different*. Not a good combination in an English boarding school I'd have thought. 'As for that bitch stepsister of yours, she's most certainly a Trotter. One bedroom to another. How many surnames does one family need?' I'm not letting him off the hook that easily,

'I'm not really a Trotter, who told you that?' Samantha shrugs. 'It…'

A knock at the door interrupts Mrs B as she heads for the stairs. Her voice carries to us as she lets the visitor in.

'Oh, Ron. Didn't expect to see you. Come on in. Sebastian's here with his girlfriend. It's about time you met.'

'Mr McMe...' I splutter as the pompous librarian strolls in. 'Wh-what are you doing here?'

Hovering in the Otherworld, the guardian grandparents look on anxiously.

'Will that ill-trained harlot remember her power, do you think, dearest one? Mayhap she could be useful in dealing with His Majesty?'

'Ill-trained? She may be a bungler now, but in the past she was one of the most powerful priestesses Egypt has known. Heaven forefend that she reconnect to that lifetime now. Her mind lacks the wisdom to use her power. Her ego is far too strong. She would it use for material gain – or world domination. No, best keep the cloaking spell tightly in place, at least for now, husband dear.'

'Fortunate it is that I had the good sense to secure a wife with sufficient training to counteract the darkest of forces, even though I had so little time with you, my dear.' He looks fondly at the gracious woman beside him. 'But now we have all the time in the world.' He pulls her close to him.

'Not so fast, husband of mine. My task is not yet finished. Our granddaughter has learned much, but I must watch over her a little longer. She is not yet sufficiently in her power to withstand His Majesty.'

'Then why not help her along? I grow impatient. That is why I drew near again. I had thought that ensuring her freedom from the constraints of her overprotective parents would be sufficient.'

'No, no. Do you not realise? That was a beginning. Not an end. I cannot do it for her. The testing time is fast approaching. We must be standing by.' Tenderly, she slips her arm through his. 'We cannot desert her, my love. And His Majesty will have need of us should she succeed.'

'As long as you do not then take on the further "education" of that American rogue. This Irish incarnation of his has great charm.'

'No...husband dear. Once was sufficient. Leave it in that other time. There is no cause for jealousy. You know that you have my

heart.' Smiling, she holds out her hand. 'Come, she has no need of us for now. This time is ours. It is your education that will continue. Come, husband, come!'

Chapter 41

Vampire claws, time hung

Ancient Khem

Silently, four donkeys are led from behind their shelter.

'Make haste, they must be in their graves before moonrise.' Agni'ti hands out the sleek agate sickles. 'Ensure that the blood is spread properly. On it our lives may depend. Remember, not a sound must they make.'

It may be an honour to serve His Majesty in the afterlife, but it is an honour that will have to wait. Agni'ti has other plans. Knives flash, blood is caught in baskets and distributed. One pool for each of the seven helpers. Agni'ti is expected to wall himself into the mastaba to expire slowly of suffocation, so no blood is needed for the aged tjaty. The entrails are quickly removed, the carcasses flung into waiting pits, followed by the offal covered with natron from the offering baskets. The desert sand will mummify them in time, but this should prevent too quick a decay. Soaring carrion birds will mark the spot assuring the *shem* priests that the requisite sacrifices have been made and that His Majesty has a retinue to serve him in the next life.

'Now, gather up the food and apportion it between us. Ensure that each man has water, bread and beer for the journey. We do not know what may befall us and the desert is a harsh taskmaster for the careless.'

With infinite care, he opens another basket. Neatly coiled within lies a strong rope and grappling hook. The next basket yields a rope ladder. Strange grave goods for a mummified Pharaoh not expected to leave his final resting place. Thank the gods no officious priest had checked them. As the shadows traverse the alcoves in the rough mudbrick walls, silent figures slip over the wall leaving a heart, the dying moon and four dead donkeys to journey through the afterlife.

Sliding through the desert towards the next village, Agni'ti murmurs, 'Let us pray we are in time.'

Behind him a raspy voice croaks out. *'Fool. Did you think to bind My Majesty when a sacred promise you have broken? My* sekhem *and my* khu *you may have been fettered to the tomb. But my* ka *is loosened to wander the earth for all time until my purpose is fulfilled. My Majesty a home shall find no matter how long it may take. I shall be eternally on the earth.'*

Agni'ti looks back. 'Over my dead body, Your Majesty. I am not done yet.' He quickly recites, *'Oh snake, take yourself off, for Geb protects me. Get up, for you have eaten a mouse, which Ra detests, and you have chewed the bones of a putrid cat. Be gone!'*

Sand whirls, dust devils dance His Majesty's rage. But nothing can stop Agni'ti now.

'I shall prevail,' he vows.

* * *

Silently he slips into the Theban palace, thankful it is the dark of the moon. The interspace when Thoth withdraws from the world to fortify himself against the mighty monsters of the night. When the Records are open to inspection. The moment the world can be changed forever.

The guards left on duty are sleepy, unsure at their post. Who will take over now the Master has departed without issue and the tjaty is gone? The Lady Yagut'd'eskia? Surely not? That evil-eyed one fled the palace in disgrace some time ago and has not been seen since.

But, when Ra rises the next morning, the tjaty is back in place. He should have been sacrificed to serve the Prince in the Otherworld. Stayed in the Prince's House of Eternity forever. But he behaves as though nothing is amiss. So they continue as before, small cogs do not argue with their masters. They merely accept the world as it is.

Chapter 42

Shedding shining light

'Come on in, Pips. It's only small, but it's home. I kept it on while I was doing my research in Egypt. Somewhere to store my thoughts.'

The bedsit is piled high with books and little else, except for a pristine computer desk with neatly aligned pens. The single bed looks lonely. Every inch of the walls is covered in printouts of hieroglyphs and demotic writings. Temples, papyri and shards of stone and pot. He seems to have covered them all. I understand why he no longer lives with Mrs B, but this... Typical student digs, I'm surprised Sebastian hasn't outgrown this uncomfortable abode. Although, there are no clothes scattered around, everything is pin neat. The stacked books don't look precarious, simply orderly. So, perhaps, not so typical student. It's a geeky workspace. The tiny kitchenette is immaculate, everything in its place.

I much prefer my own flat with its colourful pictures, cushions and throws. As soon as Tom moved out, I softened the stark minimal look he'd insisted upon. I haven't had time to redecorate yet, but have cheered it up with carefully chosen soft furnishings. Creating the right ambience is so important for me. Although, not for Seb by the look of things. But then, if he is spending so much time in Egypt or at the university perhaps...

'Okay, Pips, sit on the bed and let's approach this logically.' He grabs the lone chair from by the desk. Clearly he didn't get many visitors. 'Let's sort out where we are with all this. We can use the whiteboard. I used to plan my PhD thesis on here, but I erased it in a fit of desperation when I got back from that last trip.'

'Oh, Seb are you sure –'

'Not a problem. It helped me clear my head. Now my research funding has run out I need to get a move on, especially as my lecturing commitments start again after Christmas. I find thinking visually clarifies things – that's how the ancient Egyptians did it after all. They were the world's first mind-mappers – and multidimensional travellers. That's what the temple walls are all about. Ancient libraries describing the metaphysical and supernatural as well as the natural world. Now, what do we know?'

'Well,' I say, 'I reckon we belong together. Our hearts have been united by fire like Rumi and the Prince's book suggested. How do you feel?'

He doesn't answer, merely turns to the whiteboard and writes.

What we know

1. Twinsouls! Reincarnated?

'Let's look at what that means.' I need to be sure that we view the concept in the same way. 'In my understanding, it's two souls who have been joined in a former life and meet again. The fit is so right they instantly recognise each other. When we met, we sort of recognised each other even though we weren't certain at first. Does that make sense?'

'Perfectly, although I think I knew from the start. But where does it begin?'

'I'm not sure. The language in the book is rather obscure. It seems to imply that it happens at creation.' Picking up the familiar faded red leather book, I read aloud, *'In the beginning was consciousness. Indivisible and divine…bored with singularity Min made seti – ejaculated – and brought the Cosmos into manifestation.'*

He's listening intently. 'That's the standard Egyptian creation myth. All's clear so far.'

'But, what about this next bit? *In that manifestation two polarities were created, neither could exist without the other or the universe would collapse into chaos.'*

'That's you and me, Pips. I can't imagine a world without you.' He kisses me lightly on the tip of my nose. 'But again, it's standard Egyptian duality. Doesn't it say something about each sex finds its resting place in the other? That's exactly how I feel about you. It implies reincarnation – and meeting again over the centuries. We've been together before.'

'But…' I'm stunned. 'You seem to take it so coolly. How –'

'Never mind that. What's next?' He's raised that eyebrow I adore.

I rush on. 'We know from Randolph's intro that he was given the book in Egypt during what sounds rather like the kind of experience I've been having. Those dreams – err, let's leave that for now.' Don't want to reveal how much of a hold His Awful Majesty has exerted. 'Put the book and its contents on the board.'

2. THE BOOK

3. Dreams????!!!!

'I'm coming back to that one, Pips. Somehow I think it's more than those silly dreams Mum sent you. But we can discuss that later. Now what?'

'Well, the tomb and the binding spell seem to be important but I don't understand how His Awful Majesty got out of his cage. I know that, unlike the body, the Egyptians believed that the *ka* and sometimes the *khebit* – shadow – was not bound to the grave and could go where the body could not, but moving across time, that's a whole other ball game –'

'That's probably my fault. After all, I took the binding tablet away.' His face puckers with worry. 'I wish I hadn't done that. Since I've been home I've discovered a translation of a tomb warning inscribed on a tablet now in Scotland. The consequences of taking away such a stone were dire – as we've discovered.'

'I'm not so sure you are responsible. Although you removed the tablet, the spells remained on the door even though the seals were broken. Ergo –' It's a word I've been waiting to use for ages. But as it leaves my tongue it sticks in my throat. Rather like the furry aftertaste of His Awful Majesty's presence. Not that there's time to dwell on that now, that eyebrow is quirked again so I rush on.

'I think he got out much earlier. Perhaps he never was bound there. Time seems to be fluid, moving forwards and backwards all at the same time. I've got the feeling that His Awful Majesty has been causing trouble for much longer than we are aware.' I have no evidence, as yet but... 'Put it on the board for now and let's have another section for questions.'

4. The tomb needed more than one binding spell. Removed tablet.

Q.1 How did HAM get out? When?

He's left handed. How could I not have registered this sooner? But then, I haven't really seen him write before. His library slips were already filled in, presented with that distinctive backward-sloped looping script. Even the small space in this room has been arranged to accommodate a left hander. Better pay attention to his words.

'There's another aspect to that question, Pips. As you know, my area of expertise is threat formulae – the ancient binding and banishing spells. Tomb curses, if you will. I can translate them and have a sense of the power behind the words – what they were used for. The problem is, after my experiences in that Egyptian gaol, I know more than I'd like to about why they are necessary.' He grimaces at the memories this evokes. 'What I still don't know is *how* they were set in place. Or *why* they worked – or didn't work.'

The hollowness is back in his voice. 'Wish I'd known about that Scottish text sooner. It goes on to warn, "Indeed, the gods who rest in the midst of the mountains gain strength every day even though their pebbles are dragged away." And that's what I did, took His Awful Majesty's pebble away.'

Could it really have started when he took that binding tablet? Did time snap backwards and then rebound forwards? Or sideways? My head can't take it in, but my queasy stomach is all too certain it could be true. There's a knot rising in my throat. A panicky breathe pushing it up. Did Seb really transgress against an ancient curse? Fall foul of a malediction, a bane, a hex? There's no such thing, surely, is there? There's nothing I can say. I need to consider this. Dumbly, I urge him on with a nod.

'We know that the Egyptians used specific wording to invoke multiple realms through the use of metaphor and divine language. They used gestures that anchored them in place – you see those and the power rods on temple walls – but we simply don't know how because no one back then describes such a ceremony in detail. There were multiple levels of meaning to each hieroglyph too.' He sighs heavily, holding his head in despair. 'By using them, they increased the efficacy of their texts but didn't tell us anything more. And they don't seem to have had a future or past tense to their grammar. Everything was in the present and yet everywhere at once.'

'Is there anything specific to our problem? How the Prince can be a time-traveller, there and here at the same time, or so it seems.'

I'm groping towards an understanding. My gut *feels* what he means as it stirs uneasily. I've been moving around those multiple dimensions myself. My rational head is having a hard time catching up though. And how can we describe that sense of being in several timeframes at once, each experienced as *now*. We just don't have the language. Although there's that passage that grandpa was particularly fond of quoting. 'What we need is *Dr. Dan Streetmentioner's Time Traveler's Handbook of 1001 Tense Formations* and the "Future Semi-conditionally Modified Subinverted Plagal Past Subjunctive Intentional tense".'

'What on earth are you on about, Pips?'

He's looking so mystified, I have to laugh. '*The Restaurant at the End of the Universe*. Part of the *Hitchhiker's Guide to the Galaxy* trilogy. Don't tell me you've never read it?'

'That came out before I was born. But I guess I shouldn't be surprised that a librarian knows it.'

'It's one of my favourites. My grandfather introduced me to it when I was a child. Adams says that grammar is one of the major problems encountered in time travel, pointing out that an event will be described differently according to whether you are talking about it from the standpoint of your own natural time, from a time in the future, or a time in the further past. It's apposite especially after all we've been through. I'll play you the tapes sometime. You'll enjoy it. But do go on, you were saying?'

'There's plenty of evidence in the texts and in ordinary, everyday letters that the dead were believed to return to haunt the living and create all kinds of mayhem – I'll tell you about that later. But, of course, there's nothing about it transferring to many centuries later, except anecdotal evidence from travellers – and writers' imagination.' He looks thoughtful for a moment. 'Though there are ancient Egyptian "ghost" stories across the dynasties. I suppose that would be the same. It's just that the period in between has been extended in our case. I need to look into that.'

Seeing Seb in full lecturing mode, I smile. He's so serious, yet deeply passionate. So immersed in it all. His students must love him. There's so much I could ask, but I simply say, 'Aidan did one of his reports on that. I've been meaning to pass it on to you. It is convincing, although I don't suppose he accessed the academic sources you have.'

'Nevertheless, I'd like to read it. He sounds like a bright boy. There are a few academically approved translations of appropriate spells and rituals – along with a great deal of non-academic speculation that's probably nearer to the actual practice. Although, of course, my PhD panel won't countenance such a source.'

What is he going to do? I know how much his thesis means to him, but if they are rejecting it...he won't be able to start again, surely.

'But precisely how they were administered? No. We don't have that. There are clues, yes. It's what's holding up my PhD work. My supervisor thinks that my "nightmares" were caused by the stress of imprisonment and my vivid imagination. He won't take it as phenomenological evidence. I haven't even dared mention that I've continued to meet His Awful Majesty now I'm back and fully awake – or that you're sharing the experience.'

'It's all too real to me.' Shuddering at the thought, I go on. 'Explain phenomenology to me, it might help.'

'There's a new breed of experiential archaeologists who try to blend with the ancient landscape, to experience what those living at the time would have felt. Trying to divine the meaning behind their rituals by *doing* them, rather than trying to think their way into the words. Phenomenology literally means the study of structures of experience or consciousness.' He pauses. 'Are you sure you want to know this? I'm not boring you, am I?'

Of course he's not. I adore that he stimulates my mind as much as my body. *So sexy*. It's what was missing with Tom...but I'm not going to tell Sebastian that. Not at the moment anyway. 'Absolutely not. I've seen a few television programmes lately that take that approach. It helps you get under the skin of the past. I'm probably a phenomenologist at heart.'

'In the West, nowadays, we are used to viewing the divine world and the secular as completely separate entities. But the other-worldly aspect of life was incorporated into the everyday in ancient Egypt. They didn't compartmentalise life in the way we do. The "supernatural" world existed alongside and interacted with the everyday. It can be the same today.'

He looks enquiringly at me, but continues when I nod. 'So, for instance, standing on the top of a temple out in the desert, looking at the night sky, you share the same absolute sense of wonder and awe the old star-watchers would have felt. Feel how overwhelmed they would have been by the vastness of it. The sheer brilliance of the stars and planets. The flaming trails of shooting stars falling to earth. The mystery of the sun – and Venus—dying at night, only to be reborn in the dawn. You'd hear the strange, otherworldly noises of the desert night. It sounds like distant singing or whispered speech. The night air carries the heavy perfumes of blossom for miles. It must have been especially so when the Nile was filled with blue lotus. It's an intense smell. Almost hallucinogenic in effect.'

For a moment, his eyes look far away, the lapis turning dark as he gestures, trying to find words. 'Think of a sandstorm being whipped up, or an earthquake reducing a building to rubble. We call them natural disasters but to the Egyptians they were the gods at work.'

'Being entombed,' I interject, shuddering again at that remembered foulness. 'The pressing weight and that awful smell brings the Otherworld to life all too graphically. They must have experienced that too.'

'Yes, it's definitely a full sensory experience.' That quirky eyebrow is raised again. I nod to indicate I understand and urge him on with a smile.

'You and I have been immersed deeply enough to know the horror the ancient Egyptians would have felt around hauntings. But I don't know enough about the actual magical practices behind it,' he says despairingly, turning to write another observation on his board.

Q.1a How did binding spells work, what is power behind them?

'I know that if the requisite offerings and propitiation rituals were not made, the dead were believed to haunt the living and the assistance of priests might be needed. But you're right. I don't recall seeing anything about *how* the spells were actually put in place.' I take a slip of the, by now, cold tea, wrinkling my nose at the membraned surface, but needing the moisture.

'That's just it, Pips, there isn't. I'm not much wiser now than when I started the research. Even the most cynical of academics have to believe those letters and texts. But we don't know the *how*.' He smiles ruefully. 'I've had plenty of phenomenological proof and there's huge anecdotal evidence from ancient Egypt. But nothing *scholarly* enough to satisfy my supervisor.'

Tipping away his tea and putting the kettle on again, he continues. 'It's so frustrating. Hieroglyphs were potent, magical things. Sound was important too. Writing them on a tablet or doorpost had a multi-layered effect, as did intoning them and invoking the gods. But exactly how the effect was activated, especially in the early period, we have no idea.'

Handing me another mug of tea, he shrugs in frustration. 'The Egyptian religion is now being understood as a shamanic one. We're recognising that there wasn't a split between *heka* – magic – and religion. In the afterlife the soul existed outside of time and yet interpenetrating everything.' Futilely he tries to express with his hands what he means.

Then he puts his head in his hands, looking so downcast that I give him a quick hug. 'Cheer up, Seb. It will come right in the end. Look, why don't we have a quick walk before we start again. I don't know about you, but I could do with some fresh air.'

Chapter 43

A revulsion of the flesh

Ancient Khem

His wounds are gently bathed, a small red fish removed, salve applied and soft linen bandages bound. Beer is proffered and gladly quaffed. Goat cheese and bread follow. Thus far, this is not the reception Men'ofer envisaged from his dark-hearted captor. He looks round warily. Since handing him over to the ministrations of his *eibata,* she has not been seen.

'The Lady Yagut, where is she?' he enquires, not altogether sure he wants to know the answer.

'Attending to the messengers. She will send for you shortly. Rest now.'

But he cannot settle. He had so nearly made it. If only...

'If only you had not been so precipitate you would be halfway there by now.'

Clearly she is a thought reader. Thankfully she is now clothed in a gauzy gown but still he averts his eyes. The imperious finger beckons. 'Come. There's much to discuss.'

Following her into the central porch of the temple, Men'ofer feels a bubbling curiosity. Strange. If anything, he'd expected fear. Challenging the Lady's authority usually results in severe pain, as he'd found all too frequently during his stay here. But there is a change in her. Exultation radiates off her skin and shines from her leonine eyes. She looks...almost happy. A woman who, hithertofore, has seemed incapable of emotion so cold was her soul.

'Why do you say I would have been on my way?' It is not done to question her but he must know, whatever her displeasure.

'Everything has changed, my boy. Everything.'

'Please do not call me your boy. I do not belong to you.'

She tosses her head in exasperation. 'Oh, but you do. Do you not understand? You are my son.'

'Your son?' He shakes his head in disbelief. 'But I can't be. You only disappeared from court a few years ago.'

'I had my reasons. Your father –' She hesitates. 'Your father had ideas about you. I told him I had aborted the foetus and I fled here until your birth. You were born in that hut over there.' She points to a mudbrick structure, nestling close to the wall of the temple. 'That is your birthing house. Afterwards I returned for as long as I could bear it. Ensured I had only a daughter. No more sons for that *seba.* Then I returned here. It is where we keep your bundle, the sacred placenta from which you arose. You will need it when you stake your claim.'

'Stake my claim? To what precisely?'

'To the throne, of course. Have you not guessed? You are the child of His Majesty the Prince Khem Yar Khepher'set and he, thank the gods, is now deceased.'

Men'ofer sits down abruptly on the beaten earth floor. He can't take this in.

'But…my mother and father? Poor villagers who gave me to the temple when I was five years old? They treated me with love and great kindness in my childhood.'

'Foster parents. Agni'ti arranged it. He thought you would be safest hidden in plain sight. And we already knew that you would be hand-fasted to his daughter and brought up in the temple alongside her.'

'Mennie. Do you mean Mennie?'

'Men'en'oferet. Yes, of course. She was destined for you from the beginning of time.'

'So how could he, my father, how could he…' He bows his head to hide his tears.

'He did not know. All that he was aware of was his burning desire to overcome death. He perceived her as the perfect vessel. You were merely a hindrance.'

Yagut takes him by the arm and helps him up. 'Come. As I said, we have much to do to prepare you. You must leave at first light.'

But Men'ofer resists. 'Mes'kia. What about Mes'kia? That *sha't* is your daughter and therefore my sister. And yet you allowed…' His face colours and his blue eyes blaze as he recalls being ridden in the night. 'How could you?'

'The idea was entirely hers, I assure you. But what care you? It is a royal custom for siblings to wed. When she discovered she had a brother she was determined to find you. I did not tell her your name, yet she fell in love with you at first sight. Pulled across the centuries, or so she says. When she discovered what the Prince planned, she rescued you and brought you here. She sought to bind you to her but when I told her of your destiny she was ashamed.'

'But…but…what am I to do? A mother and a sister found on the same day, and a father found and lost again. I would rather have had anyone than that pervert sire me.'

'I agree with you, my son. But nevertheless you are of royal blood and have a heritage to regain. Come.' She pulls him towards one of the far huts, but again he resists, saying, 'It's not a heritage I desire. All I want is to rescue Mennie and be with her in the temple. For that we were born.' He stands defiant, arms folded. 'What do you say to that, my Lady Yagut'd'eskia?'

'Rescue her with my blessing and then we shall talk. Meanwhile I go north to the capital to sound out how things lie there. There is sufficient time. The court will be in mourning for some time yet.

* * *

How has he got himself into this? How can he be in a boat yet riding on the back of a massive crocodile? The Lady Yagut, he still can't bring himself to call her *mewet*, had called on Sobek to aid their endeavour. She cast a disguising spell and now even he believes he is clinging to serrated aubergine scales as reptilian legs push hard against the current.

'It will take you straight to the palace,' she said. 'When you get there, ask for Agni'ti and give the messenger this.' Taking the green-stoned gold ring from her finger, she handed it to him. 'Guard it well, my son. It may be all that stands between you and ignominious death.'

* * *

Agni'ti is appalled. The Lady Yagut. Here? Now? Kept waiting at the landing stage like a fellahin. 'Quickly man, quickly. Take me to her.'

'Her? It is not a woman. It is a young fella who carried that ring.'

'Well, let us not keep him waiting. If he was sent by the Lady, it will be important.' Agni'ti bustles down the corridor and out into the sunlight.

'Men'ofer? Is that you? And my Lord Sobek. How is it that –'

A snap of Men'ofer's fingers dispels the illusion, revealing a hollowed-out palm log.

'How far did you travel on that, boy?' Agni'ti hitches up his robe and reaches out to help the young man up, noting the battered and scratched legs. 'Looks like a few of the Nile perch may have nibbled on you as you travelled.'

'Oh those. They were gained when I tried to escape from the Lady Yagut's care.' He shrugs.

'Escape? You mean you were held captive by Yagut, escaped, and yet you bear her ring?'

'It's a long story, Agni'ti. There is much to tell but first, I beg you, take me to Mennie.'

Agni'ti shakes his venerable head. Compassion in his eyes. 'I fear that is beyond me. I can only take you to her grave. My dearest daughter is dead. Killed by the Prince. I interred her with the greatest care.'

'Nooooo...' The despairing cry rings through eternity as he falls into unconsciousness.

Chapter 44

Joy has he whom she embraces

Refreshed not only by the walk but also the quick pint and a snack we'd called in for on the way home, we're back at the whiteboard again.

'We ought to put that the hauntings seem to be unfettered by time and space. His Awful Majesty's all too real in this century as well as his own, as were the ghosts Aidan found in the museum reports. Some of them were tied to objects, but not all.'

5. HAM. Unfettered by time and space.
Q.2 How does he do it?

'What about Randolph and his esoteric school? He seems to have rediscovered the Prince's book.'

'I haven't found any mention of him being haunted by His Awful Majesty though. He had a great many psychical experiences but that doesn't seem to be one of them.' I shrug as Seb lifts that endearing eyebrow again. 'He talked to a great many of the dead and even had out-of-body sex with one or two of them.' I quickly steer my – and Sebastian's – thoughts away from that thorny topic. It'll have to be addressed one day. But... not at this moment. 'I ought to examine his personal diaries. Or ask Aidan to do it when he goes to the States to check out college possibilities. Randolph might have met Budge in Egypt. I would have thought Budge would have mentioned it in his introduction to the book though.'

Seb turns to the board, out-of-body sex seemingly out of mind – for now.

6. P.B.R. Alchemy of Night and esoteric school
Q.3 Did he encounter HAM/Budge?

'Speaking of Budge, Aidan discovered that he apparently curated a haunted mummy coffin lid at the British Museum. It caused all kinds of mayhem and had quite a story behind it. Budge refused to tell people what he'd seen. Said he'd take the story to his grave. Do you think he met up with His Awful Majesty?' The thought makes me smile. 'That would have been an interesting confrontation if the rumours of his own magical prowess are accurate.'

'I'll follow that up later. Let's put it on the board in case.'

7. E.A.W.B. Haunted mummy case.
Q.4 Did he meet HAM in the museum? Magic?

'Perhaps it's time to look at what we do know. I'm almost certain – no, make that certain – I was a priestess in training. I read magic mirrors.' My reservations about reincarnation have dissolved. My head buzzes with the knowing of it and my heart is warm and open. Eagerly I press on. 'We were in the temple together. You were my twinflame and we were about to make the mystic marriage. But I lost you. You were snatched away and His Awful Majesty took your place.'

As tears fill my eyes at the memory, Seb gets up, hugs me tight, and drops a kiss on to the top of my head. Then he writes on the whiteboard.

8. Seb priest. Pips priestess. Magic Mirrors. Snatched away.
9. Almost made mystic marriage. Souls bonded?

'Do you know our names, Pip?'

'Yes. Men'ofer and Men'en'oferet.' Up on the board they go.

'Snatched by whom? As far as I remember, the Prince swooped in just as the real bonding was beginning and then a young woman dragged me to safety. She took me to an island ruled by her dragon of a mother and –'

Another piece has clicked into place. 'I saw a woman in my magic mirror loading a boat with scrolls. She had a daughter.

They slipped away downstream. The Prince was awfully cross.'

10. Unknown woman and daughter with scrolls. Island.
Q.5 Was daughter young woman who snatched/saved Men'ofer?
The air thins and thrums. 'Cross? My Majesty enraged beyond words was. My Majesty my revenge shall one day take. She with her My Book took. Curse that *ha her sha't*.'

In unison, we incant the banishing spell and form pentagrams in the air.

'Back to the core question, Pips. Why don't the banishing spells hold?'

Q.6 Banishing spells. How to make hold?
Holding the *menat*, I consider the question carefully. 'Each time we almost get it. We know intonation is important. Gesture, too, given that the pentagrams work. I wonder if it's to do with invoking the gods? Perhaps the spell needs their support in a way we don't yet understand. Let's return to that one later.'

He adds a big red underline to the board. 'That one could be crucial.' Watching me clutch my *menat* so tightly, he adds to the board.

11. The menat and the sem.
'You know His Awful Majesty got really mad when I wouldn't let him have your amulet. I don't think we fully understand their significance either. The book only gives us a glimpse. His Malodorous Majesty seems to have a *sema* that overrides ours. I think it's Libyan gold tektite. If so, it was created when a meteorite landed in the remote western desert. Is that what gives His Awful Majesty ultimate magical power? A stone from another dimension? Oh, and I forgot, I read that amulets have to be asked to work with you.'

I droop back against the wall as he adds *sema* to the board. 'We don't seem to be getting very far, are we? It's raising more questions than answers.'

'Keep going. The answer must be here somewhere. Let's try number nine. Any idea why the Prince was able to intrude after such careful training?'

'Hmm, yes I think so. We used to sneak kisses behind the pillars whenever we could. It was forbidden. But we couldn't help ourselves.'

12. Guilty kisses.
'Well, they aren't forbidden now.' He kisses me long and deep. As my knees are buckling and I'm in danger of going back on my big decision, he abruptly releases me and records.

13. HAM has it in for Seb in a big way.
...Those tortures in that cell in Egypt. How the Prince had sneered. But there was something behind it I didn't quite grasp...the Prince was agitated by my presence. Did that mean he thought me a threat to his plans? I'm cheered by the thought that I may have more power than I realise...

My mind has wandered back to sex on the astral. Should I tell him? But, no. I can't reveal what I learned from Shelagh without permission, so I'll keep quiet for now. Instead I ask, 'What about that magical group of your mother's? How does that fit in?'

'Don't ask me, Pips. I begin to believe someone's pulling my strings big time.' But nevertheless he adds.

14. Mum's magical group. Plan for magical child. Dreams!!
He's back on that tricky subject again. Turning him aside, I add, 'You'd better question where my magical tools came from. They triggered memories for me.' I remind myself to go through those books Mrs B gave me. Perhaps the answer will be there. Although I've been asked to call Sebastian's mum 'Mimi' in private, Mimi seems too intimate somehow. She didn't want

the other volunteers getting too familiar in case it undermined her authority. I'm only too happy to oblige. In my mind, she'll always be Mrs B. Not a woman I trust, not after...

Q.7 Magical tools. Who? Why?

A thought strikes me. 'Don't forget to put Shelagh on the board too. She'll be here next week. I saw her as my nurse in Egypt.' I'm comforted by the thought of my friend returning. I so want to introduce her to Sebastian.

15. Shelagh. Nurse. Fits in where?

He looks so defeated. I want to escape from all this, to run away and 'be normal', have fun with this guy who holds my heart. Instead I say, 'There are crucial gaps in the manuscript and the end is missing altogether. It's strange. The final portion was missing off that mystic marriage papyrus I heard about on the radio too. I've got a funny feeling that the mystic marriage was only the start, not the aim of the whole thing. Did Randolph jump to the wrong conclusion?'

'Well, yes,' Seb interjects. 'The *neters* – gods – are symbolic of the forces that exist throughout the universe. Was that what he was getting at I wonder. Or was it something altogether more spiritual?'

Putting my hand over his heart, its rhythmic beat dances beneath my fingertips. 'The book talks a lot about opening the heart and we've certainly joined ours.'

Briefly his hand alights on mine, but he's not going to be distracted. 'That meditation last night showed me I was part of a divine universe. I'd even go as far as to describe it as I was that universe. How about you?'

Q.8 Mystic marriage or something else. Animism? Divine universe.

'William James said something pertinent. He described "a

continuum of cosmic orgasms against which our individuality builds but accidental fences and into which our several minds plunge as into a mother-sea." Do you think that's what's happened to us? Have we plunged into a cosmic sea?'

The echo of the firestorm that had flashed through me with such power suffuses my body once again. Didn't EAWB say something like it imbues the body with creative energy, lodging it in the intercellular structures of the bodies both material and spiritual? According to him, 'the process culminates in some kind of spiritual realisation?' I need to cogitate on that.

Sebastian isn't listening. He's reviewing the board, scratching his head. 'There's still an awful lot missing. We don't have the key. How can we make it fall into place?'

I recall how powerful I'd felt when I held back the orgasm so it infused every cell of my body. So blissful. And how womanly I'd felt wearing the blue robe. I must put it on again – and the headdress. Time to raise the flame again – take another look in the magic mirror. This time I'll use the ancient Egyptian Hathor ritual. I can handle its power now. But all I say is, 'Let's get everyone together when Shelagh comes over and see what we make of it. Perhaps if we pool our resources we'll find the answer.'

* * *

Later that night, pondering the questions and unable to sleep, I reach for the books I'd retrieved from Mrs B. Certain that the pieces are all there, I simply need to slot them together in the right way. But, as soon as I've read a few pages, my eyes droop and I slide into a deep sleep peopled with incoherent symbols and muttered voices of which I understand nothing and remember only my confusion as I awake in the light of a new dawn.

Chapter 45

Eyes that dance and wonder

'Sebastian, I'd like you to meet my friend Shelagh. I've told you about her. Shelagh, this is my –' What am I to call him? Boyfriend sounds too shallow, twinflame too intense. 'My friend, Sebastian…'

Dumbstruck silence greets my words. Bitter coldness drops around me, as though snow is whirling fiercely around the room. In late September? What could have brought about this transformation? Welcoming warmth to deadliest ice in two seconds flat. I was so looking forward to the two of them meeting. My closest friends. Confidantes. Both privy to the weirdnesses that have beset me. Allies to share it with. Help me understand. But now… It's awful.

'What is it? Do you two know each other?' There's a look of anguish on Shelagh's face. Clenched white lips and tightly drawn brows have replaced Sebastian's smile of welcome. A pulse beat quivers along his jaw, the translucent skin dancing wildly. He stares at Shelagh, blinks, and then his glance skitters away.

'Our Sebastian, is that really you?' Her eyes are fixed on him with a yearning so strong I almost taste it.

'Knew,' he says emphatically, blanking her. 'The word is knew, Pips.'

'But what, why…' I stutter in utter bewilderment, reaching out to clutch his arm. 'Sebastian, what is it? Tell me.'

'She was my mother.' He says dully, staring coldly at Shelagh before turning away. But not before I've seen the glint of tears in his eyes.

'Was? Don't you mean is my mother, Seb?'

'No, I do not. She walked out and left me when I was young.

After that I had to go to boarding school. I did not have a mother.' Pulling himself up to his full height, he bellows at Shelagh. 'You abandoned me!' Adding more quietly, 'And I never knew why.' He turns for the door.

As I try to pull him to me, he resists, wrapping his arms around himself and drawing back. Remaining resolutely standing, rigid and half turned away. Lapis eyes bruised, shining with hurt. Can what he's saying be true?

'But…how do you know she's your mother? Are you certain? If you were very young, surely, you might be imagining…and you Shelagh, how could you recognise…it's been such a long time.'

Gnawing on my lip, an old habit from childhood I thought I'd grown out of, I turn back to Shelagh. Could she have been so cruel? Walking out and leaving a child. And what about Mrs B? She's Sebastian's mother, or so he'd said. I'm still trying to get my head around that one. Could there possibly be another mother?

I look helplessly at Shelagh. 'Shelagh, I don't understand. Are you his mother? You told me you'd been happily married…you didn't mention a child. Did you leave, and if so why? What…?' My questions tumble out without a pause, my thoughts running away with my mouth.

Shelagh's shaking her head. 'It's hard to explain. I tried to put it behind me.'

'But why would you put a child behind you?' My incomprehension must surely show on my face, but her head's down, she's not making eye contact. Huddled inside herself.

'Well, hen, you see, I left out a bit of the story. Edited it like.' She's sitting down now, clutching another of her hankies and biting at a fingernail. 'You know I told you about me husband, well he were actually me second, you know.'

'No, that's the trouble. I do not know. Tell me.' Guiding Sebastian to a seat opposite her, I keep a tight hold on him.

He's desperate to pull away, torn between running out of the room and standing up and confronting this woman whom they both seem to believe is his mother. It's like an electric current running through him, one way then the other. When I have time, I'll ponder this visceral connection between us. How deeply I partake in his feelings. I sense how tightly he's held this in, for years. Now it's threatening to tear him apart. I so want to make it right for him. But, at this moment, it's more important to hear Shelagh's story. 'Do go on,' I urge, passing over yet more tissues. 'Why not start at the beginning?'

'Well, like I told you, I were going to college but I were still getting over being bothered by John.'

'John, who's John for god's sake?' Sebastian bursts in. Tremors are coursing through his body. 'Not another of your men?'

'Seb, leave that for now,' I insist gently. Thank goodness I haven't shared her Lennon experience with him, nor her Egyptian exploits. He sounds so jealous. Would he really want to know about his mother's – if she really is his mother – toy boy, a boy younger than him? And as for sex on the astral, that's best left well alone. 'I'll explain later. Do go on, Shelagh.'

'After the exams, I saw a job advertised, PA to the director of a mine out in Africa. He were only in England for a few days so it were all very sudden. Took me out to dinner, then lunch, and that were that. Two days later, I were on a plane. We got married in a tin shack. Pretty soon I were pregnant.' Her smile is far away, her eyes soft. 'Thought it were the best thing that could've happened to me. When boy were born, I took one look and fell totally in love.' Her eyes are glowing, melting violets.

Tears are running down Sebastian's face, but his voice is harsh, 'Then why did you…?'

'Shush, let Shelagh tell it in her own way. Do go on, Shelagh,' I urge, pulling him close again. Could they be right? Maybe they are mother and son.

'It were when I were breastfeeding him that I first noticed

a lump in me breast. The nurse at the mine said it were quite usual, so I took no notice.' Her face is anguished. 'Suppose I were in denial, as they say. Should have known given I'd had it before. But… You don't, do you?'

Don't you? If that had been me I'd have panicked, sought treatment even though I was marooned in the jungle. After all, she'd had a baby to think of.

'By the time he were coming up two the lump were bigger and we had a doctor by then. Sent me home for tests. They did a lumpectomy. I went back to the mine for a year, but it returned. Under me arm this time.'

She's conflated so much, collapsed time and edited her story to fit what she thought I ought to hear, still is from the sound of it. I suppose we all do that one way or another, whether we realise it or not. But, this is extreme.

'I knew it were terminal when I went back to England. Doctor said there'd be no treatment for it second time around, but sent me anyway. I told me husband – his dad,' she says nodding towards Sebastian, 'before I left. But the hospital said they'd got something new to try. A bone marrow transplant. I wrote and told the bastard, sorry, Sebastian, but he were, and he said it were better for the child if I didn't come back, 'specially if I only came home to die.'

Sebastian is sobbing now, choking as he tries to get the words out. 'How could you… You said you'd be back. He told me you were dead… I missed you so much.' He's still trying to rush out of the room, but I hold him back. More tightly this time. We have to find out the truth.

'No, but it were close. Took me a long time to recover. The treatments were horrible. Telegraphed to say I were coming back, but your dad said no and the company backed him. Said I couldn't travel to the mine without permission and, in any case, they couldn't get me long-term medical insurance. Broke me heart. But I hoped you'd forget me.'

'I never forgot you. Mimi called me a poor little motherless boy. Did her best to look after me.' His lip curls. 'But it wasn't like having a real mother.'

'Mimi? How come she's involved?' I hear my voice rising in disbelief, coming from somewhere faraway. I cannot get my head around this.

'She was Dad's PA –'

'The bitch took over when I were having treatment first time. I knew something were going on –'

The voices meld in my head. 'So she came out to Africa before you knew you were ill?'

'Yes, he said when I were pregnant that he'd have to have help, I were so sick I couldn't do me job. Mimi wormed her way in.' The accent is getting thicker by the minute. It's difficult to make out what she's saying, let alone understand it. It's like all the sounds of Babel packaged in one. I itch to shut it out. But I must think of Seb – and my friend.

'So you were all together in Africa for a while?'

'Yes. I knew when I went back that first time things'd changed. He weren't loving no more. Pushed me away. Treated me with contempt. I'd told him about the John stuff when we first met.'

Sebastian stiffens and leans forward at the mention of John. Oh Shelagh, why can't you edit appropriately. All I can do is whisper, 'Leave it till later' and hold on to his arm. Muttering, he subsides.

'He started saying I were a paranoid schizophrenic, imagining things. 'Specially when I accused him of having an affair with Mimi. I reckon he hoped I'd die.'

'Soon he pushed me away too,' Sebastian says bitterly. 'Sent me off to pre-prep school in England. Mimi was kind to me in the holidays. Even took me to school the first time. After that, I was put on a plane with the other kids and left in the care of the crew. Someone from the school met us at Gatwick. Same when I went home. Or what passed for home.'

I'm in tears now, salt scalding my face, thinking of that vulnerable little boy all alone. But he seems more composed now, as though he's got a hold on those wild emotions.

'She married him, in the tin shack, of course. Became mixed up with my mum in my mind. When Dad ran off with another woman a few years later, Mimi brought me up as her own. Had another marriage – collected Samantha along the way. She was the daughter of the guy whose wife Dad ran off with and Mimi married her stepdad, a Dutch mining engineer –'

'Stop, stop!' Married again, how could she when she was already married – my head's whirling.

'Not that I'm sure those tin shack marriages were legal, no record of them in England and the pastor handed out divorce certificates like candy. But I never forgot I'd had a real mum.' His face is crumpling, that composure didn't last long.

'Please, slow down. I can't keep up. It's like something off the telly.' My hands are over my ears now, thinking of those soap operas of which one of the volunteers at the shop is so fond. She's always telling me the ridiculous plots. 'It's all so complicated, Seb.'

'Tell me about it. How do you think it felt growing up with all that going on? Especially when Ernst was killed in a mining accident and we came home. It was easier in the end to say Mimi was my mother and Meski my cousin. But I hung onto Warner.' His face is raw. Yearning, as he half gets up then withdraws again, his shoulders hunched. 'In time, I almost believed it myself.'

'I can understand, son. When I remarried, I didn't tell me husband about you. Couldn't bear to. I buried it deep. Tried to pretend everything was okay. Almost convinced meself at times. But, I'd see a young boy with red hair and think about you growing up without me.' She shakes her head. 'I didn't know what you'd look like, but I knew I'd recognise that hair. It were me dad's. You're the spitting image…' She reaches out a tentative hand to his vibrant curls, growing back strongly now. But he jerks back.

'I guess somewhere inside I always knew you were alive and thought you'd abandoned me.'

'I'd never have –' She gulps, unable to go on.

'Dad told me before he left that you'd stayed in England to be with a man you'd met over there. Said he'd told me you were dead to save my feelings, make me forget you. But now I deserved the truth. Truth, hah! Anything but the truth. I should have known.' His face is pale and sweaty, the scattering of freckles standing out sharply against his translucent skin. His jaw is still pulsing and jumping. He looks at Shelagh imploringly. 'I searched everywhere for you when I went to uni. I had your picture. I'd never be parted from it.' He takes out a battered photo. 'It was under my pillow at school, Pips.'

I can hardly make out the creased and faded image. 'But how did you recognise her when she came in? It must be over twenty years since you saw her and you were so young.'

Is it like recognising someone from another life? Is there an instant connection no matter how long the separation? I'll have to think this through later. I need to listen as Sebastian says, 'Didn't have to think about it, I just knew. I was so angry to think I'd been missing her all that time and then there she was.' He glares at Shelagh. 'Why didn't you make contact? What stopped you?'

'Oh, I tried. I wrote to you all the time. Hoped he'd give them to you when you were older if not then. But I guess he didn't tell you.'

'No.' The reply is curt.

'Then, after a few years, letters came back marked "gone away" – they went out via the company and once he'd left I couldn't trace him. They wouldn't give me his forwarding address. I never knew he'd remarried, nor that he'd left you with Mimi. I suppose I ought to thank her.' Her smile is tremulous.

'What a pig's ear. Can you forgive me, son?' She opens her arms wide.

Standing up, he hesitates, and then reaches for his mother. Holding her as though he'll never let go. I tiptoe quietly out of the room, thankful we aren't in the pub as I'd suggested at first. I'll make us a nice cup of tea.

Chapter 46

The seeker after truth

After showering with my new rose-scented gel, rubbing in Shelagh's Egyptian oil, and donning the blue robe and headdress, I fetch Aidan's magic mirror instructions. Now it's dusk, I'm ready for the Mirror of Hathor ritual. Can I find clues in the obsidian's enigmatic depths?

I hope the dinner Shelagh and Sebastian are having together is healing some of the past hurts. Sebastian's mother! Who'd have thought it? I'm glad I didn't take up the invitation to join them. They need time alone, as do I. If I'm so shattered by it, how must they feel? I still have to get my head around it. Un-discombobulate myself: 'combobulate' – if there is such a word. Compose myself really doesn't cover it. I'm scattered to the four winds, everything thrown up in the air. It needs to fall into a new pattern. Still pieces missing though. Perhaps looking into the mirror will throw light into the situation. 'Scrying.' Another new word that I treasure. Seeking guidance.

Calling on the Lady Hathor to aid my seeing, and lighting a candle, I angle the mirror so that all I see is the brightness scintillating off the surface. It seems to bounce rather than penetrate. No light reaches the turbid depths. Taking up the incense sticks I'd also found in the shop, I light one and spiral it around the mirror. Before I have time to ask a question, the flat surface shudders. A roiling, boiling blast of sand and fury spits out. His Majesty, or is it a snake, hisses at me, sucking at my energy. Pulling me into the darkness, drawing me into his own time. I wanted to see what's behind it all, not join His Awful Majesty in his world.

Are my doubts getting in the way? My fears preventing me from seeing true? This is all too real. Too horrible for words.

His image is filling the mirror. Yanking me into that tomb of his. The rank smell is emanating from the mirror, I'm almost there. His bony arm is reaching out, dragging me...pulling me down a tunnel of darkness, sucking my energy, taking my soul who knows where... Well, yes, I do know...to ancient Egypt. I'm sliding through time into a past I never want to experience again. His pet serpents rush to haul me in, their coils exerting a surprising amount of force for what must, indubitably, be an insubstantial vision. Slapping his hand off and pushing their looping bodies away, frantically I clap my hands to close the portal, dropping a cloth over the turbulent mirror, shouting out the banishing spell.

Quickly, I turn away. I'll cleanse the mirror later.

That was not what I'd expected. What went wrong? A statement from Aidan's report comes to mind: 'employed other scryers, stating that the best of them were young, virgin, pristine, untouched.' Well, I'm young. But pristine, untouched? After those nights with Tom – and His Majesty? I don't think so.

Perhaps it's because the mirror is obsidian. The crystal book says it needs careful handling. Nothing can be hidden from it. It's supposed to be highly protective too, but it brings things rushing to the surface. Apparently it brings you face-to-face with your shadow side. The Prince can't be my shadow side, can he? A 'tenebrous animus' rather than dark enigma? He's more like my nemesis at this moment.

The scrying book says nothing about ancient Pharaohs reaching out to grab you into the stone. It seems to be a two-way portal. The past can look out in addition to the present gazing in. Perhaps that's why it needs someone experienced to work with it. If only I could remember my training from that other life. Nothing seems to stop that old perv reaching out through time. Did looking in the mirror reactivate the ties I'd cut? Why didn't I leave well alone?

Obsidian also helps to dissolve ancient traumas. Perhaps this is a catharsis, albeit a rather overwhelming one. It's protection I need right now, though, and I grip my *menat* tightly, begging Isis to shield me, swathe me in her veils.

In the Otherworld, her guardian grandmother nods. The child is doing well, calling on her ancient training, albeit still unknowingly.

At least I'm no longer enervated by my Dark Enigma's presence. When he tried to grab me into the mirror it was a shock. But I'd withstood him. I must be getting somewhere, but it's a slow process. I'll have a cup of tea and a walk in the garden. Fresh air always helps. I love the dusky garden in the starlight. What there is of it anyway, that security light that next door has installed has rather polluted my view. I can barely see the baby bats out for their flying lesson. Looking at all that sky always reminds me of the immensity of things and makes my problems seem small indeed inside the wonder of infinity. Or am I being pretentious? Never mind. It'll take my mind off things and that's all that matters.

Filling the kettle, I lay out the oriental teapot I inherited from my grandmother, and a delicate porcelain cup. That way the tea will taste as it should, or so my mother told me. Warming the pot, I measure the tea leaves carefully and let it brew. Adding a dash of milk, warily I open the door to the garden, checking the coast is clear before breathing in the night-scented air.

But something is pushing me on, convincing me that scrying holds the key. A voice is whispering about the intricate, silver-backed mirror that belonged to my guardian grandmother. Quickly gulping my tea, I go into the garage and rummage through my boxes to find it.

Such a sense of love emanates from it that, for a moment, I smile and hold it to my heart, smelling the dusky myrrh and frankincense-based perfume that's always signalled my grandmother's presence. No harm can come to me when I peer into its silvered depths, not while under her protection.

But, all I see is myself. Sketchily reflected. Not as I am now, but a husk. Fragmented and frightened. Ragged around the edges. Robbed of all beauty and presence. Helpless, eviscerated. Powerless. Soulless. Is this my true self? Surely not?

My grandmother's hand on my shoulder conveys gentle words, *'Be still, child. Look deeper inside yourself. Recognise your inner beauty. Find your core. Open your heart and be the woman you are meant to be. That's what this is about. The mirror is but a tool, as were the visions that awoke you. Let the past go. All will be well.'*

Looking deeper into the mirror, I see my soul shimmering, shining out. Now all I have to do is open my heart and *listen*. Time for another cup of tea first though.

Putting the kettle on, I see *The Ancient Wisdom of Egypt* lying where I'd set it down the previous night. Perhaps there's something about the Mirror of Hathor in there. Hmm, there's a section about using the mirror to return unwanted attention, I might try that next time His Majesty comes calling. But nothing about it being a portal through time.

I'm so confused. How I wish the author hadn't passed on. I badly need advice and might have found it there.

In the Otherworld, the guardian grandmother turns to the woman who has been her soul sister for so long. 'I thank you, Murry, with all my heart. With your wisdom to guide her, she'll come through this. Of that I am certain.'

Her companion smiles and shapeshifts into a small cat. 'Perhaps I will return.' She purrs. 'I would enjoy being a pampered pet once again.'

Chapter 47

Death shall be no sev'rance

Ancient Khem

The young priest Men'ofer is conveyed to the tjaty's private chambers, having fainted dead away. It is given out that he is ill, consumed by Nile fever from his journey. No one has the temerity to ask where he's been for all these months. His absence had been noted. As had His Majesty's hostile takeover of Men'en'oferet. His annexing of the young priestess shamed everyone in the palace. It disturbed the natural order. Repercussions were felt throughout the whole of Egypt. Premonitions of doom stalked the land. Their enemies drew near. The boundaries were elastic, unprotected. Ready to be breached. All felt for the young man who had lost everything. *Ma'at* must be recreated. The burden falls on Agni'ti's weary shoulders. Night after night he exhorts the gods and works his magic, tweaking the Records so that the balance is restored.

* * *

The faithful Lik'e'bet nurses Men'ofer devotedly for many weeks until at last, gaunt and hollowed out, he awakes again into his greatest nightmare.

'Tell me it's not true,' he pleads. But all his nurse can do is shrug miserably and go in search of the tjaty.

'Take me to her. Let me be with her. Let me commit myself to serve her through her life in the Otherworld. Please, you must allow me...' Men'ofer is beside himself as the tjaty shakes his head.

'Yours is another destiny, young man. You are to be ruler of all Egypt. Your mother has spoken.'

'No, no. At least let me withdraw into the temple. Hide from her there. She cannot make me…'

'You know full well, the Lady Yagut does whatever she pleases. There is no refuge great enough for you. You must do her will.'

Men'ofer pulls the blanket over his head and shakes in terror. Rule Egypt? Without his beloved beside him? Never. Such a thing is impossible. He has not been prepared for this. It is too much.

The Lady Yagut arrives with ostentatious ceremony the next morning. All bow down to her, prostrating themselves full length on the earth beside her barge, acknowledging that she is the legitimate successor to His Majesty. Only her son challenges her. Standing straight, refusing to bow. Dishonouring her.

But the Lady is up to the challenge. Taking his hand she raises his arm and says, 'I give you my son Men'ofer. The issue of His Majesty and rightful heir to the throne of Egypt. All honour to the Prince. May His Majesty live forever.'

As the people cheer and wave, she calls Mes'kia to her side. 'And this is my daughter Mes'kia, also heir to His Majesty. The two shall be joined in matrimony according to our custom as soon as we reach Memphis. They shall rule together for eternity.'

Men'ofer smiles tightly. 'You have won, Mother, for now. But don't think this will be the end of it. There will be no heir from the union. That you cannot force. I am forever joined to my Mennie, not this *har'her'shat*. Sister to me she may be, but Mes'kia is not my beloved, the companion of my heart. She may sit beside me on the throne but never shall she share my bed. Throughout eternity, I shall not forgive you and I shall be avenged.'

Agni'ti can only shake his head once more. Whatever will become of the land now? And how can his precious daughter be reconciled in the Otherworld without her twinsoul? There has to be a solution. He must find one soon or disaster will inevitably fall over the Two Lands and roll down the tide of time to who knows where.

Chapter 48

Whom will you embrace for your pleasure?

Sebastian's face is serious, he seems to have somewhat recovered from the shock of meeting his real mum, but it's marked him. There's a fragility that wasn't there before, even when he returned from Egypt. His eyes are weary, violet circles beneath attesting to a lack of sleep...but there's something in those eyes, a probing intensity rather than the softening that usually meets my gaze. He clearly has something on his mind.

'Come on, Pips, time to tell all. What were those dreams you were having?'

The question I've been dreading. Curled up on my huge sofa, resting my head on his shoulder, I debate with myself. Should I really tell all? What if he takes it badly? He's had so many bombshells recently. Can he handle another? But there's not much prospect for the relationship if I can't trust him. He had all those experiences with His Majesty himself, surely he'll understand. Where to begin? How to answer that insistent question?

'Well, you know you told me how His Awful Majesty came to visit you in the cells? How he tormented you and you couldn't tell if you were having a nightmare or if it was real?'

Sebastian nods, stiffening at the memory. Then sighs and nuzzles my ear. 'Yes, I remember.'

'Well, it was like that for me. Only it wasn't, if you know what I mean.'

'No, Pips, I don't. Spit it out.'

'He, er, was so *physical*. He was right there, in my world. I'd be having this lovely dream of making gentle love with you. Those were the dreams Mrs B...your mum... I mean Mimi, was sending me.' I wish I could sort out in my head what to call this wretched woman who's plagued me so. 'Though I don't think she meant them to be quite so graphic. She said she wanted me to fall in love, not have erotic dreams.' I'm glad he can't see my face. 'At first His Awful Majesty hovered on the edge, watching.'

'Dirty old perv.'

'Yes. But it got so much worse. He pushed you away and ravished me. Like he did in Egypt. He took over and I couldn't stop it. It was mindblowing. I felt –'

'Mindblowing? Ravished?' Seb lifts his head and looks directly at me. 'What do you mean, ravished?'

'I don't know how he did it, but I kept coming and coming. He'd look at me and off I'd go. Shelagh said –' Aware that I can't share Shelagh's experiences, I change tack. 'She told me it was called sex on the astral. There're books about it. It used to happen a lot in ancient Egypt. Aidan found texts –'

'Coming? You mean he gave you orgasms? You had sex with him?'

'Sort of. I couldn't help it. It's not as if –'

'How many times?'

'Too many. He –' His face reddens and his jaw clenches, I've said too much. Perhaps I should have held back. But it's too late now. I have to be honest with him, I need him to understand. If he can't, then there's no future for us. A sob sticks in my throat, strangling the words I so do not want to say.

'How often?' He's got hold of my shoulder now and is shaking me insistently.

'It got so it was every night before you came home. I didn't even have to be asleep. I managed to fight him off – most of the time. It wasn't my fault. It's been better since you were here.'

'Better? Unbelievable. How could you let him? He's a wicked old bastard who shouldn't be on this earth. It's not natural, sex with a spectre. Oh come on, Pips. Really.' His face could freeze hell.

'You don't understand. I had no choice. He did it. It wasn't as though I wanted it, or encouraged him. I didn't invite it. He...'

I'm abruptly dumped on to the floor as Sebastian stands up. 'Did you try to stop it? Or were you enjoying it too much? Is that why you wouldn't let me make love to you? Is that it? It wasn't your blasted book, it was Him. *His Majesty.* He got in the way. Exactly like He did in Egypt. You were unfaithful to me... With Him... Before... I expect you enjoyed that too.'

The look he gives me is so devoid of love that it tears the heart out of me. I lie where I've fallen. 'No, Seb, I didn't –' But, deep down, I know that, at the beginning at least, I had enjoyed the encounter with His Awful Majesty. I'm never going to admit to that though, especially not to Seb. Not even to myself.

'Oh, I can't bear it. I've been such a fool.' Tearing the *sem* from his neck he flings it at me, saying bitterly, 'You'd better have this. Clearly it belongs with His Majesty, not me.' Not giving me time to reply, he picks up his coat and rushes out of the room.

Curling into a ball, empty and quaking with cold, I throw myself onto the sofa and sob. That old black hole has opened up inside me into which I'm being sucked until nothing is left. Like that obsidian mirror – and when I lost Sebastian the first time, and when I broke up with Tom, and... Why do my relationships end like this? Futilely I cross my hands over my stomach, trying to stem the flow. If I'm not careful I'll find myself back in ancient Egypt in the arms of His Majesty. His leering presence is calling.

Desperately, I hold on to the image of Sebastian. His hands ruffling my hair. His teasing lapis eyes looking into mine. The quirk of his eyebrow. His *smell.* I shouldn't have told him. In that tarot reading I had, the cards advised me to be discreet, to hold on to secrets. I thought it was Mrs B of whom I had to beware. But it seems I misunderstood. It was Seb I should have avoided talking to. Discretion is all. Cecil Day Lewis was right, 'Love's essence – like a poem's – shall spring from not-saying-everything.'

I've ruined it. What am I going to do? I'm all alone and the nightmare is starting again. If only… But then, if I couldn't talk to Seb about this, have him here for protection, how could it work? I so want to do it right. Follow the book. Experience the Alchemy of Night.

Grabbing the *sem,* I finger it tenderly. I know it belongs to Sebastian, *I know* –

Grasping fingers reach out almost pulling it from my hand. 'That young pup was never the right partner for you, my *hennu nafrit*. With me as your lover you could own the world and live forever.'

'Oh bugger off, you old perv. Sebastian's right. You're a wicked old bastard and you shouldn't be on this earth. Begone.' As one hand traces pentagrams in the air, my other snatches the *sem* and places it around my neck. I'll keep it safe until…

What a mess. Miserably I drag myself to bed, but don't sleep. My dreams have fled. My mind constantly questions, is Sebastian right? Did I enjoy my Dark Enigma too much? I'd hardly call it lovemaking. 'Carnal ravishment', that's what it was. Pleasurable – in the beginning. Overwhelming. All consuming. Taking over my soul. But, I came to my senses when Sebastian returned. Didn't I?

Chapter 49

I am the lord of fire who lives on truth

His face hot with humiliation, pacing furiously along the riverbank, Sebastian is engaged in a bitter dispute with himself. He can't believe that Pips has been having orgiastic sex with that gruesome fiend in preference to making love with him. Wasn't he good enough for her? Yes, he lacked experience. But she'd said the dreams of making love with him were precious to her. Tender. Gentle. She'd enjoyed them, so she said, and she certainly seemed willing enough when they actually began... until she thought about that damned book of hers and called a halt. Doesn't she know how much he cares for her? Hasn't she said they are bonded for all time? Twinflames. How could she? She said she wanted to do things by her fucking book. Now he wishes he'd thrown it out of the window when he first set eyes on it. It's contaminated, foul. The Alchemy of Night? Bah! More like the pornography of inky darkness. The perversion of the damned. It's turned her head, made her imagine...

Frantically he kicks out at a squashed Coca-Cola can that's fallen out of one of the wastebins lining the riverside. So angry that he doesn't even notice when it rolls down the bank and there's a squawk as one of the nocturnal inhabitants is disturbed. By the time the flapping of wings has died, he's deep in his own inner world of furious turmoil and he lobs a crumpled fast-food carton in the same direction. But, hearing the soft hissing and the rustle of ruffled feathers settling again for the night, his rational head kicks in. This isn't him. It's like he's been taken over. Angrily he shakes himself and mutters the banishing spell. He wouldn't put it past that old bastard to be stirring up his jealousy.

What Pippa has been through, that wasn't her imagination.

They weren't nightmares either. He knows exactly how real His Awful Majesty can be. How overwhelming. How, as she'd put it, *physical*. It's not her fault. She is being haunted by a sexual predator that would stop at nothing to get his way. Who took advantage of her innocence to fulfil a past life obsession. Former life? Does he really believe in previous lives? Well, yes, he has to. He's had glimpses enough himself, they felt all too real. He was walking in the past, not viewing it from a distance.

The anguish when she was torn away from him still resonates in his heart. Now he's pushed her away. Run away, if the truth be told. Not able to face up to what she's been going through. He knows how dreadful it was for him in that Egyptian gaol. What His Awful Majesty conjured up for him. How much worse must have it been for her with him pushing himself onto her. Unfaithful to him? How could he have said that? The old perv must have forced her; she wouldn't participate willingly. Would she? She did say he had mesmerising eyes. Perhaps that's it, he hypnotised her in some weird ancient Egyptian magical way. It must have been hell for her. As it was for him in Egypt. What a twat he's been. He's waited all this time and now he's blown it.

Thrusting his fingers through his hair, its length showing him how much time has passed since he returned from captivity, he twirls the curls anxiously. Will she ever forgive him? Desolated, he fingers his neck. The absence of the *sem* feels like a part of him has been torn away. He's naked, exposed, the link to Phillippa stretched and tenuous. Why, why did he do that?

He remembers, he'd not exactly been faithful himself, back then. Equally unwillingly. Forced by Mes'kia. Ridden to orgasm by her. Bamboozled into thinking it was his beloved. Awakening too late to stop it. Was it that way for Phillippa? She said she'd been dreaming when it first started. Lucid dreaming from the sound of it. Knowing it was a dream, but unable – or unwilling – to stop it even when His Malodorous Majesty took over. He only touched her with his mind, or so she says. Hadn't penetrated her. Did she wake up and enjoy it? No, he mustn't go there. He needs to concentrate on how to make it right again. She's right to be angry with him. But they can't let the old bastard win. If he parts them this time, it will be forever.

Looking up, he realises he's reached the bridge where the river goes under the bypass. He sees the lights of the all-night garage on the edge of town. As he approaches, a lone bunch of red roses stares forlornly at him out of a bucket. Willing him to notice. No doubt feeling as lonely and out of place as he does. Picking them up, he goes to the cash window. 'Do you have any more? These are past it.'

'Sorry, mate, that's it. A bit of water 'n they'll be fine. Soon perk up. That'll be six pounds fifty.'

What? Nighttime robbery. But he hands over the money without a qualm. Then turns back to ask, 'Give me some Werther's Originals,' his guilty pleasure, 'and a six pack too, please mate.' He'll need all the courage he can muster.

Now for the hard part. Best start walking. The street lights are out. It must be well past midnight.

Chapter 50

Heavy in all my limbs

Ancient Khem

In the silky blackness of an Egyptian night, the Prince Men'ofer sits beside his beloved's tomb. He has evaded his bodyguards and made his way to this hidden cave high up in the side of the desolate valley. Agni'ti had revealed its location on his deathbed but, until now, it has not been possible to leave the capital. His mother has been too watchful. But, when he publicly decreed a festival in honour of his father and declared that he would journey to his father's House of Eternity in Abydos to make offerings, she could do nothing. Other than accompany him. But she has been laid low by a mysterious illness, crippling stomach pains – created by sticking pins into a crude clay figure bound with her hair, if she did but know it. He purloined the hair from her comb when commanded into her bedchamber to receive orders. In truth, it is she who governs Egypt. He is merely the mouthpiece for her decisions. Her rule is harsh. Already the people begin to hate him.

Only Mes'kia is aware of how, night after night, he has prayed to the gods for the dreadful demise of their mother. She has listened outside his door, pleading for admittance to no avail. With the connivance of Agni'ti, having consulted the best magicians of all Egypt, who are sworn to eternal secrecy, Men'ofer has mastered the black arts. And put them to excellent use. His undead father, watching cautiously from afar this usurper on the throne, begs to differ. He is monitoring the situation, ready to intervene if necessary.

Now the son rests in the secret cave beside his twinsoul. Excavating the short shaft, he has reached the simple wooden coffin with its inscription, *'Men'en'oferet. Beloved of her father*

Agni'ti and her twinflame Men'ofer. May she rest in peace throughout eternity. May the Lady protect her soul.' His head reposes on a pile of shrivelled rose petals. All that is left of her father's offering gift. They carry a lingering perfume that reminds him of his beloved. A smell he will never forget.

So be it, thinks Men'ofer, little realising that he has drawn to his beloved exactly what Agni'ti sought so hard to avoid. His Majesty the Prince Khem Yar Khepher'set had not, until now, known where the object of his obsession lay. But now, he can reclaim her heart. Track her soul through the afterlife and whatever incarnations she may choose for the future. Now she can be His forever.

Hissing, the Prince plunges at Men'ofer. Digging his claw-like nails into the—by now not so young—man's neck. His most detested rival. Raking his fingers deep into the yielding flesh he tears and twists seeking to decapitate his victim. There shall be no mummification for this *temum't*. Not if His Majesty has anything to do with it. Hearing a distant sound, he scoops up Men'en'oferet's heart from where Agni'ti had carefully placed it inside her wrappings. With roaring breath, the Prince causes a collapse of the tenderly excavated earth, filling in the shaft, and whirls away into the night.

Cautiously, Mes'kia edges forward. She had followed Men'ofer as he slipped off the royal barge moored at Thebes, watched as he commandeered a boat to cross the river, and then a donkey to carry him to the rocky slit in the hills that led to the afterlife. Saw the shade that followed behind. Sought a boat herself, ran as fast as she could, but arrived too late to prevent her ghostly father from attacking her beloved brother-husband.

Picking up the bone shovel that Men'ofer had discarded as he lay down to meet his love, she frantically digs out the red dirt, scraping it aside, thankful that the shaft is shallow within the cave. The solid bedrock had not yielded to Agni'ti's meagre tools. The earth had not opened before his hasty incantations.

Coming upon Men'ofer's leg, she tugs, pulling him free. His neck is bleeding profusely and he is choking in the dust. Alive, breathing raggedly, not yet a corpse, thank the Gods. But he fights her, pushing her away.

'No, no, leave me be. Let me stay here. I want to be with Mennie.'

'No. You have duties to perform. Our mother lies at the door of death. Agni'ti has passed to the Otherworld and you must return. Your land needs you. Think of the promises you made to the Gods at your coronation. You will be damned forever if you do not adhere to them. Do not become like our father, a wanderer in the desert night, a black-hearted *akh* without a home. Reclaim your heritage. Make this right. Then maybe you can meet your twinsoul again in some other life. Make the mystic marriage that was so near and yet so far. Connect your souls for all time. Come, Men'ofer, come with me.'

Tearing a strip from the bottom of her robe, she staunches his wounds as best she can. It will require all the skill of his healer-priests to repair the gaping damage to his neck. He will no doubt bear the scars for the remainder of his life.

Loading him on the donkey, she leads him into the dark Egyptian night.

Chapter 51

The bolt is sprung

Clutching a cup of cocoa, made after miserably tossing this way and that in a futile attempt to sleep, I'm heading back to bed when the doorbell rings. Throwing it open, I say eagerly, 'Sebastian, come in. I knew you'd come back, we couldn't be parted –'

'Oh yes, you could. I've told you, you're mine, *Pippi*.' Tom sneers in triumph as he pushes past me, almost filling the tiny hallway. 'All ready for bed I see, come on then. Let's get at it.' Grabbing my arm, he tugs me towards the bedroom tearing at my flannel nightdress as he does so. 'Why are you wearing this old thing? Always said you were a frigid bitch. Looks like something my granny would have worn.'

I'm not going to tell him it's my comfort blanket left over from my teenage years, only worn in the direst of moments. I pulled it from the back of the cupboard after Sebastian stormed out. Futilely, I bat Tom away. 'Get off me Tom, you can't, I won't…'

'How. Dare. You. You *nti heti*.' The roaring voice sends Tom crashing back against the wall. 'You… Misbegotten spawn of *iri nedjemem't em henen*. Remove yourself from My Majesty's presence.' A pounding wind assails the interloper, pushing him this way and that.

Tom's visibly shaken. Curling up in a tight ball on the floor, arms wrapped around his head – almost retching from the smell. Or is that from the booze he's clearly consumed in considerable quantities? Whatever, he's quaking.

For once I'm grateful for His Awful Majesty's presence. But, seeing the battering my former fiancée is undergoing, I decide to intervene. 'Leave him alone, I'm sure he'll leave quietly, won't you, Tom?'

'Not a chance, not until I find out what you've been messing with. There's something going on here and I intend to get to the bottom of it.' He's standing, defiantly. Back to the wall. Fists up. As though that could help him now.

To my astonishment, the hazy face of the ancient Pharaoh hovers over him but leaves him be for the moment. Tom obviously can't see His Majesty. He smells Him though. His nose twitches this way and that. Like the rat he is. 'What is that, *Pippi*? I've smelt it before. It's like something out of an old horror movie. What the devil have you and that redheaded git been doing? What have you conjured up?'

'Who is this person?' The creaky voice is silky, loaded with its usual menace. 'Why does he think he owns My Majesty's property?'

'I'm her fiancé, that's who.' Tom might not be able to see the cloud of phosphorescence hovering over him, but he hears the question well enough.

'What about the red-haired young devil. My Majesty believed him to be the one who was sworn to My property?'

'Oh him, he's only a temporary aberration till she comes to her senses. It's me she loves really.' His swagger is back. Pulling the remnants of his jacket around him, he enquires, 'But who might you be, O Great Disembodied One.'

'Tom, this is no time for games – or questions like that. Get out while you still can. You don't know what he's capable of.' I'm frantic now. A conversation between these two is not what I need.

'That's exactly what I want to know.' He smirks. The slick salesman he'd been coming to the fore. 'If he can see off the redheaded git, it'll clear the way for me.'

Like a cat playing with a mouse, Pharaoh swipes the smirk off his face and sends him flying. 'This, My Majesty is. Proper respect show, *ntiu*.'

But he's on his feet again in an instance. 'Can you do that to him?'

'Certain it is. My Majesty shall annihilate the *desh'retu cymotrich*. But... Why not you also?'

'Because whatever it is you want, I can help you to get it.'

Tom's got that wheedling look that I know only too well. 'Oleaginous' I would have called it, if only I'd time to savour the word. It's the look he thinks will get him anything he wants. Fawning and finagling. But, it's unlikely to have any effect on His Awful Majesty. I remind myself that Tom's destitute because he pushed his luck too far. Looks like he's doing it again. But His Awful Majesty seems to be considering the offer.

'Can you My Majesty a body give?'

Surely His Majesty isn't going to go along with this?

'If it gave me powers like you've got, you could have my body.'

Does he have any idea what he's saying? No clearly not, he's opening his arms wide, inviting the malicious presence in. Quickly, I chant the banishing ritual, shouting out the last few syllables in my head as the phosphorescent glow futilely pushes and paws at Tom's chest.

'Pah, useless it is. Were you not in My ancient land, *ntiu*? Initiated were you not?

'Well,' Tom says, smirking again, 'I had my fair share.'

'Idiot boy. Sexual activities do not an initiate make. Without training even the basest spirit embody you could not. As My Majesty says useless.'

The snarl is back, blackened teeth bared, the rictus distorted. The living dead once more. But I've got more on my mind right now, his words have triggered a thought I want to follow.

So, it would seem that Tom was never an initiate. Is it only those who were actually back there, in that ancient time, who can be violated by His Majesty? Does that mean Tom's not really involved in all this? Merely a chance bystander, as it were? One with dangerous ambitions, nonetheless. I'll give it more thought later, I need to be watchful. This hasn't ended yet.

Tom's face is crestfallen. 'I suppose *he* could, *he* was there, initiated in the proper way. *Sebastian.*' The word is spat out. The fingers making quotes are mocking. Hasn't Tom learned yet not to upset His Awful Majesty? But His Majesty is laughing, a hollow sound that could be heard all the way to the Duat. But, laughing nonetheless. Tom appears to have amused him. Who would have thought?

'Leave that red-haired spawn of the devil to My Majesty. But you, you may be a *ntiu,* but My Majesty use for you may have in future. Regain your former life you shall. On one condition.' The phosphorescent glow moves closer. 'This woman of Mine, you never trouble again. Seek your own *nedjem ndjmemit* to pleasure your nights. Come, My Majesty shall see what requires to be done.'

Breathing a sigh of relief as the two pass through the door, one having taken the trouble to open it first, I pick up the cold cocoa. Returning to the kitchen, I put the kettle on again and wash the cup. This time I'll try camomile tea.

Chapter 52

Truly, he is a foolish one

Shifting restlessly in the swampy darkness of my bed, I'm drifting fitfully towards sleep when I'm rudely yanked back to consciousness by the doorbell ringing – and ringing again. Muffled singing assaults my ears. God forbid, has Tom come back? Surely he wouldn't risk it, not after making that bargain with His Awful Majesty. He wanted success more than anything. He wouldn't give up the chance, not for me? For a moment my heart stumbles, but no, it must be a drunk. At the wrong door. What will the neighbours think?

Peering through the peephole, all I see is a bunch of roses drooping in time to the song. They look as sad as I am. Even sadder is the pair of bruised lapis eyes hiding behind them. The singing is clearer now. A rather fine tenor is crooning about love and begging for forgiveness.

Should I open the door? It's four in the morning. Rather like that Leonard Cohen song to which I can never quite remember the words. It was a favourite of grandpa's. 'Famous Blue Raincoat'? Something like that. But it's not the end of December. Even though it's been a long, long year we haven't reached the end of October yet. But the ringing goes on, and I hear him calling, 'I see you, Pippi. Peekaboo. I know you're there.'

'Sebastian…what on earth…shush…oh, you'd better come in.'

As I open the door, a bunch of roses sheepishly makes its way around it, saying, 'Sorry, sorry, can you ever forgive me,' as Sebastian halts on the threshold. 'Can I really come in, Pips? Do you forgive me?'

He looks even more like a wild bronze Byron than usual. No sign of the geeky academic now. His wayward curls are tossed every which way, eyes glittering and staring, hollow with remorse. He holds out a packet of Werther's Originals. His grin is sheepish. 'Would you like one, Pips?'

Sucking slowly and finding comfort in the familiar honeyed butteriness, I say dryly, 'We'd better get those roses into water. Then we can talk about it. But don't think I'm going to give in easily. I'm no pushover. We've got a lot to sort out.'

Chapter 53

The holy glimmer of goodbyes

'Aidan, come in. You're the first. Make yourself comfortable. You know Sebastian, don't you? You've seen him at the library. The others will be here soon.' I usher him into my tiny living room. It will be a squash but I didn't want to hold this meeting in the pub where who knows what ears could be listening. The discussion is likely to get pretty lively. Best do it in private. 'Here, sit down and I'll get you a drink.'

The room looks cosy with the fire going, even if I did have to open the French doors to let out the heat. But that meant I could bring the garden chairs in as extra seating. Aidan walks over to take one, placing himself on the edge of the action. He absentmindedly swots a moth away from his face as it flits in, drawn by the tea light lanterns I've placed on the cast iron table. The room seemed to need extra illumination, despite having all the lights on. I haven't yet organised the outside light I've been promising myself and, for once, next door has switched theirs off. I recall how I used to spend my evenings with the curtains open watching the bats swoop and dance in the half light. When did I begin to shut out the night? Tonight, though, I'd rather know what's lurking there.

'Shall I close the doors, Aidan? Are the insects bothering you?'

'No, no, you're fine. They're not troubling me.'

As I'm putting the kettle on, the bell rings and I hear Sebastian say, 'Oh hi, Mum, come on in.' To which 'mum' is he referring? It's so complicated. He still calls Mrs B mum, but has adopted it for Shelagh too. There's going to be a catfight when those two get together. Hopefully the presence of Aidan will smooth things down. I've warned Sebastian to be ready to intervene.

Hearing him introducing Shelagh to Aidan, I go in to give

her a hug. 'It's good to see you, Shelagh, thank you so much for coming. I know how difficult it is for you… Look, if you don't mind the odd moth or two flitting around, sit here by Aidan.'

Best keep the main protagonists as far from each other as possible. 'He'll look after you and it will leave the end of the sofa free for Mimi and Mr McM… I mean Ron. I still can't get used to that.' I shake my head ruefully at Aidan, 'You'd better call him Mr McMeeney, until he says otherwise. Keep up the pretence a bit longer. You know what a stickler he is for convention.'

'Pity I don't still have the dreads.' Aidan flashes his wicked grin. 'That always vexed the man.'

'I don't think he's going to need any extra stirring up, thank you very much. What I've got to say is going to stretch his mind far enough as it is.' I'm not looking forward to the next couple of hours. Despite rehearsing and revising the words, I'm still not sure how to convince the others. Let alone my stuffy boss. First of all, we've got to get the reunion between Shelagh and Mimi out the way. Bring those two on board so we all work together.

The air rustles and shivers, *that* smell seeping in. I'd thoroughly pentagrammed the flat earlier. But he's trying to find a way in. I repeat the banishing spell. We'll deal with His Majesty once we've agreed on our strategy, not before.

As I return to the kitchen, the bell summons Sebastian to let Mimi in, towing a reluctant companion behind her. 'I don't know what's wrong with you, Ron, anyone would think you were going to your execution, the face on you,' she grumbles.

'What the –' she's spotted Shelagh. For a moment there's absolute silence. Then she explodes. 'Where the hell did you come from? You're supposed to be dead. You, why didn't you tell me she was back?' Her glare at Sebastian, and the finger poking his chest, puts him firmly in the wrong. He shuffles uncomfortably and stutters.

'But, I…'

I rush forward. 'Hush now, Mrs B. I invited Shelagh here.

I know she's Sebastian's real mother. They're reconciled and I hope you will be too.' Before there can be any objection, I add, 'Look, we've saved you two a space here. Sit down, please. I'll get the tea, then we can discuss this calmly and rationally. Is Samantha coming? We need her input as well.'

'She'll be along in a minute.' The tone is sulky, the eyes constantly shifting between Shelagh and Sebastian. 'Don't see why you needed her though...'

'We can go over that when everyone is here. It really would be better to wait. Now, Ron, tea or coffee?'

There's something different about him today, not merely the body language that screams his reluctance to be here. The comb-over is no more. His hair is closely clipped to his head, shiny pate revealed to the world. That silly toothbrush moustache has metamorphosed too. He's sporting a small goatee nestling neatly around the tip of his chin. Rather like the one with which Sebastian had arrived back from Egypt. I'd been glad to see the back of that. But on Mr Mc – Ron – it's stylish. He looks years younger, although his mouth is grim.

Turning away, I push a strand of mousy hair behind my ear. Perhaps it's time I had a new haircut myself. This braid makes me look like a little girl. It's the way my mother styled it each day as I went off to school. All I've done since is butterfly clip it up out of the way. I could have it radically restyled – change the colour perhaps. Yes, that's what I'll do.

Cheered by the decision to transform my look, I hand around the cups, filling in time until there's a final ring at the door and Samantha bounces into the room.

'Hi, Aidan,' she says, 'funny you being here. Almost didn't recognise you with that wicked hair. What's going on, Seb? Who're you? Don't I know you from somewhere?' She's looking at Shelagh, who smiles tentatively.

'Yes, from a long time ago. When you were a little girl. In Africa. I didn't think you'd remember me.'

'Oh, you're the one whose picture Seb carried, the mum who abandoned him. Weren't you dead?'

'Samantha...'

'Meski...'

Sebastian nods to me to carry on.

'We'll tell you what it's about all in good time. Could we stop the questions and leave that for now? Don't judge Shelagh too harshly. You haven't heard her story yet and you might change your mind when you have. There's more to it than you've been told.' I've picked up my cup and drawn a deep breath when I'm interrupted.

'Now look here...' Mrs B is bristling, anxious to defend herself.

But I'm ready for her. 'Mrs B, Mimi, could you wait until it's time to have your say? This will go so much easier if everyone takes turns and we get the whole story – or I should say, stories. We're not only dealing with this present time you know.' Pushing aside the thought that I'm stepping into an Agatha Christie denouement, I wave away possible dissension, putting my cup firmly on the table to make the point.

Settling myself on the floor next to Sebastian, I reach for his hand and say quietly, 'Let's deal with the elephant in the room first. I want to introduce Shelagh to you all as Sebastian's birth mother. It's a complicated story with a slew of tin shack marriages and more than a touch of tragedy. Some of you know it already but bear with us. Shelagh, you're on, give us your story.'

My heart goes out to Sebastian and his mother as Shelagh pours out the tale of woe. Quietly I scrutinize the room, wondering how the others will take it. Samantha is leaning forward, absorbing every word, as is Aidan. Mimi is staring at the floor, unwilling to meet anyone's eye. It must be difficult for her to hear this. Only Mr McMeeney, Ron, seems remote, showing the coldness he so often displays at the library. He's sitting back with his eyes closed, mouth fixed in a stern line. Is he even listening? Sensing Sebastian's deep unhappiness, I snuggle closer. I'd better pay attention. I want to stay in control of the meeting. All hell could break loose at any moment.

'...it broke me heart, especially when I'd recovered and he still wouldn't let me return...'

As her voice falters to a halt, the hankie is out again. Sebastian reaches over and touches her knee. 'Go on, Mum, better finish the story now.'

'Mimi'd come out to be his PA. I were so sick I couldn't do me job, and she wormed her way in. Knew when I went back the first time things had changed. They were having an affair. She were why he wouldn't let me go back when I were cured.'

Mimi looks fit to burst. She never takes the blame in the shop, so I'm not surprised when she almost shouts, 'It was him. He wormed his way into my bed when you went away the first time. But I stopped it when you returned. Then, the second time, bastard told me you were dead. Shelagh, I didn't know, I swear to you.'

Shelagh's looking distinctly unconvinced, lifting her shoulders and her eyebrows in a skeptical shrug.

I can only shake my head in confusion. This story is so mixed up, was Shelagh thought to be a dead or a scarlet woman? It must be so much worse for Sebastian. I turn to look at him, but Shelagh has carried on speaking.

'But our Sebastian told me his dad ran off and left you too – is that true?'

'Yes, the bastard ran out on me. Left me with Sebastian, I tried to bring him up as my own. We'd arranged for him to go away to school so he could get an education. He was clearly a bright boy and the schools out there were inadequate. It was all paid in advance by the company.' Mimi shrugs. 'What else could I do? I married again and collected Meski along the way. Poor mite had been abandoned too. When Ernst was killed in a mining accident we came home. Me with my family. It's been that way ever since.' Sniffing, she waves at her two 'children.'

I'm almost sorry for her. Almost. But Shelagh's heart is softer than mine.

'I guess we've both had it rough. I were fortunate. I met a good man and had a long and happy marriage. But, no children – I never stopped missing me boy.' She holds out her hand in supplication as she surreptitiously brushes a tear from the corner of her eye. 'I forgive you, Mimi, what say we let the past go and move on? There's things to be done.'

Sebastian stirs beside me and I hold my breath until Mimi answers.

'I guess I can do that. I am sorry, Shelagh, if I'd known the truth I wouldn't have...'

It's time to intervene. One down. Several more to go though. 'Right, that's great. Now, let's move on. This is the hard part to believe for those of you who haven't been involved.' Taking a deep breath, I say, 'Seb and I are being haunted by the shade of a Pharaoh who died thousands of years ago. He's been interfering in our lives. We think we knew him before, in a previous life in Egypt.'

Ron is staring at me in disbelief. 'I never heard such nonsense in all my days. That is a seriously overworked imagination you have there, young lady. I do not believe a word of it. You cannot expect me to stay for this.' His strident voice and over-red face dominate the room as he struggles to rise from the grip of the sofa.

But, as I murmur, 'Please, humour me. Give me a chance to explain,' he reluctantly subsides again crossing his arms firmly over his solar plexus, fingers plucking convulsively at his cardigan sleeve. His face is set in a deep frown.

Aidan is nodding enthusiastically. 'Way to go, Miz Grayson.'

Mimi looks appalled. 'Haunted? By an ancient Egyptian? Anything to do with that book, lovey? I'm not sure you should have been reading such a thing.'

'Well, you did leave it there for me to find, Mrs B. Yes, I guess it had some part in it – and those other things you left. But I don't think it was the cause. He bothered Sebastian when he was in gaol in Egypt, and he'd been hanging around me even before I found the book.'

'Gaol? Sebastian, you never said anything…' Mimi's face is horrified. 'You told me you had a bad case of Pharaoh's Revenge.'

'Yes I did, Mum, just not the kind you imagined.' His grin seems to enrage her.

'You should have told me. I can't believe it. Imprisoned in that hellhole.' She bridles.

It's the only word I can think of. My lexicon of Mimi words is increasing all the time. She's more like a lion than a horse though. Is she trying to defend her cub, or simply furious that she was left out of the loop?

'You're right there, it was a hellhole. But I'm home safe now and we need to do something about His Awful Majesty. Send him back to his own time. We know quite a lot of the story. It's a weird one. There are some gaps, but we know our part in it – one or two of you were involved too.'

'I most certainly was not.' Ron huffs, pulling even further back into the corner of the sofa. Retreating into flinty stillness. 'Count me out.' He gives me an icy stare. 'As for you, Miss Grayson, you had better consider your future prospects at the library most carefully if you insist on carrying on with this charade.' He's about to say more when Aidan leans forward and interrupts.

'How about me?' He looks distinctly pleased at the prospect. 'Was I there? That'd be wicked.'

'We haven't identified you – yet. There's always a chance you were there, of course. But we know what Shelagh did, and you, Meski.'

Sebastian's ears have gone red again, there's still something he's not telling me. This is not the time to call him on it though.

'Mum. You had a leading part in that other life –'

Mrs B bridles again, looking ready to do battle once more.

I cut in quickly, 'Briefly the story is that Sebastian and I were being prepared for an initiation but, at the last moment, the Prince stepped in and took over. Meski saved Sebastian and took him to an island – the home of Yagut'd'eskia, the Prince's former wife. That's you, Mimi. Eventually the Prince killed me because I wouldn't birth a magical child for him. He wanted my heart to see him through the Otherworld when he died. Now he's trying again. We need to send him back. Do a ceremony with all of us present. Talk to him. Honour him in the old way. Get him to leave this world of his own accord. A week from today. That'll give us time to prepare. We have to get it right.' I barely draw breath, wanting to get it all out before anyone else intervenes. But…too late.

'This is all nonsense. Other lives? Ancient Egyptians breaking into the present? I have never heard such a thing. As for deliberately invoking this evil fiend, I am utterly opposed to the idea. The Bible expressly forbids us to raise spirits.' The voice splutters to a halt.

Ron is no longer calm. His cold reserve has evaporated. He's incensed. I would go as far as to say he's 'apoplectic'. The word fits his bulging eyes and engorged bright red cheeks perfectly. Visibly pulling himself together, he takes a breath and continues in a voice full of squeaky fury. 'On All Hallows Eve too. The night when the boundaries between the living and the dead are stretched thin. How could you even think of it? This is madness. What you are doing is beyond wrong. I cannot take any part it in.'

As he struggles to leave, Mimi tugs him back down. 'Oh yes, you can, Ron. What better night could there be?'

'It's unnatural, forbidden, I cannot be a part of it, not even for you, Mimi.' He harrumphs explosively. I've been dying to use that word but, as quickly as it passes through my mind, it's gone. There's no time to savour it now. I must concentrate. Mimi is continuing to reason with him, if you can call it reason.

'Ron, you appointed yourself the joint head of our magical group. It wasn't play-acting you know. We had a purpose. We have to carry this through.'

'I only did it to keep you happy. You know my heart wasn't really in it. You said if I did not take part, I would not be able to…' Realising that everyone in the room is listening intently, he breaks off muttering, 'Blackmail, that's what it was. Emotional blackmail. You can be a manipulative bitch when you want to be, Mimi. But you are not going to win this one.' Getting up, he storms out of the room and slams the door.

Seeing how his whole body shakes as he leaves, I ponder whether there hadn't been more than a little fear in his diatribe. Why is he so scared? Anyone in their right mind would be cautious, but his reaction seems excessive. The thought that he might have encountered the Prince flits through my mind. He'd have said something though, wouldn't he?

'Leave him to me,' says Mimi grimly. 'He'll be there, I promise you that. But I have a question. If I was the Queen, why aren't I being haunted by the Prince too?'

'Oh, you did a most impressive tie-cut with him, Mimi. I saw it in my mirror. You chopped him right out of your life. I expect that's why he didn't recognise you in this life. There was nothing left to hold you together.'

'I guess that explains it. You can tell me more later. Now, what do we need to do?'

'There's a formula, a particular way that the dead who were interfering with the living were addressed. A letter that has to be read out. It should be at the tomb. We'll have to fudge that one. It's a peculiar mix of praise and blame. But it seems to have worked in ancient Egypt, so there's no reason to think it won't work here. We need to write one for each of us, stating who we are in this life and who we were in that other. Saying what the Prince did to us back then – and now if he's bothered us in this present life. We've put together a kind of pro forma that can have specific details added.'

I hand them round. 'Let's draft one for each of us tonight. Then you can tweak them during the week. We'll leave Ron's until the ceremony. He doesn't seem to have played any part in that life so it will be a formality anyway. Meski, how about we start with you? Shall we tell you what we know?'

Grinning, Samantha holds out her hand for the letter. 'Okay, but I might be ahead of you. I have a few bits to add myself. This is making a lot of sense to me. Stuff I sort of saw in Egypt and haven't been able to stop thinking about since I got home. Aidan, perhaps you'd give me a hand. I've heard you've got a way with words.'

Sebastian swallows convulsively. What's wrong with him? Is this to do with what he's not telling me? But Aidan's speaking now.

'Could you include me? I'd like to do one too, if you don't mind, Phillippa. I know there's nothing to say about Egypt. But I do have things to say about my man's book. I can praise Himself up, flatter the minging old bugger. I smell Him lurking in the background. I know He's listening. But, you know, Himself's going to be astounded by what I have to say.'

'And by me,' says Shelagh, satisfaction in her voice.

Chapter 54

On the day of driving back disaster

The Otherworld

Racing into the Duat, gabbling his way through the weighing of the heart ceremony, Agni'ti makes the negative confession and apologises to the Lord Osiris for his haste. 'I need to find a way to move forward in time, I have to save her soul. It cannot be done here...but there is the fate of Egypt to consider...'

'Go forward in peace, Agni'ti. You are an initiated shaman-priest of the Two Lands. Your heart is big. Your power you have not lost. Age has not withered you. You know that time is a fluid medium that can be transcended and spiralled around. Go. Move sideways to meet yourself in the future. Find a time when you can bind His Majesty out of harm's way. He shall be released only when your daughter has found her own power, and that shall be aeons into the future. Mennie shall have need of you then.'

The Great Green God leans forward and points the way. 'A sidedoor out of eternity. Go. Leave the fate of Egypt in Men'ofer's capable hands. The gods shall guide him. Go!'

Speedily, Agni'ti exits. Sniffing the air, he exhorts the Gods to show him the way, to help him track the Prince through time. That oh-so-familiar smell of musky cloves with something more foul mouldering beneath reaches him on the wind.

Rushing forward, he sees his former master hovering over the body of a comely young woman, seducing her in her sleep. His Majesty is still trying to conceive that magical child on which he pins all his hopes of resurrection. As the young woman restlessly cries out and pushes against her dreams, Agni'ti looks through time and sees that her death is fast approaching. Her soul is stretched thin. Some tragedy has befallen her. She does not wish to live. Does His Majesty not realise that she has the plague? Is her beauty ensnaring him to the oblivion of all else? Why has he fastened on this soul? But the question has to wait until Agni'ti can place a binding spell that shall hold the Prince's soul to hers. Not for all time. No. Merely for long enough. There is no time in eternity. This shall suffice.

Tracing the magical sigils in the air, the tjaty incants, *'The Great Prince Khem Yar Khepher'set, Justified, blessed by his name, may the Gods keep His Majesty attached here forthwith to the body and soul of the young woman he covets. The shade of your Majesty shall not exist, nor shall your body. The shade of your Majesty shall not exist, nor shall your soul. The shade of your Majesty shall not exist, nor shall your flesh. The shade of your Majesty shall not exist, nor shall your bones. The place where you are shall not exist. Your name shall not be among the living. You shall be bound to this soul through eternity until released. So be it.'*

As the soul of the young woman leaves her body, the Prince growls and twists, caught in Agni'ti's trap, bound by the threads of lust and desire. 'You have not yet won, *tjaty*. I avenged shall be. Watch for me in your dreams.'

* * *

To be certain the binding spell will hold, Agni'ti visits the mummification chamber. Two mummies being prepared. Both young women. One of high royal birth, a priestess of Amun-Ra, shamed by a child conceived from a gardener. Quietly smothered during the birth before the child could see the light of day. The other the young woman to whom Agni'ti has tied His Majesty's soul. To Agni'ti's bewilderment, it is his *wowaei* who is being embalmed in the royal way. She is being substituted for the royal princess. It is her heart that will be weighed in the Afterlife. It is her coffin that shall hold the artefacts of rank. The princess is being prepared as a loyal servant. No one will examine her body closely, there shall be no scandal attached. The priests must maintain the secret at all costs. To Agni'ti's consternation, within the substitute coffin, a familiar scroll is being interred. His Majesty's precious book. How did that get there? What story lies behind that? He has no time to examine it now, but he will follow the book across time.

'Hah, Agni'ti, see how your plans go awry. You sought to bind me, but in that binding there is trickery beyond trickery. The mummy case shall tell one story. You and I know that there is another. Will you not release me now? I need to gain control of my book once again.' The voice is wheedling, seductive. When Agni'ti says nothing, it roars, 'Do as your Master says, *ntiu tjaty*.'

'Never, my Lord, we are beyond that now. My task from the Lord Osiris himself is to bind you, to prevent you from mischief. To keep you away from my daughter. I bind you to the two mummies, to their cases, to their resting place. You can read your precious book in the confines of the tomb. Eternally bound you shall be. *Isketi com niu Set ensu vi Osiris, excia Isis y Nephthys, inensui sa vasci.* So be it.'

As the young women are laid into their tomb and the doors sealed, Agni'ti hears his furious master calling, cursing, swearing to bring down the gods on his head. But it is done...for now.

* * *

Moving on through time, Agni'ti watches the tomb looters come. The arrogant fools who risk everything to disturb the dead. He sees young men gambling as to who will own the mummy case. Its contents, artefacts and the book have vanished, along with its sister case. The mummies ravaged for the treasures within their wrappings. No doubt to be sold to the eager buyers who swarm into the town. The Prince's soul shall be scattered to the four corners. The *neteru* shall keep him safely bound. To be certain, Agni'ti once again binds the Prince's soul to the lid. If it is to be removed to a distant land so much the better.

As he tracks the coffin and sees the calamities that befall those who covet it, he cannot but be elated by what happens to those who disturb the honourable dead. Who cannot let them rest in peace until the time of their rebirth. There is no need to curse these *nti hetis*. Their ignorance does that for them, assisted no doubt in this case by the malice of the spirit tied to it. His bitterness is absolute. It eats deep into his anguished soul. This is not how things should be.

What of the Prince's book? Cautiously, Agni'ti searches through time. Recognises the tome safe in the hands of a man blacker than those he has known before. Darker than a Nubian, but with the same delicate caste of features. A magician of power. The book will be safe with him. But no, a copy is made that crosses a vast ocean. The original stowed away in a hotel safe. Where, it appears, it lies forgotten until handed to a stately gentleman who walks with the aid of a stick. Agni'ti loses sight of it in the chaos of war.

Finally, he finds himself in the basement of a venerable stone building, almost as grand as a temple. Above him are displayed the treasures of his land, the fruits of incessant grave robbing. Publicly on view, a desecration beyond words. The mummies were never meant to be seen like this. A thousand souls cry out to him for release. But he cannot assist because of the one soul that must stay bound. To release all would be disaster.

He watches as three men, one the elegant gentleman who had become the keeper of the Prince's book in his beloved land, walk up the stairs. Mayhap he can track it once again. But, to his horror, they come to a stop before a glass case. Here is displayed 'the mummy case of the princess Amun-Ra'. Only he knows that it is not her body that was interred, nor the mummy it contained. And only he knows that two souls were bound together for all time. With horror, he sees that the soul of the young woman is speaking to the men. Following them down the stairs to the cavernous basement that is almost as cold as the tomb. They enter the cluttered lair of the rotund one, who tugs at his waistcoat with every step. The men are aware of her moving with them. Indeed, they encourage it. They do not see the shade that follows. The gleeful malevolence of His Majesty the Prince Khem Yar Khepher'set hovering behind them.

The girl pours out her tale of woe. Speaks of how the Prince never desisted from pestering her throughout her eternity. How he had intervened in the ritual with her appointed one. How she had been glad to die but it had not stopped His Majesty. Agni'ti had not known that would happen. Silently, he apologises to her for the torments she has endured. But your soul shall soon be freed, he promises silently. Once I have re-bound His Majesty. However, before he can act, holy water is thrown. An exorcism completed. The banishing undone.

'No, no,' he cries. But no one hears. No one heeds his warning.

The soul of the young woman disappears into the depths of eternal night, condemned forever to outer darkness. There is nothing Agni'ti can do. The Prince is free once again.

'Now to find My Book and Men'en'oferet,' The Prince hisses, leaving in a skittering of sand. 'Then your turn it shall be, *temum't seba.*'

Chapter 55

Allhallowtide

The church hall has been swept, decorated and consecrated. Dressed in my blue robe and delicate headdress, I have scoured every corner, asperged and incensed it. Dedicated it to the gods and goddesses of ancient Egypt. The walls are decorated with hangings and Egyptian posters – more treasures from the reclusive old lady that Mimi had kept 'just in case', as are the statues of the gods dotted around the room. A circle of chairs surround a gold-painted 'throne' unearthed from under the stage. I've carefully drawn a pentagram in golden glitter around it and placed pentagrams in all four corners of the room. Behind the throne, two subtly lit pillars stand invitingly at a portal to the Otherworld. Gauzy curtains cover the entrance. Behind them, a papyrus of the weighing of the heart ceremony entices the spirit home. Beeswax candles softly illuminate every surface, suffusing the air with syrupy-rich honey.

Thank goodness for amateur dramatics. I'd found most of what was needed stashed under the stage. That, and the few pieces from the shop, has transported the shabby hall into ancient Egypt. The air tingles with anticipation. Ozone crackles, another thunderstorm is brewing. Electricity plays over my skin as though I've been plugged into the mains. But, effective as the setting is, apprehension scuds through me. Can I really do this? Do I have the power?

Walking to the hall had been bizarre. Like moving through my own nightmare. Wraiths of fog hung around the streets, creeping up from the river like curled fingers from some old horror movie. A perfect stage set, except it was all too real. I shiver at the thought. Wish I'd accepted Sebastian's offer to escort me, but it seemed more appropriate to approach alone. I'd have felt less out of place if I'd worn my robe instead of neatly stowing it in an overnight bag with the other tools. The streets were thronged with raucous folk in Halloween costume. Their masks surreal in the misty sulphurous light through which giggling children weaved, trick or treating. I'd stowed sweets in my pocket to appease them. When a screaming skeleton jumped out in front of me, I'd dropped the bag. Fortunately nothing was damaged. Everything has been meticulously selected to enhance the ambience – and send His Majesty home. Hopefully I've got it right.

I'd glimpsed Tom, Spock ears atop an Armani suit. I'd know that swaggering walk anywhere. He hadn't made any effort to cover his face, too proud for that. He'd always been something of a secret Trekkie. So, His Majesty had kept his promise. Tom had finagled his old life back. That was fast. Judging from the giggling blonde in a scanty Uhura costume, he'd already found someone to keep him warm at night. Although, it's his companion who'll need warming up if the weather gets any worse.

The door slams open. Jumping with fright, dizzy with fear, my knees shake so much I can hardly stand. It's so silly to be here all alone, there's nowhere to hide.

'You're looking really good, Pips, like you did in those visions I had of you when we were back in ancient Egypt.' Sebastian leans over to kiss my cheek.

Recovering, I pull away, laughing, 'Careful. Don't smudge the eyeliner. This took me hours to get right. I should have taken up Meski's offer of help.'

'You're perfect in every way – that green enhances your almond eyes to perfection.'

The door opens again with a rush, the cold air making me shiver momentarily. A ghost going over my grave. But in which timeframe?

Agni'ti knows that the time for him to incarnate again is drawing near. It is the only way to stop His Majesty. To send Him to the Duat where he belongs. He can no longer stand guard from a distance. He must re-enter the physical world once more. He looks around, seeking the soul of his daughter so that he can be born near to her. But ahead of her in time. She will have need of his watchfulness. He will mentor her and keep her safe. This he promises – to atone for the loss of that young soul and for his carelessness in his other life. This time he will protect her. Ensure that she follows the way and does not stray. Ah, there she is, not so far into the future now. Quickly he prepares. Checks with the Lord Thoth, Keeper of the Records, the life that she is to lead. Inserts himself into her soul's plan. Seeks a position close to her, but not too close. They must not meet too soon. He doesn't want to draw the Prince to her until the time is right. He prays to the gods to keep her safe, and to keep his sight open so that he can see across the world to come. He needs all his prescience now.

As she enters with the others and looks around, Samantha says, 'It's a far cry from our tacky efforts. Feels authentic.' This time she's dressed in a chaste white robe, although her hooker heels peep from beneath it.

Her companion nods in agreement. But he's muttering under his breath, 'From ghoulies and ghosties, and long-leggedy beasties, and things that go bump in the night, Good Lord, deliver us!'

Ron is in his corn-bedecked costume, but has left the bobbing phallus behind. As he steps through the door, he says he didn't want to outshine His Majesty. Mimi tells him sharply to cut it out.

'Best not to upset His Majesty at this juncture.' His feeble attempt at humour isn't ringing true. His jiggling hands and white lips reveal how upset he is. This is one frightened man.

How did Mimi talk him round? He's here. That's all that matters. Mimi is guarding the doorway like a wary watchdog.

No way is Ron going to escape tonight. As Aidan slides around Mimi, pulling Shelagh behind him, I sigh in satisfaction.

Confidently, I step forward, the light catching the *menat* at my neck. My newly bobbed hair, darkened at the stylist's enthusiastic urging, gleams. It's a perfect backdrop for the headdress. Like that glimpse of myself I'd had in the magic mirror. Tall and assured, I raise the *uas* staff and address the group, gesturing to the chairs.

'Mimi, close the door and seal it with that sign I showed you. Then, take your places everyone please. I hope you've each brought your letter. It was important that you wrote it in your own words, from your heart.'

Mr McMeeney glowers, shifting restlessly on his chair, crumpling the paper in his hand. Mimi had probably stood over him while he wrote. But, before he can say anything, I continue. 'We are here to honour His Majesty the Prince Khem Yar Khepher'set, peace be upon him, and to intercede with the gods of ancient Egypt on his behalf. We call on those Gods and the Goddesses to be present to assist us in our endeavours.'

A sudden pressure fastens around my throat. Pulling the *menat* tight. Is someone trying to strangle me? Do I really have the power? Doubt corrodes my soul.

'Aidan, light the altar offering please.' I can barely get the words out and daren't trust my hands. I was so certain…so ready…but…quivers are coursing through me, my heart's beating so fast I'll explode. All the nerve endings in my body have come alive at once, tasting the air. Fear rattles the core of my being. Better get a grip. We *have* to do this.

Aidan jumps up and, as the wicks burst into life, frankincense suffuses the air. Breathing deep, calmed by its timeless, so-well-remembered aroma, I slowly circle the group, touching them on the forehead with the staff. Around each neck I place a single strand of beads. I hope that the larger Dalmatian Stone bead at the centre will suffice for 'spotty and very spotty'. I adore its dotty appearance. It reminds me of the Dalmatian puppy grandpa had bought me, until my mother... No, don't go there. The crystal book said that stones amplify your thoughts so I need to be careful.

'For your protection. In the name of the Lady Isis, remember who you were,' I intone. Ron tries to pull back, but is thrust forward by Mimi's unyielding hand locked against his back.

As I reach the golden throne, I pause for one final check. Everything is in place. I bow. 'I invite the Prince to join us. To sit once more upon his throne. To hear our exhortations for his wellbeing.'

In the Otherworld, Agni'ti holds his breath. Could this plan work? Or is his precious child endangering her immortal soul? The pattern is set. There is no more he can do. From this world at least.

A hot sandy blast signals His Majesty's arrival. Standing calmly, I see him outlined in the chair. Insubstantial though. Not at all the solid, light-sucking presence I'm used to. He appears uncertain, somehow hesitant. The air is not as arrogant as it usually is when he's around. I glance over to see if he's visible to the others but Mimi is busy holding Ron firmly in his seat. Samantha looks bored, buffing up her nails on her robe. Aidan is leaning forward intently, eyes firmly fixed on the throne. Shelagh has that air of quiet self-containment that so marked her out when we first met. Sebastian is staring grimly into space.

As the candles flicker in the aftermath of His Majesty's arrival, I look again at the throne. Is His Majesty already partway to his own time? Passing back into the Otherworld? Or, at least, considering it? If so, I don't want to call Him into the present again. Or, is He wary of entering a trap? Deep down, I'm certain that this ceremony is necessary. Standing before the throne, I bow again, taking out my formula and read in a clear voice.

'Greetings to His Majesty the Prince Khem Yar Khepher'set,

Keeper of the Two Lands. To the noble Prince a communication from Phillippa Ayesha Grayson, a librarian.

'Ayesha. Hah! She who must be obeyed. You kept that one quiet, madam. Anyone would think you were a heroine from a Haggard novel –'

'Hush Ron, I'm sure she'll explain later.' Mimi's hand on his arm is implacable despite the softness of her words.

'– formerly Men'en'oferet a priestess of Egypt. Oh you, noble heart of Osiris, I come to you in terror and respect. I swear to the gods that it shall be done according to what I say. I shall deposit offerings to you as soon as the sun has risen on the offering table I shall create.

'Your Majesty, what have I done against you? Why do you treat me so wrongfully? You have laid hands on me even though I commanded no wrong against you in this life or any other. I was in no way responsible for your death, nor was I the source of your debasement. Do not look at me in a manner malevolent and cruel.

'Your Majesty will recall that I was betrothed to my brother-priest Men'ofer, hand-fasted to him from childhood and undergoing the mystic marriage training over many long years. I was your loyal subject. But Your Majesty repaid my devotion by showing an evil disposition. You snatched away my beloved when we would have been bonded for all time. You defiled me and invaded my body, which you continued to do in my present life. You took away my heart. You pursued me over the centuries without my consent. You violated me and tore my twinsoul from me.'

Sensing Sebastian moving forward angrily, I smile reassurance at him, waiting to begin again until he has once more relaxed into his chair. The one I lost, restored to me. I'll keep him safe this time. But I don't vow for eternity. I've seen where that leads. No. Better to enjoy what I have for now. Let the future take care of itself. I glance around. Nothing much has changed. Ron hostile, Mimi placating him. Shelagh self-contained, Samantha bored and Aidan totally engaged. Deep breath and back to the job at hand. I can do this. I have to. If only my mother could see me now. I'm a far cry from that timid little brown mouse who took that old book home.

'Nevertheless, may the Great One favour you and be kindly disposed to you so that he will give you pure bread and the best beer with his two hands. May you wipe the slate clean and begin again. Return to your tomb, gather up your *ka*, your *ba*, your *sekhem* power, all the parts of your being and pass into the Otherworld so that you may be reborn. So be it.'

As I recede to my seat, a glow of satisfaction weaving through me, Sebastian steps forward. He's wearing a simple dark blue ghalabya with the *sem* visible at his neck. His hair is all bubbling copper curls that gleam in the candlelight. Nodding towards the throne, he says with dignity, 'Greetings to His Majesty the Prince Khem Yar Khepher'set, Justified, Keeper of the Two Lands. To the noble Prince a communication from Sebastian Warner, an academic, PhD student and archaeologist, formerly Men'ofer, an initiated priest of Egypt and mystic husband-to-be of Men'en'oferet, whom you stole from me.'

He glares at the empty chair, but hurriedly continues. 'Nevertheless, oh you, noble heart of Osiris, I come to you in terror and respect…' His voice thickens, emotion choking him.

'… You laid hands on me even though I commanded no wrong against you in this life or any other. I was in no way responsible for your death nor was I the source of your debasement. Do not look at me in a manner evil and cruel. Your Majesty will recall that I only wanted to serve the gods and my masters in the temple and be with my twinflame. But your Majesty repaid my devotion by showing an evil disposition. You stole my beloved from me. You cast me aside. You denied me my birthright. In my present life, you tormented me and caused me to be imprisoned.'

A skittering of the air and a sound like dry sand brushing

across the floor suggests that His Majesty may be preparing to say something.

Seb continues, almost gabbling. 'Nevertheless, may the Great One favour you and be kindly disposed to you so that he will give you pure bread and the best beer with his two hands. May you wipe the slate clean and begin again. Return to your tomb, gather up your *ka*, your *ba*, your *sekhem* power, all the parts of your being, and pass into the Otherworld so that you may be reborn. So be it.'

He bows towards the empty throne and returns to his seat. A faint whiff of His Malodorous Majesty passes through the hall, but the presence is far less malevolent. It's subdued, no longer *taunting*. More spoiled cabbage than sulphurous tomb rot.

An extravagantly robed priestess steps forward, lion mask in place. In an imperious voice, she holds out her letter and declaims, 'Greetings to His Majesty the Prince Khem Yar Khepher'set, Justified, Keeper of the Two Lands. To the noble Prince, a communication from Mimi van der Buerk, manager of a charity shop –'

'Erm, Mimi, sorry but you've missed a bit. Following the formula is important.' Mimi is in histrionic mode rather than ritual. But there's not much I can do to curb her excesses, except try to keep her on track. 'Stick to your script,' I urge.

'I know. But I can't say it. It's so not true.'

'Go on, please. Say who you were.'

'Formerly the Lady Yagut'd'eskia, Queen of Egypt and Wife to your Majesty.'

The air rustles ominously. His Majesty is listening intently. Becoming more physical with each passing moment. The dark mask is less transparent now, filled with something ancient, wild and foully enraged. Shadows curl around the room writhing like charred smoke, polluting the air.

Heart threating to leap out of my mouth, I hold up the mirror, willing him back on to his throne. 'Say what you can say. Lay it out for him. It's the only way. We need to get this done.'

'I know what I did against him. I know why he tried to lay hands on me. I know why I gave him the slip, the old bugger. Your Majesty will recall that I was your wife in Egypt. I was faithful to you for many years and gave you a daughter. But your Majesty repaid my devotion by showing an evil disposition. You tried to force upon me a magical child, an abomination into which you could be reborn. I told you that I had aborted the foetus. But this was not so. He was born on my island and sheltered by simple folk in Thebes before being given to the temple. That young man so callously cast aside by you was your son. The child you had wanted. He –'

'My child? You told me he was removed from life. Before birth killed. You had MY son? You kept him from MY Majesty?' He's back, at full throttle. Serpents hissing his rage.

'Yes, I did. I had to save him from your wicked schemes. I had to remove myself from Thebes and flee with our daughter –'

'Hang on, Aunty Mim, are you saying the old perv was my father too –'

But Samantha's question is drowned out by His Majesty's accusing bellow. 'With you, MY precious book you took.'

The roar, so close to her ear, causes Mimi to start and drop her script. She hadn't spotted His Awful Majesty rising from his throne to tower over her. Bending to retrieve the scattered pages, she's sent sprawling on her face. Clawing the paper to her, she resumes from the floor.

'Meski, be quiet, I'll explain it to you later. Thank the gods I did the ceremony that severed my connection with Your Majesty. May the Great One favour you and be kindly disposed to you so that he will give you pure bread and the best beer with his two hands. May you wipe the slate clean and begin again. Return to your tomb, gather up your *ka*, your *ba*, your *sekhem* power, all the parts of your being and pass into the Otherworld so that you may be reborn.'

'Bah. Reborn indeed. You denied My Majesty eternal life. Why would My Majesty listen to you, *hennu sha't*? You, whom My Majesty once loved above life itself. To whom My Majesty was to give the greatest gift. My…'

'You, you were a selfish old sod who thought of nothing but himself. Love. Hah! You knew nothing of love and you know nothing now. Look at how you've treated poor Phillippa – and Sebastian. Anyone can see they were meant to be together for all time. They are the ones who will birth the magical child, if there is to be one.'

Struggling to her feet, she advances on the minging air that is boiling with his sordid presence above the throne. 'You're a pervert. You took a child young enough to be your daughter and you violated her… you…you are a sodding disgrace and the sooner you return to your own place the better.'

In the Otherworld, Agni'ti calls out in alarm. Tries to still that vicious tongue. But, impotent, can only watch as she continues.

'I repeat, return to your tomb, gather up your *ka*, your *ba*, your *sekhem* power, all the parts of your being and pass into the Duat to be judged and reborn. Although, I'd as soon you stayed in hell forever. So. Be. It.'

Mimi stomps off to her place in the circle, sits down and folds her arms. 'So there!'

The Lady Yagut in all her glory. No wonder the pair of them argued. Both as stubborn and strong willed as each other – and nothing much has changed.

After a stunned silence, the air calms itself. The throne seems to give itself a shake as Samantha slinks forward on her hooker heels and waves her script at the waiting air. A sulky silence greets her.

'Salutations to His Majesty the Prince Khem Yar Khepher'set, Justified, Keeper of the Two Lands. To the noble Prince, a communication from Samantha van der Buerk, also known as Samantha Trotter, and, I now discover, formerly your daughter Mes'kia. Although you didn't seem to notice me much in ancient Egypt, you old git, except to leer and you –' Meski shakes her head. 'I practised this letter for hours. Determined to get to the end without faltering but I didn't know that missing piece of the puzzle. That I was Your Majesty's *daughter*.' Turning to Mimi, she asks bitterly, 'Why didn't you tell me beforehand?'

Who knows what she'll ad lib now. Mimi's tale has obviously stirred memories best dealt with away from here. Or are they? Wouldn't it be better to have everything out in the open?

Frowning, Meski resumes her script, 'Oh you, noble heart of Osiris, I come to you in terror and respect…' Her voice carefully blank, schooled into indifference. 'I was in no way responsible for your death nor was I the source of your debasement. Do not look at me in a manner malevolent and cruel.'

The air stirs and her icy control falters, her voice wavers as she continues. 'Your Majesty will recall that I was brought up in your palace as a small child. I loved my father, but you ignored me. Had me banned from your presence. Said I was not the magical child you sought. Even said that I was not your child at all. I must have been conceived through other means.' Tears slide down her face.

'I was thankful when my mother took me away. Your Majesty repaid my devotion by showing an evil disposition. You stole away the beloved of my heart. Almost killed him. I had to rescue him.'

Sebastian's face burns red. I look across enquiringly, acutely tuned into his discomfort, but he shakes his head and then nods to show he's okay. I'm not convinced, but turn my attention back to Samantha's tale of woe.

'But Men'ofer didn't want me, he only wanted his precious Mennie, and now he's got her and I'm alone.' Samantha's voice breaks again. 'Nevertheless. May the Great One favour you…'

She pauses and takes a deep breath, then rushes through the formula, ending by saying emphatically, 'So. Be. It.'

Stumbling to her seat, she wipes her eyes on her sleeve. 'Don't know why I'm so upset,' she mutters. 'He was a bastard father, like my bastard father in this life. Don't even know if he's dead or alive. Perhaps we should send them both to the Otherworld and let them stay there together. Get it on.' Her clenched fist is shaken in time to the words, flinging them both into eternity.

I admire her defiant stance, but perceive how she puts it on as a cloak over her misery. The question of Samantha's parentage is still unclear. The poor girl doesn't seem to have known her present-life father, or her mother, for long. It couldn't have been easy being brought up by Mrs B, no wonder... I'd better turn my attention back to the proceedings.

Patting Samantha's shoulder and handing her a pack of tissues, Shelagh has stepped forward in an embroidered turquoise kaftan. Her head is swathed in a scarf. She looks like a fugitive from the Sharm hotel's Egyptian fancy dress night. A rather decorous one. In Sharm, she had sat in the corner, smiling bemusedly and sipping her drink while the raucous party went on all around her. She hadn't seemed bothered by the noise. Ibra'him had been on duty that night. Attentive, if I recall correctly. Had they…? Best not think about that now. I'm not sure whether she has told Sebastian yet. Neither of them has said anything. Another secret. I'd so like everything to be neat and tidy. As if.

'Greetings to His Majesty the Prince Khem Yar Khepher'set, Justified, Keeper of the Two Lands,' Shelagh says with quiet dignity. 'To the noble Prince a communication from Shelagh Slattery, formerly Lik'e'bet, a nurse at the Royal Palace in Thebes. Servant to the priestess Men'en'oferet and before that, to your wife Yagut'd'eskia.' Murmuring the formula in a low voice, she steps towards the throne and asks, 'What have I done against you? Why do you treat me so wrongfully?'

Her colour is getting higher, as is her voice. Is she angry, or upset? It's hard to tell. I flinch as she reaches the throne.

'Your Majesty will recall that I cared for Men'en'oferet without ceasing. I was as a *mewet* to her. But your Majesty repaid my devotion by showing an evil disposition. You violated the virgin child when she were bonded to another. Used her for your evil magic.'

'What else did you do?' His Majesty's voice is silky. 'With what did you feed her so that she should not bear My child? How did you make My Majesty *sexty*, you *nedjem ndjmemit*?'

'Don't you call me an 'ore, you scumbag. You tore out the heart of an innocent child and substituted it for you own black *haty*.'

Hmm, Shelagh has a smattering of ancient Egyptian. Has Sebastian taught her, or is it far memory? I must remember to ask.

'But I know what it is to be deprived of your rightful son by that *sha't* of a wife of yours. She got mine in this life.'

Shelagh shoots a look at Mimi that would kill a lesser woman. Mimi simply smiles her cat-that's-got-the-cream smile and says calmly, 'We've been all through that. I did explain. Get on with it, Shelagh.'

'You caused Men'en'oferet to be buried without the proper rites. You're an anathema. Unnatural. I were thankful when you died and Agni'ti spirited you away. I am only sorry he didn't succeed in banishing you forever.'

She pauses, taking a deep breath and straightening her shoulders, before intoning in a quieter voice, 'Nevertheless. May the Great One favour you and be kindly disposed to you so that he will give you pure bread and the best beer with his two hands. May you wipe the slate clean and begin again. Return to your tomb, gather up your *ka*, your *ba*, your *sekhem* power, all the parts of your being and pass into the Otherworld – and stay there. So be it, you old bastard.'

Her face is furious as she takes her seat. Not much forgiveness there. Although I whisper, 'well done,' I'm not certain that riling the Prince like that was the right thing to do. But he seems to have gone quiet for the moment. Is he thinking it over?

Chapter 56

Going forth, justified

'Come on, Ron. It's your turn.' Mrs B pokes him out of his seat. She walks him to his place and goes to stand guard at the door. He won't escape this time.

'I told you, Mimi. I will have no part in this preposterous charade. Recreating ancient Egypt indeed. Speaking to the shade of an ancient Pharaoh, and a malicious one at that. On All Hallow's Eve too. Such nonsense.'

Despite his costume, Ron is clearly not about to confront His Awful Majesty. The man is unnerved. His face white and sweaty. As he turns and tries to shoulder Mimi from the door, the air above the throne thrums and hums.

'That smell. What is that smell? I have smelt it before, in the library. It's not the drains, is it?'

'No Ron. It's not. It's that malicious Pharaoh you're attempting to escape from. We have to send him back. For God's sake, get on with it.'

In the Otherworld, Agni'ti holds his breath. Needing to know how the plan will turn out. But a great sucking wind pulls him, compressing, choking, moulding, squeezing him down to the size of a pinhead. Rebirth beckons.

Not now…

Too late!

Gathering his robe around him as though for protection, Ron says firmly, 'I must say a prayer first, if you don't mind.' Before anyone has a chance to object, he says softly, '*Sanctify, O Lord, my soul, mind, and body. Touch my mind and search out my conscience. Cast out from me every evil thought, every impure idea, every base desire and memory, every unseemly word, all envy, pride and hypocrisy, every lie, every deceit, every worldly temptation, all greed, all vainglory, all wickedness, all wrath, all anger, all malice, all blasphemy...'*

The Liturgy of Saint James. I had no idea that Ron was into such things. That would have made a great opening. Wish I'd thought of it. His storming off had left the rest of us to formulate the ritual, but we could have incorporated this ancient plea. It's like the negative confession the soul made at the weighing of the heart ceremony. Was that its original source? But there's no time to contemplate this as Mimi steps in again.

'Yes, yes, that's enough, Ron. Do the proper formula. Now. I know you don't think you had any part in this, but better to be safe than sorry.'

'Erm, that is the problem, Mimi, I have come to believe that I did play a vital part in what happened to His Majesty. I doubt he will forgive me in a hurry. I am surprised he hasn't been haunting me all these years. Although in a way he has, I have had horrific nightmares ever since I was a child. It is only now that I understand them.' The hand nervously stroking his neat beard is liver-spotted. Strange, I've never noticed that before.

'Why, what did you do to him?'

'Tried to bind him into his tomb forever.' Hurriedly, he adds, 'I did it for the best of reasons, he...'

'YOU! You did this to me...you *temum't*!' His Awful Majesty has risen from his throne. Wind howls around the chamber, flapping the curtains wildly and catching the candles. For a moment there is a distinct danger of fire, but darkness intervenes. 'You have hidden yourself well, Agni'ti...' An uneasy slithering of serpent scales suggests that the Prince may be letting loose his pets. Silently, I point the *uas* staff towards them, commanding them to be still. Confident now that I can hold them with the power of my mind.

Ron stumbles, blasted by hot desert air that stinks of death's foulness. Choking, he covers his eyes and nose, desperate to breathe again.

Mr McMeeney – Ron – was *Agni'ti*? My gentle father in that other life? It can't be. How could he have changed so much? Why did I not recognise him? The man who tried to save me? Who bound His Majesty's soul? He had that much power? It's not surprising he was so vehemently opposed to this ceremony. Now it looks like I need to save him.

'Hold on a minute, Your Majesty.' My voice is firm. 'Light the candles again, Aidan. Let's have some light on this matter. As for you, Mr McMe… I mean, Ron. What exactly did you do – and why didn't you tell us? You knew we needed all the pieces of the puzzle. This might have made all the difference.'

'I did not want to believe it was true – that those nightmares were a former lifetime of mine. I was a good Christian – until Mimi got hold of me and dragged me into all her nonsense.' Glaring, he turns his back on his appalled lover and appeals to me. 'Do not make me do this.'

'I'm afraid you have to. Here, put it in your letter.' Fortunately I've bought a spare copy.

Reluctantly he takes the proffered formula. Stumbling over the words, he mutters, 'Greetings to His Majesty the Prince Khem Yar Khepher'set, Justified, Keeper of the Two Lands. To the noble Prince a communication from Ronald Arthur McMeeney, Chief Librarian, formerly…'

'Go on,' prods Mimi as he falters to a stop. 'You know you have to use your former title.'

'Agni'ti. Tjaty of all Egypt.'

'Tjaty? Over my dead body.' Incandescent with rage, the Prince is lighting up the room. He's all too physical as he roars his impotent fury. The pentagram and *uas* staff hold him in place. For now.

'Your Majesty *is* dead. That's the whole point of this ridiculous charade.'

'Don't argue with him, Ron. Get on with it.'

Right now, Mimi is even more terrifying than the Prince. She looks exactly like the Yagut'd'eskia I saw in my mirror. She could breathe fire at any moment and annihilate us all. 'Come on, Ron, do it...'

'Oh you, noble heart of Osiris, I come to you in terror and respect.' His voice is strengthening now. 'You laid hands on me even though I commanded no wrong against you –'

A bellow greets the words. "Did My Majesty no wrong? You...'

But Ron presses on. 'Your Majesty will recall that I worked tirelessly on your behalf, that I ruled the country when you yourself took no part. I kept the granaries full and the people fed. I kept your soldiers armed and your land safe from harm. I searched the land when your Queen left and gave you no comfort. I cared for your child in the hour of his need.'

Sensing that this is not the best direction to take, he hastens on. 'But Your Majesty repaid my devotion by showing an evil disposition. You killed my brother who spoke only truth. You murdered my dearest child and plucked out her heart. You would have killed me had you yourself not died. Regardless, I showed you only kindness in your last hours on the earth.'

"But not thereafter.' The roar is muted, the voice infinitely more menacing for its lack of emotion. 'It was after my death that you committed the worst of sins against My Person. Speak, tjaty, speak.'

'Yes, I admit, Majesty. I failed to inter the heart of my precious child in your body so that you could pass through the Judgement into the Otherworld. I plucked it out again and left you to wander as the unquiet dead. I interred your mummified body in a tomb far from your House of Eternity. I placed your heart in an empty mastaba surrounded by the bodies of donkeys, and failed to sacrifice myself and others to serve you in the afterlife.'

'And...' the silky voice is wheedling. "What else did you do?

Loyal tjaty?'

'I crushed your mummy and bound it into an unsanctified tomb with binding spells.'

No wonder His Majesty is furious. A funeral like that should have obliterated him forever. What went wrong?

'And…?'

'I found you again, later in time, and bound you to a coffin lid.'

'And…'

'Oh, all right. I failed to keep a sacred promise.'

''Precisely. For that delivered you shall not be.' Foulness whirls around the room. As Ron puts his hand up to cover his nose, His Majesty pounces. 'And, *ntiu,* you dare to wear the sacred sign of kingship on your insignificant chin. Imposter, be gone!'

Ron is thrust to the other side of the room by an invisible arm. His Majesty is breaking out of his magical confines.

Desperately Ron gabbles, 'May the Great One favour you and be kindly disposed to you so that he will give you pure bread and the best beer with his two hands. May you wipe the slate clean and begin again. Return to your tomb, gather up your *ka,* your *ba,* your *sekhem* power, all the parts of your being and pass into the Otherworld so that you may be reborn. May all the parts of your soul be released from the binding spell to reunite on the Other Side. In the name of the Lady Isis and Mary the Mother of Jesus I humbly entreat that you be released and returned to the Otherworld. So be it.'

As he picks himself up and stumbles to a chair, there is an absence of sound that is greater than any noise. The depths of the tomb have settled into the room. Everyone is holding their breath. Has His Majesty gone? I sniff, cautiously testing the still air. Is there the faintest trace, a memory left behind?

Or, is His Majesty waiting to see what Aidan has to say as he steps forward, holding out his arms palms up in supplication.

'Greetings to His Majesty the Prince Khem Yar Khepher'set, Justified, Keeper of the Two Lands. To the noble Prince, a communication from Aidan Doran, student, and formerly Paschal Beverly Randolph, sex magician and occultist *extraordinaire*. Oh you, noble heart of Osiris, I come to you in terror and respect… I was never one of your subjects. I am full of gratitude to yourself for teaching me the Great Work. For leaving me your book. Your Majesty will recall that, in my former life, I saved that book for posterity. Created a movement founded on its principles. Honoured yourself and tried to uphold your traditions. But your Majesty repaid my devotion by showing an evil disposition. In my present life you tried to pursue me, but I banished you without knowing who you were. Had I known, I would have spoken with Your Majesty. Learned from you. Thanked you. Honoured you. My esteemed mentor.'

How clever of Aidan, that silver Irish tongue certainly knows how to flatter the ancient shade. But his look is so sincere, he really means it. Will His Majesty think so too?

Aidan prostrates himself full length in front of the ersatz throne. 'Respect Ya Majesty.'

"Finally, someone appreciates My Majesty and offers Me what is My due. You are not like these twattling fools.' Is there a hint of laughter in the haughty voice? 'One day mayhap, who you truly are, Aidan Doran, you shall learn. Then the world must beware your power. Respect to you.'

Aidan brushes his hair from his eyes as he gets up and returns to his seat. 'Yeah, respect all round, Ya Majesty.'

Moving quickly, I take sweetly scented flowers, placing them on the offering table. Lighting a cone of musky incense, I break bread and spread it with honey. Pour beer and piles of wheat that spill over and fall to the floor.

'The offerings, Your Majesty. In abundance. Offerings that shall sustain you in the Duat until Ptah spins you on his wheel once more. *Gather yourself up. Return to the land of your birth.*

Stand before the throne of Ma'at. Face the Great God Osiris with Isis and Nephthys behind him. Beseech the Great God to admit you into the blessed afterlife. Say to him, "My heart is mine and pure, my heart is content with me. The doors of Duat open for me. May I endure and be a blessed spirit".'

I don't dare exhort him to seek forgiveness, certain his pride won't allow it. This will have to do. 'See, your heart is returned to you and an *ushabti* to serve and guide you on your way.'

I place an alabaster scarab on the throne alongside the execration figure I'd painted a soft blue but never got around to smashing. Thank goodness it had withstood the jarring when I dropped the bag. Holding the mirror up to face the throne, I command, 'Send him back.' A quick sideways glance shows it quiescent, dark and mysterious, no living being to be seen in its depths. Has he finally departed?

Sternly I recite, *'I am the Lord of Fire who lives on truth. The Lord of Eternity, Maker of Joy, against whom the otherworldly serpents cannot rebel. I am the neter in his shrine, the Lord of Slaughter, who calms the storm, who drives off the serpents, the many-named one who comes forth from his temple. Lord of the Horizon, Creator of Light, who illumines the heavens with his own beauty. Make way for me…'*

I hold up the mirror, its depths now squirming with forces I cannot bear to acknowledge. But I can direct them. Silently, I command, 'Be gone!' It's sucking at his soul, pulling him through time. 'Be granted Eternal Life in *Aaru,* Your Majesty. Be at peace. Return home. May your name live forever. So be it.'

His lips swoop on to mine, gently caressing rather than extracting the life from me. Nevertheless, they are unwelcome. Softly I murmur the words of John Donne.

'So, break off this last lamenting kiss, Which sucks two souls, and vapours both away; Turn, thou ghost, that way, and let me turn this.'

Once again, I command, 'Be gone from this world. Return to

your own. Farewell Your Majesty.'

A sound like thrashing wings, a slurping hiss, a last oscillation of the tomb. The portal closes. His absence is palpable.

Finally. Nothingness. Vast. Atavistic. All enveloping.

Slipping the now quiescent mirror into my robe pocket, I turn to the others and smile. 'He's gone. I think we can close our circle now.'

A stunned silence greets my words before the voices rush in together, tearing at my head as they try to make sense of what has happened. But I hold up my hand. 'Quiet. Please. Don't speak of it, or you may draw it back. It won't be of any value to discuss what's occurred now. Much better to let it settle. If we must rehash it, it should be outside our sanctified space.'

Quickly I circle the group, touching each of them with the *uas* staff. 'Go in peace. Remember to wear your necklaces. Now, please, everyone, go home.' Turning away, I wipe my lips. The aftertaste of His Majesty lingers. Honeyed cinnamon suffused with vile memory, will I ever be free of it?

In the Otherworld, two figures respectfully guide His Majesty to the First Gate. 'Go through with your own heart, Majesty. It has been cleansed and will bear the test.'

Beneath the Scales, Ammit settles back on her haunches. This is one soul she shall not consume. But she growls a reminder to him that it could so easily have been so.

I long to be home. A cup of cocoa in my hand. To wash away that aftertaste. I'm deflated, exhausted. Hollowed out. As Sebastian turns on the lights, I say wearily, 'Seb and I will clear this away.' The sacred space needs to be dismantled with as much care as it was set up. 'But, I'm so proud. We did it, we really did it. See you all tomorrow.'

'Okay, that's it. I'm done. Off to the pub. Anyone coming?' Samantha is already half out of the room, pulling off her robe to reveal a figure-hugging pelmet dress beneath. 'Ron? Mimi? Shelagh? How about you, Aidan? Coming?' She grins at him. 'You can be my toy boy for the night. I've always fancied one of those.'

Ron snorts and steps forward. Is he going to object on behalf of his old friend? Be the guardian of Aidan's morals? But, as Samantha grins and says over her shoulder, 'Heel, dreads-boy,' he steps back, presumably realising that she is joking. Is he lightening up at last?

Shelagh says tentatively, 'I suppose you two have things to do. Need any help?'

Looking round the room, I laugh. 'Yes, there's a fair bit of tidying up, but we can manage, thank you.'

As the door bangs shut behind them, I remember something Rainer Maria Rilke said. At least, I think it was him. *Whoever gives thanks for all circumstances receives new eyes and discovers things never seen before.* I'd loved his intensely lyrical writing when I studied him at uni. It incorporated so much wisdom. Aidan had showed gratitude and the Prince returned to his own time. Swiftly, I thank the gods of ancient Egypt and the Prince himself. Looking at Sebastian, I am truly grateful for all that has brought me to this moment.

As though sharing my thoughts, he pulls me close. 'Hmm, think of the reward that will follow. It's time for us now. But what's this about Ayesha? She Who Must Be Obeyed, eh. You kept that one quiet.'

He moves away so he can look into my eyes. The eyebrow is raised again. Blushing, I drop my head as I say, 'Oh that was my father. Apparently he was raised on Rider Haggard stories as a boy and swore that if he ever had a daughter he'd called her Ayesha so that she'd be powerful in her own right.'

'Well, it seems to have worked.' He puts a finger under my chin and drops a kiss on my forehead. 'Come on, the sooner we get this finished the sooner we can go home and relax.'

Smiling, we begin to pack away the temple. 'But, to be on the safe side, I'd like to go back to Egypt and do this properly one day.'

'I'll gladly come with you. We could even take your mothers. But I wonder, do you think...could we go home to our separate beds tonight? Start again at the weekend, have a proper date like we tried to before.'

Seeing how my eyes shine with love but must surely be etched with tiredness, he responds, 'Yes, of course, Pips, I'll see you safe to your door and then go back to my lonely bed.' But his grin shows me he's teasing and I snuggle into his sheltering arm as I pull the door shut behind us.

In the Otherworld two figures entwine, hands reaching out hungrily, tenderly touching a beloved face. 'Finally, dear heart. Our job is done. Come...'

Afterword: Truth can be stranger than fiction

This novel began with a series of dreams in which Phillippa revealed her story, ancient and modern. I simply had to get up in the middle of the night to record them. Time slid and slithered around the central characters, twisting and turning in and around on itself. Eventually they joined into one long narrative that wove through several time frames. The ancient book *The Alchemy of Night* was dictated to me by Paschal Beverly Randolph himself and, on researching his work, I found that some of it echoed his words rather too closely for comfort. Further investigation revealed that much of the Egyptian story could also be true and I have used Aidan's reports as a device to convey the historical and esoteric background.

For readers who are wondering how much of the story is truth and how much fiction, certain characters are taken from 'real life' – which as we know is often stranger than fiction. Sir E.A. Wallis Budge, who will feature with Sir H. Rider Haggard in the next volume of this trilogy, was curator of the British Museum. He travelled extensively in Egypt, collected artefacts and translated many ancient works. He was closely involved in the museum's 'haunted mummy' affair and is reputed to have said that never while he was alive would he speak of what he had witnessed but, towards the end of his life, he issued an official denial. He is also, according to my mentor Christine Hartley (the late Christine Campbell-Thomson, High Priestess of the Western Mystery Tradition), who was deeply involved in the occult and esoteric world of the time, reputed to have carried out magical rituals in the basement of the museum. Similarly his great friend, Sir H. Rider Haggard, was a Victorian/Edwardian writer who, as his autobiography shows, had many psychic experiences and travelled extensively in Egypt. There is no evidence – at least of which I am aware – that either Haggard, his great friend Andrew Lang, who belonged to the Society for Psychical Research and wrote extensively on psychic matters (Lang features in the next novel in this series), or Budge tried to exorcise the mummy case, but, according to Haggard, Douglas Murray certainly tried to and nothing would surprise me given the stories Christine told me about the metaphysical goings-on of the period. I only wish I'd recorded them at the time.

Murry Hope was indeed handed, by a stranger on a train, an ancient Egyptian papyrus detailing eight steps of the mystic marriage. Unfortunately the final steps were missing. She gave a lecture on it at the College of Psychic Studies in London sometime in the late 1980s/early 1990s, which I attended. To my knowledge, she did not write a book on the subject, but I took a liberty with this and other matters.

In case you're wondering, John Lennon has 'haunted' at least five women to my knowledge and the delightful Jewelle St James has written of her past lives with him and their contact from the Other Side.

Shelagh's young Egyptian is an amalgam of the experiences of so many older – and younger – women who go to Egypt. I've seen it so often over the years and you only have to look at online forums to see that it is getting ever more frantic and abusive. The young men are desperate to escape their country and are exceptional manipulators of the lonely. So sad in what used to be such a lovely, friendly country.

The texts and hauntings in Aidan's reports are all verifiable, as is the rather fascinating Paschal Beverly Randolph (or P.B.R. as he was known), and Aidan's sources can be followed by readers wanting to explore further. Aidan and his adventures with Paschal will be the final volume in this trilogy. I found *Paschal Beverly Randolph: a nineteenth-century black American spiritualist, Rosicrucian and Sex Magician* by John Patrick Deveney invaluable, along with online texts and Randolph's own pamphlets. Having completed the ancient book, I then found that Randolph claimed that his sexual magic was taught to him when he was initiated into the Ansairetic Brotherhood by a Nusa'iri woman one tumultuous night in Syria. I had transposed this initiation to Egypt, which Randolph visited on the same trip.

As far as ancient Egypt goes, at the time of a shift from pre-dynastic to dynastic Egypt, the capital was in the delta in the south of the country and, rather than the Valley of the Kings in Luxor (ancient Thebes), royal burials were carried out at Abydos in the south, a former capital, and the burial place of the legendary Osiris, god of the dead. At least one ruler is missing from the earliest dynastic graves, and the names of two grave-occupants not yet known at Abydos. Archaeologists are still working in the cemetery there. After I'd written this book, an academic dig report stated that an empty House of Eternity had been found with mummified donkeys buried around it and an encased heart in the centre. I had already encased this heart in a bag of sand and unmummified the donkeys – although this would have happened naturally in the hot sands.

Only much later would ancient Thebes become the centre of the flamboyant burial cult that brought us the contents of King Tut's tomb. In the earliest pre-dynastic times, minimal grave goods were interred and sacrifice of retainers was practised. Having written of Yagut as the shaman-priestess in all her awful (or should that be awe-full?) nakedness, I then discovered a statue wearing only a Bez mask and carrying a snake encrusted staff, along with a leather mask from the tomb in which it was found. It takes only a small leap of the imagination to envisage a priestess of My Lady Sekhmet, a shaman in her own right, wearing lion garb. Or, indeed, only the mask. The ancient Egyptians were proud of their bodies and not in the least prudish as statues and pictures on tombs and temples amply demonstrate.

With regard to hauntings in ancient Egypt, you only need to read the myriad domestic letters found between husband and wives, and deceased relatives, not to mention texts such as *The Instruction of Amenemhet* in which the ghost of a pharaoh instructs his successor son in how to govern the country properly, or the agony of the ghost Nebusemekh, to recognise that there was little boundary between the living and the unquiet dead. Ghosts could indeed be extremely physical and sexually active and create illness, misfortune and all round mayhem. Numerous spells to bind or banish them attest to how seriously this was taken. But little academic material is available as to precisely the way in which the rites were carried out. This is because Egyptologists who take an academic approach demand textual verification. However, phenomenological archaeologists and all those of us who work modern rituals within the context of ancient Egypt understand how important *heka,* magic, was. I would refer you to the writings of Normandi Ellis, Nicki Skully, Judith Page and others. After this manuscript was, as I thought, complete, I found a relevant blog from the Museum of Scotland at http://blog.nms.ac.uk/2017/06/23/ancient-egyptian-tomb-warnings-curses-and-ghosts/ which quotes: 'Watch out not to take (even) a pebble from within it outside. If you find this stone you shall <not> transgress against it.' Too late to assist my protagonists, although I could slip in a reference to it. But nevertheless reinforcing what I had already known and it made a perfect epigraph for this book. My thanks to Dr Dan Potter for the translation. Unfortunately I found it a day after his exhibition had closed. It would have been worth the long trip to Scotland to see it!

My own inner shamanic Egyptian journey was profoundly heightened by Alan Richardson and Billie John's *Inner Guide to Egypt.* A book of which I never tire. It always accompanies me in the Nile. In the course of my academic research, I found Jeremy Naydler's books and Kerry Muhlestein's article extremely helpful in setting out an academically acceptable understanding of something that I had recognised intuitively as soon as I approached ancient Egypt. See Jeremy Naydler's

Temple of the Cosmos, Shamanic Wisdom in the Pyramid Texts and various other works. Kerry Muhlestein will be found on www.academia.edu/526114/_Empty_Threats_How_Egyptians_Self-Ontology_Should_Affect_the_Way_We_Read_Many_Texts_in_The_Journal_of_the_Society_for_the_Study_of_Egyptian_Antiquities_34_2007_115-130.

The chapter headings are for the most part taken from ancient Egyptian love poetry and funerary texts. Also the draft works of First World War poet Wilfred Owen, whose presence in my study I was privileged to host for three months that were set outside time (see my *Book of Why*, Flying Horse Press). Thanks are due to the late Dominic Hibberd for permission to quote from the draft poems. Thanks are also due to Tesco and www.timwoods.org/the-london-slang-dictionary-project/ for their online dictionaries of street slang. They no doubt went out of date almost before they appeared on the web, but they were useful in fabricating Aidan's 'street talk', as was the young guy who gave me the idea in the first place but who prefers to remain anonymous.

For readers who are interested in the properties and mythology of crystals, see my *Crystal Bibles* and other crystal writings. There is indeed an ancient history to be discovered, see www.judyhall.co.uk and my crystal community.

The Alchemy of Night Enchiridion: the tantric sexual practises of Ancient Egypt will be available for readers wishing to consult the ancient tome and the practices therein for themselves later in 2018. *A Ravaged Shadow: the secret life of Rider Haggard* and *A Bangin Guy: a forgotten 19th century occultist and sex magician* will follow.

Aidan's reports

Magic mirrors

The use of magic mirrors for scrying – seeing what is hidden – goes back far into history. Polished stone mirrors have been found in Stone Age graves and were popular in ancient Egypt and with the magicians of the nineteenth century occult revival. The Mexican god of destiny and divination, Tezcatlipoca, used obsidian mirrors as 'speaking stones'. They are truly magic.

The Goddess of Love

In Egypt, the Love Goddess, Hathor, was the patron of music, dance and beer. This lady really liked to party. She wore the all-seeing sun disk eye of her father Ra on her head. She knew everything that went on not only on earth but in the sea and the heavens – and could get into your head as well. You had to be careful what you thought when this lady was around. There was no messing with her. She carried a shield that protected you from harm but also reflected things so you saw their true meaning. From this, the magic mirror was born. On one side the magic eye showed faraway things, you could sneak a peek into the future, on the other what was going on inside you. You had to be brave to look into the mirror. But once you did you could see your true love, check out whether someone was being faithful to you, and find out what's going on.

Medieval mirrors

The astrologer and magician Dr John Dee, who augured for Queen Elizabeth I, owned several magic mirrors and 'shewstones' (polished crystals). Lacking the skill himself, he employed a scryer (or conman depending on who is telling the story), Edward Kelly, to look into the mirrors, call up angels and foretell the future for England. His inky black obsidian scrying mirror, which originally came from Mexico, is on show in the British Museum and it still has images moving in its spooky depths. After Kelly's demise, Dee employed other scryers, stating that the best of them were young, virgin, pristine, untouched.

The modern occult revival

Although crystal and mirror gazing never really died out, it was revived by 'new' occultists early in the Victorian era. The English clergyman Andrew Lang, a friend of the novelist Rider Haggard, wrote a treatise on scrying giving many examples and offering psychological explanations. (*The Selected Works of Andrew Lang*, Kindle version.)

Mirror scrying was particularly important for the American sex magician Paschal Beverly Randolph. He learned it from his magical contacts during visits to England and also from Baron Jules Denis du Potet de Sennevoy in Paris. Du Potet practised mesmerism and performed before Napoleon III. He used drugs and somnambulism to induce trance states when working the magic mirror to connect to the dead and to 'celestial spirits' that had never had a body. Swedenborg, founder of mesmerism, used a magic mirror to collect the scryer's 'magnetism' to power the seeing. This work was continued by Cahegnet who wanted to reach the highest states of consciousness. He created the complex mirror used by Paschal Beverly Randolph and his followers.

First off a mirror had to be consecrated. For Randolph, this seems to have involved shooting off on to the mirror. If sexual fluids from a woman could be added, so much the better. The mirror also had to be bathed regularly and was put out in the sun and moonlight to recharge. The mirror was also charged with magnetism. 'Magnetism', the animal force, was important in inducing clairvoyance – an ability to see beyond everyday awareness. According to Randolph, 'A mirror is the means of a better, and far more reliable clairvoyance than nine out of ten would suspect' (*Guide to Clairvoyance*). But, he says, 'There is another secret about them which can only be revealed to such as have and used them! – and not then till they shall have proved worthy of the knowing' (*Eulis*). He hints that this may involve sexual magic and the charging of the mirror with sexual forces and fluids. French writers were more open about this. Randolph used different mirrors for 'fortune telling', 'seeing absent friends', magical work and what he called 'creating ethereal lanes through which magnificent supernal realities could be seen'.

The Theosophist Madame Blavatsky also wrote about magic mirrors. She seems to have known about the sexual dance with which the Brahmins of India charged up their Muntra-Wallah mirrors. Virgins first gathered black 'parappthaline gum' and left it to settle for forty-nine days. Two brides and two grooms carried the gum in pots to the sacred fire and performed a 'sensual dance' around it. By the end of the ritual the gum had become rose coloured. It was smeared on a glass plate and left to dry to form a mirror. An English Colonel, William Gifford Palgrave, who wrote about the ritual, was allowed to look in the mirror and saw a large inheritance resulting from the death of one of his relatives. Which came true. Apparently these mirrors were found all around the world (*Paschal Beverly Randolph, the biography*).

The Mirror of Hathor: the magic mirror ritual

Traditionally carried out in the hour before sunset, the Mirror of Hathor ritual should be done once you have bathed in rose oil and changed into clean robes, but fresh clothes will do fine. Use a double-sided bronze, silver or crystal mirror if possible. If not, an old-fashioned hand mirror will do the job. The clearest side shows you what is deep inside yourself or tells your fortune, a duller side turns back bad vibes. Burn rose incense as it is Hathor's scent.

- Invoke the Lady Hathor, mistress of prophecy, music and joy. Invite her presence at your side to show you anyone's past, present and future; or use a traditional invocation to Isis:

  Blessed Isis, celestial mother, nurture and care for me and support me in times of affliction. Help me to seek out and reunite the lost fragments of myself and to penetrate the mysteries of past, present and future.
- Place the mirror so that it catches the last rays of the sun, or light a candle and place it to the side so that the light reflects in it.
- Tilt the mirror so that you cannot see your own face unless you want to see into yourself (but be ready for a bit of a shock if you do).
- Cover the mirror with smoke from the incense or breathe on it.
- Ask your question.
- As the smoke clears, watch the images that form deep in the mirror with your eyes half closed.
- When you have finished, clap your hands over the mirror to clear the images.

Interpreting the images

If the mirror is double-sided, one side is your inner self, the other the outer world.

If an image is moving away, it is an old one. The past may still be influencing you.

If the image is coming closer, it is current or something new is coming into your life.

Images on the left connect to actual physical occurrences. Images to the right or centre are symbolic and metaphorical.

Anything near the top is urgent. Things to the side are less important.

Big images are Very Important.

A Ritual for Banishing the Badass Guys
Aidan Doran

Aleister Crowley (12 October 1875–1 December 1947) was a phat occultist who popularised ritual magic in the West and founded a new religion, Thelema, which he got from an Egyptian spirit, Aiwass. Crowley was the first rudeboy. The role model for the 1920s cult classic black-and-white film *The Magician*. The newspapers of the 1920s and 1930s demonized him, dubbing him 'the wickedest man in the world'. His philosophy was 'do what thou wilt' and he appealed to people who wanted to revel in excess. He died penniless and forgotten in a boarding house in Hastings. But, twenty years after his death, his 'magick' was part of the crazy sex, drugs and rock 'n' roll lifestyle of the 1960s. Crowley was a heroin addict and a member of several occult organizations, setting up the Ordo Templi Orientis. A prolific writer and poet, he was also a world traveller, mountaineer, chess master, artist, yogi, social provocateur and bisexual sexual libertine who swung both ways. Before Crowley, magic was for initiates only. It had to be earned and took years of practise. But magic – which he spelled 'magick' – to obtain wealth, happiness and power can be practised today by anyone as it isn't a secret no more thanks to Crowley.

In his writings, the self-styled Great Beast says that you must create a safe space for ritual work – and he tells you how to banish the badass guys when they come calling.

According to Crowley, his practices stemmed from ancient Egypt and the badass guys were as bothersome then as now. Some of the Undead were real psychos. Proper whack jobs. His 'Lesser Banishing Ritual of the Pentagram' gets rid of the badass guys, but Crowley says in *Magick in Theory and Practice* 'those who regard this ritual as a mere device to banish spirits, are unworthy to possess it. With it you are sealed off from the outer world of ignorance and darkness, from the false and the unseemly, and are attuned to the Light.'

The ritual uses the five-pointed star pentagram to create a safe place in the astral as well as the physical world in which you may safely engage in magick. The pentagram has supremacy over lying, deceitful spirits, in other words the badass guys and the Undead. The usual magical preparations are required: bathing, clean robes and sanctified space. Also the study of appropriate books, meditation and focused intention – and a specially regulated breathing pattern. This creates an aura around your body described by Crowley as 'a natural fortress within yourself, the Soul impregnable'. He calls the aura 'the outworks'. The aura has to be sensitive to impressions so it knows when the badass guys are near, but it also needs protection so that nothing gets through it. In what Crowley describes as an ordinary man the aura should be 'bright and resilient'. In a magical adept it is 'radiant'. When you're ill the aura becomes weak, flabby, torn at the edges, cloudy and dull. It lets the bad guys in.

The Banishing Ritual

- Draw a five-pointed star on the floor with chalk or your finger, or imagine it. You can do it with a magick wand if you want. Start at the top and trace it in front of you. It will burst into fiery flames. Return to the first point to close the star.

- Stand in the centre facing the east. Breathe slowly and regularly, fully releasing the breath before you inhale again, with a long pause between the breaths.

- Raise your hands to your forehead with your hands together as though praying. See light streaming down to form a ball above your head. Intone the word *Atum* as you do so.
- Bring your hands to your heart. Draw a fiery pentagram in front of you.
- Place your hands over your heart, turn south and draw another pentagram.
- With your hands over your heart, turn to the west and draw another pentagram.
- With your hands over your heart, turn north and draw another pentagram.
- Say: "I call on the gods of ancient Egypt to protect me, filling the space around me with Light. For about me are the flames of the pentagram." [Crowley says if you prefer the Archangels you can substitute: Before me Raphael, behind me Gabriel, on my right hand Michael, on my left hand Auriel.]
- See the light above your head coming in a beam of light straight down through your body towards the centre of the Earth anchoring you. This is your protection.

Ghostly goings-on in Ancient Egypt and elsewhere
Aidan Doran

Most of what we know about the dead in ancient Egypt comes from the tombs, the Book of the Dead and other texts, and from letters written from the living to the dead – or the Undead. The post-death state wasn't that different from life. People feasted and played, had sex, and life carried on almost as normal – most of the time.

Many of the magical practices of the Egyptians were concerned with preventing or counteracting disturbances from the actions of the Undead. The ancient Egyptians believed the dead lived in the Otherworld. They demanded respect to keep them content. The relatives visited the tomb regularly and made offerings. If not, the dead were vexed. They became the Undead. The *Oxford English Dictionary* says that the word means 'clinically dead but not put at rest'. The Undead could put the evil eye on the living and caused illnesses and bad things to happen. Letters were left for the dead, and spells to protect the living. There were helpful spirits who could be called upon but the malicious Undead who had not passed the entry test for the Otherworld were damned for eternity and they were the ones to watch out for. Most Undead didn't travel very far from their tomb, although a few did with dire consequences as we'll see.

The Undead in Ancient Egypt

In one text, a wandering spirit has been causing trouble and the High Priest deliberately invokes the Undead to settle the matter. The Undead, Nebusemekh, pours out his agony at his tomb having collapsed leaving him with no home. The saddo complains about being exposed to winds in winter and overheated in summer, left hungry and without food. Offerings have ceased to be made and he cannot be sustained in the Otherworld so he becomes Undead. To keep him quiet, Nebusemekh has to be bribed with a new tomb and offerings and he isn't afraid to negotiate for what he wants.

The High Priest Khonsemhab climbs up on to the temple roof. He invokes the gods of the sky, the earth and the underworld; the south, north, west and east directions, saying: 'Send to me that august spirit.' When Nebusemekh arrives he tells him: 'I am your friend who has come to sleep tonight next to your tomb so that I may help you.' The High Priest asks him to tell him his name, his father's name, and his mother's name that he may offer to them. Names had potent magical power in ancient Egypt.

Then the High Priest of Amun-Re, King of the Gods, says to Nebusemekh: 'I shall have a sepulchre prepared anew for you and have a coffin of gold and zizyphus-wood made for you. I shall have done for you all that is done for one who is in your position [dead].' The High Priest intends that the spirit will live safely – and quietly – in the Otherworld and not exist as an Undead.

The saddo tells the priest that he was an important person. He boasts that his Pharaoh gave him four canopic jars and a sarcophagus of alabaster. He was laid to rest in a tomb within its shaft of ten cubits. But now the ground beneath has collapsed and dropped away so that the wind blows and 'seizes his tongue' – though it doesn't stop him complaining. He moans he has been promised his tomb will be restored four times but nothing happened. The High Priest replies: 'I shall have five men and five maidservants devoted to you in order to pour libation water for you and have a sack of emmer [wheat] delivered daily to be offered to you. Moreover, the overseer of offerings will pour libation water for you.'

But the spirit is a minging old bugger and complains: 'Of what use are the things you do?' He wants a nice solid rock tomb that won't wash away again.

The High Priest sends out his men to find a suitable burial site. The three of them return and say: 'We have discovered the excellent place to make the name of the spirit endure.' The text tells us that 'they sat down before him' and 'made holiday', in other words, had a party. The text ends at the point where the High Priest returns to spend a night at the new tomb and so we don't know whether the old bugger was satisfied with his new tomb or not.

Hauntings happened to ordinary guys too. A husband wrote a formal letter to his dead wife moaning about the troubles she'd brought upon him. He reminds her how well he'd treated her when she was alive and how he doesn't deserve her evil because he is one of the good ones. He sets out what he's done since she died three years ago and reminds her that he hasn't had sex with any other woman since. He has to write the letter, go to her tomb and read it, and then tie the papyrus to the statue of her in the tomb so that her *ka*, who lived in the tomb, would understand. We don't know whether the letter worked.

Similarly, in another letter, Heni writes to his deceased father Meru asking him for assistance in preventing someone called Seni from appearing to him in dreams. Apparently Seni thinks that Heni was responsible for his death. Heni begs his father to guard him at night so that his dreams can no longer be disturbed. Many similar letters exist.

The Undead on their travels

The Undead could travel, especially when attached to an object or a part of their previous body. In his memoirs Sir Alexander (Sandy) Hay Seton, 10th Baronet of Abercorn, tells how in 1936 he and his wife, Zeyla, travelled from Edinburgh to Cairo. This trip made Sir Sandy believe that his family was forever cursed. They stayed at the luxurious Mena Hotel, and Abdul, one of the staff, told them that his brother could show them a newly discovered tomb. After an early breakfast they were taken into a shaft being excavated in the shadow of the pyramids. The baronet said: 'I had a feeling in my bones that something was going to happen over this and it was only with the greatest of difficulty that Zeyla cajoled me into going with her. I wish earnestly to God that we had not gone!'*

Ushered down thirty roughly hewn steps, they were led into a cramped and airless room. On a stone slab the disjointed remains of a female skeleton lay in hardened mud. The tomb had been flooded by the Nile, which caused much damage. Sir Sandy quietly whispered a brief payer for the lady's soul and left to smoke a cigarette. Husband and wife had their photo taken and returned to the hotel. But, secretly, his wife had removed a bone and placed it in her pocket. She confessed to her husband at dinner that evening and showed him the bone which, according to Sir Sandy, looked like a grotesque, heart-shaped digestive biscuit. It was packed away in her travelling trunk and forgotten.

When Sir Sandy and his wife returned to Edinburgh, Zeyla showed the bone to dinner guests. As it amused them, she decided to display it in a glass case in their drawing room. Within an hour of the bone being set upon the table, stones from the parapet crashed down almost hitting the departing guests. During the next weeks the family's sleep was disturbed by many bumps, bangs and thuds. The Undead was moving around.

Sir Sandy locked the drawing room door and kept watch. After several hours when nothing happened, he went to bed. He repeated this for several nights and finally gave up, going to bed at his usual time. Some hours later his hysterical wife woke him saying someone was wrecking the drawing room. Their nanny had already reported hearing footsteps and noises from the room. Taking a poker from the fire, Sir Sandy went downstairs to investigate. When he unlocked the door chaos greeted them. Furniture was overturned and books were flung about but the bone was undisturbed. The windows remained locked. Sir Sandy thought they had a poltergeist and was determined to destroy the bone but his wife was vexed about that idea. His nephew Alisdair Black saw a strangely dressed figure, wearing a sheet, going up the main staircase and many other incidents occurred.

When a newspaper reporter from the *Daily Express* nosed on to the story, he was lent the bone to keep him quiet. He returned it without incident but was seriously injured in a car crash shortly after – as happens to many people involved in these ghostly goings-on. Another reporter, from the *Scottish Daily Mail* this time, took the bone to photograph but became seriously ill with peritonitis the very next day.

At a Boxing Day party one hundred guests were present when the bone hurled itself across the drawing room as the guests were served cocktails. The party didn't last long after that! A furore erupted and Howard Carter, the guy who'd found King

Tut, wrote to Sir Sandy warning: *'inexplicable things could happen and would continue to happen.'*

One day while Zeyla was out, Sir Sandy had his uncle, a Benedictine monk, exorcise the bone and burn it in the fireplace. His wife never forgave him and they got a divorce. But Sir Sandy said peace had returned to his house.

These are by no means the only contemporary reports of ghosts remaining behind to roam the landscape and haunt the living. In Egypt, Pharaoh Khufu (*c*.2589–2566 BC) is still said to emerge from his Giza pyramid at midnight dressed in the traditional armour of Egypt. People in nearby houses are surprised to find the ancient ruler entering their homes today and commanding that they leave. He thinks he is still in his own time. At Tel el Amarna, Pharaoh Akhenaton is said to drive a chariot pulled by a black horse. Many unbelievers have seen him. So imagine what it was like in ancient times when people actually believed it was not only possible but quite normal.

You don't need to have a body to have a ghost. In 1885 a museum was built in Cincinnati, USA, to house artefacts being brought back from Egypt and elsewhere. A century later it began to be haunted but the source of the ghost is not a mummy. It's a sarcophagus in the Ancient Egyptian Room. Purchased in 1976, it remained in a storeroom for a decade. When it was put on display in the 1980s, people immediately began to report strange happenings. A featureless cloud of black smoke would rise up from the sarcophagus, head for the ceiling, and disappear. One day a security guard was taking a nap in a storage room immediately above the sarcophagus. He reported feeling great dread and a sense of something being very wrong. A vile face looked out at him. Terrified, he tried to escape but the face floated in front of him, blocking his way and following his every move. Eventually the spectre tired of playing tag and dissipated and he was able to get out. Other guards reported scary stuff in the same room. One heard ghostly footsteps and another, someone whispering in a strange language. Was the former occupant of the sarcophagus upset by its removal to a strange land? Was he protesting at a tombless non-burial that he was not consulted about? His coffin being put on display for all to see? The ancient Egyptians would certainly have believed so.

It is reported that the disused platform of the former British Museum tube station in London is haunted by a mummy wearing only a headdress and a loin cloth. Apparently, while the station was still open, a national newspaper offered a cash reward to anyone brave enough to spend a night alone there. No one was.

The priestess of death

There are other reports of ghostly happenings within the British Museum itself caused by a haunted mummy case lid – often said to be cursed as well. At the time, Sir E.A. Wallis Budge, keeper of the collection, refused to comment on what he experienced saying he'd take it to his grave, but his staff were loud in their protests. One keeper reported seeing a horrible yellow face rising up from the case. Other staff heard 'wracking sobs and loud knockings'. Budge is even said to have suggested that the mummy caused the First World War and he moved it to a place of honour to placate its owner. Peter Underwood in Haunted London (1974) states, 'It does seem indisputable that from the time the mummy case passed into the possession of an Englishman in Egypt in about 1860, a strange series of fatalities followed its journey and even when it resided in the Mummy Room at the British Museum, sudden death haunted those who handled the 3,500-year-old relic from Luxor.'

In 1934, Budge finally issued a statement saying, "No mummy which did things of this kind was ever in the British Museum. The cover never went on the Titanic. It never went to America." (Marjorie Caygill, *Treasures of the British Museum,* Harry N. Abrams, Publishers, 1985, page 102.) But although Budge might have scoffed at the idea of a curse, at soirees, dinner parties, and the paranormal "ghost clubs", so beloved of the Victorians, it was avidly discussed. In 1904 a dashing young, and ambitious, journalist named Bertram Fletcher Robinson scooped a front-page typically tabloid article in the *Daily Express.* Headlined 'A Priestess of Death', about an allegedly haunted mummy, it reported, 'It is certain that the Egyptians had powers which we in the twentieth century may laugh at, yet can never understand.' People flocked to the museum to see the case.

The mummy case had been purchased in Luxor and the four men involved supposedly became the first victims of the curse. The various stories circulating say, for instance, that the man who bought Amen-Ra walked into the desert a few hours later and was never seen again. The day after the visit to the Luxor excavation another of the young men was shot accidentally by an Egyptian servant and his arm had to be amputated. The two remaining men returned home, but one of them found that he was financially ruined as his bank had failed and the fourth man fell ill, became unemployed and was forced on to the street selling matches. In another story the finder, Murray, and his friends drew lots to determine which of them would buy it. Murray won and the case was packed up and on its way to his home in London the same evening, with equally dire consequences. Having returned home after being shot and losing his arm to gangrene, Murray unpacked the case and, instead of beauty, found the object 'chilling and ominous', the face on the board now being full of malevolence. The case ended up in the British Museum.

In 1890, Murray contacted the museum to ask if he could hold a séance in the Egyptian Room with his colleague, the journalist W.T. Stead, who wrote one of the first articles about the 'mummy's curse'. According to Budge, 'they wished to hold a séance in a room and to perform certain experiments with the object of removing the anguish and misery from the eyes of the coffin-lid.' Stories like this sell newspapers. Murray was turned down, but the papers reported the story anyway, mixing together the abortive séance, the creaky old ghost story, the coffin lid and Douglas Murray into what www.darkestlondon says is 'a composite nonsense tale that's survived for a century.'

The mummy was allegedly bought from Murray by a London businessman who donated it to the British Museum after his house nearly burned down and three of his family were injured in a road accident. One of the workers that had unloaded the mummy at the museum broke his leg, a second one died mysteriously and the truck carrying Amen-Ra reversed trapping a pedestrian. A journalist photographer who reported the story of the curse allegedly shot himself when his photograph of the sarcophagus showed a human face. Dire events indeed.

At least one prominent Spiritualist was said to be involved in a rescue circle to release the tormented soul. The case was even rumoured to have been on the Titanic when it sunk but this isn't so. The story of the mummy's curse still persists, however.

In the 1899 novel, *Pharos the Egyptian*, by Guy Boothby, Pharos asks the son of a famous Egyptologist, "And pray by what right did your father rifle the dead man's tomb?" He continues by asking, "Perhaps you will show me his justification for carrying away the body from the country in which it had been laid to rest; and conveying it to England to be stared at in the light of a curiosity." Was he talking about the priestess of Amen-Ra? The reconstruction in Piccadilly of Seti I's tomb, in 1821, was a sensation and started a craze for 'mummy unwrapping'. Notable surgeons publicly unwound mummy bandages and chiselled away at the bitumen preservative for hours on end in front of fascinated audiences. This morphed into horror stories in film and fiction where the dead unleashed vengeance on the living. Boris Karloff played the reanimated magician Imhotep in the 1932 horror film *The Mummy*. It was but one of a long line of tales that culminated in Indiana Jones and his 'Temple of Doom'.

Douglas Murray was a member of the 'Ghost Club', a group

of ardent Spiritualists. From the upper echelons of society, he knew many diplomats, colonialists, painters and writers and was a friend of Wallis Budge and William Flinders Petrie. He drew on his contacts to spread the story of his curse.

What the Egyptians believed and what could be done

The Egyptians believed that after death the soul went through the weighing of the heart judgement and, if it passed, took a trip into the next world. If not, it became the Undead, damned to wander for eternity. In the Otherworld an *akh* – transformed spirit – could be activated. The *akh*, like the Undead, could mess with the living. *The Instruction of Ani* warns:

> Satisfy the ancestral spirit, do what he demands.
> He causes strife in his house.
> Hearts are set against one another.
> Keep yourself clear of what he abominates.
> Remain unscathed by his many spiteful actions.

If an *akh* was vexed it could cause blindness and other ills. Amulets were worn around the neck to fend off the attentions of the evil Undead. But an *akh* sniffing a water lily was a symbol of rebirth so perhaps the spirit hoped to be born again? It was important that the old body was kept in good nick. In the *Book of the Dead,* Budge cites the *Papyrus of Ani* in which the deceased says, 'Homage to thee, O my father Osiris, thy flesh suffered no decay, there were no worms in thee, thou didst not crumble away, thou didst not wither away, thou didst not become corruption and worms; and I myself am Khepera, I shall possess my flesh for ever and ever, I shall not decay, I shall not crumble away, I shall not wither away, I shall not become corruption.' He goes on to point out that different parts of the person could go wandering after death and interact with the living. This was due to the bits getting separated, by accident or design.

The god Osiris was in charge of the *akhs* and if they misbehaved he could be called on to keep them in order. Being bad seems to have been common. According to the *Penguin Book of Myths and Legends,* night assaults by the Undead involved touching, kissing and sexing as well as illness, misfortune and nightmares. In trying to prevent this, nothing was left to chance. Spells had to be performed in the correct way and the pronunciation had to be perfect.

There were texts to repel 'every dead man, every dead woman, every male enemy, every female enemy who would do evil.' All the wack-jobs and the badasses. One spell says, 'Get thee back enemy, dead man. Do not enter into his prick so that it goes limp.' The *Papyrus Leiden* contains spells against nightmares and night terrors and 'adversaries in the sky and earth'. According to the Chester Beatty *Dream Book,* to keep bad guy nightmares away you had to invoke Isis, then rub bread marinated in beer, herbs and incense on your face. You need to know the name of the bad guy as this has power. If the spells and letters didn't work, then 'execration figures' were made from clay or bowls inscribed with the deceased's name or the name of an enemy to be overcome. The figure or bowl would be smashed, destroying the evil through substitution.

An important part of Egyptian closing rituals after banishing the Undead was to make a necklace out of carnelian, lapis lazuli, serpentine, 'spotted stone' or 'very spotted stone', shiny silex, breccia and 'little jasper' beads. This was worn around the neck for seven days. Then the badass guy was well and truly banished and could not return.

And finally, another contemporary ghost story

This tale is on a ghost story site on the internet but the writer insists it's a true account of being haunted by the ghost of an ancient Egyptian. It bears out what the previous information shows, the 'dead' are very much alive in another world and can interfere with the living in the present time no matter when they lived. The writer describes an ancient Egyptian figure that holds her down at night and 'takes advantage of her'. On one occasion he elevated her off her bed and moved her across the hallway to the guest room, and then back. When he visited again she asked him why he was bothering her. She's sure no one will believe her but 'a white owl showed up in my room. I was very scared and I asked the owl to go away. He started flying away. Then I said, "Wait, unless you came to answer my question." I kid you not, but right after I said that the owl came back and right when it came back, I passed out and fell asleep. In my sleep I saw some kind of ancient Egyptian palace with me lying on a tomb and my ghost was in my dream standing over me sad that I had killed myself.' So it looks as though she may have committed an act in a former life that drew him to her in the present. She goes on to say that when she began to date a guy she 'liked very much' the ghost returned. 'I woke up suddenly from the ghost. He was being very aggressive. He was pushing me down like he has in the past. Then I saw him grab my shoe because he wanted to stab me, but I kept begging him to stop and luckily he did.'

Two weeks after that he returned again and had sex with her, which she pretended to enjoy. She asked him to show his face, which she hadn't seen before. He was very handsome. Then she had a dream in which the ghost and the guy she was dating appeared. She ran to the guy she was dating and hugged him and the ghost looked sad and went away. It didn't stop him returning though. 'A few days ago my ghost was in my room again. He didn't do anything. He was just sitting on my bed.'

Sources:

The Book of the Dead, Sir E.A. Wallis Budge Dover edition

Haunted Cincinnati and Southwest Ohio, Jeff Morris, Michael A. Morris, p. 71

Extreme Hauntings: Britain's Most Terrifying Ghosts, Paul Adams,

Eddie Brazil www.googlebooks.co.uk
Religion and Ritual in Ancient Egypt, Emily Teeter, Kindle version
The Penguin Book of Myth and Legend, www.amazon.co.uk
Magic in Ancient Egypt, Geraldine Pinch pp.147-160
http://seeksghosts.blogspot.co.uk/2012/12/haunted-object-cursed-egyptian-bone.html
http://www.touregypt.net/ghoststory.htm#ixzz3BtZm9emW
http://katiestringer.files.wordpress.com/2012/02/letters-to-the-dead-paper-edited.pdf
*still to be verified

Paschal Beverly Randolph
Sexual Magician, Occultist and a Bangin Guy
Aidan Doran

Paschal Beverly Randolph has been described as the greatest unknown metaphysician of the nineteenth century. An alchemist, sex magician, magic mirror salesman, mason, Supreme Grand Master of the Rosicrucians, abolitionist, doctor and psycho-phrenologist, archaeologist, politician, Civil War activist, world traveller, poet and writer, he was the founder of the Ansairetic Mystery System of sex magic. He had a huge but forgotten influence on Aleister Crowley and Western Occultism. He was a guy who made enemies very easily.

Born a bastard on 8 October 1825 in the Southern United States, Randolph was a 'free man of colour', an African American of mixed race at a time when slavery was still rife. Madame Blavatsky and other occultists referred to him disparagingly as 'the nigger' though she made extensive use of his magical writings. She later fell out with him and became involved in a protracted magical battle to obliterate him. One or the other may have died as a result. He became a friend of Abraham Lincoln's and fought against the iniquitous slave trade. Lincoln was assassinated in 1865 and Randolph accompanied Lincoln's funeral procession but was asked to leave the train because other passengers objected to his colour. Not everyone shared Lincoln's humanitarian principles.

According to Randolph, his father was a plantation owner and his mother a free woman of Spanish, Eastern Indian, French, Oriental or Royal Madagascan blood – depending on who he was talking to. When it suited him he denied that he had any African blood at all – Madagascar being a separate country in his eyes. His mother died when he was young and, abandoned by his father, he was left in the indifferent care of his half-sister. He was taken in by an English actress, Harriet Jennings, and her husband George Jennings, a gambler but, 'cuffed and kicked about,' he begged on the streets of New York to survive. He became a bootblack, cleaning shoes for a living. At age fifteen he ran away to sea but was bullied and beaten. He had little schooling and was self-taught.

He acquired linguistic skills and profound esoteric knowledge of sex magic and clairvoyance – taught to him, he said, by initiates in Africa and Asia. He became an important figure in the early American Spiritualist movement, was part of the early free love movement, wrote a treatise on scrying with magic mirrors in 1860 and founded the oldest Rosicrucian order of the United States in 1873. By this time he was a doctor who specialised in sexual medicine and tried to liberate women trapped in Victorian marriages by his ideas of 'true sexuality'. In 1874, Randolph published his most famous work, *Eulis,* which included a long treatise on 'Affectional Alchemy' – using sex in a magical way. Randolph created his own Ohio-based publishing house writing over fifty books on sex magic, alchemy, elixirs, scrying and other topics.

Randolph was very fond of women but didn't have much luck with them. He had several lovers, whom he claimed he'd known in other lives. Mert La Hue 'dines while I starve'. A six-week one-sided affair with 'La Blondette' led to him writing *Casca Llanna,* about the mashin urge. The affair made him cynical. In the book he describes strongminded women as cruel vampires who deceive men and laugh at them up their sleeves. He said that the women's rights activists of his day had 'cast steel souls'. He complains that with love kisses still warm on his lips they will without a word of notice part from him forever. A year before his death Randolph married, and his wife bore a son, Osiris Buddha Randolph. Earlier he had been married to an American Indian woman, with whom he sold medical formulas. They had three children although only one survived infancy.

The Great Free Love Trial

In 1871 Randolph was arrested. He'd been conned by two so-called mates into publishing a book apparently promoting free love and the practice of birth control. He was dobbed to the police by them, accused of making an obscene publication. One of the bad guys offered to drop the charges if Randolph signed over his books to them. It was a fiendish plot to get control of Randolph's copyrights. Judge Chamberlain, who'd read the material, had Randolph released from The Tombs gaol. But Randolph turned the situation to his advantage. Using his notoriety, he wrote to the local papers and enclosed copies of his published works so that readers could judge for themselves. He also wrote a potboiler of an autobiography, full of pathos trying to get the public on his side.

The book included a mock trial by representatives from all countries of the world, which many people believed had actually happened. In it he repudiated the practice of free love saying that in twenty years of practising as a doctor he'd never seen anyone made happy by it. Later he would write, 'no man is free who has not command over himself, but suffers his passions to control him.' However, he had already written about twin souls that proceeded from God in pairs and which had special 'eternal affinity' for each other and this idea was incorporated into the sexual magic he founded. He seems to have been undecided whether it would flourish past death as one soul could outstrip the other in its spiritual development and wouldn't hang around and wait.

Randolph and the dead

For years Randolph had been performing as a Spiritualist medium, talking in trance to the dead. In 1873 he published *The New Mola* which revealed a great deal about his supernatural work. He describes a Toledo circle in which seven people sat in twilight. The mediums were a lady and a gentleman (Randolph).

'A phantom hand moved through the air, across the table, pulled at a gentleman's beard and faded away in dim phosphoric vapour' [Deveney, p. 205]. He also describes, 'the most magnificent spiritual pyrotechnics and *thousands* of electric scintillas dancing mazy waltzes about the room...broadening out into sheets of living vapour, irradiating the room with pearly light.' He quickly became involved with Kate Corson, the medium in question, who published the book. He married her despite having a wife living in Utica and possibly another in Chicago.

But Randolph had other dealings with the dead. In a letter written to the *Religio-Philosophical Journal* in 1866, he boasts of his nightly mashing with the spirit of a dead woman. She was one of the Undead who roamed the earth calling out to him when he was asleep. He said that they met and mingled 'high and holy ayont the fence of flesh and passion.'

Held in the bounds of love

Randolph returned to Europe and Asia and then privately published what he called the *Secret of the Ansaireh Priesthood of Syria*. In it he says, 'There is a moment, frequently recurring, wherein men and women can call down to them celestial – almost awful – powers from the Spaces, thereby being wholly able to reach the souls of others, and hold them fast in the bonds of [a] love.' He also said in the letter sent out with it that it would not be possible for him to remain much longer on the earth [Deveney, p. 209].

Randolph then left on a trip to the Pacific Coast and, when he stopped off in Owen's Valley, California, he received death threats but found enough precious metals to fund the remainder of his life.

Randolph's suspicious death

Randolph died in Toledo, Ohio, at age forty-nine under suspicious circumstances. An eyewitness, Mrs Worden, told the local paper that he was acting strangely that morning. He apparently said that in less than two hours he would be dead. When she moved away she heard a shot and turned to see Randolph falling. It was ruled suicide from a self-inflicted wound to the head. However, it is said that he was in a magical duel with Madame Blavatsky and she turned a pistol on him from a distance. Allegedly R. Swinburne Clymer, a Supreme Master of the Rosicrucian Fraternity, made a deathbed confession stating that, in a fit of jealousy and temporary insanity, he had killed Randolph.

Source: *Paschal Beverly Randolph, a Nineteenth-Century Black American Spiritualist, Rosicrucian and Sex Magician,* John Patrick Deveney (State University of New York Press) and online texts and articles.

Ancient Egyptian Glossary

asitsow – ignorant, uninitiated

Ba - the soul

behau – coward

bend'ti – breasts

Central sun – chakra

desh'retu cymotrich – wavy haired one

Duat – the Otherworld, the afterlife

ebien – wretched; poor man

eibata – servant, slave

esu – light minded; unstable

eges't – vile, wretched

Finger of Hathor – third (ring) finger of the left hand, believed by the ancient Egyptians to link directly to the heart via the 'vena amoris', vein or pathway of love.

God's Plenty Below – vulva or testicles

ha'her'sha't – foul-faced bitch

haty – the physical heart

heka – magical power

henn – penis

hennu nafrit – beautiful woman; literally 'beautiful vagina'

ib – the metaphysical heart

im bar – embark

iri Nafre't – to have intercourse with a virgin

iri Nedjemem't em henen – to have intercourse with yourself; masturbate

Ka – etheric body

khabit – nipple

kat – vagina

kher heb – lector, funerary priest

kheroti – virgin

Ma'at – cosmic balance

menat – female amulet
mewet – mother
nedjemit ndjemu – sexual pleasure, 'love joys'
nedjem Ndjmemit – whore
neteru – spirit powers/the four gods of the directions
ntiu – worthless ones, the damned
nti heti – senseless fool
nti hati deshretyw – worthless inhabitant of the desert
Quema – creation
sau – male masturbation
seba – devil
Sekhem – magical power
sem – male amulet
sema – amulet having overall power
seti – ejaculation of sperm/impregnation
sexty – castrated, impotent, disempowered
sha't – bitch
temum't – a damned person
tjaty – vizier or chamberlain
uas staff – symbol of magical power
ude – ejaculate; 'to shoot off'
wowaei – virgin maiden

Aidan's Street Talk Glossary

ballin – successful, doing well
bangin – sick, good, sexy
beast – really cool
buggin – crazy
give im the air – ignore him
mashin – intercourse
minging – ugly
peng – good looking
phat – wicked, evil
rank – disgusting

rudeboy – street hardened
vexed – angry or irritated
wack – boring, crazy
wicked – cool
yakin – talking

Roundfire

FICTION

Put simply, we publish great stories. Whether it's literary or popular, a gentle tale or a pulsating thriller, the connecting theme in all Roundfire fiction titles is that once you pick them up you won't want to put them down.

If you have enjoyed this book, why not tell other readers by posting a review on your preferred book site.

Recent bestsellers from Roundfire are:

The Bookseller's Sonnets

Andi Rosenthal

The Bookseller's Sonnets intertwines three love stories with a tale of religious identity and mystery spanning five hundred years and three countries.

Paperback: 978-1-84694-342-3 ebook: 978-184694-626-4

Birds of the Nile

An Egyptian Adventure

N.E. David

Ex-diplomat Michael Blake wanted a quiet birding trip up the Nile – he wasn't expecting a revolution.

Paperback: 978-1-78279-158-4 ebook: 978-1-78279-157-7

Blood Profit$

The Lithium Conspiracy

J. Victor Tomaszek, James N. Patrick, Sr.

The blood of the many for the profits of the few... *Blood Profit$* will take you into the cigar-smoke-filled room where American policy and laws are really made.

Paperback: 978-1-78279-483-7 ebook: 978-1-78279-277-2

The Burden

A Family Saga

N.E. David

Frank will do anything to keep his mother and father apart. But he's carrying baggage – and it might just weigh him down ...

Paperback: 978-1-78279-936-8 ebook: 978-1-78279-937-5

The Cause

Roderick Vincent

The second American Revolution will be a fire lit from an internal spark.

Paperback: 978-1-78279-763-0 ebook: 978-1-78279-762-3

Don't Drink and Fly

The Story of Bernice O'Hanlon: Part One

Cathie Devitt

Bernice is a witch living in Glasgow. She loses her way in her life and wanders off the beaten track looking for the garden of enlightenment.

Paperback: 978-1-78279-016-7 ebook: 978-1-78279-015-0

Gag

Melissa Unger

One rainy afternoon in a Brooklyn diner, Peter Howland punctures an egg with his fork. Repulsed, Peter pushes the plate away and never eats again.

Paperback: 978-1-78279-564-3 ebook: 978-1-78279-563-6

The Master Yeshua

The Undiscovered Gospel of Joseph

Joyce Luck

Jesus is not who you think he is. The year is 75 CE. Joseph ben Jude is frail and ailing, but he has a prophecy to fulfil ...

Paperback: 978-1-78279-974-0 ebook: 978-1-78279-975-7

Tuareg

Alberto Vazquez-Figueroa

With over 5 million copies sold worldwide, *Tuareg* is a classic adventure story from best-selling author Alberto Vazquez-Figueroa, about honour, revenge and a clash of cultures.

Paperback: 978-1-84694-192-4

On the Far Side, There's a Boy

Paula Coston

Martine Haslett, a thirty-something 1980s woman, plays hard on the fringes of the London drag club scene until one night which prompts her to sign up to a charity. She writes to a young Sri Lankan boy, with consequences far and long.

Paperback: 978-1-78279-574-2 ebook: 978-1-78279-573-5

Readers of ebooks can buy or view any of these bestsellers by clicking on the live link in the title. Most titles are published in paperback and as an ebook. Paperbacks are available in traditional bookshops. Both print and ebook formats are available online.

Find more titles and sign up to our readers' newsletter at http://www.johnhuntpublishing.com/fiction

Follow us on Facebook at https://www.facebook.com/JHPfiction and Twitter at https://twitter.com/JHPFiction